the dead
of winter

NOVELS BY PAULA GOSLING

The Dead of Winter
A Few Dying Words
The Body in Blackwater Bay
Death Penalties
Backlash
Hoodwink
The Wychford Murders
Monkey Puzzle
The Woman in Red
The Harrowing
Solo Blues
The Zero Trap
Fair Game

the dead of winter

PAULA GOSLING

THE MYSTERIOUS PRESS

Published by Warner Books

A Time Warner Company

Mysterious Press books are published by Warner Books, Inc.,
1271 Avenue of the Americas, New York, NY 10020.

 A Time Warner Company

The Mysterious Press name and logo are registered trademarks of Warner Books, Inc.

Library of Congress Cataloging-in-Publication Data

Gosling, Paula.
    The dead of winter / Paula Gosling.
      p. cm.
    ISBN 0-89296-511-8 (hard)
    1. Sheriffs—Michigan—Fiction. 2. Great Lakes Region—Fiction.
  I. Title.
    PR6057.075D42   1996
    823'.914—dc20   95-39099
                                                      CIP

Printed in the United States of America

First printing: January 1996

10 9 8 7 6 5 4 3 2 1

For Elaine Green—wonderful agent,
wonderful friend, and terribly missed.

the dead
of winter

JANUARY

The surface of Blackwater Bay was white—a dirty gray white that dully reflected the light of the overcast sky. Iced over to a thickness of two feet or more, the frozen windswept expanse stretched from Perkins Point to the horizon, where the open, deeper water of the lake lapped at its crusty edges.

Across this temporary plain, many small structures were scattered. Like a cocoon, each structure held an occupant, wrapped in layers of clothing to twice their normal size against the frigid winter temperatures, and all—without exception—hunched over in an unconscious imitation of Rodin's Thinker, or the central figure in a laxative ad. What held their attention was simply a hole in the ice.

They sat, variously, on stools, old beer crates, tattered hassocks or broken chairs that had been rejected for any more respectable use. These figures were contemplative, quiet, and often slightly drunk.

Frank Nixey had been on the ice since seven that morning. Already, his feet were numb. His hands and face were numb. His brain was numb. He had four small perch in his creel, and a determination not to return home until his wife's mother had gone back to the city.

Suddenly he stiffened, grew hot, then cold, then colder still.

Right at his feet, a hideous face had appeared in the ice hole. A face that couldn't possibly be real, couldn't possibly be *there,* yet there it was.

The skin was white where it wasn't torn. The nose was mostly bone. What remained of the lips were pulled back in a weird smile exposing slightly uneven teeth. And a small black hole was visible in the middle of its forehead.

The face was staring up past Frank as if lost in thought.

He knew that if it spoke to him, he would have to go all the way home for clean underwear. But it did not speak. It just bobbed up and down in the hole, the water lapping gently at its ears.

For a long moment Frank stared down at it. Gradually the face sank again, the greeny-black water closing over it until it disappeared from view.

Groggy from the cold and stunned by the shock of this unexpected visitor, Frank Nixey shouted down the hole, the force of his breath making ripples in the water.

"Hey, buddy, what you doin' down there?" he called.

But answer there came none.

ONE

The house at Perkins Point stood on a gray stony bank that rose abruptly from the shore to a height of some thirty feet, an overhang of grass edging it like glowering eyebrows. The bluff was topped by big trees, their branches weaving black lace around the house that seemed to glare down at Blackwater Bay in Victorian disapproval. Its once-white clapboards needed painting. And on this bitter morning long glittering icicles of random lengths, like daggers pointing accusing fingers at the snow-covered unkempt grounds, hung from the remains of the original gingerbread trim.

Appearance to the contrary, the house at Perkins Point housed not a miserly old recluse, but six relatively young people sharing accommodation while pursuing busy separate lives. This meant the predominant factor governing the maintenance of the old house was not stinginess but simple procrastination.

Standing behind the highest window of the house at Perkins Point, Jess Gibbons paused momentarily, her brush caught halfway through her long hair, and stared down.

The general atmosphere in the ice-fishing village that

stretched out below her was usually one of leisure, thoughtful-
ness, and reflective repose. Because of their thick clothing and
the low temperatures that slowed their blood flow and numbed
their limbs, ice fishermen rarely moved at more than a slow
shuffle.

Yet down on the ice, a man had emerged from one of the
more ramshackle huts and was *running* toward the shore.

She watched him weave an apparently random path between the other huts. His almost panicky loose-kneed
progress made her smile. Drunk was the likeliest explanation, even at this early hour. Sometimes they arrived still
slightly tight from the day before and just kept themselves
on a nice level glow all the day through.

She supposed an alcoholic haze compensated them for sitting there freezing their backsides off. She liked a drink as
well as anyone, but meeting a dead fish face-on would have
sobered her up instantly, so it would have been a real waste
of good liquor as far as she was concerned. At the far too
rapidly ripening age of twenty-nine, there still remained
better things for her to do. Although, she thought with a
wry grimace, they certainly weren't coming thick and fast.

Unlike the wrinkles around her eyes.

Turning her hair into the single braid she habitually wore,
Jess glanced from the patterns and colors of the ice-fishing
village below to a large, unfinished patchwork quilt top
pinned to the cork-covered wall on her left. There was a medieval feel to the temporary village that mushroomed annually on the bay—blues and oranges predominated, but there
were also touches of yellow, green, crimson, and ochre—that
she was trying to capture in her quilt. She drew a deep
breath of dissatisfaction, seeing so much work still undone,
gauging how little time was left in which to do it. An im-
pressionistic interpretation of the colorful huts against the
pale ice, the quilt was intended to be her entry in an international quilt show to be held in Houston that summer. It
didn't look like she was going to finish it in time.

She scowled into the mirror over her bureau.

She'd had flu over Christmas, but that only partially explained the defeat in her eyes and the shadows under them. Lying in her big warm bed, staring at the sloping rafters of the white-painted attic ceiling, she'd had ample opportunity to examine her life and found it wanting.

Look at you, she told herself in the mirror. Jessica Margaret Gibbons, where is thy sting? Look over there at what you planned to wear today. Look at the expression on your face — do I detect any life? Do I see any hope? No. I see a pointed chin, long dark hair, big eyes, a sulky mouth, and joyless resignation. I see a nose with character and a person with none.

How dare you feel so superior to those men down on the ice. Why, after a few more decades of teaching at the local high school, ice fishing will probably begin to look like hysterical fun to you. As you grow older you'll learn to play bridge, and after that it won't be long before the wild world of shuffleboard will beckon, followed by knitting, falling out of rocking chairs, terrifying small children by forgetting to put in your teeth, and, eventually, death. A brief life, and a dull one.

She turned away from facing the Wicked Witch of the Attic and returned to the windows—an infinitely more interesting view.

The running man had reached a mooring ladder on the seawall that edged the bay at a lower point, and was climbing up it with some difficulty, his big boots becoming wedged between each rung. He was closer now—and looked more shocked than drunk. She was pretty sure the man was Frank Nixey, which meant his burst of energy could be caused by anything from ants in the pants to bats in the belfry, depending on how long his mother-in-law had been staying.

Funny he should run that way and not toward the parking lot further up where all the fishermen normally left their cars and trucks. She watched him for a moment, then shrugged and turned back into the big room.

She had returned to Blackwater a couple of years earlier, to take up the job of teaching home ec at the local high school.

Although—or perhaps because—she'd grown up in Blackwater Bay, her first days back had been odd. There was comfortable familiarity coupled with the classic sensation that everything was smaller and slightly grubbier than she had remembered. And there were ghosts. Among the crowds of young people surging through the familiar halls between classes she had seen fleeting images of her old friends, and even of herself—bright-eyed, hopeful, fresh, looking forward to conquering the world. Then she met those same old friends in town and saw the changes in them—the slightly bowed posture, the acceptance of responsibility, the first tiny inroads of time's passage.

At first this had depressed her, but as the months passed, the ghosts disappeared from the halls. The contrasts between then and now lessened, and blurred, until the old friends she greeted in town seemed perfectly normal and her own reflection brought no shock or sadness.

Until this morning, that is. Facing the start of the new term, she'd seen herself clearly—and been dismayed.

She seemed to be reaching out to embrace middle age like some long-awaited lover. Beige sweater, beige skirt, sensible shoes, sensible attitudes, sensible life.

No!

Dammit, girl, don't be beige today. New year, new start. Right? Right. How would you have dressed ten years ago? Do it, she told herself. Start taking chances again. Do it. Scare the students half to death. Scare yourself. Do it!

After a quick browse through the back of the closet, she made her choice. She stuffed the bottom of a new red cashmere sweater (Christmas present from her parents, who apparently still believed in her wild, artistic heart) into the top of a long black jersey skirt (from her younger sister, who apparently had begun to despair of her *ever* rising from the dead), cinched her still-slim middle with the big silver buckle of a wide leather belt, stuck her feet into a pair of elderly cowboy boots (acquired at a sale years before), and slipped on a wildly abstract needlepoint Joseph's vest of many colors (self-constructed for a college project). Throwing a couple of silver chains around her neck and putting on heavy Mexican silver earrings as she clattered down the stairs, the new/old Jess burst into the kitchen just in time to see the last drop of milk cascade over Tom Brady's cereal. Her brief ebullience drained away.

"Gee, thanks, Tom," she said.

He glanced at her, unrepentant. "You always drink your coffee black, and you never eat anything for breakfast anyway."

"That's not the point—"

"Oh, yes it is."

"She might have wanted something more substantial this morning," said Jason Phillips, who was seated across from Tom polishing off bacon and eggs. "I could cook you up something in a jiffy, Jess."

Jess shuddered as she turned up the heat under the kettle. "No, thanks, Jason. I'm a bit keyed up this morning."

"Everyone else has left," Tom continued defensively. "Anyway, I'll be bringing milk home tonight with the rest of the groceries, since it's my turn to do the shopping. Have you put everything on the list that you want?"

"Yes, thanks. Chip and Pat and Linda have gone already?"

"Sure. They are dedicated to their profession, you know. They believe in getting a head start on the little bastards."

She poured boiling water from the kettle onto instant coffee and hitched herself up onto the counter to swing her heels while she drank it.

"Whereas you and I—" she began.

"Have surrendered our ambitions already," he concluded

calmly, and turned over a page of the newspaper. "We no longer give a damn."

"I hope you aren't including me in that category," Jason said mildly. He stood up and carried his plate to the sink, running water onto it and then leaving it there. He was tall and elegantly thin, with golden hair that drooped over his forehead, causing most women to want to brush it back for him. His recent arrival had caused serious flutterings in the classrooms, and the fact that he dressed like an escapee from *Brideshead Revisited* did not help. He was, in short, an adolescent female student's dream—sensitive, intelligent, and unreachable—a role he seemed more than satisfied to play. He also happened to be an excellent teacher, which provided Tom Brady with further reason to dislike him.

Jess owned the house at Perkins Point—an inheritance from the unmarried aunt who had first instilled in her a love for quilt making. The only way she could afford the gradual renovation and upkeep of the old place was to take in housemates, and she presently had five—all young, all single, and all teachers at the local high school—an arrangement that raised a few eyebrows in the town. But despite what seemed like a perfect setting for scandal, it had not been forthcoming. No wild parties, no passionate liaisons, no violence, nothing. Just six people living at the same address. It was a serious disappointment to some.

The sexes were currently at par. The three women were Jess herself, Pat Morrison, who taught art, and Linda Casemore, who taught biology. The men were Tom Brady, who taught physics, Chip Chandler, who taught physical education and coached the football team, and the newest addition to the group, Jason Phillips, who taught chemistry. They were an amiable group that had never properly jelled, in the sense that each lived his or her life individually and only occasionally thought of themselves in the collective sense. The house at Perkins Point was more hotel than home, which was as Jess had hoped when she began the venture.

Jess smiled and turned to Tom. "As for not giving a damn, you can speak for yourself, Mr. Brady. I have, as of ten minutes ago, decided to start giving a great big damn again," she announced.

"Why?" he inquired, turning a page of the newspaper without looking up.

"Because I don't want to become an ice fisherman."

He lowered the paper and looked at her. She looked as bright as a robin, and her eyes were sparkling. He felt a sudden sense of danger, and was uneasy. She'd looked like that in the playground when at the age of eight she announced a diabolical plan to terrorize their third-grade teacher. There'd been quite a turnover of teachers in that class. *Pace,* mentors, he thought. We knew not what we did. "What has ice fishing got to do with it?" he wanted to know.

Jess explained about the ice fishing and the knitting and eventual death wearing beige and black. "No more Miss Middle Age for me," she announced.

"Admirable," said Jason. "Face up to life, that's what I say. Face up to it and grab with both hands. *Carpe diem.*"

Tom looked over the top of the paper at him. As usual, Jason was gazing steadily at Jess and sycophantically agreeing with everything she said. Tom, with an effort, suppressed the usual impulse to kick his fellow resident in the backside.

Jess put her coffee mug down and rummaged in her huge handbag for a cigarette. By the time she found one, Jason was ready with a light. She drew a luxurious lungful and exhaled with gusto. "Ah, that's better." She spoke as one who held a science degree and knew all the pitfalls, but just didn't give a damn. Not that morning, anyway. Gripping the edge of the cabinet, she held tight until the room stopped spinning around her. "Let's just say today is the first day of—"

"Don't," Tom pleaded. "Don't say it. *Please.*"

She grinned at him, glad he was there to witness her initially faltering steps back to being somebody—anybody—again. Tom had always been there for Jess, from the third grade on. When she was worried, when she was hurt, when she was afraid, it was always Tom she'd turned to for support and a laugh. All through grade school, high school, and college, she and Tom had always been part of the same bunch. Their inevitable summer romance at the age of seventeen was now only an embarrassing memory. "Our three months of hormonal madness," Tom called it. Short it may have been, but it had proved sufficient time in which to learn that they could never, ever, *ever* be interested in one another romantically.

Probably.

After that episode they had maintained a dignified emotional distance, always friends but never quite as close again. They drifted apart after college, each eventually married, each eventually divorced. But when she'd returned to Blackwater Bay, she found that he, too, had come home to teach. They had met at the school and chose to continue their friendship as if nothing had interrupted it. Continued it cautiously and neutrally, neither ever referring to the years in between. There seemed to be an unspoken agreement between them to keep it light now, keep it easy. Even so, he was the brother she'd never had, and the thought that he might not be there for her never entered her conscious mind. For Jess, Tom was one of life's constants, like the grass and the sky and the bay and the annual ice fishermen.

Jess decided to let her inspirational lecture lapse. "I think I just saw Frank Nixey running out of his fishing hut," she said. "He was staggering all over the place."

"Probably drunk," Tom muttered, his eyes on the newspaper.

"I don't think so."

"Who is Frank Nixey?" Jason asked.

"Oh, come on, he's always drunk," Tom said, turning over a page and running a finger down the basketball scores.

"Who is—?" Jason began again. He looked at the two of them and despaired. They had known one another for so long their conversation was almost a kind of shorthand, difficult for a newcomer to comprehend. Their affinity was complete, along with their communication, even though the latter had lately been less than amiable.

"No," Jess corrected Tom. "He's usually a little . . . a little . . ."

"Drunk."

"Tiddly."

"Drunk."

"Merry."

Tom lowered his paper to stare at her. "Merry? You call the most miserable man in Blackwater *merry?*"

"Why is he miserable? Who is he?" Jason persisted.

"He's a man who is living off a generous pension for an industrial injury which no longer really troubles him," Tom said. "As a result he has nothing to do but read, watch TV, fish, and hang around the Golden Perch drinking with his buddies."

"And he's miserable?" Jason asked in astonishment.

"It also means he's around his wife a lot," Tom explained. "That would be enough to make any man miserable."

"What a terrible thing to say," Jess admonished him. "Dixie isn't that bad." Tom just looked at her. "I mean, I know she's a little . . . but he could . . ." He went on looking at her. "If her mother would just . . ." He was still looking at her. "Well . . ." She shrugged. "You know what I mean."

He turned back to his paper. "I never know what you mean," he grumbled.

"That's because I never mean the same thing twice," she said, grinning at the back of his neck. He needed a haircut, as usual. Not especially tall, all bony elbows and knees, Tom always reminded her of a messy little boy who never could keep his shirttail tucked in. Especially when he wore those wire-rimmed glasses he'd found in a sixties retro shop and had fitted with his own prescription. From the way he was squinting, it was a prescription that needed updating. He's sliding too, Jess thought. Letting go instead of taking hold. We're a sorry pair.

Tom remembered the sixties with great fondness. He had come about as close to being a flower child as digging in the garden with a spoon could bring him, and his devotion to that gentler dreamtime was in direct conflict with his true personality. He had a mind that was both practical and scientific, which annoyed him, as he really wanted to be a lyrical poet and read aloud in coffeehouses. The last time he'd been to a coffeehouse he'd ended up in the kitchen helping the owner mend one of the espresso machines, and by the time he had emerged to read his one and only poem, everybody had left.

"Go away," he suggested. "You're confusing Snap, Crackle, and Pop. They prefer a quiet, contemplative life, and you're jangling all over the place."

She sighed. "Have you seen Cleo and Twister?" she asked. "Has anybody fed them?"

"I fed them," Jason said, bending down to retrieve his briefcase from beside the kitchen table. "And they've both been out."

"Right," Tom said. "For exactly one minute each. They're probably in the living room by the radiator, recovering from the shock." He was back behind his newspaper.

"Thanks." Jess smiled at Jason and went to say a few words of encouragement to her cats before leaving. Jess's two cats were annually traumatized by winter. Each time it arrived they acted as if it were a personal betrayal and entirely Jess's fault. They disapproved of low temperatures, were deeply dismayed by snow, and holed up as soon as the first flake fell.

She discovered them sitting close together, nose-to-nose like a pair of bookends. They looked up with a startled air, for all the world as if they had been discussing some secret plan.

"Now, why do I get the feeling you've been up to something?" she asked them. Probably because they had, she thought. They had been having bursts of very odd manic activity lately, and she was beginning to worry a little about them. At the sound of her voice the two cats began to purr. Making a carefully equal fuss of them, Jess glanced around the room. Quite a few things had been dragged out and scattered about—a banana skin from the wastebasket, a scarf from the hall, a couple of books knocked to the floor. Apparently they had been bored during the night. She rebasketed the banana peel and tidied up. Then, giving them each a final scratch behind the ears, Jess put on her coat and gathered up her own books. "Anybody want a lift?" she shouted toward the kitchen.

"Ready when you are," Jason said, appearing suddenly. "My car is in the garage, remember?"

"Of course," Jess said, and raised her voice. "Tom? Coming?"

"I'm taking the van, it's my turn to do the shopping tonight," Tom called out. "I told you that. You never listen to me anymore. It's all over. I *knew* it would end like this—"

She smiled to herself. "Bye," she shouted, and went out.

Tom heard the door slam, and sighed. Well, Brady, you handled that well, he told himself sarcastically—congratulations.

As usual when Jess had breezed into his view and out again, she left behind an emptiness he had only recently recognized. The fact was, he had fallen in love with her and didn't know what the hell to do about it. There had been no warning at all. He'd merely looked up one day and there she'd been, suddenly different, suddenly a problem. They had known each other for so long that it had never occurred to him his feelings could change in this way. It made him cross and irritable that his mind and body could have mounted this sneaky attack on an otherwise orderly and sensible existence. God knew he was acquainted with enough women. Surely there could have been *one* who could have volunteered to save him from the ignominy of falling for his best friend.

He felt like someone who had been handed a huge and ungainly package to carry around. How did one bring a sudden lust into the conversation? What would be the right moment? Should he send flowers from "a secret admirer"? Push a sloppy poem under her door? Should he corner her on the stairs, drag her by the hair to his room, or stand up in the middle of dinner and ask her if she fancied a quick roll in the hay? And how to handle that terrible silence that might ensue, that look of embarrassment, perhaps even of pity, that would cross her face? Sorry, she would say, sorry, Tom, I just don't feel that way about you, can't we just stay friends?

He folded the newspaper and smacked it down on the table. "I am a horse's ass," he announced with great feeling, and glared out at the snow-filled garden, wrapping his arms over his recalcitrant heart. Not for the first time he considered moving out and leaving the path clear for Jason, the slimy bastard.

From the day he'd arrived, Jason Phillips had done everything he could to make himself look good to Jess—all the things Tom could not bring himself to do because he had left them undone for so long. His face twisted into an unconscious sneer as he thought about Phillips. *Jason* was a *sweetheart*. *Jason* had accompanied Jess to a quilt show in Hatchville and another in Grantham, even going so far as to pretend to enjoy it. *Jason* was constantly praising her work, her looks, her ideas, even fussing over her rotten cats. Anything and everything he could do to cut Tom out or make him look an insensitive dolt, Jason did. Tom felt certain there would soon come a time when he would be forced to knock sweet *Jason* on his tidy, ingratiating ass.

Maybe he would do it the day he moved out. But, of course, if he moved out he would only see Jess at school, not coming out of the bathroom in her old blue robe with a towel wrapped around her head, not bending over her quilting frame with her glasses at the end of her nose, not rosy-cheeked and shiny as she stood by the stove stirring something, not . . .

"Oh, hell." He stood up to rinse his cereal bowl and, after putting it in the dishwasher, reached for the Zantac tablets in the cupboard. He didn't know whether it was his unresolved conflict over Jess or the unruly students in his physics classes, but *something* had given him an ulcer. He glanced at the clock. Eight-fifty—and he still had things to do. As he turned away from the dishwasher he managed to stub his toe on the table leg. It was the last straw. "Oh, *shit!*" he shouted to the unfair world.

Outside, the wind was thin and cold as a stiletto. Jess ran for her car and found, with relief, that the lock was not frozen. It started easily, too—another reason to be grateful. Winter mornings were always a challenge in Blackwater Bay, and the first morning back to school after the holidays was not one on which to be late. She glanced back at the house. If he didn't get a move on, Tom would be late. Did he care? She was beginning to doubt it. He had been so glum over Christmas. His had always been a wry outlook on life, but recently there had been a painful edge to his humor. She wished she knew what was wrong. She wished she could do something about it, but Tom was as prickly as he was funny, and she didn't want to hurt him. She hoped that if he needed something—anything—he would ask. Surely they were close enough for that.

As they started down the road, she quite expected to see Frank Nixey running along, but there was no sign of him. A few hundred yards further down the lane she saw some fresh ruts in the snow where a car had been parked beneath tall bushes. So he'd cut through someone's yard to get out onto the ice this morning rather than use the official entry a mile further up the coast—how typical.

"He must have been making good time," she said half to herself.

"Who?" Jason asked.

She'd almost forgotten he was there. "Frank Nixey," she said. "It was the way he was running that was so odd. Almost . . . as if he were *afraid* of something."

"What on earth could frighten anybody at this time of the morning?" Jason asked.

Jess shrugged and carefully negotiated her way over some nasty frozen ruts in the ice-packed road. "Maybe he thought his kerosene heater was going to explode," she said.

"Or perhaps he caught a shark," Jason suggested blandly.

Jess giggled. "I think the worst thing any of them ever catch out there is pneumonia," she said. She turned onto the main road and started through town, looking along the sidewalks as she did so. Suddenly she spotted Frank Nixey standing by his car outside the post office, his face as white as a sheet. He seemed to be catching his breath, looking around wildly. She looked back in the rearview mirror and saw him go into the sheriff's office. "That's funny," she said.

"Now what?" Jason asked patiently. He was fumbling in his briefcase, shuffling papers around. He hadn't seen Frank Nixey.

"Oh, nothing," Jess said, driving on. But she was frowning.

TWO

"God Almighty, Frank, simmer down! It's *not* that I don't believe you," shouted Sheriff Matt Gabriel.

"White as a fish's belly," Frank Nixey shouted back. "Just floated up and floated down. Hello and goodbye. I saw it, I tell you, I saw it as plain as day. Come up like a dumpling in the stew, went down like—"

"I got it, I got it," Matt interrupted, making notes on the report sheet.

"—like a doughnut in the coffee," finished Frank, his face flushed beneath his old fishing hat, which sat askew over one ear, dangling hooks dangerously close to his eyes. "You got to do something, Matt. He's under the *ice*. He could be *drowned* by now."

"He *is* drowned by now." Deputy George Putnam added his voice to the confrontation. "For crying out loud, Frank, use your head. He was already drowned when he came up like that."

"Right up like a thing in one of them balls that you ask questions to," Frank nodded. " 'You could be right' and 'Maybe not' and—"

"What is he talking about, George?" Matt asked wearily.

For the past twenty minutes they had been listening to Frank Nixey tell and retell of his encounter with the Creature from the Bottom of the Bay. Each rendering of the tale became more lurid and more sinister, as Frank moved about the office with the exaggerated steps of someone who is afraid of being thought drunk, thereby merely verifying the diagnosis. He was enthralled by the excitement of it all. The only thing better that could have happened to him was attending his mother-in-law's funeral.

"Didn't you ever have one of those black eight-ball things when you were a kid?" George asked Matt. "Full of oil or something. You asked a question, then turned it over, and little pieces of cardboard floated into a glass window at the bottom. They had 'answers' printed on them. Dumb stuff that could mean anything." George looked at Matt's puzzled face. "Came up at random." Matt shook his head. "It was a *game*," George said.

"Oh." Matt bent his head to the report again. On the wide window ledge Max, the office cat, had turned around in order to watch Frank Nixey's perambulations. People who came to the sheriff's office tended to offer a cat more in the way of entertainment than passing pedestrians or the weather. Tracking the odd flake of snow as it drifted down was as nothing compared to the fascination of watching yet another overexcited human windmill himself from wall to wall, babbling incomprehensibly. It made up for the bad mousing in winter.

"You shudda seen it," Frank shouted. "Come right up and—"

"I *have* seen it," Matt said.

That stopped him. "You what?" Frank demanded. "You seen it, too?"

"I have seen a body come up from the bottom of the lake," Matt said patiently. "We get one every once in a while, Frank. I agree, it isn't the most pleasant of sights . . ."

"Come up just like a trout rising, went down . . ."

"Like an old tire sinking?" George suggested.

"Yeah," said Frank in a more subdued voice. "Like that."

"The Lakes can hang on to people for quite a while," Matt went on. "You know that, Frank. My God, you ought to, you've lived here all your life. Sailors off the big ships, fishermen, suicides, drownings. It takes a while sometimes, but eventually—"

"They say Lake Superior never gives them up," George put in. "Too deep, too cold. Bottom probably littered with corpses from one end to—"

"Never mind, George," Matt said. He put down his pen. "Tell you what, Frank—we'll come out and have a look, okay? It's not very likely he'll come up again, but we'll have a look."

Frank stood beside Matt's desk, shifting from one foot to the other, looking from one man to the other. "So are you going to chop through or what?" he finally blurted.

Matt and George exchanged a glance. "How long did it take you to chop your fishing hole, Frank?" George asked.

"I dunno, maybe an hour."

"And how big is it?"

"About a foot and a half across, maybe less. See, you never know how big a—"

"And how big is Blackwater Bay?"

"Oh."

"What do you think all the other fishermen out there would say if we started hacking up the ice? Presuming we had nothing else to do for maybe a month?" George asked.

"But—"

"We have to wait, Frank," Matt explained. "If it survives the winter intact, the body will probably wash up over by Butter Beach, or further along the shore, depending on how and when the ice lets go of the bay."

"I see. You got it down to science, like," Frank said.

"Just nature, Frank," George said. "Just ebb and flow."

"Who?"

"The cold water will preserve him pretty well, although if the fish get real hungry—"

"Ugh," said Frank, going a little pale. "You sure got a lousy job, Matt."

"It isn't *all* fun and games, Frank," Matt agreed solemnly. He went on to explain some of the dynamics of drowning, the processes of underwater putrefaction and saponification, and the problems the ice presented.

When the chastened and nauseated fisherman had left, George looked over at Matt. "It may not be fun and games, but it sure gives me a laugh now and then. I thought his eyes were going to roll right down his cheeks when he first came in."

Matt leaned back in his chair and threw his pencil on top of the report. "Then you believe him?"

George was caught off guard. "Don't you?"

"I don't know, not for sure. These ice fishermen, they sit out there half-canned most of the time, breathing in fumes from those oil heaters of theirs, falling asleep over their lines. It's a wonder to me they don't fall in."

"Well, maybe one of them did," George pointed out. "Maybe that's where the body came from."

"If it exists."

"Yeah, well—how do we find out for sure?"

"We wait to see if anyone else reports it. Or you could put on your scuba gear and go down to take a look," Matt said.

George paled. "Oh, hell, Matt, I can't cover the bay by myself. The ice hits bottom in some places near the shore, you know. There's channels and blind alleys under there, I could get trapped and frozen up, and even if the guy exists he could be practically next to me and I wouldn't see him because of the ice pillars or he could be wedged in a crack and so could I, and anyway if he *doesn't* exist, I could be risking death or double pneumonia for nothing."

"I know, I know," Matt sighed. "Plus in this weather you

could only stay down twenty minutes at a time, anyway." He considered the situation. "We could call the State Police Barracks and ask them to send over some divers."

"They'll say the same thing probably," George said. "I mean, you're right, we only have Nixey's word for it, he could have made it up, or imagined it. What the hell." He took a deep breath. "But if you want me to give it a try, Matt, I will. It's just that—"

"It's just that you don't like the idea of coming face-to-face with a floater under the ice," Tilly Moss said from her desk, only the top of her head visible over her computer. "We understand, George."

"That's got nothing to do with it," George said defensively.

"Oh yes it does."

"Oh no it doesn't, dammit."

"Knock it off, you two," Matt said. Most of the time he could put up with the amiable wrangling of his two most frequent companions, but for some reason it irritated him this morning. George Putnam, twenty-seven, was muscular, ambitious, as energetic as a Great Dane puppy and with about the same amount of brains and common sense. Tilly Moss, in her late forties, and long a fixture in the sheriff's office, was George's opposite. She was overweight, content with her life, extremely bright, and as organized as a Swiss bank. Matt turned to her. "Have we got a current list of missing persons, Tilly?"

"Yes, somewhere. It's not a very long list," Tilly said. She pressed a few buttons and, beside her, the printer chattered briefly. She ripped off the paper and held it out across her desk. Matt stretched to take it.

"A *current* list . . . that's a good one," George chortled, relieved that Matt seemed to have dismissed the idea of his going under the ice for a look around. "It was the current that brought him up—"

"Like a dumpling," Tilly chuckled.

"And sent him down like a—"

"Not many on here," Matt said, ignoring them. "Seems like everyone is keeping pretty good track of one another at the moment."

"Very reassuring," Tilly said.

"Yeah," George agreed in a snide voice. "I *hate* carelessness."

Matt glanced up over the top of the printout. "You're getting skittish, George. A nice cold swim would probably settle you right down."

"Very funny," George muttered. He gazed across at Matt, filled as usual with conflicting emotions. He idolized the big man and at the same time coveted his job. Matt Gabriel, at thirty-something, was a handsome man, well over six foot, with auburn hair and a lineman's build. Women and men liked him immediately and rarely found any reason to change their minds—unless, or course, they chose a criminal course of action. All smiles stopped then.

Matt glared gloomily at the list of missing persons. It was getting harder and harder to be sheriff of Blackwater County. He had been elected to office after his father—the previous sheriff—had died (in bed, as had all previous sheriffs of Blackwater County). He had been teaching philosophy at a small college upstate, and leaving academia behind had seemed a small sacrifice. He had been wanting an excuse to return home since his acrimonious divorce, and he had assumed the job would allow him plenty of time for peaceful contemplation and perhaps even to write a book or two. He scowled. Fat chance.

Not long after his return, Blackwater Bay had suddenly caught up with the twentieth century via two cases of homicide.* Matt had only solved the first with the help of Jack Stryker, a vacationing homicide detective from Grantham, the nearest big city. The second he had solved on his own, but it had been a chastening experience. Blackwater having been revealed by the media to be lacking in police amenities if not

*See *The Body in Blackwater Bay* and *A Few Dying Words.*

ability, civic pride alone might have forced modernization, but the media fuss had also attracted the attention of someone in the state capital. As a result, state and local money had flowed into and irrevocably changed the Blackwater Bay County Sheriff's Department, creating what Matt considered to be a fast-growing monster.

He now had to supervise more deputies (i.e., think up things for them to do), schedule the rotation and servicing of more vehicles, and serve as a liaison with the state law enforcement network (with attendant interference in return) every time a major crime took place. There was even talk of a helicopter, which had excited George Putnam almost beyond their control. There had been much posing and bragging about how he was going to take flying lessons and add wings to his deputy's badge. Unfortunately for George's reputation among the young women of Blackwater, the Greenleaf Air Force Base was just across the bay, and its junior pilots were always eager for flying experience. In the end, the rather hefty expenditure of buying a helicopter had been deemed unnecessary when compared to the cost of an occasional fee to the air base. George had been sulking about it ever since.

All these changes would have been bearable if it had not been for the fact that Matt now had to expect a media circus to come to town every time anything remotely interesting occurred on his patch. The finding of a floating body under the ice might just qualify, if there were no other news items available when the story hit the news desks in Grantham.

This was because, for some indefinable reason, the media had decided it *loved* Blackwater Bay County. It was as if it had discovered a permanent crazy season. Tilly said it was because it was small, self-contained, and had plenty of bars, but in fact everything about it enchanted the newsmen and newswomen—from its old-fashioned homes to its old-fashioned morals. They had begun to treat it as if it were a private zoo, viewed with a kind of prurient nostalgia.

In a way they had a point. Blackwater Bay County *was* an anachronism. Created during Prohibition because of the large amount of freelance "importing" of booze from Canada across the lake, its law enforcement agency had been granted unique powers backed by some questionable procedures. After Repeal it had seemed to the state legislators to be more trouble and red tape than it was worth to re-amalgamate it with the large county from which it had been carved. The locals had gotten used to it and made it clear they would cause trouble if forced to "return to the yoke"—a felicitous phrase thought up by the then editor of their local weekly newspaper, the *Blackwater Bay Chronicle*.

So Blackwater Bay County remained splendidly isolated, and was largely forgotten as a legal entity. There were occasionally a few ripples during state election years, but inevitably procrastination prevailed on the basis of "if it works don't fix it." And until recently Blackwater County had gone on working just fine.

Departmental activities had consisted mostly of traffic and nuisance control during the summer, and damn-all in the winter, for the population of Blackwater waxed and waned with the sun. There were off-season high spots: for example, the Howl—a strictly local version of Halloween—and the Ice Festival, which was coming up soon. This latter was made up of novel winter sports, such as wife-sliding, beer sculpture, snowball wars, and Ski-doo racing. That had been the top and bottom of the local wild life.

But no more.

Now everything was up-to-date in Blackwater County. They'd gone about as far as they could go. Suddenly they'd had winos, homicides, panhandlers, burglaries, assaults, drugs, holdups, vandalism, chicken races on the highways, even a couple of warring teenage gangs—in fact, a taste of practically everything that made living in the nineties so *special*.

In the past few months there had been the added distrac-

tion of the office being extended, renovated, and redeco-
rated. The combination of paint fumes, overwork, and computer foul-ups had made them a little edgy with one
another.

And now this damn body had appeared.

George stood up abruptly, before Matt could give further
consideration to the question of under-ice diving. "I'm
going out to have a look down Frank's fishing hole," he announced stoutly. "It's the least we can do." And the quickest
way to get out of here, he thought to himself.

"Good God, George," Tilly said in mock astonishment.
"Do you mean you are voluntarily going out in the freezing
cold?"

"Crime does not wait upon good weather," George said in
a portentous voice.

Matt and Tilly watched him put on his leather jacket and
make his exit into the icy outer world. As he slammed the
door behind him a few snowflakes were blown into the room
and settled on the linoleum, where they slowly melted away.

After a moment, Tilly spoke. "Matt," she said. "Do you
still think George is cut out for police work?"

"Well, I can't imagine him doing anything else," Matt
said sadly. "And believe me, Tilly, I've tried."

THREE

As the morning progressed, a great many people learned just what it was that had sent Frank Nixey flying to the sheriff. The speed of the communication was matched only by the complexity of its route. George Putnam told three people, they in turn mentioned it to four more, and so the web spread far and wide, by word of mouth, phone (and, in the case of Mr. Pugh, the town's deaf undertaker, sign language) until, via the janitor, one Digger Wells, it reached Heckman High.

Jess Gibbons had learned much more quickly than her fellow teachers, however, through the simple expedient of telephoning her younger sister, Emily, during her first free period, in order to verify a lunch date for later in the week.

There were three "Gibbons Girls." Jess was the middle girl and Emily was the youngest. Their older sister, Abbi, had broken free of Blackwater and was presently an advertising copywriter in Grantham. Rebels all, they had cut their individual swathes in Blackwater society during their teen years, but now were settling down into their respective chosen careers. Emily was a reporter on the *Blackwater Bay Chronicle,* published twice a week and owned by their father.

"From what I can gather, Frank Nixey caught a dead body and then threw it back," Emily told Jess. Behind her voice could be heard the *ping* and *brrapp* of a computer game.

"Too small?"

"Too big, more likely. Frank Nixey would never hack a hole in the ice any bigger than he had to," Emily said. "I'm surprised he even bothered to drop a line down—everybody knows he only goes out there to get away from his wife."

"I assume, from the sound of your computer, that you won't be putting out a special edition?" Jess said.

"Nope. A dead body on its own—if it exists at all—isn't enough to get the presses rolling over here. You know how Dad is about speculation," Emily said idly.

"Yes—he's against it on a cost basis," Jess said, reiterating one of their father's many journalistic dicta. At the other end of the line the noise of the computer game altered slightly, and Jess smiled wryly. She could visualize Em tapping the keys with her free hand, no doubt caught up in some complex game or other. Nice to know her call was so riveting.

"You haven't had a riot up there at the school, by any chance?" Emily asked with a perfunctory display of interest.

Jess glanced down the long hall—empty, for the moment, of racing, shouting students. "Not yet. They've just come back from Christmas vacation, remember. They haven't had time to get *really* bored."

"They will."

"Well, this time I'm ready for them."

"Oh? You sound funny—what's up?"

Jess took a breath. "I don't know if it's funny, but I've decided to take hold of my life, not to sit around waiting for it to turn into something magical."

There was a silence. Then—"Hello? Hello?"

"What's wrong?" Jess asked.

"I think I've been disconnected. I was talking to my sister and then this strange woman broke in—"

"Very funny. I mean it, Em."

"Well, small hips hooray—I *was* beginning to think of you in the same category as one of our old-maid aunts. What brought about this change of heart—has Tom proposed?"

"Good Lord, no! Why on earth should you say that?"

"Oh, just put it down to my romantic nature."

"Ah, yes, how *is* Dominic?" Jess knew this was the way to get Emily off any other subject.

"Wonderful, as always." Dominic Pritchard was the young lawyer to whom Emily had just become engaged.

"Hmmmmm—so all is still magic and mystery between you two?"

"It was last night. This morning I might return his ring."

"Why?"

"Well, it's almost eleven o'clock and he hasn't called me yet. I think he's cooling."

"You can print an announcement in Friday's edition saying you're no longer responsible for his ills."

"Was I ever?"

"From the day he met you."

"I love you, too. Well, I'm glad to hear you're rejoining the human race."

"I never left it."

"The evidence is conclusive—you are twenty-nine and teaching home economics in a small midwestern town."

Jess was stung. "Well, you're just a reporter on—"

"*I* have ambitions. Goodbye." Even before she'd hung up the phone, Jess could hear Em's computer respringing into violent and noisy life. She started back to her classroom just as the bell rang, irritated as usual by her younger sister's ability to get under her skin. Suddenly the long empty hall became a maelstrom far louder and more dangerous than any computer game could ever create. Shouts, laughter, overlapping conversations in voices high, low, and breaking, locker doors slamming, the slap of sneakers on the granite floor, and the occasional snarling altercation filled the air. Things were rapidly getting back to normal—there would be at least one fistfight to break up after lunch. Wonderful things, hormones.

As usual, she tried to maintain an aura of dignity as she pushed through the throng, but she was too well liked by the students to maintain a lofty distance for long. By the time she had regained the relative peace of her classroom on the top floor, she had heard about two broken romances, fourteen Christmas presents, and some student party that had gotten badly out of hand.

Because she taught both needlework and cooking, Jess had the unusual benefit of two long classrooms that were permanently her own. It was a mixed blessing. Both rooms had large windows overlooking the athletic field, which meant there was a lot of light—a definite benefit. The definite drawback was that she and her students froze in winter and suffocated in summer, despite every effort made by Digger Wells to provide the necessary balance between radiators and air conditioners. Heckman High—more properly the Cecil G. Heckman Memorial High School—had been built just after World War I, to a classic high-ceilinged design. But time and technology had moved on, and no longer combined comfortably with twenties architecture. Indeed, if Digger Wells had not had a tendresse for Jess Gibbons, and therefore was predisposed to do his best for her, it is likely that she would have had to reposition the equipment every winter so as to have each sewing machine facing an open oven—or give up the needlework side of home economics entirely.

This she would have been loath to do, for, in addition to being a good and inventive cook, she was also a gifted needlewoman and had found an outlet for her creative abilities in the world of the art quilt. She had won several prizes and had lately been doing quilted wall hangings and lap quilts on commission. She was one of the leading lights of the Blackwater Bay Magpies, the local patchworking group. As she was, at present, in the throes of designing a quilt based on the patterns of ice-fishing huts made on the frozen bay, Jess was less than delighted at the news that there was a body floating around out there under the ice.

She had a brief, macabre thought: why not enclose a small felt figure within the quilt, a sort of symbolic image? The existence of the figure would be known only to herself—and to whoever, in the dim and distant future, might have cause to cut up or mend the quilt. Whether she would actually do such a thing depended on who the body was, how it had gotten there, and so on. Perhaps it could be a kind of memorial.

And perhaps, she decided, this morbidity was another sign of encroaching old age. She'd be reading obituaries aloud next.

In fact, the appearance of a body in the bay was mercifully rare. She couldn't remember hearing about anyone drowning in the bay in winter—skaters usually preferred the smaller ponds, which had smoother surfaces, unscoured by the winter winds and unbroken by the vast and changing pressures of the Great Lakes. She crossed the room and looked out of the window, hugging herself for warmth both within and without. As her teaching rooms were on the top floor, she was able to glimpse the bay itself just above the tops of the trees. It was easier to see it in the summer, when it glittered and reflected the blue of the sky. Now the band of pale gray ice simply merged with the overcast. The snow, which had been falling sporadically all morning, was falling faster now. The town, the bay, and the huts would be freshly shrouded in white by tomorrow. Shrouded? She shivered. Trust her obviously twisted subconscious to throw up a word like that.

It was not only odd that there should be a body out there under the ice, it was sinister. She didn't like it. She wondered, briefly, whether she should change the design of her quilt, which was fairly far advanced. Perhaps the huts could be changed to sailboats, the background to blue instead of gray and white . . .

Just then the girls in her next class started to filter into the room behind her, chattering and shrieking like seagulls.

"Okay, okay, settle down and get out your projects, please. I want to see what you accomplished over the vacation."

There were twenty students in this class, listed as Art Needlework 5050 but known more casually as "the patch class." Jess and the art teacher, Pat Morrison, had found that their specialties complemented one another, and so they had joined forces to produce the 5050 course, which combined design and craftswomanship. To join the class the students (usually but not always girls) had to demonstrate unusual ability, which gave rise to mutterings in the faculty offices about elitism.

Surprising support came from both Decker Moseley (American history) and Francine "Frankie" Ahearn (school secretary and ardent feminist), who both pointed out the historical and herstorical importance of The American Quilt. Their combined arguments won over the conventional heart of the principal, Mr. Dutton, and the class had now been offered for two years, with considerable success.

As Pat was one of the six teachers who lived at Perkins Point, she and Jess were good friends and found plenty of time for gossip in between teaching and advising. Pat was long and lean and not particularly beautiful, but her face was vividly alive, and her gray eyes were fascinating—each luminous iris rimmed with black.

"You heard about the Falconer party, I suppose?" she muttered to Jess during a quiet moment.

"Yes. What a hoot!"

"I don't think the Falconers will be doing much hooting when they get back from their ski vacation in Colorado. I hear the damage runs into the thousands."

Jess glanced across the room, where a subdued Chrissie Falconer was bent over her appliqué wall hanging of brightly colored tropical fish. "I thought she looked a bit down."

"Down and out, if old man Dutton has anything to say about it. He's waiting for the parents to come back so he can expel her officially. There were drugs, you see."

Jess was far from shocked. "Wow—so they smoked a little grass. Don't we all?"

Pat scowled at her and glanced at the class. "You're incorrigible," she whispered.

"Better that than a hypocrite," Jess whispered back. "If you ask me, grass is preferable to alcohol. People don't get into fights or stab, shoot, and run cars into one another on grass, but they do on booze, right?"

Pat pretended to draw something on the pad in front of her. "Well—maybe. If it had been only grass I don't suppose there would have been such a big fuss about it. Matt Gabriel is as broad-minded as you are on the dreaded weed, but he got riled up quite a bit over Chrissie's party, I hear. There must have been something more serious."

"Well, she looks pretty miserable," Jess said. "I'll have a word with her." Within her burgeoning "new" self, she felt a need to put things right for everyone else as well. It was a trait which had led her into trouble more than once in the past. Looking at Chrissie Falconer now, Jess felt a return of the old impulses, the tingling nerve ends that told her This Girl Can Be Saved.

Pat Morrison looked at her with something resembling alarm. "Jess," she said softly. "Let her alone."

"What do you mean?" Jess was truly astonished.

"I mean maybe she deserves to be taught a lesson," Pat murmured. "Whatever actually happened, how it happened or why, it might have been for the best. Ever since Chrissie was elected Homecoming Queen last fall she's been a bit . . . well . . . difficult."

Jess stared at her colleague. It was unusual for Pat to speak badly of a student, being of a normally generous and positive turn of mind, as was Jess herself. "You sound like you don't like the girl."

"I don't like people who think they *deserve* the best without earning it," Pat said reluctantly. "She's pretty, she's bright, she comes from a well-to-do family—"

"No wonder everyone hates her," Jess said, amused.

"Okay, I take your point. But ever since they put that tin crown on her head, she'd been acting like . . ."

"Like a queen?" Jess asked. She leaned closer. "Tell the truth now—were you always last to be chosen for the team?"

Pat grinned sheepishly. "Yup."

"Me, too," Jess said. "I had knock-knees, wore thick glasses, and had a rotten hand-eye coordination. I also got all As and let everybody know about it. I was definitely not Miss Popularity, and I remember what it was like being on the outside of everybody else's good times."

"Ditto," Pat said.

"So, under the circumstances, maybe we ought to be more sympathetic toward Chrissie rather than less," Jess continued. "She had a lot further to fall."

"I crouch corrected," Pat said with a smile. "Go on, save the poor little bitch's soul—see if I care."

Jess chuckled and moved across the room to take the empty chair beside Chrissie. "That's coming on beautifully," she said untruthfully. Normally the girl's hand stitching was exquisite, but the work she'd done so far that morning was uneven and scrappy.

"It's crap," Chrissie said unenthusiastically. "I don't seem to be able to do anything right at the moment."

"I heard about your party getting gate-crashed," Jess said in a sympathetic voice. That there was an empty chair next to Chrissie was in itself was unusual—invariably Chrissie had a group of sycophants around her. "It must have been awful."

Chrissie shrugged. "I can get a summer job and help pay for the damage," she said. "It's the other thing that my parents will go ape-shit about."

"The drugs?"

Chrissie's head drooped and her hands grew still, pale against the deep turquoise of the cloth that lay across her knees. "I told him it wasn't my fault, but he wouldn't listen."

"Who wouldn't listen?"

"Sheriff Gabriel," Chrissie said with deep contempt. "The bastard."

"He's usually a very fair man," Jess protested. She had always had a soft spot for Matt, and had hero-worshiped him during her own adolescence.

"I'll bet," Chrissie said sourly. "I'll bet he helps old ladies across the street and then charges them with jaywalking."

"Don't be silly. He was doing his job."

"Some job, arresting kids for nothing."

"Look, I'm sure he didn't want to, but some drugs are very dangerous, Chrissie. He has a responsibility to protect you."

"I didn't need that kind of 'protection,'" Chrissie muttered. "I had to call my father's lawyer in the middle of the night. It was this whole big *thing* . . ."

"You shouldn't have thrown a party with your parents away," Jess reminded her gently.

"I know *that*," Chrissie said impatiently.

"But that's half the fun, I suppose," Jess added.

Chrissie managed a faint smile. "You got it," she said. "If only those guys hadn't started wrecking the place, there wouldn't have been a problem. Things were fine up till then." She giggled. "*Really* fine."

"Because of the drugs, you mean?"

Chrissie shrugged and was quiet for a minute, then suddenly flared up. "I don't see what business it is of anyone's, anyway, what I do in my own private home. They weren't against the law, he said. They were experimental and just . . . well . . . fun things. Perfectly safe, no problem."

"Who said? The person who sold them to you? Another student?"

"It doesn't matter," Chrissie said, subdued by her own vehemence—several of the others students had turned to stare.

"Well, it does matter," Jess told her. "If somebody supplied you with illegal substances . . ."

"It wasn't *like* that," Chrissie interrupted her, her hands suddenly crumpling the material of the wall hanging. "It was more like a . . . like a test."

"You mean a dare," Jess said disapprovingly.

Chrissie's head came up suddenly, and there was a flash of defiance in her eyes.

"No . . . I don't mean that at all."

"Well . . ."

"I don't want to talk about it, Miss Gibbons. Thanks for taking an interest, but it's my problem, not yours." There was utter dismissal in her voice. "Excuse me, please—I'd like to see the nurse. I'm having cramps." She stood up and threw her work onto the table. "Can I have a hall pass, please?"

"As you like," Jess said, realizing that she could take this no further for the moment. With luck the girl would relax, perhaps take her into her confidence in time. They had always had a good relationship before, but Chrissie's humiliation was still raw. She had tried to get too close too soon.

She could have kicked herself. Instead she wrote out the hall pass and watched Chrissie leave the room.

"I hate to say I told you so, but—" Pat began.

"Consider it said," Jess snapped. "I, too, crouch corrected."

FOUR

The gulls, swooping over the huts of the ice fishermen, saw little below to attract or interest them. Ice fishing had become so organized over the years that the Blackwater Town Council had extended their winter trash-collection routes to encompass the temporary encampment. Naturally they did not allow their heavy trucks out onto the ice, but placed large Dumpsters at the edge of the bay.

The Icemen, as they called themselves, were aware that the Council could end the ice fishing anytime they chose by preventing access to the bay (although it would have been self-defeating, since the ice fishing and the festival that closed the season produced a mini-tourist boom in the doldrums following Christmas). As a result the Icemen were fairly responsible about policing the area and bringing their nonorganic trash to the Dumpsters at the end of each day. (Everything else went "down the hole" to draw the fish.) The gulls did not appreciate this ecologically sound approach and continued to dive and shriek in frustration over an area that in summer provided them with a wide range of excitement and nourishment.

So, when the first scream emanated from the hut of Frog Bartlett, it went largely unheeded by the rest of the population of Ice City, who assumed it was just another gull fight. However, when the screaming continued, and Frog himself burst out of his tacky hut and started running in circles while wildly waving his arms, quite a few men left their lines and emerged to see what the hell was going on.

It transpired that Frog, too, had seen the man under the ice.

"He looked at me, he looked right at me!" Frog screamed. This in itself was considered unlikely, as locals were of the opinion that Frog Bartlett was the ugliest man in Blackwater Bay County. He was equally burdened by a sensitive nature and a voice that, while normally basso profundo, could rise in vexation or terror to a soprano that Kiri Te Kanawa might envy.

It was in that range now.

"Jesus, Jesus, he musta fell in, he musta fell in!" Frog squealed frantically. "Gedda ax! We godda get him out!"

"Who?"

"Who?"

"What the hell's going on?"

"Whatsa matter?"

"Hey, Frog! Cool it!"

The other men, skidding a bit on the occasional slippery stretch of ice between the huts, crowded around the nearly hysterical Frog, whose unappealing face had now turned puce, tinged with gray around the edges. Their collective breath rose and mingled in clouds.

Frog was still windmilling his arms, turning around and around, staring into one face after another. "A guy! A guy! Under the ice! I seen him! His face just come up and he looked me right in the eye! I tell ya! He's trapped under there!"

"Come up like a dumpling in the stew?" asked a laconic voice from the edge of the gathering crowd.

Everyone turned. Frank Nixey was regarding them with a knowing expression. "Up like a trout, down like a stone?"

"Well . . . yeah . . . sort of," Frog allowed.

"Dead," Nixey said.

They all stared at him.

"He come up under *me* about eight o'clock this morning,"
Nixey continued, enjoying the unaccustomed attention.
"God knows how long he's been floating around under there."

As one man they stared down at the ice between their
boots and began to shuffle uncertainly. Was that a ghostly
knocking that they felt?

"I thought he was someone got drunk and fell in his fishing hole," Frog said, his voice sliding back down the scale.
Being of a reclusive nature, he had not heard of Nixey's "dis-
covery" earlier, and the whole experience had been a considerable shock to him—almost as bad as the sight of himself
in the mirror each morning.

"Nope," Nixey said, assuming a professorial attitude.
"He's been down there for a while. See, these gases sort of
form from him rotting inside and—"

"How come you know about this?" someone asked from
the back of the still-assembling crowd.

"Because the sheriff told me, that's how," Frank said. "I
went to him the minute I seen the guy, and he said he was
probably a floater, they come up and go down like that, and
there wasn't nothing he could do about it. So. There."

"You mean he . . . it . . . is just . . . sliding along . . .
under the ice?" a youngish voice quavered.

"Yup," Nixey said with a proprietary tone of authority—
after all, he'd seen it *first*.

Frog was drawing a visual line from Nixey's hut to his
own. "Current from the channel must be moving him," he
croaked, his voice back now to its usual deep timbre. "Sort
of pushing him along."

There was a collective shiver and a multiple clearing of
throats. Everyone was either looking down at the ice or up
at the sky—avoiding one another's eyes.

"Can't we do anything?" the youngish voice asked.

"Nope," Nixey said. "Just keep fishing, is all."

Nobody seemed in a hurry to resume that particular occupation, considering what they just might hook on the line.

"You know," someone said in a speculative voice, "if you're right about the current and so on, we might be able to figure his general direction and . . ."

"And what?" Frog asked cautiously.

"Well, I don't know." It was Mel Tuohmy, one of the barbers from Spelter's on Main Street. Old man Spelter put a hut out on the ice every year and, since he contended that hair grew slower in the winter, he allowed his barbers to take turns using the hut during the week. "Send a diver down, maybe?"

"Send him down where?" somebody wanted to know. "By the time they get divers over here the thing could be anywhere."

"Well—why don't we organize a watch?" somebody suggested. They turned to stare at the big idea man. He proved to be a city dweller who only came to Blackwater for the winter fishing.

"What do you mean, a watch?" Frog asked suspiciously.

The city man looked embarrassed. "Well, we all watch for it, and if it comes up again—"

"Grab it?" someone asked in a sarcastic tone.

"Well, maybe," the city dweller said. "Put a hook in its collar or something, anyway. Then the authorities could just— sort of—reel it in. Or follow the line . . ." His voice trailed off.

There was a silence.

"That's not a bad idea," Frog Bartlett said slowly.

"Thanks," the city dweller said shyly. He'd never really spoken to any of these men before, other than to pass the time of day, although he had been fishing the winter bay for many years.

"I mean, now we all *know* it's down there, we can sort of *expect* it instead of being scared out of our goddamn wits," Frog continued. "Especially those guys who are fishing beyond Nixey and me."

"Yes, indeed," said the city dweller sadly. His hut was
well out of the area Frog was indicating. But still, it *had*
been his idea. So much for those sarcastic things his wife
said. What did she know about a *man's* world? The city
dweller hitched up his L.L. Bean dungarees and leaned closer
to hear Frog Bartlett's strategy.

FIVE

The faculty lounge at Heckman High was not designed to inspire its patrons, or even to raise their broken spirits. Rather, it was a shabby, stained retreat from the bright shocks of adolescent reality. Its original pastel colors had faded into restful neutrality beneath years of grime and cigarette smoke, its furnishings castoffs and leftovers from garage sales gone wrong or contributions from vindictive parents who'd decided the broken springs of their old chairs were one way of getting back at the teachers for the lousy marks given to their sons or daughters. No two pieces had originally matched, but in this, too, time had leveled all.

Every time Jess walked into the teachers' lounge she had a momentary vision of achieving a wondrous transformation with slipcovers and paint, but the impulse inevitably passed. Life was complex enough, and anyway, she was certain that a spruced-up faculty lounge was the last thing any of them really wanted. Bright colors would be hard on the eyes, and they would have to keep it *tidy*. Nobody wanted to keep it tidy. Nobody wanted to be stimulated or startled into a higher level of awareness. God forbid. All they required was a quiet place to hide, and regular blood transfusions.

Jess sank down beside Tom Brady on what had been a chartreuse and purple sofa, a perfect icon of the sixties, placed beneath the windows in the vague hope that sunlight would eventually fade it. It was invariably the last place left to sit because it was also perfectly located to catch icy drafts and direct them onto arthritic necks and shoulders rounded from years of correcting papers.

She gazed around at her colleagues, the walking wounded in the continuous war of confrontation that passed for modern education. Many of them had been teaching when she herself had attended Heckman, and she had been startled on her return to find not only that they were still there but that many of them hadn't been all that much older than she was now.

"I don't know who to feel sorrier for, Mrs. Culhammer and the kitchen staff serving what passes for food in this place, or the kids who are desperate enough to eat it," Jess announced. "I suppose I'll have to have another inspirational talk with the old bat."

"It won't do any good," said Betty Hardwicke, from a few feet away. She peered over the top of her *Grantham Free Press*. "Mabel Culhammer is as deaf as a post and just as immovable. Save your energy."

"Anything in the paper about Frank Nixey's body?" Jason Phillips asked. "At least now we know what was wrong with him this morning."

"You heard about that, too, did you?" Tom said, looking up. "I understand it was only a glimpse of a body."

"Maybe not even that. I spoke to Glen a little while ago," Betty said. Her husband, Glen, was one of the sheriff's deputies. "He says it was only a glimpse of what Frank *thought* was a body. Matt isn't sure whether to believe him or not, apparently."

"Is he giving him the benefit of the doubt?" Jason asked.

"I think so. George Putnam believes him."

"Hah," Jess said. "George Putnam believes you can get rid of warts by rubbing them with a dead rat and then burying it in the moonlight."

Tom turned to stare at her. "He does?"

She flushed. "Well, you know what I mean." Jess had had "confrontations" with George Putnam from childhood. His idea of winning her heart then was putting frogs down her dress. He still operated on similar principles, only the methods were a little more sophisticated—like throwing pretzels at her in the Golden Perch while loudly discussing her bust measurement with his cronies. Since some of the senior students of Heckman High occasionally dropped into the Golden Perch, this did little for Jess's attempts to maintain an air of dignity and authority—an upward struggle at the best of times. For some reason her fine-boned build made her even more desirable in the eyes of George Putnam. He was big and muscular and yet had a strange hankering for the delicate. Perhaps that was why the very sight of her seemed to turn his brain to oatmeal.

"Even the *thought* of a body drifting around under the ice is enough to give me nightmares tonight," Betty said, going back to her paper. "I don't want to think about it."

Tom glanced at Jess before returning to his book. "Don't tell me—you're already thinking of putting a little body in your quilt."

She stared at him. "My God, how did you know that?"

"Because that's what I would do," he said, turning a page. "You're not the unicorn you think you are."

"But you're the hippopotamus I think you are," she retorted.

He rubbed his stomach absently. "Everybody puts on a little weight at Christmas."

"Not me."

"Only because you had the sly cunning to catch the flu and go into a maidenly decline, leaving the rest of us to finish up the leftovers and wash all the dishes," he pointed out.

The door of the lounge burst open, and Milly Hackabush,

one of the gym teachers, came in, followed by Chip Chandler.
"Hey, did you hear about the body under the ice—"
"We heard, we heard," came a chorus of voices.
Milly looked disappointed. "Well, I only asked," she said,
and closed the door behind her. "Any guesses as to who it is?"
There was a sudden silence. Until that moment, that par-
ticular angle hadn't occurred to them. They looked at one
another, then shuffled in their various broken-spring seats.
The thought of a body—any body—was not the same as the
thought of *somebody's* body.
"Nobody's missing, are they?" Fred Naughton asked.
More silence.
"I mean," Fred went on, "everybody's turned up for classes
this morning, haven't they?"
Further silence.
"Some of the kids are missing," someone said in a small
voice. "Just the usual goof-offs and truants, though."
"Glen said there was no way of knowing whether it's a
young person or an old person," Betty said, reluctantly low-
ering her paper once again. "Frank Nixey wasn't making
much sense, apparently."
"He never does," someone muttered.
"Anyway," Betty continued, "there are always kids absent
after Christmas."
"And runaways," Chip said. "There are always a few runaways."
"Old people wander off, too," someone said.
"I meant are we sure there are no teachers missing," Fred
said irritably. He had taught mathematics at Heckman High
ever since he graduated from college. He had been happy in
his work, but now his entire existence revolved around his
new obsession—avoiding the horrible possibility that he
might have to stand in for someone else and teach a subject
he knew nothing about. It had already happened once this
semester, and he was still reeling from the experience.
"Just Ed Martin," somebody said. "At least we know you

didn't bump him off, Fred. Although the rest of us might have."

There was general amusement. Ed Martin had been the defaulting teacher Jason Phillips replaced—a bombastic long-haired egotist totally unsuited to handling teenagers—or colleagues. He wore his hair in a trendy ponytail, and felt it his duty to inform those teachers whose methods he thought old-fashioned (everybody) just what were the very newest theories and methods in the profession. He himself had been a replacement for a much-loved teacher who had died the previous term, which made things even more difficult for him, but if he'd been even halfway pleasant he would have been accepted. It was not to be. After making himself generally unpopular he'd abruptly quit, two months into the term, leaving the principal, Mr. Dutton, no alternative but to press Fred Naughton into teaching both beginning and advanced chemistry until he could organize a replacement. Fred had been the only teacher whose schedule allowed it. He had proved an unmitigated disaster, replacing Martin's biting sarcasm with nervous insecurity and general dither. Until Jason arrived, there had been much muttering about final-exam results being affected—especially those of the seniors, who were worried about getting into college. In the event, Jason had managed to quickly rectify the situation, bringing the students into line and up to speed in no time. He was—as a result—the new apple of Mr. Dutton's eye. And, while Jason might not get on with everyone on the faculty (or at Perkins Point), he was a big improvement over Martin, and he could do no wrong as far as the rescued Fred Naughton was concerned.

"I heard there was a big party that got out of hand at Chrissie Falconer's house," Chip said after a moment.

The others looked at him and then one another, apparently startled by this piece of "inside" information.

"There was?" Jason asked.

"I heard something about it, too. You must have heard about it, Betty," Jess said. "From Glen?"

"He did mention something about a party, but he didn't say whose place it was," Betty said, folding her paper in resignation. She was a slight, very pretty woman with an exquisite complexion, china-blue eyes, and silvery hair that framed her face softly. She taught computer science, and her sweetly feminine appearance hid a brain like a bacon slicer. "Are you certain it was the Falconer girl? She's a very good student, aside from her atrocious spelling. I never thought she was the type to turn wild."

"Oh, it was Chrissie, all right," said Jess. "She was absolutely miserable in class this morning. And the thing that scares me is that apparently there were plenty of drugs available."

"Kids are always smoking grass," Chip said in disgust. "It slows them down and takes away their aggression. If I catch one of my boys smoking it—" His threat hung in the air, accepted by all, for he was a tough coach and wouldn't allow any trouble from "his boys."

Chip Chandler was big and muscular and conventionally handsome—cheekbones like baseballs, a noble nose, granite jaw, curly hair, clear sun-crinkled eyes, the whole works. So handsome, in fact, that he was regarded more in awe than actively desired by the girl students. To them he was as gorgeous as any Hollywood star, and as unreachable. In this they were absolutely correct, for Chip would never be caught by any covetous female. He was good-natured, relatively bright, kind, generous, and gay. This latter aspect of his personality was discreetly guarded—he had at the moment no wish to come out, as it would probably affect his job. His housemates at Perkins Point were aware of it. They all protected him—even Jason—from the officious interest of the PTA and the less liberally minded members of the faculty because they knew his lifestyle would never find its way into the school. Chip was drawn to older men, not teenage boys, and had a deep and ongoing relationship with an artist who lived in a converted lighthouse some thirty miles up the coast. His residence at Perkins Point was sporadic. It was mainly, for him, a place to change clothes and get mail. He was in full-time residence at the moment only because his lover was abroad preparing for a British showing of his work.

"Not just kids smoke grass," Jess said, thinking of the small stash in her blue and white ginger jar. "But apparently these were hard drugs."

"Crack?" someone asked.

"No, thank God," Betty said. "More on the line of LSD and Ecstasy."

"Good Lord," Fred Naughton said. "Junkies."

"Not quite," Claude Trickett told him. He taught both chemistry and physics and was head of the science department, a stocky, sandy-haired man with a rather forced jolly manner. "The term 'hard drugs' means addiction, and LSD is not physically addictive the way heroin and crack are." He beamed at them. "I've even tried it myself, under medical supervision, of course. Very interesting experience, although not one I'd wish to repeat. You can get hooked on the sensations, I imagine, but not if you're sensible."

"That's the whole point," Jason snapped. "Since when are adolescents sensible? They're just intent on getting a rush, whether it's from the boy next door or speed." He glanced around. "Both kinds—drug and car."

"We haven't had a drug problem with kids like Chrissie before," Milly Hackabush said slowly. "Some kids, yes, you expect it. Inevitable. But her crowd—I don't like the sound of it."

"Oh, come on," Jason said disbelievingly. "There's a drug problem *everywhere,* on every social level. Why should the wealthy young of Blackwater Bay be immune? Down in Grantham they were openly dealing in the hallways of the school where I taught and everybody was buying. It was terrifying."

Jess, Tom, and Chip exchanged glances. They'd taken Jason into the house at Perkins Point out of sympathy—he was in his late twenties, single, and in need of friends.

They'd since had cause to question the wisdom of their charitable act, for he'd proved to be moralistic, judgmental, inflexibly opinionated, and was too fastidious to take out the garbage. He was devoted to Jess's cats, so she was prepared to put up with his exasperating ways, but Tom was less than delighted with having Jason in the house, because in addition to refusing garbage duty he always seemed to be somewhere else when anything muscular needed to be done—usually gazing soulfully at Jess.

As a result any hard work was left to Tom and—if he happened to be around—Chip.

"I'm afraid Jason is right, Claude," Betty said quietly. "Scientific interest is one thing, but making money out of vulnerable adolescents is quite another. Glen has mentioned it, too. It was only a matter of time before these ghastly people spread out from Grantham and Hatchville looking for new buyers."

"Jesus," Tom muttered in disgust. "Bodies under the ice, drugs—what next?"

"Aliens from outer space?" Jess suggested brightly.

"Oh—your relatives in town again?" he said, and went back to his book.

Jess looked at him with a frown. She was more than accustomed to his sarcastic banter and was usually amused by it, but there seemed to be a glum undertone to it today. "Who let the air our of *your* tires?" she asked.

He sighed and closed the book over his index finger to keep his place. "My portable generator blew up this morning, and according to Claude there's no money for another one until next September."

"Why not ask the PTA?"

"I'm afraid the PTA is about wrung dry by now," Claude said regretfully.

Out in the hall the bell rang for the next period, followed by heavy groans and a general rising. Betty Hardwicke put her paper away, and Claude and Jason went off arguing amiably about an article in *Scientific American*.

Jess stared down at Tom. "Don't you have a class now?" she asked, just managing to resist the impulse to do him serious physical harm. He'd been absolutely impossible lately and she was tired of it.

"Nope. I have a double lunch hour on Mondays and Fridays, remember?"

She smiled sweetly at him. "Obviously they feel the science department is overstaffed." He looked up, alarmed, and she grinned. "Gotcha," she said. Then she remembered that he was doing the shopping that evening. "Hey, don't forget my lamb shanks."

He made an elaborate show of leaning forward to look at her legs. "Very nice," he said.

SIX

Fate is sometimes kind to those in need of a story to build a life on. That may be why, two days later, it *was* the city man who made The Catch.

"I . . . I tried to be efficient," he was saying. White-faced, he was waiting outside his bright red Orvis state-of-the-art arctic igloo tent when Matt and George drove over the ice. Quite a crowd had been waiting with the city man, although none had seemed eager to enter the tent. The weather had changed for the better, and although it was still bitterly cold, the sky was an amazing blue with an occasional meringue of clouds being blown across by a frisky wind. Whitecap weather—if the bay hadn't been frozen solid.

The city man—whose name was Treacher—had apparently seen the cloth of the dead man's jacket as it bobbed up in his fishing hole and made a grab for it.

"But it was rotten," he said with chattering teeth. "So I . . . I sort of rolled him over . . . and got a hook around his belt buckle." He managed a long breath. "Unfortunately—"

Matt waited. He had a feeling that what was coming was less than delightful. There was a certain something in the air—

"Unforunately," Treacher continued, "I must have . . . punctured . . . that is to say . . . pierced . . ."

"You made a hole in him with the hook," George said impatiently.

"Oh, Jesus," somebody in the crowd said. "Is *that* what it was."

"I figured the wind had changed direction and was blowing from Lemonville," somebody else commented. Lemonville was famous locally for its ghastly smell—produced by a cellophane plant that had been built there a few years before.

"Even Lemonville never smelled like *that*," Frank Nixey said sullenly, resentful that somebody else had hooked what he thought of as *his* catch. "I thought the devil himself had farted."

There was a general burst of laughter, and Treacher looked—had it been possible—even paler than before. "In the end, I let him go," he murmured.

"Oh, shit," George said.

"Oh, but the line is still attached," Treacher said eagerly. "I ran it out a little, then anchored it to my chair. You can pull him back." He paused. "If you really want to."

"You did a good job on this, Mr. Treacher," Matt said firmly, with a glare at Nixey. "It can't have been very pleasant for you."

"Nn . . . no, it wasn't," Treacher said, brightening a little.

"You acted quickly, that's the main thing, when you realized the cloth wouldn't hold," Matt continued, raising his voice slightly to reach the back of the crowd. "I don't suppose there are many who would have thought of the belt— or had the nerve to do anything about it."

"I'm in the Coast Guard Reserves," Treacher said, pulling himself up straighter. "They train us, you know. About . . . things like that." He didn't think it necessary to add that until this moment he'd never had any reason to make use of that training, and that as soon as he got back home he was going to resign, because as far as he was concerned if all bodies looked and smelled like *that,* the Coast Guard could *keep* their damn brass buttons.

"We'll have to widen the hole, of course," Matt said, looking around. "Can I borrow an ice ax from somebody?"

"Oh, there's one inside," Treacher said. "Everything's there."

As Matt and George entered the tent, they saw what Treacher meant. Everything *was* there. In fact, the interior of the hemispherical tent looked like the city man had bought out Abercrombie & Fitch, with a side trip to Herman's in case he had forgotten anything. Unfortunately, being as well made and windproof as it was, the expensive tent had managed to contain a great deal of the putrefaction gases Treacher had inadvertently allowed to escape from the body.

George gagged and turned to leave.

"Hang on, George." Matt, glancing around, noticed a vent flap in the tent's side and opened it. After a moment there were curses from outside and the sound of shuffling feet as the crowd backed away or circled the tent to stand upwind. Matt smiled to himself and went over to the hole in the ice. There was a line attached to the elegant folding chair that so recently had held the executive backside of the unfortunate Mr. Treacher, and when Matt tugged on the line he sensed a considerable weight on the end of it. When he let go, the line slowly pulled taut. The channel current was still at work.

He straightened up and looked around. "We can't pull this guy up in here," he said. "We'll have to get Treacher to clear it out and move it—then we'll put up screens before we start chopping out the ice. You go back to the car and radio Tilly to ring the Coroner's Office and send Hardwicke and Boomer over here with screens, perimeter tape, ropes, and anything else they think we'll need."

George looked relieved, and left the tent. A moment later Mr. Treacher entered, cautiously. Matt smiled at him.

"This is going to be a messy job, Mr. Treacher, and you've got a lot of nice stuff here. I think you'd better move it to a new spot," he said gently.

"Maybe it's time I packed up, anyway," Treacher said resignedly. "The season's nearly over, and somehow the whole thing has . . . that is to say . . . I think I'd better—"

"Come back next year?" Matt suggested.

"Right," Treacher agreed.

"We will need a statement from you, and you'll probably have to testify at the inquest if there is one, but if you leave your address and so on, I'll be in touch," Matt continued. "I'm really very grateful to you for what you've done. If we had been forced to wait until the thaw, it would have been a lot more difficult to locate and identify the body." He gestured vaguely.

"I think I know what you're saying," Treacher said quickly. "The fish . . . the ice . . . the rocks . . ."

"Exactly," Matt said, relieved not to have to go into the revolting details. His stomach wasn't really any stronger than George's, he just had tighter throat and jaw muscles. "Can I give you a hand with your things?"

By the time Hardwicke and Boomer arrived with the necessary equipment for protecting the scene and retrieving the body, Mr. Treacher's expensive fishing outfit had been efficiently stowed into an amazingly compact pair of specially constructed trunks that fitted exactly into the rear of his Mercedes station wagon. All that remained, in solitary state, was his splendid chair. It sat next to the open hole with the thin strong line still attached to one of its sturdy legs.

"Looks like a goddamn throne," Frank Nixey muttered, thinking of the battered wooden chair rescued from his wife's old kitchen set that even now was waiting for him in his hut.

"Getting to be good business now, ice fishing," Mel Tuohmy said. "You should *see* some of the stuff you can get."

"All *we* ever needed was a hole and a line," one old-timer said out of the corner of his mouth. "Maybe a blanket on a couple of sticks to block the wind."

"Different now," another grizzled veteran of the ice murmured back. "No stamina, no guts. All the comforts of home they've got to have. Bring portable TVs, some of them, for the football." He shook his head in disgust at the weakness of the modern generation, then considered the seat next to the hole as the deputies began to set up the screens around it. "Wouldn't *mind* a chair like that, though. Fishing gets me in the back now."

"You, too?" his friend said.

"Cuts just like a knife, right here . . ." They lowered their voices, discussing their respective twinges and the comparative virtues of various liniments and treatments.

Once the screens were in position, the deputies took turns chopping at the ice, widening the hole but taking care not to disturb the taut line that disappeared down into the water. Open to the sky now, the dark water showed a hazy greenish tinge, and lapped at the underside of the ice, which flexed slightly under the pressure of the men walking over it. There was little danger of their going through—the ice was a good two feet thick out here. The chopping wasn't easy, but eventually the hole was widened to about three feet across.

"I reckon that's enough," Matt said as Hardwicke, Boomer, and George straightened up to get their breaths. "We'll be able to bend him through—he's long past rigor mortis now. It's just a matter of not losing an arm or any pieces of skin or flesh. If he's been under a long time, the skin of his hands might come off and we'd lose any chance of getting prints."

George made a sound of disgust. "Aren't we going to wait for the coroner's guys?" he asked plaintively. "They probably have special equipment for keeping all the bits together."

"They're here," Hardwicke said, pointing to a dark car making its cautious way over the ice toward them. "I'd better move the patrol cars, or there'll be too much weight concentrated in one spot."

"Good idea," Matt agreed. "We don't want to end up under the ice like our floating friend, do we?"

SEVEN

"Well, he sure as hell didn't drown," George said when they had settled back in the office. "Unless somebody decided to shoot him after he was dead."

"Maybe he committed suicide, then fell into the water," Tilly suggested from her desk. They had given her a brief description of the body and its recovery, a description she had received with interest while exquisite shudders shook her considerable bulk.

"No powder marks," Matt said, leaning down to give Max a stroke as the tomcat plodded past resolutely. Being a thoroughly professional rodent control officer involved making regular inspections of the premises throughout the day and night, and it was time for the next patrol.

"Powder marks could have washed away," Tilly pointed out.

"I suppose so. There may be some grains still embedded in the skin. If so, the autopsy will show them. They'll examine the wound pretty closely and it's accessible enough—right in the middle of the guy's forehead," Matt told her, then glanced across the desk. "You all right, George?"

His chief deputy was looking a little green. Again.

It had been an unpleasant business, to say the least. To tell Tilly there had been a dead body with a bullet hole in the forehead trapped under the ice was not to fully describe the soapy, dead white of the flesh, the damage done by the ice and winter-hungry fish, the rotten rags of clothing that clung to it. Or the smell.

Especially the smell.

"Oh, sure, I'm fine," George said negligently.

"Then you're ready for lunch?"

"Well—"

Matt was not a cruel man, although the sight of George Putnam trying to play the casual cop accustomed to dealing with such situations had been almost laughable out on the ice. Had they been alone, George could have thrown up with impunity—it was not unusual for even experienced cops to be sickened by floaters—but the crowd of fishermen had made George defensive and caused him to curse loudly and strut around with his chest out and his teeth clenched against digestive rebellion. Now, in the close warmth of the office, the memories were coming back to him.

"I think what we both could use is a stiff drink," Matt said. "If you'll pardon the pun."

"Great," breathed George.

"I'll need reports," Tilly called after them. She was their conscience, translator, and coffee maker par excellence. She had been office assistant to Matt's father before him and knew more about police and legal procedure than even Matt did. It was Tilly Moss who kept things properly organized in the Sheriff's Department of Blackwater Bay, and they all knew it. She had a warm heart and tight lips. Burdened with an invalid mother, she was nevertheless consistently supportive of "her men"—Matt, George, and the other deputies.

She sighed as Matt and George went out. It was true that her life was a bit more pleasant now that the building conversion was complete. She had her own office, as did Matt, and the files and storage areas were vast compared with what they had struggled with in the past. However, old habits died hard. Inevitably, in the few moments of peace that came along, both she and Matt ended up sitting around in the outer area of the office as they had always done, chatting with any deputies who happened to be around, passing the time of day with folks who dropped in, and generally making themselves comfortable. The architect had intended the outer office strictly as a reception area with a desk for the on-duty deputy or deputies. As a result of their using it like a living room, a great deal of clutter accumulated out there, and this meant she had to regularly spend time redistributing things to their "proper" places.

Due to the amount of walking back and forth this required, she had lost ten pounds already without even cutting back on one of the many doughnuts she and the staff enjoyed during the working day. Indeed, the enlarged Sheriff's Department of Blackwater County probably would be unable to operate without the constant supply of fresh doughnuts Tilly brought in every morning, picking them up at the Ring-a-Ding Doughnuttery on her way to work. Had anyone been able to chart productivity in the department, it would have become immediately obvious that on Tilly's days off the lack of doughnuts could be related to a drop in general activity. No doubt one of the college students they employed during the summer would eventually produce a master's thesis on the correlation of carbohydrate input and police efficiency.

As Tilly was reluctantly getting to her feet to tidy up the morning's debris and call Max into the kitchen for his usual lunch of tuna fish and doughnut crumbs, Matt and George were gratefully settling down at the bar of the Golden Perch. George had *nearly* turned tail as they opened the door and were engulfed by overwarm air carrying the smell of beer and fried fish, but he had rallied and managed to make it to the bar without disgracing himself.

"Two whiskeys, straight up," Matt said to Harlow

Wilcox, the bartender. The huge white-haired man raised an eyebrow.

"Middle of the day?"

"Had a floater out on the bay," Matt said with a barely perceptible tilt of his head toward George. "We could use a steadying confluence."

"Ah," Harlow nodded, and produced the required stabilizers.

There were plenty of bars in Blackwater, but the Golden Perch was one of the oldest. It was also considered to be one of the better venues because of its very excellent adjoining restaurant. Ladies often lunched there, and the evening atmosphere was both elegant and expensive. The bar itself, however, was primarily a masculine enclave, dark and leathery in nature, and popular with local businessmen. It was a little early in the day still, and there were not many patrons lining the long mahogany bar that had been a central feature of the place since the turn of the century. A few stools further down its gleaming length, Shad Billmore leaned forward and called to Matt. "Anybody local?"

"Stranger to us," Matt said. "We'll be looking for help on the identification, if you'd like to drop over to the morgue in Hatchville."

"How long in the water?" Billmore asked. He was an insurance man and knew a little about a lot of things, including death.

"Some weeks, I'd say."

Shad grinned. "No, thanks. I'll leave it, if it's all the same to you."

"We'll be circulating a description and getting a drawing done for the TV and newspapers," Matt said, sipping his drink. "But if you hear of anybody missing, we'd appreciate the input."

George got down suddenly from his barstool and made for the men's room. Shad watched him go, then winked at Matt. "The delicate deputy departs." He took a swig of his beer.

"A few weeks in the water isn't pretty," Matt observed with a slight edge to his voice. He didn't much like Shad Billmore, who was a somewhat sleazy new addition to the local population, and in any event he thought George had done damn well to last as long as he had without puking. He'd had a few uneasy moments himself.

"The way things have been going around here, I suppose your latest corpse will turn out to be some missing Hollywood star," Shad was continuing with slightly sadistic glee. "When can we expect the television people this time?"

"Never, I hope," Matt said glumly.

"Didn't the guy have any ID?" asked Wilcox, who was accustomed to ask for such things, particularly during the spring and summer influx of students hell-bent on a high time.

"Nothing," Matt said.

"You mean he was naked?" Billmore butted in again.

"No. He was wearing what was left of a jacket, shirt and trousers and underwear, still had one shoe on, and wore a signet ring on his little finger," Matt said. He did not add that when he'd tried to remove the ring, the finger had come off, too. Or most of it, anyway.

"Class ring, something like that?" Wilcox asked, playing detective as he moved up and down the bar, dusting and re-arranging.

"No, just an ordinary run-of-the-mill onyx ring," Matt said. "Nothing engraved on it, no symbols or anything."

"Damn," the bartender said, putting back one bottle and starting to polish the next. "Tough one."

"You sure you never saw him before?" someone standing behind Matt asked. He turned and saw that several men had gathered around, listening to what few pieces of information he had. It was the scene on the ice all over again, but in darker, warmer, and more comfortable surroundings.

"A stranger, like I said," Matt told them. "When the coroner has finished with him, we'd appreciate anybody coming forward who thinks they might be able to identify him. And, of course, we'll be in touch with other towns around the lake and bay to check out their missing persons."

"The Soo Locks are still froze over. No big international ships coming through now," somebody observed. "Got to be from around the bay somewhere."

"Could have gone in on the Canadian side," somebody else put in. "You sure about the time in the water?"

"Just a guess," Matt allowed. "Could have been longer, I suppose. But after a while . . ." He stopped, glancing at the bartender. Disgusting details were not going to do much for his lunch trade. "Cold water slows things down," he acknowledged. "Hard to say."

"Sure hope we don't hold a policy on the poor bastard," Billmore said with a raw laugh. "We have to pay out double indemnity for accidental drowning."

"Oh, it wasn't a drowning," somebody at the back said. "The guy was shot." Matt recognized one of the men from the ice-fishing community who'd come in from the cold.

There was a shocked silence.

"That true, Matt?" Harlow Wilcox asked, his flicking towel stilled for once.

"He had a hole in his head," Matt said. "I don't know if it was a bullet hole or not. We'll have to see what the coroner says." But he knew.

And they knew he knew.

There was a collective sigh, part regret, part anticipation.

There was going to be a hot time in the old town.

Again.

EIGHT

The monthly meeting of the Blackwater Bay Magpies was in
full chatter. Outside, a whining wind complained around
the corners of the old house at Perkins Point, but within all
was cozy and warm. Some of the ladies were working on
their own projects, but six of them were sitting around a
large frame that had been propped up on four chairs in the
living room of the house at Perkins Point. They were working on a group quilt that was to be auctioned off for charity
at the Ice Festival, and the final stage of quilting had been
reached. The subject under discussion, however, was not the
sewing, but the body that had been under the ice.

"They still haven't the least idea who it is," one of the
ladies was saying.

"It's not as if we have so many people around here in winter that one could disappear and nobody would notice," said
another.

"Probably somebody from the Canadian side," put in a
third. "Very casual, Canadians."

"But very tidy," said the first lady. "It doesn't seem to me
it would be something thrown in from that side."

"Thrown in?"

"Well, it was murder, wasn't it? It said in the *Chronicle* that the man was shot. I don't suppose he was *swimming* when somebody plugged him, do you?"

They agreed that the possibility was slight.

Jess glanced at Betty Hardwicke, who was opposite her. "Have you heard anything more about it?"

Betty shook her head. "Glen says that getting fingerprints from a body that's been in the water as long as that one was is a slow process. If it works—and it doesn't always—they should know after the weekend. But as Mona said, nobody's been reported missing, and finding out who he is might not really get them any further. He's been dead for weeks, so the killer, whoever it is, has had plenty of time to cover his tracks. Where would you go from there if *you* were the sheriff?"

They thought about this.

"I'd find out who was missing from other places around the Lakes," Margaret Toby said, stabbing her needle into the fabric so forcefully that for a moment the quilt shook.

"Ouch!" someone exclaimed, and a fingertip was sucked reproachfully.

"Sorry," Margaret murmured. "And then I'd set them out in order of who is most likely to have been murdered, and who might have wanted them dead, and then . . ." She trailed off.

"Yes?" asked Betty pointedly.

"I see what you mean," Margaret conceded. "It kind of keeps widening out. Could take a lot of time."

"Of course, even if the person isn't from around here, there might be some local connection," Mona Pickering said. She was secretary to the law practice of Crabtree and Putnam, and accustomed to seeing one thing lead to another. Usually, she said, from bad to worse. "That might give them a lead."

"And it might mean them spending the rest of the winter on wild-goose chases," said Pat Morrison from her arm-chair in the corner. She had recently completed a wall hang-ing and had a sketchpad propped on her lap working out designs for her next project. "Haven't we got plenty of trou-ble in our town already without that?"

Several of the ladies stopped stitching and turned to stare at her. "What do you mean, plenty of trouble?" someone asked.

"I think she means the drugs," Jess said. "There have been reports of drugs found at a local party."

Margaret Toby snorted. "Plenty of people have the odd joint of grass—so what?"

Now *all* the ladies stopped stitching and turned back to stare at Margaret. After a moment she noticed the silence and looked up. "Well?" she asked, of no one in particular.

"I think you've shocked some of the ladies," Jess whis-pered, trying not to laugh.

"Oh, for goodness' sake," Margaret said, looking around in exasperation. "I know all of you, and especially you, Hester Crabbe. I knew you when you were in your flaming youth and not averse to the odd snort of cocaine, either, at some of those college dances you went to along with me and some of these other so-called ladies."

"Well, really," blustered the bosomy and blessed Mrs. Crabbe, a leading light of the local Methodist church.

"Of course," Mrs. Toby went on imperturbably, "we didn't know how destructive cocaine was then. It was racy, and we tried it. Reefers, too—that's what they called joints then. *And* Hester made bathtub gin, *in* her bathtub, I might add."

There was a momentary lack of oxygen in the room as all the ladies drew in a simultaneous gasp of astonishment, dis-may, and delight. Hester Crabbe's face went crimson.

"You're in serious danger of becoming a bad influence, Margaret," Jess said. "We younger Magpies are stunned by these revelations of your lurid past."

Mrs. Toby looked across the quilt at her. "Balls," she said,

and went on stitching. There was another silence and then
an explosion of laughter. By the time Tom came to see what
was going on, several of the ladies were wiping their eyes on
the corners of their incomplete quilts.

"Any first aid needed here?" he inquired.

"No—but tea and coffee wouldn't be turned down," Jess
said over her shoulder. "We are badly parched." She knew
without looking that Tom was swallowing whatever smart re-
mark came into his mind out of respect for what he assumed
were ladies of delicate sensibility, stitching away at their
dainty needlework. Little did he know, she thought, and enjoyed imagining his expression as he nearly strangled on what
he would have normally said in response to such a request
from her.

"Well, I'll put the kettle on for you," he finally conceded.
"Glad to."

When he had gone, there was another ripple of laughter,
followed by the usual, "oh my's" and "dear me's" as the ladies
gradually regained their equilibrium.

"It's all very well and good remembering our flaming
youth, as you put it," Betty Hardwicke pointed out. "But,
from what I've heard, the drugs at this party were a little
more dangerous and the children a lot more into them than
we ever were."

Margaret Toby frowned. "You don't mean that—whatsit—crack, do you?"

"Not yet. But it can't be far behind," Betty said. "I understand the kids that were involved were from families who
are overgenerous with allowances and undergenerous with
their time and interest. We're not talking about poor kids
looking for escape, which is terrible enough. We're talking
about bored rich kids looking for kicks, kids who are apt to
turn destructive because they figure their parents can afford
to pay for their shenanigans. After all, they always have."

"Caroline Falconer will just *die* when it comes out," Mona
Pickering said, ending the dance around not speaking aloud

the names of those involved. Although it remained unreported in the *Chronicle,* it appeared that they all knew something of what had gone on at the Falconer girl's party.

"Why didn't Matt throw them in jail?" someone asked Betty.

"He did," Betty said. "For all the good it did him. They just laughed at him—and their lawyers had them out before morning. Like I said, we're talking money here, and money talks back. Glen says he's not worried—they've known all those kids since they were born, and they know they're not going anywhere. It's when the cases come to court that the trouble might get out of hand. And poor old Matt, with an election coming up this year."

"The lawyers had a duty to protect their clients," Mona said, sticking up for her employers, whose firm represented most of the aforesaid wealthy families of Blackwater Bay County. "Especially since most of them were still under eighteen, and the parents were . . ." She paused delicately. "The law is perfectly clear," she finished, and bent her head over the quilt again. The conflict between her duty to her employers and the wish to gossip was clear, and the ladies didn't press her, although they would have dearly loved to hear the details of what had been said in the offices of Crabtree and Putnam the morning after.

Emily Gibbons could have told them, as she was engaged to a young attorney employed by Carl Putnam, but she had quickly learned that her loyalty to Dominic outweighed both her work as a reporter and her participation in these monthly gabfests. Unlike Mona Pickering, she felt no conflict. If something could hurt Dominic, it was not even considered. Of course, if Dominic could point her toward information she could gather herself, that was quite another thing. She could follow a trail as well as anyone. What she discovered was up to her, as was what she revealed of it. Tonight she was saying nothing, and continued to stitch her tapestry pillow cover. After a moment she put it aside and got up.

"I'll give Tom a hand with the coffee," she said.

Jess nearly maimed herself with her needle in astonishment. The recent changes in her younger sister had been profound and totally unprecedented. Theirs had always been an edgy relationship, filled with rivalry and, on occasion, claws—but beneath it they loved one another deeply. Still, they knew one another's weaknesses only too well, and made few allowances for them. Voluntary assistance in any form of domestic activity was definitely not usual for Emily.

"Why don't you bake up a few cookies while you're out there," Jess suggested, and got, to her further surprise, a smile. Not exactly a nice smile (that would have indicated a brain tumor at the very least), but a smile nonetheless.

"I'll settle for whatever you've done," Emily said mildly, knowing perfectly well that Jess would have prepared something fattening and totally delicious for the ladies. "If I like it, I might leave a few for everyone else."

Jess turned her place over to one of the other ladies and followed Emily out to the kitchen. Could it be that Emily was growing up at last? The possibility seemed a remote one, but Dominic Pritchard was a pretty powerful influence. She highly approved of her prospective brother-in-law, who was funny, good-looking, and extremely bright. He was also modest, a very endearing quality in someone so gifted.

Tom had put two kettles on to boil and was leaning against the sink laughing at something Emily had just said. When Jess came in, he put on a quick scowl.

"Listen, I am not your butler," he began.

"I know you aren't," Jess said. "And I appreciate the fact that you denied yourself the pleasure of telling me so in front of my guests."

"Oh. Well." He looked confused. "I don't mind putting the kettles on—as long as I get a few cookies."

"Help yourself—there's plenty," Jess said.

Tom and Emily exchanged a glance.

"Are you feeling all right?" Emily finally asked.

"I was wondering the same thing about you," Jess said, pausing with her spoon suspended between the tea caddy and the teapot.

"I knew it," Tom said. "Bubonic plague."

"It's just that I get the feeling you know more than you're saying about this body they found under the ice," Jess said to Emily.

"Well, I don't," Emily said with an edge to her voice that revealed frustration. She was small and shapely, a sexier version of her two older sisters, with light brown hair and chocolate-brown eyes. Her appearance was in direct contrast to her personality, which was sharp and brisk. "Until they get an ID on him, there's really no story at all. I'm hoping he'll turn out to be Elvis, myself."

"It's probably just some old drunk," said Jason Phillips from the doorway. He was dragging a piece of string at the end of which was a cloth mouse. Both cats were following it with rapt attention. He jerked the string and they pounced, rolling about and batting it with their paws.

Emily glanced at him and then looked at Jess with a raised eyebrow. "This is our newest addition, Jason Phillips. Jason, this is my sister Emily. She's a reporter on the *Chronicle*."

Jason jerked the string again, more absorbed in the cats than anything. The overhead light glinted off his glasses as he glanced at Emily and then away. "Oh, that weekly thing with the blue stripe at the top?"

"*Bi*weekly," Emily snapped. "Tuesdays and Fridays."

"I thought it was a supermarket giveaway," Jason said vaguely.

"I don't know how you got that idea," Tom said. "You never go to the supermarket."

"No, that isn't my job," Jason said mildly. "I do the laundry and deal with the dry cleaning and . . ." He paused.

"And?" Tom asked, leaning forward.

"And whatever else needs to be done," Jason finished.

"Hah!" Tom snorted, but a glance at Jess told him this was the wrong time to challenge Jason on his lack of contribution to the household chores.

"The *Chronicle* has been serving Blackwater Bay County for over a hundred years," Emily began hotly. "We're on the wires and have broken many stories . . ."

Jason wasn't listening. "What are all those women doing here?" he wanted to know. "I have some work to do."

"It's a sewing group I belong to," Jess said. "I told you last week that they were coming, Jason. We have monthly meetings in rotation and this time it was my turn to be hostess."

"It's very awkward," Jason said. "I need the dining room table and it's all covered in *food*."

"It costs fifty cents," Emily continued. "It's not free."

"Why don't you go up to my room and use my big table, Jason?" Jess suggested with a nervous glance at Emily, who seemed in imminent danger of creating a headline or two herself by spontaneously combusting. "Just move the fabrics onto the bed."

"All right," Jason said, turning away. The cats, light-headed now and obviously entranced, followed the trailing string and the bouncing mouse out of the kitchen. The door swung shut behind the small parade.

"You're welcome," Emily shouted after him.

"Em," Jess said, mildly reproachful.

"Well, he'll probably mess your stuff up," Emily said. "My God, what a rude bastard. Why did you ever let him in here?"

"Something I have often wondered myself," Tom said with a meaningful glance at Jess.

She bridled. "I thought he would be a nice playmate for you, Tommy dear. If Chip leaves in the spring as he's threatening to do, you'd be outnumbered by women."

"I know," he said in mock rapture. "It would be perfect.

All I'd have to do is carry the heavy stuff and replace burned-out lightbulbs. In return my socks would be darned, my shirts ironed, my brow smoothed, my troubles listened to . . ."

"A sultan's existence," Emily observed.

"Exactly," Tom agreed. "I'd've had it made. But now that . . . that . . ."

"Drip," Emily supplied.

"Thank you. That drip, that dweeb, that damned nerd arrives, courtesy of Our Lady of the Misfits, here . . ."

"Well, thank you very much," Jess said, mystified by his sudden venom. "I asked *you* here, didn't I?"

"Just goes to prove my point." Tom grinned. "You're a sucker for a sob story."

"What was your sob story?" Emily wanted to know, as she filled up the milk and cream pitchers.

"Oh, that I was madly in love with a home economics teacher who wouldn't give me the time of day," Tom said lightly.

Jess glanced at him, startled. "That's not how I remember it," she said.

"Well, that's how it was," Tom said firmly. "How it is."

They stared at one another. Tom looked away first, turning to put the milk carton back into the refrigerator.

"Can I have a comment for publication, sister dear?" Emily asked sweetly.

Jess looked at her, picked up the tray, and went into the dining room. The door swung shut behind her. Emily looked at Tom.

"How long has this been going on?" she asked.

"It hasn't," Tom said into the refrigerator.

"But now it is?" Emily asked sympathetically.

He closed the door and leaned his head against the cool surface. "Pardon me while I go and hang myself," he said.

"I'd appreciate it," Emily said sincerely. "I could use a good story for the front page." He gave her a weak grin and went out into the hall. Emily picked up the second tray and went into the dining room. The ladies had gathered and were still chattering like the Magpies they were. As they chose their refreshments, Margaret Toby made an announcement.

"We've worked it out—about the dead man under the ice," she said.

"Oh?" Jess asked, handing out cups.

"Absolutely."

"And?"

"Obvious, really. He must have fallen out of a plane and gone into the lake further out!"

Emily and Jess exchanged glances over the table.

"Of course," Jess said. "How could it have been any other way?"

"I'll start calling the airlines in the morning," Emily promised. "Who knows? Somebody might have noticed a door hanging open."

NINE

Things had begun to change after the retrieval of the body.

Quite a few of the huts had been taken down or dragged off to be stored in garage or boathouse until next year, and the ones that remained were not exactly hives of activity. Those men who stayed loyal to the ice trudged out rather truculently each day, stubborn looks on their faces and fierce dedication in their hearts.

The enlarged hole from which the sheriff and his men had dragged the body had frozen over thinly and the scar was slowly filling in with drifting snow. It was encircled with warning flags to prevent someone falling into it and starting the whole process over again.

"The thing kind of puts the kibosh on dropping your line into the water," Frank Nixey complained at lunchtime in the Golden Perch bar. "You get to wondering what *else* is under there."

"About a million bucks' worth of Prohibition booze," Shad Billmore, the insurance man, said. He was still making a strong bid to settle down in Blackwater, but the locals just weren't interested in buying more insurance. He was spend-

ing more and more time, and more and more money, in the
Golden Perch. It had soured him, and he was on the lookout
for new avenues of endeavor. Most of them seemed blocked
by snow.

"Nobody's ever snagged any of that bootlegger booze,"
Frank said regretfully. "They generally threw it overboard in
the shipping channels as soon as they spotted the Revenue
boats. Too deep for a grapple or line out there." Prohibition
had been a lively period in Blackwater Bay history, what
with Canada being so close and the locals being of an anar-
chic and enterprising turn of mind. Only something as
bizarre as Prohibition could have produced a place as quirky
as Blackwater Bay County, and the locals were grateful for it.

"You hear what happened to Tyrone Molt yesterday?" old
Snakehips Turkle asked. Heads were shaken. Snakehips
leaned back and fondled his beer glass. "Well, there he was,
fishing quiet like you do, and suddenly this big black hairy
thing bursts up out of the hole and knocks him flying."

"Jeeesus!" somebody said.

"He figured the devil himself had come to get him and he
lit out running. Reckon he left a brown trail behind him as
he went. I sure would have."

"What the hell was it?" somebody asked, expecting the
Creature from the Black Lagoon or another body at least.

Snakehips grinned. "Dog," he said.

"Dog?" There were murmurs of disbelief.

"Yep. Turns out Curtis Wainright was in the next hut,
and he'd brought his son's pup with him for company.
Retriever, it is. Big black retriever, still young enough to get
excited when Curtis was trying to gaff something and it
went right into the water after it. Instinct, I suppose. Poor
dumb thing must have swum around under the ice, pretty
desperate, near drowning until he come to Molt's hole and
burst out heaving for breath and damn well terrified hisself.
Molt had to go to the doctor for some more heart pills."

There was much laughter combined with commiserations

for Molt, a local car dealer, and various exclamations of amazement. Didn't that just beat all? somebody said. Imagine how you'd have felt yourself, that big black thing coming at you when you were least expecting it, what with this dead body and then—

The mention of the body cast them all back into despondency again. The laughter faded, and more beers were hastily ordered.

Billmore had been thinking. "How many dead people do you tend to get here in a year, anyway?" he asked. "Do you grade them by weight or condition? We could average it out, figure the odds on somebody hooking anything bigger than, say, a teenager, and then we could set up a pool, winner takes all."

"That's not funny," the bartender said. Harlow Wilcox had been tending bar in the Golden Perch for over twenty years and there were some that said he owned the place and others that said they didn't think he owned it, but on the other hand, who did? Nobody knew.

"Only trying to cheer up my man here," Billmore said. "Give him another drink. Ease his pain."

"I'm not saying we're chicken or anything like that," Frank continued, accepting the drink with his usual salute. "But it's not the same. You sit there and you look down into the water and it looks . . . different. Not friendly."

"And it looked friendly before?" Harlow asked.

"Well—it didn't look *un*friendly," Frank said.

"You dwell on things too much, Frank," the big bartender said, wiping the bar down for the fifteenth time. Condensation was a real problem in winter, what with the central heating on and everybody breathing hard when they came in from the cold wind and started stomping snow off their boots. Not everybody considers these various aspects of running a good drinking place, Harlow always said, whenever folks expressed a wish to buy a little bar and grill somewhere when they retired. Harlow said he would never retire, they would just find him dropped down dead behind the bar one day, and he would be obliged if they would put a maraschino cherry in his mouth and bury him as he was, towel around his waist and a swizzle stick in his hand, thanks for the memory. "You're too sensitive," Harlow added, and pushed the salted peanuts toward them.

Frank sighed. "It's my one-sixteenth Indian heritage," he said.

"Yah," Harlow agreed solemnly. "Like you say."

"I feel closer to the spirit world, sort of, than most folks do," Frank said dreamily.

"What kind of spirits are those—whiskey or gin?" Shad wanted to know, and laughed appreciatively at his own joke. The other two men ignored him.

"Maybe somebody ought to do something about it," Harlow said. "What about Old Fishguts—he still got his powers?"

Frank brightened. "Say! That's an idea."

"Who's Fishguts?" Billmore asked.

Harlow glanced at him. "Old Indian medicine man lives up the river."

Shad put on a burlesque expression of amazement. "An Indian *medicine man*?" he said. "Cowabunga!"

"He's pretty old, mind," Frank mused. "Got arthritis bad, I hear."

"Can't be much of a medicine man if he can't cure his own arthritis," Shad said disparagingly. "I mean—can he?"

Frank finally deigned to look at him. "He probably would cure it if he thought he *should* cure it," he told Shad. "Some ills are sent for teaching, you know."

"And some come just for fun?" Shad asked.

Frank turned away. "You don't understand."

Harlow looked at the insurance agent with a degree of pity—after all, he was a regular customer and deserved respect. Well, some respect, anyway. "Fishguts has done some impressive things in his time," he said. "A lot of folks around here got Indian blood in 'em. I'm one-sixty-fourth myself, and even I've seen things I couldn't explain."

"What things?" Billmore, the modern skeptic, asked.

"Spirit things," Frank muttered. "You wouldn't understand." He glanced up at Harlow. "I'll ask Fishguts if he can do something to get rid of the bad feelings out there," he said decisively. "It wouldn't hurt to ask him, would it?"

"Hell, no," Harlow said. "Especially if you take him some medicine for his bones."

"What does he like?" Frank asked.

"Johnnie Walker Black Label," Harlow said promptly. "All he ever drinks."

"Well," Frank said, nodding. "He would."

"That is some classy Indian," Shad put in. "A regular Champagne Charley, hey?"

Harlow glared at him. "He's a full-blood. They've got to have the best stuff."

"Why?" Billmore asked. This sounded like a good wheeze to him. He might start to claim Indian ancestry himself.

"Purity," Frank told him.

"Oh, yeah?" Shad said.

"Yeah," Frank said, beginning to look irritated.

"Why?" Shad asked.

"Because—" Frank paused and looked at Harlow.

"Because you got to have a straight line through," Harlow said, thwacking his towel on the bar to get a fly. The fly escaped. They always did—Harlow never aimed to kill, just spook.

"Yeah," Frank nodded, folding his arms across his chest. "You got to have a straight line through."

"Through to what?" Billmore was getting irritated, too.

"Through to the ancestors," Frank said.

"The ancestors?" Billmore echoed blankly.

"Who else are you going to ask?" Harlow wanted to know.

"Ghostbusters?" Billmore suggested.

Frank sighed heavily and turned slightly away from Billmore. "What kind of break are you offering on the Lions game on Saturday?" he asked Harlow.

The talk turned from dead bodies to athletic ones, but it was clear that Frank Nixey's observations concerning the drop in fishing enthusiasm had been accurate. There were a lot more fishermen in the Blackwater Bay bars than there were out on the ice. It did not bode well for the Ice Festival—a situation reported to the local newspaper by Dominic Pritchard, who had been quietly consuming a steakburger in a rear booth of the Golden Perch when Frank Nixey's despair had overtaken him.

"And, from what I understand, Frank is going to see some kind of Indian medicine man," Dominic told Emily.

Emily nodded. "Probably Old Fishguts."

"I think that *was* the name Frank said," Dominic agreed. He was relatively new to Blackwater Bay, having arrived the previous summer, but whereas someone like Shad Billmore would never learn to fit in, Dominic had blended into town as smoothly as a drop of butter into good hollandaise sauce because he had a streak of irony that allowed him to appreciate the more esoteric aspects of Blackwater life. He was pretty much liked by everyone. "Is there a story for you in this medicine man?"

"Well, maybe," Emily allowed. "Especially if Old Fishguts does his stuff in full dress."

"Is he likely to?"

Emily considered. "I think he should be encouraged to," she said. "From the looks of things, the Ice Festival needs all the help it can get this year. We're putting the profits into furnishing the new extension to the library—we've got all that room and nothing to put in it at the moment."

"How about a few books?" Dominic suggested.

"Absolutely not. Every damn library you go into is full of books," Emily said. "What *we* want is . . ."

"Is what?"

"Something different."

"Pigeons?"

"Isn't it time you got back to suing someone?" Emily asked sweetly.

"Absolutely not. Every damn lawyer I know is suing someone," Dominic countered, unwilling to depart any sooner than he had to, especially as she was wearing the Blue Sweater That Shrank a Little in the Wash. It had shrunk just enough, in his opinion, and was the pièce de résistance of her wardrobe. Particularly as Emily was an expressive speaker— when she waved her arms things moved about. Just enough. He leaned back a bit precariously in the editor's well-bro-ken-in chair, knowing he was safe there for at least another twenty minutes because as he'd left the Golden Perch he'd seen Mr. Gibbons walking toward the Ventnor Hotel, and it was Rotary day. His own boss, Carl Putnam, was also a member. "What's the latest on our floating mystery man?"

"Ah—he is a mystery no longer," Emily said. "They've just identified him. His name is Albert Vernon. He's an ex-con and apparently bad news all around. Especially for the person who shot him."

"And you're just sitting here bandying words with me when you could be writing the scoop of the week?"

Emily grinned and indicated her new state-of-the-art computer. "It's already written and on the wires. I'm hoping Matt will have more information for me before we go to press, though. It's pretty thin."

"You're so efficient," Dominic said, putting on a smitten voice with just the smallest edge of mockery on it.

"True," Emily agreed drily. "It's the sweater that does it."

"And who made the ID? Somebody local?"

"No. The FBI identified him through his fingerprints. He's apparently from New York. Nobody has the least idea what he was doing around here."

"So we still have a mystery dead man?"

"Right."

Dominic sighed. "I thought you told me this town was dull off season."

Emily lifted her chin defensively. "It is. Or it was, until fairly recently. Do you suppose the earth's center of gravity has shifted without anyone realizing it and Blackwater Bay is now situated where New York used to be and as a result we're all being adversely influenced by Manhattan's stars?"

Dominic sat up straighter. "You could be right. Or *maybe* some crazy mystery writer has settled on Blackwater Bay as a perfect locale for mayhem and could even now be planning to bring a whole range of horror, crime, and panic into our lives."

They stared at one another in wild surmise.

Then Emily shook her head. "No," she said. "That's going *too* far."

"I suppose so," Dominic conceded reluctantly. He brightened. "It's probably just aliens from outer space."

"Ah," Emily nodded comfortably. "Now, *that* I can believe."

"What's next?" George Putnam asked Matt. "I mean, do we contact New York, or what?"

"We do," Matt said.

George sat up. "Really?" This was big stuff. Grantham was one thing, but New York was where all those TV cops worked. *NYPD Blue,* he was ready!

"Last known address from the FBI files was somewhere in upper Manhattan," Matt said. "I suppose we'd better find out what precinct that would be, and start with them. Would you like to do that?" he asked George.

His chief deputy, faced with real as opposed to television drama, backpedaled. George hated calling strangers on the phone, even to complain about something. In fact, especially to complain about something. Face-to-face, George was fine.

Even brave and bold, on occasion. There was just something about the telephone . . . about a voice without a face . . .

"Should be you," he said. "Senior officer, homicide case, all that . . . it should be you."

"But it will end up being me, as usual," Tilly said resignedly. "What's the address, Matt?"

He passed it over as he'd taken it down from the FBI. "I suppose I should have asked them which precinct."

"No reason they should know," Tilly said, reaching for her ever-ready notebook and looking up the number for 1 Police Plaza, New York, which Matt had known all along that she had. She glanced across the top of her VDU. Poor George. At this rate he'd never grow up.

When she got through to the right department, Tilly switched the call through to Matt's phone. He identified himself and explained the situation. "The FBI confirmed the prints our coroner lifted as belonging to one Albert Vernon, last known address on 114th Street. The number is—" He paused. "You're kidding." He covered the phone. "This guy knew Vernon's name right off. He's wanted for questioning in New York on some gang killing." He uncovered the phone again and listened. "Yeah. Sure, I'll fax them through right away. What do you want us to do with the body? Have you got any idea about next of kin, or what?" He listened a little more, made some notes, said his thanks, and hung up. He leaned back and stared at the ceiling, his hands clasped across his belt.

"Well?" George and Tilly asked.

"They're going to try to find next of kin, but they want to see the prints first, to make sure it's him."

"The FBI was sure," George said irritably. "Don't those guys trust anybody?"

"New York cops?" Matt grinned. "No, George. They don't trust anybody. And from the way things seem to be going around here, I don't think we should, either."

TEN

The *Blackwater Bay Chronicle* hit the streets of town at about the same time as the first contingent of inquiring reporters arrived from Grantham. They made no contact with the *Chronicle*, supposing—quite rightly—that the staff (especially Emily, whom they'd met before) would be less than forthcoming with any further information.

So, naturally, their first call was on the sheriff, who told them only what they could have just as easily read in the *Chronicle*: the body found under the ice had been identified through the FBI as Al Vernon, late of upper Manhattan, a wanted man who had a suspected connection with organized crime, and that many people, including most of the New York City police force, were grateful that he had turned up dead on somebody else's doorstep.

Why this particular doorstep? He couldn't say.

Did Vernon leave any family? According to the NYPD, absolutely none. His bosses, whoever they were, were not ready to claim him, either. There was a not very grief-stricken girlfriend who would no doubt miss the weekly beating Vernon used to give her, but she had shown no indication of wishing to travel to Blackwater to celebrate her deliverance. The funeral would be sparsely attended. Indeed, there would be no formal service at all, much to the disappointment of Hugh Pugh, local undertaker, who had been informed the process was to be a simple burial followed by a light dusting of hands, charges to the town.

Further than that, the sheriff had nothing to say.

No, he really didn't know anything else.

And he was very busy.

Goodbye.

The visiting reporters decided that all this evasion was an attempt to cover something up. What they didn't realize was that it was honesty—something to which life in the city had not accustomed them. Matt really didn't know anything more than he was saying.

But as red rags to bulls, so quietude breeds curiosity in the news-hungry, and the reporters decided to stick around for a while. This required accommodations, and—these particular reporters being penurious as well as curious—their need led them to the outskirts of town and the White Gull Motel. When they checked in, they mentioned why they were in town—just in case the manager, one Billy Ash, might know something. Unlike Matt, he did, but like Matt, he did not offer it.

Billy Ash was not a man to offer anything for nothing, as clearly evidenced by conditions prevailing in the White Gull Motel. But he *was* a man for whom opportunity was God. When Billy Ash realized that the reporters were interested in a man called Al Vernon, and when he then read the article in the *Chronicle* about the city having to pay for the funeral, he perked up considerably. To his rather limited imagination, there seemed a possibility that if the city would pick up the bill for a burial, then it might be inclined to pick up other bills that the late and unlamented visitor had run up.

Like his unpaid motel bill, for example.

So, like the visiting reporters, he went to ask the sheriff.

"Well, why the hell not?" Billy wanted to know, when Matt revealed that the possibility of the city paying Vernon's outstanding bill was an unlikely one.

"If they started paying all the outstanding—" Matt began.

"I pay my taxes, don't I?" Billy asked.

"I'm sure you do, but—"

"And this guy died owing me money!" Billy continued with growing outrage, unknowingly pacing the same path that Frank Nixey had paced before him. Tilly had already observed that the new linoleum was not going to last long at this rate.

"The thing is—"

"I want justice!" Billy shouted. "And I want my sixty-two fifty, plus tax!"

"Death cancels all debts!" Matt shouted back.

Billy blinked. "What?"

Matt spoke more quietly. "According to the law, death cancels all debts. If a man dies owing money, and leaves no estate or heirs, the debt dies with him. That's it, Billy. That's the way it is."

"You're making that up," Billy said truculently. He had a feeling things were not going to go his way, after all.

"Afraid not. Sorry," Matt said. "Now listen, Billy—did Vernon skip out or just not come back?"

"What do you mean?" Billy was *real* disappointed, and stood glaring at the base of Matt's desk, longing to give it a hefty kick. Wouldn't you just know it? It was the story of his life, the little guy always gets it in the neck, the low man on the—

"Well, what about his car?"

"What about it?" Just one good kick, Billy was thinking.

"Is it still at the motel or what?"

"Naw—it went with him."

"He drove it away?"

"How the hell should I know? It was there and then it was gone. It didn't come back and neither did he."

"Do you know the license number?"

"Sure—it's wrote down on the register, like it should be. I know the rules. It was a rental, I think."

"And did he take his luggage with him?" Matt asked.

"Nope, *I* got *that*," Billy said triumphantly. "When he didn't come back, I put it in the storeroom."

"Ah," Matt said.

Sensing disapproval where there was none—a lifelong habit of his—Billy's natural belligerence returned. "It's mine by default, that's the law, too. I got a right to sell it to 're-cup my losses,' it says somewheres. I know about that, I've done it before. People are just—"

Matt glanced at George, who raised an eyebrow. "How much luggage of Vernon's do you have, Billy?"

Billy's eyes narrowed. "Why?"

"It could be important. There might be something in there that could lead us to his killer."

"Oh, yeah?" Billy looked more cheerful suddenly.

"It's possible. I'd appreciate it if—"

"A hundred bucks," Billy said. "You can have it for a hundred bucks." He noted the expression on Matt's face. "It's mine to sell—I had extra expenses."

"What expenses were those, Billy?" George asked.

"Well, he left the place in a hell of a mess," Billy said. "I had to get somebody in to clean it up special."

Matt leaned forward in his chair. "What sort of mess did he leave it in?"

"Hell of a mess. Furniture thrown around, stains and rubbish and all sorts of crap all over the place. He was some kind of a pig, believe me. He never let the maid in none of the days he was there, the bastard. If I'd known how he—"

"What kind of stains, Billy?" George interrupted.

Billy, somewhat carried away by his new diatribe, stared at George. "What?"

"Pizza stains? Bloodstains? Puke stains? What?"

"Oh." Billy looked at him for a minute. "All kinds."

Matt spoke quietly. Too quietly. "Are you telling us that six or seven weeks ago you had a customer disappear from his room and when you went in you found the furniture thrown around and what could have been bloodstains and *it didn't worry you?*"

"Why should it?" Billy wanted to know. "Bastard had skipped on me. Like I said, he was a slob. You'd be amazed at the kind of—"

"Didn't it occur to you that something might have happened to him?" George asked.

"Well—" There was a long pause while Billy thought this over.

"No," he finally said. "I just figured he was a slob."

"A slob who threw the furniture around and bled freely just for the hell of it?"

"I don't know if they were bloodstains, do I?" Billy protested self-righteously. "Neither do you. Anyway, they were brown, not red." He leaned forward and spoke confidentially. "They could have been anything, couldn't they? Lots of things are brown, you know. Some of them not very nice. People do that, you know. They get drunk and they shit on the floor, on the beds, they think motels are just—"

"You could be charged with withholding evidence, Billy," George said.

"Evidence of what?" Billy countered.

"Evidence of a crime."

"What crime?"

"Murder."

"You don't know that. You don't *know* that!" Billy shouted, suddenly pale.

"And destroying evidence."

"I didn't destroy nothin'!" Billy shrieked.

"How do you know?" George was enjoying this, pressing hard while Matt simply stood up and started putting on his hat and coat. "There could have been fingerprints, letters with addresses on them, bloodstains, maybe a bullet stuck in the wall—"

"Hah! I would've noticed a bullet hole," Billy said.

"Not necessarily," Matt said. "Come on, Billy, let's go."

"Go? Go where?" Billy began to back away.

Matt sighed and gave George a reproachful glance. "To your storeroom, Billy. I want that luggage. We can stop off and get a warrant if you like—"

"A hundred bucks!" Billy said, making a final stand.

Matt looked at him. "How much was the bill—the actual bill, Billy? Sixty-two fifty, I think you said?"

"Well—"

"I'll see what I can do," Matt promised.

"Shee-yut," Billy said. Something in Matt's expression told him this was the best he was going to get and he was lucky to have it. Matt was not pleased with him, and things could get a lot worse before he got his sixty-two fifty.

Which was true.

Things could get a whole lot worse.

ELEVEN

Chrissie Falconer sat in Jess's tiny office, sobbing her heart out. Not only had every one of her chicken Kievs leaked, but her cheese soufflé had also exploded, a double culinary disaster leading to a hard lesson on oven cleaning.

Jess let her have a few minutes of feeling sorry for herself, hoping she would get it out of her system. Before the disastrous party and its subsequent humiliation, such an event would have left Chrissie laughing. Now she was blaming everything—even the faulty chicken—on Matt Gabriel.

Jess sighed. She had her own thoughts to straighten out. Particularly in reference to what Tom had said at the Magpie meeting. "Hopelessly in love with a home ec teacher who wouldn't give him the time of day"—wasn't that it? Another of his snide comments—his snide *irrelevant* comments—or truth? And, if the truth, what was she to do about it, if anything? Oh, she was being silly, it couldn't possibly be the truth. She frowned. Was there a *new* home ec teacher in the area? Hatchville? Lemonville? Tom went out a lot, and she'd always assumed he was out drinking with buddies. Maybe she was wrong. Could he be seeing another teacher, one she hadn't met?

Chrissie gave another huge sobbing sigh, dragging Jess's attention back to the present problem on the other side of her desk. Outside her office, the girls in the cooking class were happily clearing up, chattering like birds in the bright sun that flooded through the high windows. Somehow their normality made Jess even more impatient with this lovely girl, who had so many natural and material advantages and yet felt so wronged. She had to find a way to help Chrissie deal with it.

"Chrissie, if there were drugs at your party, Sheriff Gabriel was quite within the law to arrest you. It was your house, so you were supposedly in charge of what was going on there."

"Oh, sure, like I *was*," Chrissie said defensively. "Like when there's about a *zillion* people running around, I'm supposed to know what they're all doing at any given *moment*? Give me a break."

"If things were getting out of hand, you should have called the police yourself," Jess said, hating the prissy sound of her own voice, but knowing it was necessary.

"I was *going* to," Chrissie said. "But the neighbors beat me to it. And he got there so *faaaast*—"

"Oh, I see. You mean before you could flush all these drugs you had down the john?" Jess asked in a tone of pleasant inquiry.

"Well. Sort of. I guess so. Yeah," Chrissie conceded.

"What did you have?" Jess asked in as casual a voice as she could manage. "Uppers, downers—that kind of thing?"

Chrissie looked at her oddly. "You know about stuff like that?"

"Well—yes."

"Personally?"

Jess was cornered. She began to straighten the things on her desk. "I have smoked grass," she conceded, feeling childishly embarrassed. "When I was at college."

"Oh, grass," Chrissie said negligently. "*Everybody* smokes grass."

Jess had a momentary image of all the teachers—from the principal on down—lost in a dreamy haze behind fat joints, the school falling to rack and ruin around them. "Not everybody, Chrissie," she said gently. "And I don't really advocate it as a regular occupation."

"Oh, well, sure, you have to say that, don't you?" Chrissie acknowledged with a tone as good as a wink. "Being a teacher and all."

"I am also a person, and I still don't advocate it on a regular basis. There have been studies to prove that prolonged regular use of—"

"Well, there you are," Chrissie said eagerly, her face suddenly suffused with hope. "Studies, research—people are trying to find out about *good* drugs, you know. Drugs that tap into the natural receptors, imitate endorphins and all that stuff. Somebody will come up with a benign painkilling drug soon, and it will be a real boon to mankind."

Although she knew that Chrissie was a good student, Jess hadn't realized the girl was so scientifically oriented. "Will it?" she asked. "I wonder."

"What do you mean?"

"Do you think nature intended man to be anesthetized against reality? Do you think we would make anything like the progress we have made if we were all high on something? Our brains would drift freely, yes—all very pleasant, I'm sure. But you have to be sharp, logical, constructive, to create anything new—"

"But that's what I'm *saying*," Chrissie said, leaning forward earnestly. "Suppose there were drugs that would *free* someone like Stephen Hawking from all his pain so that he could think even more deeply, or some pill that would open the mind of someone like Picasso or Beethoven so that physical constraints didn't matter, they could create new and wonderful things . . ."

Jess raised a hand to stem the flow of rhetoric. "Or imagine they had, until they woke up and found it was dross," she said. "That's been the experience of most people who have tried hallucinogens, you know. Like the dreams you have under any anesthetic—they don't make much sense." She tried to lighten the discussion. "My favorites are things people write down in the dark and then read in the morning—like 'The skin is mightier than the banana' and 'The entire universe is permeated with a strong odor of turpentine.'"

Chrissie wasn't listening. "But don't you see, there *are* new drugs that *clear* the mind, that *do* produce insight, that release creativity and allow a person access to all the unused mass of the brain so that new powers can be utilized. Telepathy, telekinesis, all the things people have been certain were impossible *are* possible, once you have the *key*." Chrissie's eyes glowed with a messianic fervor, and Jess stared at her, feeling ice at the bone. This wasn't Chrissie talking, these were someone else's words in her mouth.

"Are you saying you had such drugs, Chrissie?"

"No!" The response was too quick, too sharp. "No, of course not." She got herself under control and adopted a casual tone. "I'm just speaking hypothetically. For the sake of the discussion. I'm just saying suppose, that's all. Wouldn't it be great? Wouldn't it be a real step forward for us to discover our mental capabilities as well as—"

"I have to say I have my doubts about doing it through artificial means," Jess said. "So-called 'discoveries' often have a dark reverse side. While there may be a need for drugs that kill pain without side effects, there is also a great risk in looking for them. Other things get discovered along the way. Drugs that *dull* the mind, for example. In the hands of a dictator such drugs could be used to enslave a population. Or drugs that cause a person to become self-confident could be used in stronger dosages to stimulate soldiers to fight and kill until they dropped dead themselves. Perhaps those gate-crashers of yours had drugs like that. What—exactly—did they do?"

Chrissie ran off a series of descriptions that made Jess's blood run cold when she mentally added up what the repairs would cost the girl's parents. "And you think behavior like that is acceptable?" she asked gently.

"Well, of course not." Chrissie seemed to consider what Jess had said. "Okay—I see what you mean about risks, but we have to take risks *sometimes,* don't we?"

"Sure. But it's one thing to take a risk yourself, and quite another to risk the lives of others. If those gate-crashers took a drug for a thrill, that's one thing and bad enough for them—dangerous, too—but when it causes trouble to other people, then that's something else entirely. If there *are* drugs like that loose around here, it could be very dangerous. Are you *sure* you don't know who these people were?" she asked, and immediately realized she was pressing too hard. Damn, she thought. Damn.

Chrissie's mouth had thinned, and her grip on her book bag had tightened. "Even if I did, they couldn't pay for anything," she said.

"How do you know, if they were strangers?"

"You could tell."

"From the way they dressed?"

"From the way they *smelled,*" Chrissie sniffed. "Anyway, the minute they heard the sirens they took off—and left us holding the whole bag."

"So none of these gate-crashers were actually still around when the sheriff arrived?"

"No." From her tone of voice and the way she shifted on the hard chair, it was obvious Chrissie wanted to avoid the subject of identities. Was that, Jess wondered, because of what the gate-crashers could say if they were arrested? Or because they didn't actually exist, but had been thought up as an excuse for the mess Chrissie and her friends themselves had made while high on some strange new drug?

Jess looked upon the girl and despaired. Smooth soft skin, delicate features beneath big blue eyes, a glorious tumble of silken blond hair, a bouncy sensual body full of health and hormones—with so many natural gifts, why does someone like this want drugs? I could understand it in myself, she thought wryly. After looking in the mirror on any bad morning I could easily be sold some magic pill to erase those first wrinkles and tighten up that incipient double chin. To say nothing of double thighs. But in someone so young . . . and then she thought of that glow in Chrissie's eyes when she spoke about new drugs, and she felt ice in her bones again.

Someone is getting at them, she suddenly thought, utilizing that other aspect of youth . . . that wonderful thing called aspiration, when they believe they can change the world, bring order out of chaos and save mankind. Someone is playing dirty with their dreams.

For money? Or just for a power trip?

"God, I'm so *tired*," Chrissie moaned in her affected, exaggerated way. "My parents get back tomorrow night, and there's so much left to *doooo*."

"You mean nothing's been cleaned up?" Jess asked, coming back to the present with a horrified bump. "It's all still—"

"Oh, people *came*," Chrissie said vaguely, after blowing her nose. "They *did* things. Mr. Putnam arranged it. But my mother will just *lose* it because the stupid *painters* didn't match the *color* in the *dining* room right, and Daddy's going to be *furious* about the MG, I just *know* it. And it wasn't my *fauuuuulllllttt*!"

"But it *was* your fault, Chrissie," Jess said firmly. The girl's eyes widened. "Accepting the responsibility would be an important step in growing up."

"I don't want to grow up if it means everybody *blaming* you for everything that goes *wrong*," Chrissie said sulkily.

"Well, you're going to grow up whether you like it or not." Jess smiled. "Time passes, Chrissie. You can't change facts, and the fact is you gave a party at which drugs were available. It was at your home, by your invitation, and you were therefore responsible in law for what took place there. The courts only look at facts."

"Courts?" Chrissie gasped. "You mean I have to go to court?"

"Well," Jess said slowly. "Wasn't your birthday in October? You're eighteen now. If Matt put you into jail and your father's lawyer had to get you out, then I assume a charge was brought against you. That means appearing in court to answer the charge. I don't imagine it will be too—"

The bell suddenly rang and there was a clatter of footsteps outside the office door as Chrissie's fellow students made a rush for the hall.

Chrissie stood up suddenly, clutching her book bag to her admirable chest. "I have to go to my next class," she said. There were tears in her eyes, and she looked terrified.

"What class is it?"

"Math."

Jess sighed. Fred Naughton would not look kindly on a class missed for what he would term "emotions." Perhaps she could find some time later to talk to Chrissie about the drugs. Someone had to find out what was going on. If it had any connection with the school, it was her duty to protect both the institution and the students. It was any teacher's duty. If it meant Chrissie or any other student saw her as old-fashioned and fuddy-duddy, so be it.

"Okay, Chrissie, go on to your next class—we can clean the oven on Monday," she said resignedly. "But I want to talk to you again about this."

"Yes . . . okay . . . sure . . ." Chrissie was backing away, obviously glad to escape. She went out, still clutching the book bag as if afraid someone would snatch it from her.

Jess sat slumped beside her desk for a moment, wishing there had been more time. If only she could have gotten the girl to talk more about these drugs, whatever they were. Maybe she could have found out who was filling her head with all this rubbish. Or perhaps together they might have identified at least one of the gate-crashers and gotten a lead somehow.

But there was never enough time, and she wasn't Chrissie's counselor, either. Who was? Falconer—F—that would be Mrs. Beecham, counselor for girls A–G. Fat chance of any sympathy there, Jess thought to herself. Beecham was hell on wheels about the Evils of Modern Society, and no doubt had been one of the first to give Chrissie a dressing-down. Now she herself had added to the censure. Well, it needed to be done, but she hoped she could be more sympathetic than some of the others. On this morning's showing, perhaps not. Chrissie had looked seriously scared when she'd left the office.

She sighed in temporary defeat, then looked up with an effort to greet her next class. Freshman cooking—thirteen-year-olds, bright-eyed and still awed by high school. She thought suddenly of a Hart Crane poem about "bright-striped urchins" playing on the beach.

> O brilliant kids, frisk with your dog,
> Fondle your shells and sticks, bleached
> By time and the elements; but there is a line
> You must not cross nor ever trust beyond it
> Spry cordage of your bodies to caresses
> Too lichen-faithful from too wide a breast.
> The bottom of the sea is cruel.

"This Al Vernon was almost as disgusting alive as he was after being dead for a couple of months," George said as they started looking through the contents of the two cheap suitcases that Al Vernon had left behind at the White Gull Motel. "Do you suppose he ever washed his socks, or did he just wait until they walked out of his life of their own accord?" He picked up a particularly repellent piece of underwear and dropped it onto a pile that was forming beside the table. "I'm glad we had to wear gloves."

"The gloves were for things like papers and objects," Matt muttered. "In case somebody's fingerprints are on them."

"Yeah, I know," George said. "But, like I said, I'm glad." He pulled out a clotted handkerchief and dropped it with dainty distaste.

"Here's something," Matt said, extracting a small wad of newspaper clippings from the elasticized section at the back of the larger suitcase. He flipped through them quickly, then returned to the top one. "They all seem to be about Luca Ritto."

"Oh, shit," George said, his hands suddenly still. "He's that *guy*."

"What guy?" Matt asked.

"You know, you know—"

"Do I?" Matt asked innocently, watching George go through the pantomime of hitting himself in the forehead as if trying to jar his brains loose—which, indeed, he was.

"The *guy*," George said. "The *Mafia* guy."

"I don't think we're supposed to use the word 'Mafia' anymore, George," Matt said patiently. "According to these clippings he seems to have been something in organized crime—"

"*Exactly!*" George said.

"And he happens to be Italian—" Matt continued.

"*Right!*" George said.

"And he was tried and convicted for murder," Matt concluded.

"Yeah, the murder of his biggest rival, Somebody or Other Pescatori."

"Sam."

"What?"

"Sam Pescatori."

"Yeah, right, but he was always known as Somebody or Other Pescatori," George said, snatching the clippings from Matt and flipping through them. "There, see? Right there—

Somebody or Other Pescatori. Because he was always saying that."

"Saying what?"

"That it was 'somebody or other.'"

"Somebody or other what?"

"Somebody or other that did it."

"Did what?"

George was getting very impatient and did not see the twinkle in Matt's eye. "Did whatever it was. Like if anybody blamed him for anything, he'd say, 'It wasn't me, it was somebody or other.' It was never him, see?"

"So he was an innocent man? This Ritto killed an innocent man?"

"No, no, *no*." George sighed. "Look, it's all organized by what they call families, see?"

"What is?"

"*Crime*. In New York. Chicago. Las Vegas . . ." George came to a slow halt, realizing he was being taken for a ride on this one. "You *know* all this, Matt."

"Sure. I was just testing you."

"Oh, yeah. Right." George was disgusted with himself for being drawn, and went back to the suitcase, muttering. Matt continued to read through the clippings, one by one. When he had finished he leaned against the table.

"Very interesting," he said.

"I'm glad you liked it," George said grumpily.

"It says here that Ritto was pretty well convicted by the testimony of one person."

"Al Vernon!" George said, straightening up with a triumphant look on his face.

"No—somebody named—sorry—somebody or *other* named—"

"Very funny."

"Named Peter Murphy."

"I'll bet," George scoffed.

"What do you mean?"

"That's the name they *gave* the guy."

Matt shook his head. "No. That was his name, apparently. It says he went into the witness protection program afterward, but at the trial he was Peter Murphy."

"Oh, yeah? And who was he, this Murphy guy? What's a mick doing in the Mafia? Sounds like an old movie title—*A Mick in the Mafia*—great part for Cagney, right?"

Matt chose to ignore this. "Apparently Mr. Murphy was an accountant of sorts. Young, idealistic, and so on. And when he found out who he was really working for, he made it his business to expose them. Hence the trial, hence the conviction."

"That sounds like a movie I saw, too."

"You see too many movies, George."

"There's not a lot of other stuff to do around here in the winter," George said. "Anything else in those newspaper stories?"

"Just that Ritto swore to kill Murphy when he got out."

"And is he out?"

"I don't think so," Matt said. "It says here he was sentenced to life—which means at least seven years. These clippings are only about four years old."

"Of course, he doesn't have to be out to get this guy Murphy offed, does he?" George mused. "He could put out a contract."

"True." Matt was opening the second suitcase.

"And if Al Vernon was an enforcer type . . ." George was getting excited.

"According to the NYPD—suspicions only. They said he was what they call a soldier, he did whatever had to be done."

"So maybe he agreed to a contract on this Peter Murphy."

"Maybe," Matt said, gazing down into the second suitcase without much enthusiasm. This was apparently the repository for Al Vernon's *really* dirty laundry.

"But Peter Murphy took *him* out instead."

"Uh-huh."

"But . . ." George was getting there. "That means that Peter Murphy is here—in Blackwater Bay somewheres."

"Or was," Matt said. "A man can move a fair distance in two months, George."

"Not if he's set up a new identity, not without causing a lot of talk or curiosity."

"And can you think of anyone who left town hurriedly in the past eight weeks or so?" Matt asked.

"Well . . . no, not running flat out or anything. But that doesn't mean he wasn't . . . or that he didn't," George persisted. "Just that we haven't heard. I mean, he could have been anybody."

"Somebody or other?" Matt suggested wryly. He felt down the sides of the suitcase and noticed something flat and hard in a side pocket. He reached in gingerly and extracted an address book.

"What's that?" George asked.

"Well, it's a book, with alphabetized pages, and a leather cover with 'Addresses' embossed on it in gold. Speaking as both a logician and a law enforcement officer, I'd say it was a frog. What do you say?"

"I say look under 'M,'" George said.

"For 'Murphy, Peter'?"

"Right."

Matt obligingly opened the little book to the page marked "M." "No Murphy listed here," he told George.

"Damn," George said.

"There is another familiar name, though," Matt said. "Moss, Victor."

"Son of a bitch," George said gleefully. "A connection."

"Everything comes to he who waits," Matt said with some satisfaction.

"And he who looks through dirty laundry," George added, starting to replace the rags and tatters of the deceased Al Vernon, late of New York, found floating in beautiful Blackwater Bay with a bullet hole in his head.

TWELVE

For Jess the weekend came as a welcome relief from the vicissitudes of both students and faculty members. Despite the fact that they had just had a supposedly refreshing three-week break over the holidays, her colleagues were already complaining about the workload or the weather or the food or one another.

When she got up on Saturday morning, fresh snow was falling past her window, and when she looked out she saw about two inches had accumulated during the night. So much for going into the city to check out the January sales!

In truth, Jess was glad to accept isolation—it gave her an opportunity to continue work on her wall hanging without feeling guilty. She was annoyed to see that so many of the fishing huts had disappeared from the ice, though. She would have to continue arranging the fabric pieces from memory. Not that she was attempting an actual re-creation of the scene before her, but it helped to have the right atmosphere. Normally there were at least eighty huts scattered across the ice of the bay. Now there couldn't have been more than fifteen or twenty, reducing the opportunities for creative variation in her picture.

The unwelcome visitor from beneath the ice had certainly undermined the prospects of the Ice Festival, she thought, as she went downstairs to make breakfast. How many people were going to feel like having fun at a grave site—even a temporary one?

She entered the kitchen and sighed with pleasure. It was easily the best room in the house, the one in which she spent the most time, and the one on which she had spent the most money.

The arrangement of duties at Perkins Point was not really fair—but it was sensible. Everybody else took turns shopping and cleaning, and Jess cooked all the meals. During the week this was difficult, as it meant working after a day at school, but on weekends Jess enjoyed her assignment, and on this snowy morning the kitchen seemed to her particularly cozy and welcoming.

She set the coffee going, turned the oven on, and began to grease the muffin tins. While she was stirring the muffin mixture, Tom arrived looking less than chipper. His shirt was buttoned wrong, with one side hanging lower than the other and the collar was awry.

"Late night?" she asked as he helped himself to coffee.

"More like an early morning," he said, adding sugar and cream.

"Anybody I know?" she asked rather carefully.

"No," he said.

"But you did have a date?"

He ignored this. "Do I see real oatmeal?" he asked.

"You know you do. There's bread for toast, or you can wait a bit for blueberry muffins."

"I'll stay myself with oatmeal and wait for the muffins, thanks." He slumped down on one of the chairs beside the old pine table, scratching his head with one hand and raising his mug of coffee with the other.

Jess finished spooning the muffin mixture into the tins and slipped them into the oven, setting the timer as she did so, then wiped her floury hands on her apron. "I wonder where those cats have gotten to."

She went into the living room and found the two cats intertwined in front of the embers of the fire that had blazed so merrily the night before. Both Tom and Jason had been out, but the rest of them had spent a pleasant evening wrangling amiably over which television program to jeer at while pretending to mark papers or prepare lesson plans. Or, in Chip's case, to work on his play book. The football team was doing well this year, and hopes were high for getting the trophy back from Lemonville.

The cats had hugged the rug in front of the fire then, and they did not seem to have moved since, although their mutual proximity indicated a wish to be warmer. Twister and Cleo got along well enough, although there were occasional periods of snit, and the odd altercation on the stairs. Normally they settled themselves in invisibly defined areas of territory, but this morning they were like kittens, wrapped around one another and snoring slightly. Twister always had a tendency to snore, as he had a sinus condition, but this morning even Cleo was emitting tiny buzzes indicative of deep feline repose.

She patted them, smoothed them, and they responded quite normally, stretching and sighing, but they did not wake up. When she went into the dining room to collect a dish to hold the fresh-baked muffins, she saw why the cats were so tired. They had set up a confetti factory the night before—papers that had been left out on the dining room table were torn to shreds and scattered the length and breadth of the room.

Jess's "Oh, no!" brought Tom in from the kitchen. He stood beside her, appalled.

"Oh, great," he said. "Whose were they?"

"Mine—and Jason's," she said. "He was working on lesson plans before he went out. Thank God Chip took his play book upstairs. What on earth got into them?"

"Boredom, probably," Tom said. "They haven't been going

out much, remember, because of the weather. Guess they had a lot of energy stored up—and it had to go somewhere."

"Jason will want them destroyed."

"Oh, don't be ridiculous," Tom said impatiently. "He's almost as nuts about those two cats as you are, he's always playing with them. You can do the plans again. You have the whole weekend."

"But I was going to work on my quilt."

Tom shrugged. "Your choice. I don't see why you have to do such elaborate lesson plans, anyway. All you have to do is sort your fabrics for sewing and gather up a few recipes."

"Oh, very amusing. I could say all you have to do is list a few theories that are so old they might as well be hewn in stone."

"I'll have you know physics is one of the fastest-developing sciences in the world," Tom said, looking stung to the quick. "Quantum mechanics is a thousand times more complicated than the recipe for muffins."

"I don't teach muffins," Jess retorted. "Well, I do—but only to freshmen."

"And I only teach Newton to freshmen."

They glared at one another. Then Tom grinned. "Why don't we get together and teach Fig Newtons?"

Jess grinned back. "You know, I've always wondered why they're called that. I think I'll set the girls a challenge—find out why fig-filled cookie bars are called Fig Newtons. A box of them to the first girl to report back with the best explanation."

"Ah—creative teaching," Tom said wryly. "I am inspired." He folllowed her back into the kitchen. "I am also damned hungry all of a sudden. When are those muffins going to be done?"

Saturday and Sunday breakfasts were usually the best meals of the week. Jess believed in A Good Start to the Day on weekends, because during the week nobody had enough time to do more than snatch at a cornflake or two. This particular morning, while Tom cleared away the evidence of the cats' mischief, she set about producing eggs, bacon, sausages, grilled tomatoes and mushrooms, toast, and the aforesaid oatmeal and muffins. When the others arrived, there was the usual feeding frenzy, followed by leisurely conversation over the second and third cups of coffee.

The fresh snow meant some changes of plan. Like Jess, the other women had been considering driving down to the January sales at some of the shopping malls that edged the city of Grantham. The city itself was some way to the south of Blackwater Bay—and was one of the twentieth century's saddest victims. Its once splendid heart had been eaten away, leaving a "doughnut" of a virtually destroyed city center surrounded by variably affluent suburbs. For years city officials had been mounting one campaign after another to "reopen" and revitalize the downtown area, but success had so far eluded them. By day the big business buildings were active, but by night the streets below them were the domain of criminals, junkies, and prostitutes. Nobody shopped downtown anymore, but circled the city for both basics and bargains.

"The heck with the sales," Linda Casemore said. "I'll only buy clothes I wouldn't have looked at a month ago and will hate as soon as I get them home. It's always the same." She sighed and reached for another muffin. Linda was short and round and tended to buy anything that fitted. "I could use some new sheets, though," she continued. "I might risk it. It's only a matter of getting out to the highway, after all— they should be clear."

"I'll come—we can take my car," Pat suggested. She drove a four-wheel-drive RV, necessary to accommodate all her art and weaving equipment. "It should get you through anything."

"Don't you want to come?" Linda asked Jess.

"No—I have plenty to do here, and plenty of bills that need paying," Jess said. "The snow has saved me from the bargain side of The Force."

"What force is that?" Jason wanted to know.

They all looked at him. Was there a person alive who hadn't seen *Star Wars*? Apparently so, for he gazed at them in earnest inquiry.

"The Force that compels women to spend money," Tom explained. "If Newton were alive today, he'd have listed it as one of his laws of motion. The Purse empties in direct ratio to the Savings Promised—something like that."

"Ah," Jason nodded. After a moment, he added, "That's quite funny."

"Have another muffin, Jason," Jess said before anyone could speak. He had taken the news about the destroyed lesson plans very well, and she was grateful to him for not demanding that she have her wicked cats put out into the snow immediately.

It was after meals that Jess had her finest moment—walking away from the table without having to do the dishes. This, too, was part of her deal—when she cooked, she did none of the cleaning up. To be fair, she washed utensils as she went along, so there was not much for the others to do except clear the table, then load (and later unload) the dishwasher, but the feeling of release never failed to delight her.

She climbed the stairs and in her room again looked out onto the frozen bay. Snow was still falling, and a light wind was stirring and swirling the flakes, making spiral patterns against the dark gray sky. Suddenly the scene began to change, and she leaned closer to the window.

Had another body been found? There were people pouring out onto the ice, more than she was accustomed to seeing even at the height of the season. And they were definitely not all fishermen, for there were women and children, too. Had she gotten her dates mixed up—was it the Ice Festival already? No—there were no booths, no racetracks laid out. Then, for a moment, both the snow and the crowd parted, and she saw the focus of their attention.

Old Fishguts had arrived.

THIRTEEN

The snow had stopped falling, and there was a great silence over the bay. Back onshore there was a faint crackling as a slight wind stirred the naked branches of the trees. Overhead the clouds were thinning slightly, the dark gray becoming paler, brighter, higher.

"What's he doing now?" Shad Billmore wanted to know. He raised himself onto his tiptoes and tried to peer over the bulky shoulder of Frog Bartlett.

"He's listening," Frank Nixey said in a hushed voice.

"To what?" Billmore asked snidely. "The sound of one hand clapping?"

Old Fishguts raised his hands and intoned, "I have heard the mermaids singing each to each."

His eyes met Matt Gabriel's across the scar of the hole through which Al Vernon's body had been drawn from beneath the ice. Old Fishguts blushed high on his prominent cheekbones, and then he winked at Matt. Not many of the listeners would have recognized the quote from T. S. Eliot—but then, not many of the listeners knew that Old Fishguts, whose real name was Vern Whitefish, held a master's degree

in English, which he had gotten on the G.I. Bill from
Grantham University after World War II. This was the kind
of thing a really good medicine man kept from his trusting
followers. No sense in muddying the waters. Or diluting the
whiskey, for that matter.

"Do you think they will sing to you?" Matt asked, countering the quote with apparent innocence.

"Ugh," said Old Fishguts, more traditionally.

He began to shuffle to the right, then to the left, then
back, then forward again to the shallow lip of the ragged circle in the ice.

"Now he's getting warmed up," Frank Nixey said enthusiastically, prodding Mel Tuohmy in the ribs. "*Now* we'll get
some action."

"Especially if the old faker falls in," Shad Billmore said.

Nixey whirled around. "What did you call him?" he demanded.

Billmore stepped back, startled by Nixey's snarl. "An old
faker," he said.

"Oh," Nixey said, and turned back toward the action.
Billmore, after staring at Nixey's back, moved forward
again. He didn't want to get too far away from Frank, because Frank was obviously the kind of man who believed in
things. Things like Indian spirits. And—maybe—life insurance.

Old Fishguts was in a difficult position. What with
arthritis, the cost of living, and a wish to reexplore some of
the more esoteric aspects of the Beowulf legend in the original Old English, he'd more or less been ignoring the mys-
tic side of his heritage. On the other hand, there was within
him a true core of Native American feeling and belief, to
which he still felt a loyalty and a calling. When you added
to this the innocent trust of Frank Nixey and the others,
something within him had stirred. These people had come
to him with open hearts. They were worried, fearsome, and

hopeful. He felt he could probably help them. And there wasn't much on TV that afternoon.

So, wearing as much of his medicine man regalia as he could find, stuck away as it had been in odd drawers and trunks and paper bags around his place, he had come to the water. Or, rather, the ice.

Over his usual thick winter underwear he had drawn buckskin trousers, heavily fringed, and a buckskin tunic (Old Frontier Trading Post Catalog, 1948). The latter item had been elaborately embroidered by his middle daughter while she was laid up one summer with a broken leg. She had copied the motifs out of a library book. She had made her choices purely on the basis of aesthetic beauty, and to be fair she had done a very nice job overall. But such were the limitations of her education in her own tribal lore that there was a wider range of symbolism in the patterns that now adorned her father's chest. They represented no fewer than nine separate Native American tribes, four elemental gods, and eighteen animal spirits.

Around his neck hung many strings of varicolored beads, a leather thong with a silver Thunderbird medallion, and a string of eagle bones (all from the Old Frontier Trading Post Special Anniversary Catalog, 1966). On his head he wore a beaded bonnet embellished with gull feathers, made with great love and reverence by his eleven-year-old grandson, who had also referred to a library book (*Fireside Tales of the Indian Trails,* by N. J. Fenstremmer). (The Whitefish family were all big readers.) While Old Fishguts had learned some things at his grandfather's equally arthritic knee, the ethnic section of Grantham University Library was the source for most of the ritual that Old Fishguts was now desperately trying to remember.

None of this is to say that Old Fishguts was a fake. He did have true Native American blood, as pure as it could be considering the times present and past, and he did have psychic abilities, as had his father and grandfather before him. The trouble was that Old Fishguts had been interfered with. Logic and reason had been brought to bear on his mind— that is to say, white man's logic and white man's reason. There had been grade school, then high school, then the army sending him to help reconstruct postwar Germany, then the degrees from the university, then his wife and kids throwing at him what seemed like an endless stream of information from the *National Geographic,* Hollywood, *Saturday Night Live,* and PBS. In short, he had been "educated" as a modern man, and as a result he did not trust his Native American heritage as much as he might have.

Had he but known it, there was considerable power gathered around him as he stood there in his favorite cowboy boots (Sears, 1964), his tweed overcoat (Hudson's, 1989), and his knitted scarf (Kmart, 1992), freezing his buckskin ass off and wondering what to do next. Had he made exactly the right moves and said exactly the right words, he probably could have blown the whole crowd off the ice and into the trees.

Instead, he made the moves he'd read about in white men's books, mixed with what he could remember from his grandfather's rather terrifying childhood instruction, and so only caused a faint quiver in the ice and a feeling of unease in those closest to him.

People further back just thought he was nuts.

"Oh, hey yah, hey yah, hey yah, hey," said Old Fishguts, hopping on his left foot.

"I love this ethnic stuff," George Putnam said. Matt and his deputies were there to make certain things did not get out of hand. And because there was not much happening anywhere else. They stood with their arms crossed, facing the crowd.

"Oh, go yah, go yah, hi yah, hey," said Old Fishguts, hopping on his right foot.

"My mother loves this kind of stuff, too," George continued. (George's divorced mother collected authentic Aztec and Toltec artifacts from reputable dealers. George's young stepmother collected gold artifacts from the shopping channel.)

"Ah mishna, go yah, ixnay, hey," said Old Fishguts, turning in a circle slowly and raising his arms to the sky.

"I go more for the Celtic stuff," said Glen Hardwicke, shifting from one foot to the other as the cold from the ice penetrated his boots. "Old World, not New World."

"I never saw anything like this at all," marveled Duff Bradley, who was relatively new to the area and had grown up strictly inner-city. "Except in the movies, of course. *Dances with Wolves*, right?"

"Oh, right," Matt agreed. "*Last of the Mohicans*."

"What about *Geronimo*?" George wanted to know.

Glen looked at him. "Well, what about him?"

"The movie, I meant," George said. "Jack Palance."

"It wasn't Jack Palance," Matt said. "It was Chief Thundercloud."

"I never saw that one," George said.

"No—I mean Geronimo was *played* by Chief Thundercloud," Matt explained. George looked at him, squinting against the bright overcast.

"A real Indian?"

"I believe so. Of course, Geronimo has been played by other actors in other movies with different titles. A lot of people played Geronimo."

"Yes—but not many won," Glen said.

They all chuckled and then gradually realized that Old Fishguts had stopped his chanting and was glaring at them across the scarred ice.

"Sorry," Matt said.

"This isn't easy, you know," Old Fishguts said glumly.

"I know, I know. I'm sorry," Matt said.

"Needs concentration."

"Of course," Matt said. "I think you'd just about got up

to the part about ragged claws scuttling across the floors of silent seas," he added blandly.

"Humph," Old Fishguts muttered, suppressing a grin.

On the other side of the frozen-over ice hole, the audience watched this exchange restlessly, waiting for Old Fishguts to resume action. "What are they arguing about?" Frog Bartlett asked Frank Nixey.

"Damned if I know," Frank said. "Something about claws in the sea."

"Maybe it was a clause, like in the bylaws or something," somebody suggested. "Maybe he's got to do this in a certain amount of time, or something."

"What time?" somebody else asked.

"About eleven o'clock," he was told.

They all turned back to Old Fishguts.

"Kallikak and Michimac," Old Fishguts resumed, calling out to the sky overhead.

"Them's old Indian gods," Frank Nixey said smugly.

"Hell they are," Frog Bartlett said.

"Hell they aren't!" snapped Frank.

"They're old fort names," Frog said. He regarded himself as something of an authority on the military history of the state.

"Yeah, but those forts was named *after* old Indian gods," Frank riposted. "So there."

"Could be," Frog surrendered. "Could be."

"Was," Frank muttered.

"Gitchee, gawmmee," Old Fishguts said.

"And a pound of salami," Shad Billmore said disgustedly. "He's not doing *anything*."

In the distance, there was a long, slow roll of thunder.

Frank, Frog, and the others turned to glare at Billmore.

"So?" Billmore asked weakly. "Thunder. Big deal."

"In *January*?" Frank asked, with heavy meaning.

Billmore shrugged. "It happens."

"Not here it don't," Frog said, glowering at the insurance

salesman from under eyebrows that hung over his piggy eyes like fur-covered bananas. "Not ever."

Old Fishguts, fortified and enthused by the thunder, which had impressed him as much as anyone, picked up the volume and began to get into a real syncopated rhythm. Hopping from one foot to the other, he circled the iced-over hole, chanting and waving his arms, and then—without warning—produced from the pocket of his tweed overcoat an old Folgers coffee can which he had previously filled with a few assorted items, and threw it, hard, onto the thinner ice that filled the hole.

It went through, splashing icy water up onto those nearest the hole—himself, Matt, and the deputies.

"Hey!" shouted George, leaping back. "What the hell was that?"

"Spirit request," Old Fishguts said. "Wait."

"Son of a—" George began to mutter, then jumped back—as they all did—when there was a rumble under the ice and a fresh gout of water squirted up through the hole and foamed over the edges, flooding the harder ice for about ten feet around the hole and melting the freshly fallen snow that was layered on top of the ice.

"Shit!" shouted old Fishguts, more startled than anyone. At his feet thrashed a fish. "I mean . . . Howamugga!" he said, regaining his equilibrium. He bent down and picked up the fish, and made as if the fish was speaking to him. Closing his eyes and nodding, he waited a minute, then threw the fish back into the water. The thin ice that had previously covered the big hole was now shattered, and floated in small pieces on the surface of the gray-green water as it lapped the sides. Old Fishguts hunkered down and began to rock back and forth on his toes and heels, humming to himself. Matt, alarmed by the explosion and worried that the old man might fall into the water, laid a hand on his shoulder.

"Hmmmmmm . . . no problem . . . mmmmmm," Old

Fishguts said out of the corner of his mouth. "Hmmmm . . . low center of gravity . . . hmmmmm . . ."

Matt withdrew his hand but stood ready should the old man begin to slide toward the open hole.

"Baaalaaaawaaalaaamaaalaaacallaballaa," muttered Old Fishguts. He stood up. Raised his arms.

And screamed at the top of his voice.

It was a truly magnificent effort, combining the maniacal shrillness of a panicking schizophrenic with the violent deep-throated despair of a rutting bear who has just lost the scent of a passing female.

George instinctively reached for his gun and nearly shot his foot off. Frank Nixey and Frog Bartlett jumped back, slipped on the wet ice, grabbed one another, and went down in a heap, dragging Shad Billmore with them. They all began to curse and scrabble around, attempting to regain their feet. The people around them either reached out to help them or began to laugh—either way accomplishing little. There was a general churning around and melee, as people in the back pressed forward to see what the hell was happening, hampering efforts to help their fallen comrades even further.

Old Fishguts turned to Matt, ignoring the shouts and shoves and general flailing of his audience. "That's it," he said.

"That's *it?*" asked George in a shaken voice.

"That's all she wrote," Old Fishguts said. "I run out of ideas."

"What the hell did you throw in there?" Matt wanted to know.

"Army surplus grenade," Old Fishguts said. "Sealed it in with a few handfuls of gravel and had a piece of string running through the lid—pulled the pin out before I threw it in. Never really thought the son of a bitch would go off like that, though. Scared the hell out of me."

"You and me both," Matt said. "You could have put us all under."

"Sorry about that," Old Fishguts said. "Made a good show, though, didn't it? Worth coming out for, I reckon."

"You'd better tell them the show is over," Matt said.

Old Fishguts turned back to the waiting crowd and held up his arms. "The evil spirit of the dead one is gone," he shouted, "and haunts this place no more. Fish in peace."

There was a moment of silence, then a scatter of applause. Then the crowd began to retreat, talking, laughing. As they walked back toward the shore, men punched one another amiably and waved their arms, women nodded and giggled, children skipped and chased one another, all apparently satisfied.

Frank Nixey had finally regained his feet. "You *sure* it's safe now to fish here?" he called across to Old Fishguts.

" 'Scuse me, got a few skeptics left," Old Fishguts muttered to Matt. He turned to face Frank, Frog, and Shad Billmore, who had remained behind. He raised his arms once again and bent down over the hole in the ice, hummed a little, then straightened up and cupped his hands to his mouth. "Fish say they are ready to bite now. Not depressed," he called across the hole.

"Great," Frank said. "Thanks." He turned away and started toward the shore. Shad Billmore grabbed his arm.

"You mean to say you *believe* all that hopping and humming and carrying on?" Billmore demanded. "You believe that the fish were *depressed*?"

"They weren't bitin'," Frog Bartlett said.

"That's because you weren't *fishing*," Shad said, turning to face him. "You were all in the bar tying one on."

"Same thing," Frog said, and walked away, leaving the insurance man even more outraged than he had been before the whole performance began. He glared across at Old Fishguts and the sheriff, then stomped off—his departure somewhat marred by his slipping on the wet ice once more and skidding for several feet with windmilling arms before regaining his balance.

Old Fishguts had a splendid face. His dark saffron skin was like crumpled parchment, paler where it was stretched smooth over his high cheekbones. His nose was a noble prow that jutted out over a mobile mouth. On that mouth there was now a wicked grin.

"I enjoyed that," he said. "There's nothing like the roar of the greasepaint, is there?"

"You're not wearing greasepaint," George objected. He had thought the performance unconvincing in the end, although the distant thunder and the grenade had added a certain element of drama.

"I wasn't going to use the grenade unless I had to, but then I heard that squadron of jets taking off from the air base—"

"Is that what that was?" Duff asked.

"If the snow hadn't stopped when it did, we wouldn't have caught it," Old Fishguts said. "But they usually take off for practice about now, and I had my hopes that the humidity might play a few tricks with the direction."

"I hope they paid you well," Matt said with a smile.

Old Fishguts looked hurt. "I don't take money for this, Matt. If they want to give me a present of some fine whiskey, well, it would be bad manners to refuse, wouldn't it? Anyway, I was getting restless hanging around the house. I'm waiting for a replacement board for my computer so I can get on with the research for my doctorate, and until it arrives I can't do a damn thing. That's the trouble with getting dependent on the new technology, of course. Makes fools of us all."

"Well, so much for the old technology, then," Matt said. "Let's go, boys. I want to get over to see Vic Moss before dark."

"Thing is, Matt—" Old Fishguts said.

"Yes?" Matt walked along beside the old man, steadying him over the wet area of the ice.

"There may be another one down there," Old Fishguts said.

Matt stopped. "What?"

The old man shook his head. "I don't know . . . it was kind of faint . . . but I think it said there was another one down there. Or there would be soon."

Matt stared at the old man, who looked back at him with the clear, honest, innocent eyes of a child.

"You're serious," Matt said. "You mean that fish . . ."

Old Fishguts shrugged. "Hard to say who was speaking," he told them. "But the message was along the lines of 'the bad one will not rest alone.'"

"Now wait a minute," George said.

"Might mean there's another one up here, of course," Old Fishguts went on, starting again toward the shore. "It was kind of faint, like I said. These things so often are. I've forgotten how to focus, you see. It takes a young man to really focus." He moved away, hands behind his back, the gull feathers on his beaded bonnet waving gently in the wind of his forward movement.

Matt watched him go, then sighed.

Information received.

FOURTEEN

Vic Moss was the head of local organized crime.

Naturally he denied this.

And nothing had ever been proved.

Although his interests ran invisibly in many directions, what Vic Moss did openly was to run a very exclusive country club and inn, which catered to a very odd assortment of people.

River Hill was a magnificent pink-brick mansion in the Federalist style, with white columns at the door and black shutters on all the many-paned windows. The club had an interesting membership encompassing a variety of names—all of which represented money and/or excitement of one kind or another. They stayed in the beautifully decorated suites and ate gourmet meals. By day they played on the delightful nine-hole golf course or the tennis courts or the squash courts, and swam in the elegant pool that occupied a separate glass-domed enclave. By night, they gambled and gamboled. Many things were on offer at River Hill.

According to the existing statutes, gambling was permitted in Blackwater Bay County. In practice, it was not encouraged. Unless, like Vic Moss, you had "contacts"—in which case you were granted a special license that permitted private "gaming" by those *resident* within a particular establishment. Now, it would have been immediately apparent— if inspected by someone with more than ten fingers and ten toes—that River Hill frequently had many more "residents" than rooms, especially on weekends. Fortunately for Mr. Moss and his people, such inspections came rarely, and always with plenty of warning.

After a little unpleasantness at the gate, Matt and George passed up the graveled sweep of the drive and parked their car behind the main building. Matt appreciated the fact that it would never have done to have a police car spoil the façade of River Hill or the look of its extensive grounds, now mantled in a spotless cloak of freshly fallen snow.

Unless, of course, one wished to make a point.

This time he felt it would pay to be discreet. Matt Gabriel, like his father before him, was a pragmatic man. He knew that crime is always with us and that even if he'd had a staff of thousands, it could not ease the evil from men's hearts. So he was, in a way, grateful to Vic Moss, because Vic controlled the services he provided with an iron hand, staying well within his own boundaries. He even had been known to cooperate with the law when one of his "employees" crossed one of those invisible boundaries, because he wanted trouble even less than the law did. Trouble might be bad news for its victims—he didn't much care about that one way or the other. But trouble was bad for business—and he *did* care about *that*.

This was the first time George had been in the River Hill Club, and he was fighting hard to keep his jaw from dropping. The interior was, if anything, more impressive than the outside.

Thick Persian carpets overlaid the glossy hardwood floors in each room, while the halls were carpeted wall-to-wall in imported Axminster apparently woven to order, for it featured a tiny RHCC monogram repeat just one shade darker than the main color. There were sofas, chairs, escritoires, and tables of many styles, but all in period. On the walls hung paintings and portraits, no one of which was of later date than the house itself. But while the original owners of River Hill might recognize the style of the furnishings, they in their time would never have benefited from the deep warmth of underfloor heating, much less lavish indoor plumbing, elevators, and television sets. But these modern innovations had been added so discreetly that they in no way jarred the overall feeling of stepping back in time, albeit a shinier, richer evocation of older days than could have been accomplished then.

Each of the main rooms they were led past or through on the way to Vic Moss's inner sanctum was done in a different color, yet all within the period palette—a deep rose-pink, a clear pale green, a dusky blue, a bronzy gold—these were the tints of the silk wallpapers, the brocade upholstery, and the rich heavy draperies that framed the small handmade glass panes of each tall window.

While he vaguely appreciated that he was in a setting few people ever have an opportunity to see, much less enjoy, George was excited by something else. Only the eagle eye of a man well up on the latest articles in *Modern Lawman* could have spotted them—the tiny openings for security cameras that surveyed every inch of every room. George prided himself on noticing such things. In a way he was a little miffed that someone like Vic Moss should be employing state-of-the-art technology that properly belonged on the right rather than the wrong side of the law.

Matt glanced at him and smiled. "The club itself is a legitimate business, George," he said quietly. "It deserves to be looked after like any other."

"Yeah, okay, but—"

"I'm sure the surveillance tapes are put to very good use," Matt said.

"Good for who?" George wanted to know.

"No one has ever complained," Matt said.

"I bet no one ever dared," George said. "My God—the blackmail and—"

"I don't think that's a word Mr. Moss would like, George," Matt cautioned him softly, with a glance at the flawlessly tailored back of the man escorting them. "I don't think those are the kinds of subjects we're here to discuss today. All right?"

"Sure, sure," George muttered. One day he would be sheriff, he thought. One day he's see this kind of thing—whatever it was—stamped *right* out.

Vic showed no surprise at their intrusion—but then, Vic rarely showed surprise or anything else except the faint flicker of a smile when amused. He was a villain of the old school, a Hollywood gent, with the cheekbones of a lion and the eyes of a *Tyrannosaurus rex*.

No relation to the sheriff's right-hand woman (as she frequently pointed out), Vic Moss had grown up on the streets of Grantham, a handsome boy with a talent for spotting the main chance. At the age of nineteen he had been taken in hand by one of the great ladies of the afternoon, a woman named Delilah Armbruster, a legendary madam whose establishment had serviced the whole of the northeast side of the city—the side where the money lived. She educated the young Vic in the arts, trained his palate, taught him how to dress, how to mix with society, and how to get the last drop of juice out of every orange in the bowl.

When she died, something in him had closed like a fist. She left part of her estate to him as a nest egg to make a beginning. Some would argue that the uses to which he put it were less than inspiring, and undoubtedly illegal, but they were profitable. He invested the profits and, again, they grew. At the same time, *he* grew into a handsome man, tall, spare of form, beautifully dressed, prematurely silver-haired, utterly without malice *or* morals. As far as he was concerned,

if something had to be done—be it a mauling or a mani-
cure—it had better be done, and done quickly, then never
spoken of again.

He rose to his feet, all courtesy, when his assistant showed
the two visitors into his immaculate and surprisingly modern
office. Here the wood was ebony, the upholstery was the soft-
est, palest suede, the oyster curtains and carpet were plain and
rough-textured. No plants or flowers, but starkly lit African
carvings hung on the pale walls, and the painting behind the
desk was a bold, masculine abstract in black, white, and scar-
let.

"Sheriff Gabriel, good afternoon," Vic Moss said, reaching
across his desk to shake hands. "It's been a long time.
Please—make yourselves comfortable. A drink? Coffee, perhaps?"

"Nothing, thank you," Matt said.

"I wouldn't mind a Coke," George said. Vic nodded to his
assistant, who withdrew.

"My deputy, George Putnam," Matt said.

"Ah, yes—Carl's son," Vic said easily. "I know your father
well, Mr. Putnam. A fine man."

"Oh. Yes," George said, a little startled by this revelation.

A faint smile flickered across Moss's face. "A fine oppo-
nent, I should have said. We have crossed swords several
times in court. I respect him. I don't know whether he
would say the same about me. I rather doubt it," he concluded wryly.

The assistant returned with George's Coke and an amber-
colored drink for Vic Moss, then stood behind the desk, to
Moss's left, staring at them.

"You have no objection to my assistant, Mr. Logan, being
present?" Moss asked.

"None at all," Matt said. "The reason we've come to see
you, Vic, is that we have a problem."

"Anything I can do," Moss said easily.

"It concerns a dead man," Matt continued.

Moss's face remained expressionless. "Oh? I find it's usually the living who create the problems," he observed.

"Well—we pulled a corpse out from under the ice a few days ago—"

"Ah, yes, I read about it in the papers," Moss nodded. "Name of Vernon?"

"Yes. Did you know him?"

Moss shook his head. "I'm sorry, I didn't," he said with what sounded to George like genuine regret. "I heard you'd been asking for information. I would have been in touch if I had known anything about him."

"Of course," Matt agreed, accepting the lie as legal tender. "The thing is, Vic—the man had your name and phone number in his address book."

"Many people do."

"Yes. But we checked out his telephone calls at the motel where he was staying, and several were made to this club."

"Oh, really? Perhaps he was trying to book a room," Vic suggested. "He was never put through to me."

"I see." Matt looked at Vic, who returned his glance with a faint smile. There was no way to tell whether he was lying or not, and Matt did not feel inclined to ask him to question his staff. Not now. Not yet. He cleared his throat. "We've also found out that this man worked for people in New York. People I think you might know."

"Like Luca Ritto," George put in.

Moss turned his gaze on the deputy, and suddenly George wished he'd kept his mouth shut.

"I know the name, of course," Moss said softly. "I read the papers like everyone else. I do not know him personally. He is not the kind of man I would want to know, you understand. Only from the newspapers, I assure you."

"Does the name Peter Murphy mean anything to you?"

Vic Moss leaned back in his chair—until that moment Matt hadn't realized he'd been leaning forward—and re-

garded him levelly. Beside him, the assistant stirred and
then was still.

"Should it?" Vic asked.

Matt sighed. He saw no point in pretending. "Peter
Murphy's testimony put Luca Ritto behind bars. Murphy then
went into the witness protection program. It occurs to me that
perhaps Ritto put out a contract on Murphy, and this Vernon
took it up. What bothers me is why he came to Blackwater
Bay—unless he knew—or somebody knew—that Peter
Murphy was here. This would be useful information for Ritto
and his organization, information for which they would pay
well."

"I have no doubt of it," Vic said. "People like that are always interested in information."

"Exactly."

"But why come to me with this? I don't deal in information."

"Not personally. But perhaps someone on your staff, or one
of the members of your beautiful club, might know something?"

"I think not," Vic said. "Really, I think not."

"Can you be sure?"

Moss looked at him. "Should it worry me? Would I want
to know this?"

"I think so," Matt said. "I think it would be better for
both you and me to know now rather than to find out later."

"Ah," Vic said.

"The thing is, Vic—I don't like mysteries. I fully intend
to get the person or persons who killed this Vernon, even
though he seems to be a man better dead."

"I appreciate you have to do your job," Vic said.

"Thank you," Matt said.

George was lost. He'd finished his Coke, he had detected an
unpleasant bulge in the vicinity of the assistant's armpit, one
of the masks on the right-hand wall seemed to be glaring at

him, and despite the time of year it was very warm in the office.

"I suppose you will have to approach the FBI on this," Vic said after a moment.

"I have no alternative," Matt said. "Probably tomorrow."

"Ah," Vic said again. "That's a pity. I imagine the federal government may be difficult to deal with."

"I hope not," Matt said. "The trouble is, they have no reason to trust me or anyone else. Trust is so important, and so rare, these days."

Again, that flicker of a smile. "Loyalty is always valued. Its loss is a blow to the heart of any family."

"As is loss of respect. I don't think the FBI has much time for respect. If this murder does concern their interests, then they'll be looking in all the corners."

"Well, that's where the rats usually are," Vic said.

"I don't like the idea of outside interests causing trouble in my county," Matt went on. "Either the government or anyone else. We have a nice quiet place here, and I'd like it to stay that way as long as possible."

"I entirely agree," Vic said. "If I hear of anything that might be helpful, I will notify you immediately." He stood up.

"I'd be grateful," Matt said. He stood up, too. As George followed suit, the assistant's eyes met his, and they were just like Moss's own—dark, cold, and heavy-lidded. George wondered if he had a forked tongue behind that thin-lipped mouth.

"I appreciate your seeing us, Vic," Matt said. "Thanks for your time."

"My pleasure. Deputy, give my regards to your father next time you see him."

"All right," said George. "I will." He wondered how his father would react to this message from the dark side of the moon.

They left, following the silent assistant back through the

body of the club, sensing people near but seeing no one. George wondered if they were closed for the winter.

"Do you mind telling me what that was all about?" he asked Matt when they had returned to the car. Matt started the engine and rolled forward around the house and onto the drive, avoiding the worst of the ruts in the icy snow.

"It was an exchange of information," Matt said.

"It was?" George didn't remember any facts going back and forth. Nothing but polite nothing seemed to have passed between Matt and Moss. "Why should he tell you anything? And why should you want to know anything he knows? He's just a crook in a fancy suit."

Matt glanced at his deputy and smiled. George had so much to learn. "We could do a lot worse than having Vic Moss running the vice around here."

"You *like* having him here?"

"Of course not. But I like the alternatives even less. The corrupt are always with us, George. Vic Moss may run women and numbers and very possibly a little dope out of River Hill—although I believe he's always had a strong bias against drugs—but he keeps his people and his operation in line and out of trouble. He's as interested in a quiet life as I am."

"I still don't see why you should bother to tell him anything."

"There is the possibility that Vernon was actually sent to kill *Vic*—hence Vic's name in the address book."

"So let him take his chances like anyone else. Anyway, why would a New York hit man be sent to kill a nice quiet crook like Vic Moss, for crying out loud?" George asked snidely.

"Because Vic has loyalties and connections to the Pescatori family that go back a long way."

"No shit? I didn't know that." George turned to face Matt, putting his seat belt under serious strain.

"It's hardly public information," Matt said. "I only knew

because my father told me about it a long time ago. There were loans and investments made at a time when Vic looked as if he was losing what he had built up. Everything has long since been repaid, there are no official obligations on either side—but obligations exist, nonetheless."

"Okay, but I still don't—"

"The Rittos are still interested in taking over the business enterprises of the Pescatori family—which was the reason Ritto killed Sam Pescatori in the first place. Even though Ritto is still in jail, the war goes on."

"I didn't know that."

"They don't send many dispatches from the front."

"I guess not."

Matt saw that George was still unconvinced. "Peter Murphy put Ritto in jail, now Peter Murphy is living somewhere under an assumed name, right?"

"Yeah."

"And the Pescatori family, being grateful to him for putting away the man who killed one of their own, would be prepared to lend a hand now and then to keep him safe, wouldn't they?"

"I guess so."

"Well, if Vernon wasn't after Vic himself, it occurred to me that Vic might be shielding Murphy as a favor to the Pescatoris. Perhaps having him right there in the club, as an employee, and that Vernon intended to pressure him into exposing Murphy."

"You're kidding."

"No," Matt said rather grimly. "I'm guessing, simply because of all those newspaper clippings Vernon had with him."

"Would Vic have told him?"

"No. But he might have killed Vernon, or had him killed when Vernon tried to get him to expose Murphy."

"Well, why the hell didn't you ask him that?"

"I did."

"The hell you did."

"I asked him simply by going there. He knows he's a suspect now."

"You told him you were calling in the feds."

"Yes."

"Are you?"

"I'm going to have to ask them if Peter Murphy is living in Blackwater Bay or not. I don't think they'll tell me, but they will want to know why I'm interested, and so I'll have to tell *them* about Vernon and the clippings. That could start them poking around, which is not something Vic Moss would welcome and neither would I, because it might bring more trouble to Blackwater. I hardly think this is the right place for a gang war."

"So you went to *warn* Vic Moss?"

"I went to ask him to check out his people. If Vernon came to kill Vic, or to kill Peter Murphy—whoever he might be now—then it may be because someone in Vic's organization gave a tip-off to the Ritto family, which would have been very disloyal and stupid of him or her. Alternatively it's also possible that someone in Vic's organization killed Vernon without having been ordered to do so. Maybe this person did it to protect Vic himself when he was being threatened. Either way, I've given Vic a chance to turn the person or persons responsible over to me. It would avoid a lot of trouble for both of us. He took the point. He told me he would do what he could."

George was aggrieved. "Dammit, I was sitting right there and I didn't hear any of that."

"I guess you weren't listening." Matt smiled, and drove out of the gate onto the highway, heading back toward Blackwater Bay.

FIFTEEN

They were, without a doubt, the most beautiful green eyes Jess had ever seen. So entranced with them was she that the man behind them had to repeat himself twice before she snapped to attention.

"They are both in excellent shape, Miss Gibbons. I can't find anything physically wrong with either one. Have you been paying them enough attention?"

"Oh, yes—I feed them as soon as I get home from school and play with them afterward. And they both sleep on my bed at night." Oh, dear, she thought. That tells him far too much about my sex life—or lack of it.

"What's your major?" he asked.

"I beg your pardon?"

"You said when you get home from school—"

Jess drew herself up. "I'm a teacher," she said. "I teach home economics at Heckman High."

"Good Lord," the vet said, blushing. "I'm sorry."

"I suppose I should be flattered," Jess said—and she was. She didn't believe in his "mistake" but appreciated the effort behind it. "But it should tell you the trouble I have maintaining authority over there."

"I can imagine." They grinned at one another.

Dr. Geoff Kelly had taken over the veterinary practice of Dr. Marlow, who had retired to Florida at the end of the previous summer. Jess, who had taken her pets to Dr. Marlow from childhood, had been hesitant about visiting a stranger—even one who had taken over the same practice. Now she was rapidly trying to think up new difficulties about her cats so that she could come regularly. Dr. Geoff Kelly was gorgeous—in his midthirties, dark auburn hair, those green eyes, wonderful bone structure—she was a sucker for bone structure—and a build that spoke of fitness far beyond the standard required for operating on a canary— or even on an elephant.

"How about mice?" Dr. Kelly asked after a moment.

"I don't mind them," Jess said.

He laughed. "No—I meant, do you have any?"

"I once had a gerbil, but—"

"In the *house*," he interrupted. "The cats' erratic behavior is also indicative of hunting frenzy. If their nice winter doze had been interrupted by mice the other night, they would have been all over the place chasing them. Didn't find any heads or tails lying around, did you? Well-fed cats usually can't finish a whole mouse."

"I didn't notice any," Jess said, startled. "You know, I never thought of mice. But it's an old house, so I suppose . . ."

"If they worry you, set a trap or two in the basement," he suggested, stroking both Cleo and Twister at once, his long-fingered hands moving smoothly over their backs. Much purring ensued, both in the cats and—less audibly—in Jess herself. She wouldn't have minded a few strokes from those nice hands herself.

The vet continued, unaware of the reaction he was precipitating. "However, in the interests of the cats I'd say let them get on with it. It's excellent exercise for them, and from the state of their stomachs, I'd say they could use a little dashing and chasing after all these weeks of sleeping in front of the fire."

"They *have* put on a bit of weight," Jess admitted, knowing full well she overfed them because she was too soft-hearted to resist the sad meows both cats had perfected. Even their whiskers expressed deep starvation whenever they cornered an adult with access to a can opener.

"Well, that's fine," Dr. Kelly said encouragingly. "A lot of women raise the roof at the thought of mice in the house."

"I don't think that would help to get rid of them," Jess said.

"Probably not," he agreed. They grinned at each other a little more.

"Well," Jess finally said. "Thank you for seeing them."

"My pleasure." He turned to check his notes. "I'll send you a reminder when they're due for their next boosters."

But that's a year away, Jess thought. I'll have to think up another mystery disease, after all. Ah, well, there's always teeth cleaning. She gazed at her cats with affection. Dear things—and so much to go wrong. Eczema, ear mites, depression—the possibilities for trips to see the gorgeous Dr. Kelly were endless. Expensive, of course, but endless.

"Are you settling down well in Blackwater?" she asked, as she began to cajole the cats back into their carrier. They were not in the mood, and a tussle ensued.

"Yes, thanks. A lovely little town—and really nice to be by the water. Or, I suppose it will be, next summer."

"Oh, it's fun in the winter, too. There's an Ice Festival coming up soon. Your family will enjoy that." She was wrestling with Twister and avoided looking at the vet.

"It would—if I had a family," Dr. Kelly said, also avoiding eye contact. "At least it made moving here easy—no ties, no complications. I found a nice apartment over on Walnut Hill—"

"One of those new condos they just built?"

"That's right. Terrific view down over the town and the bay." Their hands touched as they thrust Cleo in after Twister and slammed the wire door shut. Jess was sure she felt an electric shock pass between them—but it was probably just static from the cats' fur. "I see on the notes that you live out on something called Perkins Point—where's that?" he asked.

"You can probably see it from your place," Jess said. "A big ugly Victorian house on the shore north of Paradise Island."

"I'm afraid I don't know where Paradise Island is."

"Almost center of the bayshore—a little to the right, facing out. We're a little to the left of center."

"Politically or geographically?"

"Take your pick. There are six of us living there."

He raised an eyebrow. "A commune?"

"Nothing so racy. I'm the landlady, and I have five house-mates—all teachers, all very anal-retentive, so much staking of territory goes on. Nothing communal about it."

"All women?"

"Nope." Jess hefted the cat carrier and started toward the door. "Three men, three women."

"Good odds," he said with a twinkle in his eye.

"Depends on the game," she retorted.

"Do you like games?" he asked.

She smiled. "Depends on the odds," she said, and left him smiling after her. She went into the waiting room to pay her bill and met the icy blue eyes of the young woman behind the desk. Uh-oh, she thought—speaking of staking out territory, here's a claimant already.

"Hi," Jess said, putting the carrier down on the floor. "What do I owe?" If her expression is anything to go by, I owe her an apology for living, she thought, as the girl slapped down an account in front of her and prepared to write on it.

"No pills or shots?"

"Annual boosters—and good advice," Jess said.

"Twenty bucks," the girl said. Jess didn't recognize her.

"Are you new in town, too?" she asked with what she hoped was a friendly, defusing smile.

"Hardly. I'm Mandy Turkle."

"Oh, sorry."

The girl regarded her with the disdain of any eighteen-year-old for an elderly lady of twenty-nine. "I heard about you coming back to teach at Heckman—you've got one of my cousins in your patchwork class. Jill Pederson."

"Oh? I didn't know she was a—" Jess caught herself, then went on. "She's *very* good. We're hoping she'll join the Magpies when she graduates."

Mandy sniffed. "She's not hanging around this dump after she finishes. She's getting out, she says. Going to art college." From Mandy's tone, she didn't believe a word of it, nor did she want to believe it. There didn't appear to be much love between the two girls. A clear case of negative and positive Turkles, no doubt. The Turkle family bloodlines crossed most others in Blackwater County, and the Turkle traits were usually dominant. Negative Turkles were sly, lazy, and general disasters that rarely waited to happen. Positive Turkles were ambitious, hardworking, and told you all about it. Whenever the two strains crossed, the lucky genetic recipient usually went into politics.

This girl must have graduated from Heckman last June, Jess thought, but I don't remember her. Dr. Marlow's wife had been his receptionist, so the delicious Dr. Kelly must have hired Mandy from—where?

"Do you like working with animals, Mandy?"

"I like it better than working at the shoe factory," Mandy snapped. "I took a special course at night, so I could move up. And I did."

"You certainly did," Jess said. "This is quite a responsible job. You'll know you're making a difference here."

Mandy raised her eyebrows and glanced toward the examination room. "You bet I will," she said, and the inference was clear.

So, Jess thought, as she went out into the cold, it's not going to be a clear run, after all. The vet has a pet Cerberus at the gate who plans to collar him for herself. Well, we'll see.

She never could resist a challenge.

As she made her way across the small parking lot, she began to shiver. Glancing up at the sky, she noted that it was filling with heavy cloud cover, low and dark. "I don't like the look of that," she said to the cats as she placed their carrier on the backseat. "I think I'll stop at the supermarket on the way home and stock up—before the hoarders get there."

This was an old family joke, but one that had particular meaning in this instance. Jess Gibbons was many things, but foolish was not one of them, and thus she was among the few who were fully prepared for what was to come.

The word "cold" does not begin to encompass what began to descend on Blackwater Bay that evening. Slowly, insidiously, the temperature began to slide downward and continued to do so through the night. Somewhere around dawn, the snow began to fall, tight little pellets of icy snow that filled the air like fog, blowing and billowing down the streets and between the houses.

The snowblowers, plows, and salt trucks came out, but it was a losing battle as the hard snow built up. Light flakes make for easy shifting, but this was pellet snow, ice-heavy and dense. Snowblowers became clogged because it packed so tightly and weighed so much, and eventually even the snowplows were defeated, crawling back to their garages for maintenance and preparation for the time when the snowfall would stop and the drivers could assess the best way to clear it.

But the snow *didn't* stop.

It continued to fall all day and all through the following night, sometimes in flakes, but mostly still in the icy pellets that tapped against the windows of the houses in ghostly

Morse code. The wind howled and snarled down the streets. People turned up their heating and took stock of the contents of their cupboards and freezers. In many houses there would be some strange and meager meals eaten over the next few days, for the television and radio reports now told them that the entire Midwest was in the grip of one of the worst blizzards in twenty years. They didn't need the radio to tell them—they knew.

Blackwater Bay was socked in completely. The highway to the north and south of it was completely impassable. The minor roads that led into the farms behind it were simply gone, lost beneath the vast white sea of snow that obliterated everything except houses and tall trees.

For three days the snow fell.

When it finally stopped, and the sun came out, the vista was both breathtaking and heartbreaking.

It was, in its way, a jeweled scene, with the diamond glitter of ice and the blinding white of the snow sharply contrasted against the vivid deep blue of a cloudless sky. But the black tracery of the leafless trees had become misshapen with the asymmetrical jagged wounds of wrenched-off branches. Young trees were down everywhere, broken-backed by the weight of the ice. Isolated farm animals that had survived the cold floundered helplessly in the drifts. Birds, which must eat their own weight every day simply to live, circled endlessly in a hopeless search for both familiar landmarks and food. Everywhere on the invisible road were the mounds that indicated abandoned vehicles.

For the first few hours of daylight there was a vast, crystal silence over Blackwater and the surrounding area. Then, as people awoke, there began to be heard the thin gleeful shrieks of children offered an endless white canvas on which to make their mark, and the weary shouts of adults emerging to face the task of reestablishing communication with one another and the world outside.

By midday the air above the endless white pastures was

crisscrossed with the droning of mechanical insects as helicopters from Greenleaf Air Force Base across the bay and those of the Highway Patrol and other emergency services came out to assess the situation and—if necessary—be of help.

Bales of hay were tossed down to hungry cattle. Abandoned cars and vehicles were noted and mapped for investigation, should they contain passengers trapped by their own foolishness. Paramedic teams were lowered to isolated farmhouses to aid the sick. The Sheriff's Department opened a communications center in town and began to coordinate needs with solutions.

Radio and television stations broadcast warnings and information: Do not attempt to shovel your walks unless absolutely necessary, especially if elderly or unaccustomed to physical labor. Those in need of assistance please telephone the following numbers. If no telephone available, place a red blanket or a large red piece of clothing outside your house and someone will try to get to you. Do not let children or pets go outside unaccompanied. Feed the birds.

There was no sign of a thaw. According to the weathermen, the cold would continue for at least another week, and—worse news still—more snow might be on the way. But a start had to be made. One by one the snowplows edged out of their garages and began to chew away at the massive weight of the snow, throwing up wedges and piles that were house-high in some places. Their main task was to clear the highway north and south so that help and commerce could get through.

Little by little, things began to return to a new kind of normal, where roads were canyons in the snow, where houses seemed suddenly lower, where meals were makeshift and people stayed in, huddling around fires or television sets, close to one another, grateful for any warmth.

Some were not so lucky.

SIXTEEN

Matt Gabriel stepped outside of his office and took a deep breath of the icy biting air, almost enjoying the sensation as it froze the hairs in his nose and penetrated his chest with a sharp, knifing pain. He breathed out, feeling the hairs in his nose thaw, and then freeze again as he inhaled more gently.

He frowned. It was the quality of the air that was so eerie, he decided. Sounds seemed to carry for great distances, but they were distorted and disconnected. The bark of a dog was recognizable, but there were odd sounds the origin of which he could not locate—sharp cracks, dull thuds, the hollow sound of a door slamming, the call of a young child, the chunk of an ax blow, pings and whines and odd gasps that seemed to have no human connection. And yet, between the sounds, the air seemed to hang like a blanket over all, muffling one's own noises and movements.

Main Street was a Christmas card, one he wished heartily had not been sent. The roadway had been cleared to two car widths only, and parked cars—marooned under thick blankets of white—meant that large delivery trucks could not pull aside and therefore periodically blocked traffic completely while they unloaded as quickly as possible.

Drivers were generally patient with one another, but a doctor on his way to a heart attack or a birth naturally needs priority over a bread delivery, and is inclined to say so—loudly. It seemed to Matt that his men were engaged equally in traffic control and diplomacy and, as they were all exhausted, the latter duty was growing more and more onerous. The road still had snow on it, but it was dry and dirty snow, as much like frozen dust as anything, except where salt had muddied it into slush. It made a nice skid-pan, so that in addition to large trucks occasionally blocking things in both directions, there was also the odd car that had slewed broadside to traffic which needed to be manhandled back into line.

There was no hope from the weatherman, either. Continued freezing temperatures meant that a thaw was not forthcoming in the near future. At least, Matt thought, it kept the burglars at home. Behind him, the door opened and George stuck his head out.

"Matt—I think we've got a problem."

"Her car is gone," said Mrs. Falconer. "Also her goose-down coat and boots, but I can't say what she was wearing underneath. She has so many clothes I can't keep track."

"Any suitcases missing?"

"No—the ones she usually uses are still in her room," Bill Falconer said. He and his wife, Caroline, had finally made their way home, only to find their daughter, Chrissie, missing. "We've called all her friends. She's not staying with any of them. She hasn't left a note or anything." He bent down to rub the ears of an elderly retriever who seemed to be leaning on him for support. "When we came in, Shandy here was practically hysterical, kept barking at us and running in and out. From what we could see, he hasn't been fed for several days, which isn't like Chrissie at all. She adores Shandy—he's got a liver problem and she's been taking him to that new vet for shots twice a week since before Christmas. She's always been a reliable kid—wherever she is, she'd find some way to get back here and feed him if she could. And he needed his medication, too."

"The blizzard trapped a lot of people—" Matt began, but Falconer rushed on.

"Fortunately the dog flap is on the lee side of the house, so he could get out to do his business, and he could get water from eating snow. But he was pretty weak and wobbly, and his eye trouble has started up again. When I get my hands on her . . ." Slowly he ran down. Matt could see he was diverting his concern for the girl onto the dog, turning fear into anger as a way of not thinking about what could have happened to Chrissie, something so drastic that it prevented her from caring for her beloved dog.

Mrs. Falconer was standing in her dining room, hands on hips, glaring at the walls. She turned to join her husband and Matt in the hall. "One of the neighbors told us about the party," she said, thin-lipped. "Anything you'd care to add?"

Matt shrugged. "Gate-crashers who turned nasty, according to Chrissie. When we got here, the place was in quite a mess—"

"So I see," Bill Falconer said.

"Oh, much worse than this," George put in brightly. "You should have seen it *before* the cleaners came in."

"Oh?" Caroline Falconer raised an eyebrow. "What, exactly?"

"Well," George began. "There were the wine and beer stains halfway up the wall, and—"

The Falconers stared at him. Bill spoke first. "Wait a minute. The Newcombes just told us there was a noisy party and that you'd been called to quiet it down—they didn't say anything about damage."

"Oh," Matt said. "Well, you'd better talk to Carl Putnam

about that. He arranged for the cleaning and the repairs and—"

"Repairs?" The Falconers spoke as one.

"And the repainting—"

"Repainting?" Again, in chorus.

"Well—"

"Why on earth was Carl Putnam involved?" Bill wanted to know. "People in town know I'm good for any bills Chrissie might run up."

"Well, when I took Chrissie in, she was allowed one call—"

"You *arrested* Chrissie?" Caroline gasped. "Why?"

"I'm afraid there were drugs on the premises, Mrs. Falconer."

"Marijuana?"

"And other things. Pills, mostly."

"Oh, my God," she moaned, and went into the sitting room, sinking down onto the sofa and running her hands through her sleek blond hair. "We never should have left her alone. She promised us . . . she swore . . ."

"I can't really take this in," Bill Falconer said.

Matt felt sorry for them. Bill Falconer owned a very successful agricultural supply business situated west of town and had recently expanded into office equipment. His wife was a former model and worked part-time in real estate, mostly as a hobby. The two were normally a magazine-cover pair, but their natural good looks were already considerably undermined by their fraught journey back from Aspen. Blocked by the blizzards, it apparently had been a series of bad connections, long waits in small airports, a train into Grantham, and then collection by a friend with a Range Rover to cover the final weary snowbound miles. Now, beneath their ski-slope tans, they were haggard and stunned.

"I'm really sorry," Matt said. "I thought Carl would have contacted you about all this by now."

"We left our hotel and went to stay with some friends who

have a lodge," Caroline explained. "It was only for the last few days—we didn't think to leave a number at the hotel. We did try to call Chrissie, but never seemed to catch her at home. We left messages on the answering machine, but she never called back." She looked up. "Now I can see why."

"Do you think she's run away?" Bill asked Matt. "Knowing we were coming back and so on?"

"I don't know," Matt said. "She's been going to school regularly." He smiled encouragingly. "I'm sure you'll find she's staying with some friend you haven't thought of."

"We've been through the Rolodex on her desk," Bill said. "It took quite a while, but I don't think we missed anyone." He frowned. "What about these gate-crashers you mentioned? Who were they?"

"Chrissie claimed they were from Hatchville, and that she didn't know who they were," Matt said.

Bill's glance was sharp. "Claimed?" he asked. "Didn't you believe her?"

"I think she may have known them—if they existed at all. You see, when we got here there was no sign of them, and it did occur to me that they were a convenient explanation for whatever had gone wrong at the party."

"I can't believe I'm hearing this about my daughter," Caroline wailed. "She's such a good girl, we've never had any trouble before . . ."

"I know that," Matt said. "That's why I didn't put up any opposition to her release. Maybe it would be better if you called Carl Putnam now. He can give you the details. Meanwhile, we'll start asking around and see if we can get a lead on who she could be staying with. She might have been visiting a new friend and got trapped there by the storm. Not all the phone lines are back in action, otherwise she might have phoned a neighbor about the dog. If she's as devoted to him as you say, I'm sure she's worried, too."

"I'd probably strangle her if she walked in right now," Bill Falconer said angrily—and unconvincingly.

"Every kid goes through a bad patch," George volunteered. "She was last year's Homecoming Queen, wasn't she?"

"Yes," Caroline said with somewhat jaundiced pride, pointing to a silver-framed photograph on the piano— Chrissie in her crown and cape.

"Sometimes that changes them," George said ponderously. "Has an effect on them psychologically, makes them vulnerable to influences."

"Influences?" Caroline asked.

Matt glared at George, who had obviously been reading the pop psychology column in *Modern Lawman*. "I think George means that if she got accustomed to the limelight, perhaps she felt she had to do daring things to keep getting her friends' approval."

"Also guys," George said. "Guys start hanging around."

"Oh, Lord," Caroline Falconer moaned. "Not that Joey again."

"Joey?" Matt asked.

"A very unsuitable boy who came to the house several times after last year's Howl," Bill explained. "I think Chrissie had given him the wrong impression or something." His expression sharpened. "Say—he was from Hatchville."

"Do you know his last name?" Matt asked, reaching for his notebook.

"No, I'm afraid Chrissie only introduced him as Joey," Caroline said. "He was one of those boys with a great deal of hair, all in clumps. And an earring—well, several earrings, as a matter of fact, all in one ear. Like a Ubangi."

"A what?" George asked.

"You know—those African natives who put rings around their necks and so on? He had a whole line of rings through one ear, all around the edge, like a fringe."

"Joey," Matt said, writing. "With hair and earrings. I'll check with the Hatchville police—he may be known."

"If only for his foul mouth," Bill said. "You should have heard him when I made it clear he wasn't welcome around Chrissie." He paused. "You should have heard her, as a matter of fact." He shook his head. "I suppose it's trite, but—God, kids today are weird."

"Kids have always seemed weird to everyone but one another," Matt said, putting his notebook away and putting on an encouraging smile. "If they don't drive everyone crazy, they feel they've failed somehow."

Bill smiled. "I suppose so."

"Well, don't worry. I'll get out a call on the car, but I'm sure she'll come through that front door anytime now. However, I would like to take a look at her room, if you don't mind. Just in case I might see something you've missed."

Mrs. Falconer looked up from where she was leafing through the mail that had accumulated during their absence. "It's a terrible mess—we've only just gotten back and—"

"Good," Matt assured her. "Then it will tell us a lot more than it would have if it had been cleaned and tidied."

"Oh." She looked suddenly pale. "You mean if something happened to her there . . . you mean . . ."

"I mean she might have made a note of a phone number or address on some scrap of paper," Matt said quickly. "Little things can tell us a lot—"

"It's the third door on the right at the top of the stairs," Bill Falconer said, moving across to place a reassuring hand on his wife's shoulder.

Matt nodded and went out, with George trailing after him. Behind him, Matt heard Caroline Falconer begin to cry, and Bill Falconer say, "Oh, God, Caroline, try and stay calm."

"Think she's a runaway?" George asked, as they went toward the stairs.

"I think it's a good possibility," Matt said grimly. "When

she realized they actually were about to appear, she probably lost her nerve. Funny about the dog, though. Leaving him like that when she was so devoted. I don't like that, much. For once I'm glad about the drugs."

"Because it means we can look for her?"

Matt glanced at him approvingly. "Right. We can class her as absconding rather than just missing. She will have to answer the drug charge, and so we can pull out all the stops to find her."

Matt stopped by the front door and looked up and down the street—one of the best ones in town, lined with large single homes surrounded by big gardens. The landscaping was now the same for all of them—flat white broken by mounds of white. None of them had shoveled their walks—their gardeners were stuck at home, too. There was no broken snow on the pavements, either—not that any of these people ever walked anywhere.

He glanced back through the half-open door to the living room, and saw that they were both trying to distract themselves with the mail. It looked like there was quite a bit of it—mostly late Christmas cards, no doubt. As he watched, Caroline opened yet another envelope, glanced through the contents hurriedly, then tossed it aside and reached for another. He returned to his reflections.

The uppermost question in his mind concerned when Chrissie had left home. Before the blizzard? During? She could have left anytime in the past three days, but the likeliest period was sometime between Friday night and Saturday evening when the blizzard really took hold, because her car—a small sports model, according to her father—would never have made it over the roads once the snow really got serious. Had she intended to return? If not, then what about the dog? It didn't seem likely she would just abandon her responsibilities to a beloved family pet when she had carried them out so conscientiously before. If she had made arrangements for the dog with a neighbor, why hadn't they done what they'd promised?

There was a brief cry from the living room, and he turned to look through the open door. Mrs. Falconer was holding a piece of paper out to her husband, who took it, read it, then turned pale.

Matt went to the doorway. "Is it a note from Chrissie?" he asked.

Bill Falconer looked momentarily confused. "Why . . . no," he finally said. "Just another bill. I guess they'll be coming in quite frequently now, from what you said."

"I expect so," Matt agreed. His eyes were on the paper in Falconer's hand, but Falconer turned away and put it on top of a stack of others he had apparently culled from the accumulated mail.

Matt nodded and started toward the stairs, then paused again. It had not been a bill at all—there had been no heading, no commercial appearance at all. It had been a letter. Why had Falconer lied? Matt could think of only one reason. And it was not one he liked. He started to turn back yet again, only to find that Falconer or his wife had closed the living room door.

"Well—are we going up or not?" George asked.

"Yes, right," agreed Matt. As they started up the stairs he looked down at the closed door and wondered whether he should have gone in and demanded to see the piece of paper that had startled and upset the Falconers so much.

Had it been a note from Chrissie, after all?

Or a note *about* her—demanding ransom?

Matt felt sudden despair. The way things had been going lately in Blackwater Bay, a kidnaping seemed almost like a natural progression.

SEVENTEEN

Matt and George went up the curving stairs that wrapped around the large entrance hall of the Falconers' Georgian-style house, their feet sinking into thick moss-green carpeting. After opening a door or two they found Chrissie's room, unmistakable in its chaos and the combination of fading childhood and burgeoning femininity. There was a smell of stale cigarettes and some flowery perfume in the room.

Outgrown dolls were heaped artistically on a chintz-covered chair, behind which was propped a hockey stick and, oddly enough, a pair of crutches. Matt vaguely remembered a springtime hockey game and a clash of vixens that resulted in someone's ride to the hospital—apparently Chrissie's. In place of pride, suspended on ribbons over the dressing-table mirror, the Homecoming Crown, all gold foil and stick-on stars. On the lace-canopied bed a patchwork quilt in cherry pink and white thrown back, exposing the pale pink sheets and pillows. One slipper on its side, another peeking out from beneath the flounces. Along one wall, low bookshelves overflowing with school texts and murder mysteries and tomes on skin care and hair care and how to mend a broken heart and how to analyze your handwriting/character/ boyfriend/career prospects. A window seat with a very bald teddy bear.

The room was dim, for the curtains were still drawn. Matt went across and opened them, letting the harsh reflected snow light stream in, reducing the impression of a cozy retreat to one of something recently struck by lightning.

As, indeed, it may have been. To Matt, however, the lightning was more that of a careless teenager than any kind of struggle.

He went over to the bedside and inspected the table there. A couple of glasses stood next to the alarm clock. Using a pen, he slid open the drawer in the bedside table, revealing, among other things, the edge of a packet of condoms. An opened packet. Gently he lifted the covers on the bed, but there was no used condom there or beneath the bed itself.

"We'll want the bed linen for semen stains and anything else they can pick up," Matt said. "It looks like she wasn't alone before she disappeared."

"And how do you explain that to her mother?" George wanted to know.

"I don't," Matt said grimly. "If she wants to work it out for herself, she can. If we can get a blood type, it might help. He obviously got rid of the condom or condoms."

"But not the glasses," George said. "That was dumb."

"They're probably wiped," Matt said. "Everybody knows about fingerprints these days."

"Unless he panicked," George observed, bending down to examine the open texts and notebooks on the desk opposite the window. "She was doing geography—glaciers."

"Appropriate," Matt said. He poked at the cigarette butts in an ashtray beside the two glasses. One brand, no lipstick. Didn't prove anything. Saliva tests might. How far could he go when this was not officially a crime scene?

No posters on the walls, he noted. A couple of fairly bland watercolors bracketed the bed. Opposite it, above the bookcases, was a large patchwork hanging, abstract in design, colorfully embroidered and beaded—presumably Chrissie's own work, for it was out of place in these conventional adolescent surroundings. He looked at it for a long time and decided that, in his limited opinion, the girl showed talent in that direction.

"How rich do you suppose the Falconers are?" he asked George, who was going through the desk drawers slowly and carefully, examining each item.

"A lot of girls her age keep a diary," he said over his shoulder. "We might get lucky." He straightened up. "How rich? I don't know. Why?"

"Do you think it would be worthwhile kidnaping Chrissie?"

George looked amazed. "Do you think that's what's happened?"

"I don't know." He told George about the letter and the Falconers' reaction to it. "I might be imagining things."

"Why don't you go down and ask them?"

"Because if it *is* a ransom note, one thing it would have certainly said was not to go to the police. They wouldn't tell me."

"Well, if the house is being watched, which seems a little unlikely in this weather, they would have seen us arrive. It's too late to pretend we aren't involved. Just take it."

Matt shook his head. "They'll have hidden it by now. They'll be trying to decide what to do. If it is a kidnaping—"

"I can't believe it," George said. "He has his own business, but he's not in the money class that attracts kidnapers."

Matt made a face. "I don't suppose I really believe it, either." He put the idea away, not dismissing it entirely, but setting it aside against the moment—any moment—when further evidence might present itself.

His eyes kept going back to the bed. Had someone been in it with her before she left? The bed was too rumpled to tell—all the pillows were crumpled, the entire surface wrinkled. Was she a wild sleeper—or had something else gone on? Condoms—used the night she left or just available in the drawer in case? Two glasses—used the night she left or sometime before? There were several old mugs of coffee on the desk, one well overgrown with mold. As she had not taken those down to the kitchen to be washed, so she might not have taken glasses from her bedside table. One glass could have held a soft drink from earlier that evening or water the night before—it didn't necessarily indicate a second person. It did, however, *suggest* one. And that would make kidnaping less likely, for he had never heard (yet) of a kidnaper who slept with his victim before taking her. The bed was rumpled, but the rest of the room was only untidy. No—it looked like Chrissie had left of her own free will.

So, what would send a young girl out into the night? Because the curtains had still been closed and the blinds drawn, he assumed it had been in the night or early dawn. Had she run out of cigarettes—or just run out? Had she run away *with* her maybe-bedmate or *from* him?

He sighed, and went into Chrissie's bathroom, her own small pink bathroom, the door to which he had first mistaken for a second closet. Surely a girl with her very own bathroom . . .

It was very neat, in contrast to the bedroom. He was virtually certain that a socially active woman like Mrs. Falconer had a maid, and that the maid was told to ignore Chrissie's room in order to force the girl to acquire tidy habits. A towel had been dropped over the side of the bathtub, dry and stiffened into a curve. All the other chrome surfaces were shiny, but there were water spots on the tub faucets, and there was a slight residue—bath oil or bubble bath—in the bottom of the tub itself. Quite dried out now, of course, but still discernible. So Chrissie had taken a bath that last night or morning. Before her expected guest had arrived or after he'd gone? It was certainly not the action of someone being forced to leave.

He opened the medicine cabinet over the basin. Stuffed—neatly, but stuffed—with cosmetics and skin-care products. A bottle of aspirin, another of some pills for period cramps, a half-filled bottle of cough medicine (he sniffed it and it *was* cough medicine) and another of mouthwash (ditto). Toothbrush and toothpaste. A prescription medicine bottle—labeled for a general antibiotic but empty. That and the cough medicine said that Chrissie had probably had a winter throat or chest infection in late November—the label had been dated by the dispenser of the prescription, a large discount chain. Another prescription medicine bottle, three-quarters full, marked "phenobarbital." What the hell would that be for? Some kind of barbiturate, obviously. Sleeping pills? What did a teenager need with sleeping pills? Dated in mid-December. Her doctor was Dan Rogers—his own doctor. He'd be talking to him soon.

George appeared in the doorway. "No diary," he reported. "Anything in here?"

Matt showed him the prescription bottles. "Know what she'd be taking that for?"

"No idea," George said.

"Yeah," Matt agreed, putting the bottle in his pocket and switching off the bathroom light. "That's my problem, too. No ideas."

They went downstairs, and Matt knocked on the living room door. "We're leaving now," he told the Falconers, who peered out at him, pale-faced. "We've taken a few items from your daughter's room for—"

"Why?" Mrs. Falconer demanded.

"For examination," Matt said, hoping she wouldn't press for any details. She didn't. He'd scribbled a receipt for the items and gave it to Chrissie's father.

"That's fine, that's fine, whatever you have to do," Bill Falconer said hurriedly. "We've thought of a few more people we can call, places she might have gone. We'll let you know the minute we find her."

"Fine," Matt said, and looked at them more closely. "Is there anything else you'd like to tell me?"

Falconer shook his head. "No, nothing. What would there be?"

"I don't know," Matt said. "I just wondered. We'll be in touch."

"Good. That's . . . good," Falconer said, still standing behind the half-open door. "I appreciate it. We both do."

There seemed to be nothing more to say. Matt gave them a half-salute and left with George, carrying the sheets from Chrissie's bed and a few other small items.

"What's the matter?" George asked, as they floundered back down the unshoveled walk to the car. Matt had paused to glance back at the house.

"They were pretty eager to get rid of us, all of a sudden."

"Probably want to cry in private," George said.

"Maybe," Matt said. "But I think I'm going to have the house watched, just in case."

Under the ice in the bay, another body was shifted back and forth by the current from the Black River as it squeezed beneath the ice and flowed out toward the great lake. Pale hair moved over the face and back again, gently, softly, covering and uncovering the wide-open eyes, pressure shifts in the ice above it causing eddies to swirl and pluck at the arms and legs. Fish nibbled at the areas of exposed flesh, leaving little ragged edges. Bits of flesh floated away and were consumed by other creatures that crawled along the muddy, sandy base of Blackwater Bay.

EIGHTEEN

Grapevines do not thrive in postblizzard conditions.

Therefore it was not until the day after the snow stopped that Jess made contact with the outside world.

Perkins Point had taken the full force of the storm, and the big house was isolated by head-high drifts of snow. The lawn furniture had been almost completely obliterated—only one corner of the pine swing frame protruded, giving brief perch to a very irritated robin. The house itself was mercifully undamaged—not even a shingle had blown away. It was wonderfully quiet now that the wind had died down. There was just the snap and crackle of the fire as Jess sat before it, her pieced wall hanging stretched over a quilting frame. The storm had allowed her to complete it, including the little figure she'd embedded in the wadding between the layers. She had embroidered the name—Al Vernon—on the little figure. No one would know about its presence but herself.

The design of the wall hanging was an abstract one, using the lines of little fishing huts as a starting point, the "map" of their distribution providing an attractive linear pattern, which she had enhanced with beading and embroidery into an overall impression of winter on the bay. The background colors were muted grays and off-whites, the fishing huts bright and angular against the gentle curves of the bay and the hills around it.

As she followed the lightly drawn quilting pattern with her needle, she could hear Pat's radio playing quietly upstairs—she liked to listen to music while she painted. Linda and Chip had gone out earlier on their skis, pushing themselves along what they guessed was the road, looking to see what the chances were for negotiating an escape in Pat's four-wheel-drive RV. Schools were closed until further notice, and the unexpected extra vacation was like a late Christmas gift.

Both Tom and Jason were with her in the living room, but she might as well have been alone for the amount of company they provided. Each was deeply engrossed in a book, breaking the silence only occasionally with a sigh, a turned page, or a glare that was as loud as a trumpet.

Jess didn't know what the problem was. She had heard them earlier, bickering in the kitchen, and last night there had been a louder altercation upstairs. They sat on opposite sides of the room, bracketing her like rival claimants to a mutual possession. She had tried several times to start a friendly conversation, but the effort had been too much.

Because she hadn't realized the line had been repaired, Jess jumped and stabbed herself with her needle when the phone rang.

"I'll get it," she said, gratefully abandoning her handiwork and sprinting for the hallway.

The caller was, of course, Emily.

"Hi."

"Are you just standing by your phone ready to call people as their lines are reconnected?" Jess asked as she sucked her injured thumb. "Is the *Chronicle* so desperate for news?"

"Well, thanks. I was just interested in knowing whether

you were alive or dead out there. I can take my business else-
where if you prefer," Emily said huffily.

"I was just kidding. It's nice to hear a new voice, even
yours."

"My, you just get more charming by the minute, don't
you?"

"Sorry. How are you? More to the point, where are you?"

"I'm at the office, of course. *Some* of us have made an effort
to emerge from hibernation."

"The schools are closed, there was no point—"

"I know, I know. As luck would have it—and I *mean*
luck—I was at Dominic's when the blizzard started. So,
rather than try to get back home to Mom and Dad, I was absolutely forced to remain in town."

"Gee whiz, what rotten luck," Jess said, grinning.
Dominic Pritchard had an apartment over Daria Grey's art
gallery. Emily officially still lived at home, but was more
often found at Dominic's than at the old Gibbons homestead
outside town.

"Yes, terrible for us, we had no one to talk to but each
other, and the heating conked out so we had to go to bed to
keep warm."

"Well, of course. A simple matter of survival."

"Uh-huh. The downside being that once the snow
stopped I had no excuse for not making it in to work. All I
had to do was walk across the street. Not that it was as easy
as all that—you should see the height of the heaps left by
the snowplows—I literally can't see one side of the street
from the other. They've had to cut little tunnels through
every twenty feet or so to allow people access to stores. Are
you okay for supplies out there?"

"We're fine," Jess assured her. "I saw the bad weather
building up and did a little hoarding on the way back from
the vet's on Saturday. We usually have plenty of everything
on hand, anyway, but we're getting damned fed up with
dried milk."

"Which cat needed the vet?"

"Both, really. Annual boosters—but I also wanted to see if there was any reason why they've been acting so crazy lately. He says they're perfectly healthy—just getting stir-crazy and so I should play with them more. He, by the way, is gorgeous."

"So I hear. Mary Anne Hinckley took her schnauzer out there and drooled so much that the guy tried to give *her* a distemper shot."

"Are Mom and Dad okay?"

"Fine. Worried about you, but I told them Tom would have gotten word out somehow if there had been any problem. Mom and Dad also got to the stores and stocked up before the hoarders got there. Family trait, obviously."

"What's it like in town, aside from the snow heaps?"

"A lot of people falling over—but that's only because the bars are open. To be honest, I think that no matter how loudly they complain, most people are enjoying the challenge. At least we know that it will eventually end—it's only snow, not war or an earthquake. And at least none of you are about to go into labor. We're getting in an amazing number of stories about brave women giving birth in lonely farmhouses—there must have been some big drunken party somewhere, nine months ago. Then there are men having heart attacks while shoveling snow, cars stuck in weird places . . . we could practically run the front page from 1937 when the last real blizzard struck, just add in the part about some people having to dig out their satellite dishes in order to get CNN. Oh—one thing. Do you know a student called Chrissie Falconer?"

"Of course—she's in my 5050 class. Why?"

"She's disappeared."

Jess actually shook the phone. "What?"

"I said she's disappeared," Emily shouted.

"I can hear you, I just couldn't believe what I heard."

"Why not? Isn't she the runaway type?"

"Well . . . no." But Jess felt suddenly guilty. She had been pretty hard on Chrissie when they'd spoken last Friday. Had she triggered off something in the girl? Scared her sufficiently to send her running? "Well . . . she was very depressed."

"About what? She wasn't pregnant or anything, was she?"

"No, of course not," Jess snapped. Although, she thought suddenly, anything was possible. "It was about this business with her New Year's party getting out of hand, having to pay her parents back for all the damage and so on. I had her in tears in my office last Friday."

"That's very interesting," Emily said slowly. "Maybe you ought to talk to Matt Gabriel about that."

"Why?"

"It just seems the kind of thing he should know," Emily said rather evasively. "You know, state of mind and so on?"

"I suppose you're right. Her counselor wouldn't be any help, that's for sure. Mrs. Beecham is very big on keeping accurate records, very bad on actually talking to her girls about unwieldy things like emotions."

"God, I had Beecham, too. I still have bad moments when I hear her voice saying, 'Pull yourself together, Gibbons.' " There was another pause. "Listen, tell me more about drugs at the high school?"

"Such as?" Jess asked warily.

"I'm not sure—I keep hearing things about Chrissie's party."

"She had some gate-crashers," Jess acknowledged.

"Wasn't it something *more* than just gate-crashers?" Emily asked in a meaningful tone.

"You mean you know it was. Dominic told you," Jess said in an accusing tone.

"No," Emily said triumphantly. "You just did. There *were* special drugs, weren't there?"

So Carl Putnam had been successful in keeping it quiet, Jess thought. Now she had given Chrissie away herself.

"Em, listen . . . the girl's disappeared, maybe run away. Isn't that enough for her parents to deal with? If you start running sensational stories about teenage drug parties and so on, it will just make it worse for them."

It had always been a bone of contention between them. "It's not sensationalizing if it's a fact," Emily said. "I mean, what other reason could Chrissie have had for running away?"

"I don't know," Jess said.

"So . . ." Emily prodded. "What can you tell me?"

"Nothing, Em."

"Nothing? Not even a quote on what a super girl she was, how you're all worried about her, stuff like that?"

"All you like of stuff like that, but nothing about anything else, until I talk to the sheriff."

"Aha—so you think there *is* something else."

"Listen, you were the one who said I should tell him about her state of mind."

"Oh, yeah. Well, you should."

"I will."

"Fine."

"I'll call him right away."

"Good."

"As soon as you hang up the phone, Em," Jess said pointedly.

"I want to thank you for cooperating with the press," Emily said. "We won't forget your kindness."

"Em . . ."

"I know. I am just a guttersnipe, a parasite living off the garbage of society, a rooter-out of scandal and misery . . ."

"Goodbye."

Eventually Emily said her farewells. But they were not final, and they both knew it. Jess sat beside the phone for a while, thinking. Then she went to the kitchen and put the kettle on.

As she prepared the three mugs of coffee, Jess reflected on

her last conversation with Chrissie Falconer. There was no doubt about it, she'd mentioned things like trials and jail and facing up to responsibility. It might have been enough to send Chrissie into a tailspin and frighten her into running away. Jess didn't flatter herself that she played much of a role in the girl's life—she was only one of her many teachers, after all. But her words might have started a train of thought that eventually precipitated Chrissie's flight. And then there was the way she had clutched her book bag, as if afraid some-one would take it from her.

How often we say things without realizing how they af-fect the hearer—casual words casually spoken and taken to heart. Like those spoken by Tom the other night, which still nagged at her.

She and Tom had more or less avoided being alone to-gether since then, their mutual edginess making things worse rather than better. Both seemed to sense that some-thing between them had gone awry. That was why, despite the inimical atmosphere in the living room, she had been glad of Jason's presence there.

When she had originally decided to have housemates, she had automatically assumed they would all be women. Then Tom, such an old friend, had pointed out to her that it would be very useful to have a man about the house to do difficult chores that might require physical strength. Not to take away from women's abilities, he said, ever the political animal—but sometimes mindless brawn was required. Like moving furniture, or removing large blown-down branches from a lawn (this had been pointed out while he was doing that very thing). Or replacing shingles (ditto). And, watch-ing him up the wobbly ladder, she had seen the logic of his suggestion. Especially as there had been so much repair work to do when she first took over the house.

So Tom had been the first housemate, giving rise to much ribald conjecture on the part of their colleagues. Pat Morrison came along the week after, as "chaperon," she claimed, and it had been just the three of them through the first winter, Tom and Pat exchanging effort for rent. They had worked hard, evenings and weekends, enjoying the challenge. They had converted the kitchen, living room, dining room, and Jess's attic aerie. Then they had gone to work on the bedrooms, redecorating Tom's, then Pat's, then doing up two others, after which Linda Casemore and Chip Chandler had joined them. And all had gone along nicely.

Then Jason Phillips had appeared at the school, replacing the impossibly ultra-trendy Ed Martin. Because Jason had arrived at an odd time, he'd had to stay at a motel, and spent most of his time in the teachers' lounge moaning about the cost. He'd looked so forlorn, and seemed so innocuous, that she had taken pity on him and moved her bed up to the attic, surrendering her own bedroom.

All right, it had been a mistake, she accepted that. For all his faults, she liked Jason, but it had become more and more apparent that Tom and Jason would never get along. They were oil and water. Of course, being her oldest friend, Tom had priority, but she certainly wasn't ready to ask Jason to leave. Not yet. The extra rent was useful, and he was providing a buffer between herself and Tom at the moment. What confused her was why one was needed. Well, their little personal problems weren't important now. She needed to talk to Tom about Chrissie—he was so levelheaded and calm about things.

"I've just been talking to Emily," she said on her return to the living room. She set down the tray with the coffee mugs.

Tom glanced up. "Might have known our first call would be from Em."

"She had a piece of rather unpleasant news."

"Oh?" Tom turned a page.

"Yes. Chrissie Falconer has disappeared—probably a runaway."

They both lowered their books to stare at her. "You're making that up," Tom said.

"Nope." She sipped her hot coffee as she handed each of them theirs in turn. "Her parents came back from their ski vacation yesterday and found her car gone and the girl ditto. Matt Gabriel is looking for her everywhere."

"Who's Matt Gabriel?" Jason asked.

"The county sheriff," Tom said. "You must have seen him around town—about six foot four, red hair, square jaw, fists like cantaloupes—"

"And the smile of an angel," Jess put in.

"Oh, for crying out loud, you haven't still got a crush on him, have you?" Tom asked in disgust.

"Always will," Jess said. "Anyway, isn't it amazing about Chrissie?"

"It's unbelievable, considering the kind of girl she is," Tom said, closing his book without marking his place, an unheard-of action which told her he was more upset than he wanted to acknowledge.

"I think it had something to do with the drugs," Jess said.

"Drugs?" Tom was startled. "What drugs?"

She reminded him of the party. "We were talking about it on the first day back, remember?"

"Oh, yeah."

"I know she was upset about it, and we had a talk a few days ago. She was very defensive about drugs, but the words she used sounded like someone else, not Chrissie. I think someone has got hold of these kids, Tom. Maybe one of the senior boys who thinks he's God's gift to chemistry. Ring any bells, Jason?"

"Sorry?" He had been gazing vaguely out of the window.

Give me strength, Jess thought. "Are there any senior boys in your chemistry classes who might be capable of making these—what do you call them—designer drugs?"

"Why would they be seniors?"

"Chrissie is a senior, so she would only be impressed by a senior," Jess said, sitting back down at her quilting frame and carefully placing her coffee where it couldn't spill onto the cloth. "Or—wait a minute—we just had the Christmas break. Boys were back from college, too. Weren't there a couple in last year's graduating class who went on to major in science?" She picked up her needle and carried on with her quilting—its regular rhythm helped her think.

"Three," Tom said. He named them. "But I don't think any of them would be likely candidates. They were all pretty serious boys."

"Remember your first year in college? How long did *you* stay serious?" Jess challenged him.

He smiled reluctantly. "About two weeks. I see what you mean. You think they may have gotten involved in something."

"It's possible. *Somebody* had gotten Chrissie into drugs."

"It could have been me," Jason said suddenly.

The other two stared at him.

"I only meant—I gave a talk on drugs to the Science Club shortly after I arrived here," Jason said, looking worried. "About their possibilities for good and the hope they offered for curing many of the world's problems. One of the students there could have taken me more literally than I intended. You said she wasn't talking like herself—maybe she was talking like me."

"And, by the way, Miss Look-out-for-Sexism," Tom said, "where do you get off asking Jason if one of the boys in his classes is capable of making drugs? What about the girls?"

"Touché," Jess admitted. "You're absolutely right. One of the *students*, then. Any bright sparks, Jason? Any who might have taken you too literally?"

"Several, I'm afraid," he said, frowning. "I'm a very good teacher, you see."

"Are you?" Tom said expressionlessly.

"Yes. Apparently I inspire students sometimes—quite without realizing it."

"Ah, so, grasshopper," Tom said with a glance at Jess.

His ironic tone went right by the bespectacled egotist on

the other side of the table. "Yes," Jason said vaguely. "I can think of several boys who might qualify, Jess. Two, in fact, who have a very rebellious attitude, very independent. Back-talkers, if you know what I mean."

"You mean they actually argue with *you?*" Tom asked in tones of amazement.

"Hard to believe, I know," Jason said. And for a moment—just a moment—Jess thought she glimpsed something behind Jason's spectacles. Laughter? Sarcasm? It was gone before she could confirm it. Does he realize we laugh at him? she wondered. Does he play to it? Has he been bam-boozling us all this time? She couldn't really believe it. And yet—

"Why bring this up?" Tom asked her.

He knew her so well. "Em thinks I ought to tell the sher-iff about my talk with Chrissie. About her 'state of mind.' She was very depressed, Tom, despite all her fine talk. And I didn't make things any easier for her by pushing the 'taking responsibility for our actions' angle. I might have scared her more than I realized." She glanced out the window and shiv-ered. "Suppose . . ."

"Suppose what?"

"Well, it did occur to me that she might have used some drug or other that deepened that depression and made her decide to kill herself. Freezing to death is a good way to go, once you get past the first chill. Or so I've read."

"Yeah, I've read that, too. You've got a weird mind, Jess."

Jess nodded. "I know." She stood up and went over to look out at the vast, featureless expanse of snow that led down to the edge of the bluff and the frozen bay beyond. Idle words. What had her casual, idle words led a young girl to do? "She told me she expected her parents home on Saturday night. Suppose—like someone taking an overdose only when they expect to be found in time—suppose she took some pills and then went out into the blizzard and lay down, expecting her parents to find her. Unfortunately for Chrissie the blizzard got worse and worse and her parents didn't get home until yesterday. By which time . . ."

"She was lost and gone forever," Tom said. "Little darling, Clementine."

"That's rather insensitive," Jason remarked.

"I hardly knew the girl," Tom said.

"That's no reason to be so—"

"So what?" Tom flared.

"So—flippant."

"It was a bit . . ." Jess began.

"Et tu?" Tom asked, glaring at her. "I'm sorry. I have a green outlook—waste makes me angry. Useless, pointless, youthful death makes me angry. Is that so difficult to understand?" He stood up, hurled his book to the far end of the sofa, and stalked out of the room.

"Well!" Jason said. "How childish."

Jess stared after Tom in dismay. Too late, she had remembered something she should never have forgotten. Jason was wrong. Tom wasn't insensitive at all.

Quite the opposite.

Because his own little sister, Tildy, had killed herself at the age of fifteen, while he had been away at college. She had called him but he had been out on a field trip and had gotten her message too late. When he'd called back a day later, Sheriff Gabriel had answered. Not Matt, but his father, who had been sheriff before him. Jess remembered going to the dormitory and helping Tom pack, because he was crying too hard to see what he was doing.

"I must say—" Jason began.

"Shut up," Jess said. "Just shut up."

NINETEEN

Dr. Dan Rogers was a man of medium build whose power far exceeded his appearance. Even-featured, with a small mustache and a precise manner, he was the terror of the hospital nurses and interns, who flinched at the sound of his metallic snarl, and the darling of his patients, for whom his voice was soft and sympathetic.

Rogers had his office in an attractive brick building which he shared with a dentist. It was situated near the local hospital, where he was now chief of staff, and he divided his time between the two venues. Pinning him down for ten minutes in either place had not been easy.

When Matt caught up with Rogers in his private office and told the doctor about Chrissie's disappearance, he was surprised to see how worried the doctor became. When he showed him the bottle he'd found in Chrissie's bathroom, Rogers added exasperation to his worries.

"So wherever she is, she doesn't have her medication?" he said. "Oh, Lord, preserve me from casual adolescents."

Matt frowned. "What exactly are these for, Dan?"

Rogers sighed. "When Chrissie was small she had meningitis. There was a little scarring of the brain tissue, and since then she has been prone to occasional attacks of what we call petit mal," he explained.

"Epilepsy?"

"Yes—but in so mild a form that it was easily controlled. I made sure she had regular checkups, of course, and once a year she saw a neurologist, but the attacks were no more than a brief occasional inconvenience. Chances are anyone watching her during one of them might not even notice anything was wrong."

"So she was all right as long as she took her pills."

"Yes. But between Thanksgiving and Christmas she had two much more severe attacks, not quite grand mal, but very disturbing. Both times she had been with a friend, who was able to describe to her what had happened. The wicked thing was, she refused to tell her parents about them."

"Why do you suppose that was?"

Rogers frowned and picked up a green pencil, twirling it between his fingers, watching it and not Matt. "She said it would stop them going away on their vacation and that they deserved their break. She planned to tell them when they came back."

"Wasn't that risky?"

Rogers shrugged a shoulder. "Yes—and I told her so. But she was eighteen and she had a right to make her own health decisions. I tried to reason with her, but she was adamant. So I increased her dosage of phenobarbital as a precaution and insisted she go for tests. She finally agreed to that and promised to be very quiet and careful in the meantime. She was due to go in for the tests on Monday, but when they told me she hadn't come in, I naturally put it down to the blizzard."

"I'm afraid she didn't keep her promise about being quiet, either," Matt said.

"Oh?" Rogers stopped twirling the pencil.

"She threw a big party on New Year's Eve. We were called

out because of the noise and found drugs on the scene, although she herself seemed okay to me."

Rogers came forward in his chair, scowling. "Drugs? What kind of drugs?"

"Marijuana . . ."

Rogers frowned. "Oh—well, I suppose a little of that wouldn't have harmed her. Not that I approve of course, but—"

"There were also uppers and downers, Ecstasy and some other tablets nobody could or would identify. I've sent them to the state forensic labs—"

"Damn!" Rogers exclaimed angrily. The pencil hit the desk and flew off at an angle. "That idiot child! No wonder she didn't want to go into the hospital for tests!"

"What do you mean?"

"Well, blood tests would have revealed these other drugs she was taking. No wonder her condition had worsened—if she was playing around with psychedelics. She was a bright girl, she should have *known* that was the cause . . ."

"It's often the bright ones that get caught," Matt said. "They have curiosity to go along with the IQ, they are often bored and restless because they aren't challenged enough by school or life—especially the wealthy ones who never have to struggle for anything." He thought back to the wildly tumbled bed in Chrissie's room. "Is it possible she could have had a grand mal seizure and afterward wandered out into the blizzard?"

Rogers's eyes widened. "My God—what a terrible thought." He looked out at the waist-high layer of snow that lay everywhere. "You mean she could be under there somewhere . . ."

"It's only a thought," Matt said. "I have to consider every possibility."

"But how could you even begin to look for her?"

"Her car was gone—finding that is our first priority. We're physically checking the area around the house, of course—but if she drove or wandered any distance before collapsing . . ."

"You'd have to wait until the thaw," Rogers finished for him.

Matt shifted uncomfortably. "Well—if we knew that she was dead, there wouldn't be the pressure there is in looking for a live girl, hard as that sounds. We could use dogs and electronic equipment to try and locate her body—and we will if it comes to that—but I'd rather assume we'll find her alive."

"Mmmmm." Rogers considered. "Sometimes there *is* a period of fugue following a seizure, so that couldn't be ruled out, but in Chrissie's case I'd have to say it was unlikely—she'd be more likely to fall asleep. Mind you, no two cases of epilepsy are the same . . . and hers was in the process of change, so she could have gone to grand mal after taking something stupid."

The bed was still in Matt's mind. "How about after sexual intercourse?"

"Less likely. But an epileptic seizure can be set off by something as simple as a flashing light, in some cases."

"In Chrissie's case?"

Rogers looked really worried. "There's no way of saying, because we haven't been able to run any tests, have we? God knows what state her brain is in if she'd been dropping acid or taking Ecstasy or whatever. *Damn!* And to think I was worried about a brain *tumor*. I never suspected she was doing drugs—she just wasn't that kind of girl."

Matt stood up. "That's the trouble, though, isn't it? They're never that kind of girl until they become that kind of girl—and then it's too late."

The Hatchville Police Headquarters was a very modern building, set on a sidestreet just off the town center. It smelled of new paint, new equipment, new everything. The new chief of police smelled of Brut and wore his uniform with pride. Which was understandable, seeing as it had been hand-tailored at his own expense.

Although he was new to his title, Chief Henderson was a long-serving officer. As an old acquaintance he took Matt's gentle teasing with good grace.

"Look," he said, "it was my wife's idea, not mine. She said it would raise morale if the chief looked good."

"And has it?"

"Well, funnily enough—and I hate to admit it—people do seem to be paying a little more attention to their appearance."

"How are the arrest figures?"

"Up."

"Well, maybe she was right."

But Henderson shook his head. "Hell, no. I'd like to think so, but the figures are up because the offenses are up, simple as that. We are in the midst of a little crime wave, Matt. Everything is up—burglary, robbery, vice, violence—the whole schmear. I'm going to wear this fancy uniform out long before my retirement comes up."

Matt laughed. "Still chasing squad cars, Harry?"

"Like a rabbit out of the gate." Henderson smiled. "The click of handcuffs is my favorite sound. And I have good men now. We got rid of . . . excess baggage."

Matt had heard of the cleanup that Henderson had instituted on becoming chief. Until then the Hatchville force had been, if not exactly dirty, then tinged with gray. Certainly if Henderson's predecessor had still been in office, Matt wouldn't have bothered to come calling, knowing that his reception would have been frosty at best. He and the old chief had not seen eye-to-eye on a lot of things, particularly on the caliber of men required for the job. Now, looking out at the bustling office, Matt saw a lot of new faces, young faces, with sharp eyes and hard jaws. Henderson's new broom had swept pretty clean, although there were still some potbellies behind the desks. A few potbellies were not a bad thing, Matt conceded, provided the experience behind them was useful. Some of the early retirees from the old Hatchville force had come to him looking for a job. He had all he needed, he'd told them. All he ever would need.

Now he was beginning to wonder.

"How about drugs, Harry? Drug arrests up?" he asked.

Henderson looked suddenly uneasy. "Why do you ask?"

Briefly he brought Henderson up-to-date on Chrissie Falconer and his discussions with Dr. Rogers. "When we broke up Chrissie's party, we found grass, of course, but also uppers and downers, Ecstasy, and all the usual. We sent it all to the state lab for analysis."

Henderson nodded. "Yes, we've been watching the whole drug scene come up from Grantham. It's been like watching the Mississippi, rising a little higher, coming just a little further up the state each month. I don't know how to stop it, frankly, except to keep banging away at known dealers. We've had reports of something new being available—getting word of some funny side effects, too. A couple of doctors reported problems in patients who admitted taking this new stuff. This girl—"

"Chrissie Falconer."

"Yes. Do you think she'd been dealing?"

Matt shook his head. "If she was, it certainly wasn't for the money or the peer influence—she had plenty of both."

"For the stuff itself?"

"I don't think so. She was getting it from somewhere, obviously—but the quantity on hand was because of the party. I think she had just begun to dabble, because Dr. Rogers said her physical troubles started sometime between Thanksgiving and Christmas. And I think she was getting a little scared, too. Unfortunately, not scared enough."

"Drugs are insidious, Matt. Something new on the scene all the time. The DEA can't keep up with it."

"I know. It's like that fungus they found that grows underground to a huge size but only pops above the surface here and there," Matt agreed. "As to where she got it, I'd like to talk to a kid named Joey," Matt went. on. "A bit of a wild boy according to Chrissie's parents. I don't know his last name, but I gather he has a distinctive hairstyle and a lot of earrings . . ." He gestured around the rim of his ear.

"Joey Ritto," Henderson said immediately. "A real smart-ass and a troublemaker. He's in and out of here like we had revolving doors, but his family has money and the lawyers just walk him every time."

Matt tried not to show his shock at the name. "Family has money?"

"Oh, yeah. Father has that new music store in town, big place, with a coffee shop attached, makes a thing about letting kids listen to the latest discs before they buy. Naturally it's become a hangout for all the dregs, of which—if you ask me—Joey himself is the worst. Cocky little bastard, full of himself, big with the girls, all that. You know the type."

Matt leaned back in his very comfortable leather chair. Henderson, for all his cleaning up of the men, obviously had a tendency to nest-build that must have been proving an expensive expression of thanks from the Hatchville civic budget. "That's an interesting name—Ritto."

Henderson looked at him wearily. "Tell me about it. I know what you're thinking, I read the papers, too. But Papa Ritto, when asked, denies all connections with any murderer, takes dramatic offense. A coincidence, a common Italian name, can't a decent man live in peace, et cetera, et cetera, et cetera."

"And yet you note a rise in local crime. When did the Ritto family move in?"

"Last year, around April. He bought the old Tilman department store downtown, and had it gutted and redone. There's Papa Ritto, Mama Ritto, and four *lovely* Ritto boys, of which Joey is the oldest and the worst. Even the eight-year-old looks like potential trouble. Latin temperament, they say, when the teachers complain. But Papa Ritto has made some friends in the business community, because his shop draws a lot of customers into the downtown area. And he keeps the place clean, doesn't allow trouble on the premises, so it all looks very respectable."

"That's interesting, Harry. Maybe he was sent as a forward scout. It would make sense to put someone in under a legitimate cover to make contacts and start building an infrastructure. A couple of weeks ago I wouldn't have thought it possible, but now—"

"I don't like this, Matt," Henderson said uneasily.

"It gets worse. As you probably know, I have a body on my hands."

"The guy under the ice."

"Right. At first he seemed right out of left field, someone who should never have been in Blackwater Bay—but there he was. And the NYPD tells me he had connections with Luca Ritto."

Henderson's thick gray eyebrows went up, like caterpillars fleeing toward his hairline. "Oh, shit," he said.

"My feeling exactly. And there's a question of having to contact the FBI about someone who might have been placed locally in the witness protection program. I was about to do it last week, but then the blizzard hit. As soon as things settle down, I'm going to have to talk to them, though. No rush—nobody's crying over him."

Henderson tipped his chair back slightly and contemplated the ceiling. "I knew things were looking too good."

"I've been to see Vic Moss," Matt said.

Henderson's eyes met his as his chair dropped back down. "Did he say anything?"

"Yes and no."

"Good old Vic, the natural communicator." Henderson smiled grimly. "I've always had a kind of soft spot for the son of a bitch, though. He keeps things under control."

"I know. But if the Ritto outfit is starting to take an interest in us, he's their natural target, because of his connection with their enemies, the Pescatori family. And because he's so successful, within his limits. It may be that's *why* they're taking notice of us. My iceman might have been sent to put Vic out of business in the quickest and most permanent way as part of a Ritto war plan to take over the whole Pescatori network. I don't think Vic is working *for* the Pescatori family, he's his own man, but if pressed he'd support them. He's very vulnerable, and so are we. We could end up right in the middle of a family battle of the worst kind, and if that happens, all the new uniforms in the world aren't going to help us, Harry."

"I thought you were looking sharper," Henderson said.

"They forced it on me. They've been forcing everything on me—uniforms, computers, a new office and jail, cars, men—and I was beginning to resent it. Now I'm wondering if they knew more than I did. That they knew about what was coming our way and figured we should all be prepared."

"My God, Matt—you're not telling me that there might be someone in the state capital with brains, are you?" Henderson pretended dismay. "This could be very dangerous. It could set a precedent."

Matt stood up. "Don't worry, Harry, it won't last. The minute the politicians realize there's someone among them who's smarter than they are, he'll be out on his ass, heading some corporation or other. Wish I knew who he was, though—I'd appreciate some input on this."

Henderson stood up, too. "Well, all I can offer you is my files and my men—talk to whoever you like, including the Ritto boy and his old man. If the shit is going to hit the air conditioner, we might as well share an umbrella."

Reaching across the desk, they shook hands.

TWENTY

Tom Brady had walked out of the living room because the thought of Chrissie Falconer—of any young girl—deliberately killing herself was unbearable. Jess had followed him into the kitchen, watched him slam pots and pans around in a parody of clearing up. Gradually he'd calmed down, pressing the memories of his vulnerable, confused, pregnant little sister back into their special mental cupboard and locking the door. The most likely explanation was that Chrissie had run away, of course. After all, if her car was gone, what else could it be? Jess's suicide theory just didn't hold water.

But as he'd calmed, Jess had boiled. Anybody who gave pills to vulnerable young women was a killer or as good as, short-term or long-term. The real culprit, if there was a culprit, was not the unhappy Chrissie, but the person or persons who had made her so.

Jess always maintained that she never knew what she thought until she heard herself say it—and she now presented Tom with a prime example of becoming convinced by her arguments. Watching Jess pace around the kitchen as she built up her theories about Chrissie Falconer, Tom had the feeling that she was getting *too* excited. Her cheeks were flushed and her eyes were bright, always a bad sign. She was about to get *involved*. Her next action proved him correct.

"Going somewhere?" he asked casually, as she went out into the hall and came back carrying her ski boots.

"I'm going in to school. I want to look in Chrissie's locker to see if I can find out anything," Jess said.

"Wait a minute, Nancy Drew," he said, "The school is locked up."

"Oh, that doesn't matter—Digger will let me in," Jess said, sitting down and starting to work her feet into the boots.

"What makes you think he'll be there?" asked Jason. He'd followed Jess into the kitchen and was peering hopefully into the cookie jar.

"He's always there," she said confidently. "He'll have the heating on to keep the pipes from freezing, and he'll be checking on the roof."

"Why the roof?" Jason wanted to know.

"Flat," Tom said. "The weight of the snow could be a problem. It's happened before."

"Yes—about ten years ago—in what is now my cooking classroom," Jess said. "You can still see the marks where they had to replaster the ceiling."

"I'm going to come with you," Tom announced, suddenly getting to his feet.

Jess looked up in surprise. "You?"

"Me." He looked down at her. "Well . . . what?"

"I've just never known you to exert yourself unnecessarily before," Jess said.

"This is necessary," he said grimly, going out into the hall to get his own ski boots. Fortunately Chip and Linda had brought everybody's skis down that morning. Poles, too. Only Jason was without his alternative form of transport, a situation that seemed to worry him not at all. Jess clumped after Tom into the hall, leaving Jason staring after them from the kitchen table.

"Why? I'm hardly apt to get lost."

"And if you fall into a snowdrift?" Tom snarled, disentangling the ski poles. "You're so small we wouldn't find you for weeks." He glanced at her. "Maybe we should put a little flashing light on the top of your hat, just in case."

"Very funny," she said grumpily, and went over to look out of the window beside the door. "There are bound to be plenty of people around—I'll stick to the roads."

"How can you be certain where the road *is*?"

"I'll just stay between the telephone poles," she said reasonably.

He was sitting on the lower steps, fastening his boots. "We need a few things, anyway. Milk, for one thing. Eggs."

"Chip said he'd get them."

"All right, *I* need a few things," he said, irritated by her arguing. Didn't she realized she needed looking after? This whole Chrissie thing was getting out of hand. "Some blank floppy disks."

"Well, that's a real good excuse," she said.

"You don't even have an excuse," he snapped. "You could perfectly well wait until the road is cleared to snoop in Chrissie Falconer's locker—the plows are sure to get up here by tomorrow afternoon at the latest. Then we could take Pat's RV."

"What for?" Pat, at the top of the stairs, wanted to know.

"To go to the school," Tom said over his shoulder. "Jess has some wild idea that there are some 'clues' there."

"Clues to what?"

"Oh, Pat, you haven't heard," Jess said, looking up at her. "Chrissie Falconer has disappeared. I'm sure she must have been high on drugs."

"Why?" Pat asked, coming down the stairs and edging around Tom, who was wrestling with a recalcitrant strap.

"You heard her," Tom growled. "Suddenly we are in the midst of a *mystery*."

"Why are you getting suited up like astronauts, for crying out loud?" Pat asked.

"I want to go to the school," Jess said stubbornly. "Chrissie may have left her book bag in her locker last Friday. While we were talking I got the feeling there was something in there she was sort of protecting."

"Like what?" Pat asked.

"Like maybe five pounds of best Mexican sinsemilla, fourteen magic mushrooms, and a big bottle of pills marked 'Whoopee Drugs, teenagers for the use of,' " Tom said, standing up and stomping his boots on the floor. "Also a bill of sale stating her source for all these items, signed and sealed with a big thumbprint. You know—the kind of stuff *every* kid carries around with her when attending class these days."

"Oh, Jess," Pat said. "Leave it."

"I'm bored sitting around here," Jess said. "It's one thing to choose to stay indoors, but quite another to *have* to stay in. You'd think I'd be loving it, having a chance to quilt in peace, but it's driving me crazy. I just have to get some fresh air."

"I see," Pat said, obviously not seeing at all. "And what is Tom's excuse for going out into the wild white world?"

"He says he needs things." Jess gave him a hard stare. "Personally I think he's just as nosy as I am."

Tom gave Pat a long-suffering look. "Somebody has to look after her," he said.

"I entirely agree." Pat returned both looks with interest. "And somebody has to look after you, too. I think you're *both* insane."

"But if there *is* something that might help the sheriff, don't you think he should have it as soon as possible?" Jess asked, zipping up her jacket.

"I can't see what difference a day or two would make," Pat said with a shrug of her shoulders.

"Neither can I," Jason said, coming into the hall. "I think they're wasting their energy." He looked at Jess. "Why don't you just call this lovely sheriff of yours and tell *him* to take a look in Chrissie's locker? He could go over himself and make the janitor open it."

Everybody stood still, looking at Jess.

"Jason's suggestion is perfectly reasonable—the sheriff only has to drive over to the school, not ski cross-country," Tom said.

"I'm going," Jess said flatly. "I want to go and I'm going."

"I knew I should never have used that word," Tom said glumly, as Jess opened the door and icy air poured into the hall. "The minute I said it I knew it was a mistake."

"What word?" Pat asked.

"Reasonable."

"Isn't it beautiful!" Jess enthused, as they stood staring down the road that led away from the house. The white world was stark and delineated. Very little color showed anywhere, giving the impression of an etching rather than a painting, and every surface had a faint glitter that made them blink hard.

"Looks aren't everything," Tom grunted, pushing off between Pat's RV and his own battered van. He could hear a swish as Jess caught up with him, and then the sound of his own breath took over.

"Hey, what's the hurry?" Jess gasped, after a few minutes of concentrated effort.

He glanced sideways. Damn the woman, anyway. How could she look totally right out here in a reflected glare that should expose any woman's worst flaws? No, good old Jess, his heart's underminer, had to look flushed, bright-eyed, eager and excited. If he hadn't wanted to bed her so much, he could cheerfully have socked her.

"I want to get this over with," he managed to say.

"I feel a bit guilty, hoping that there will be something incriminating in Chrissie's book bag," Jess said, half a mile down the road. "I mean, suppose it leads to someone we *know*."

"Like Jason?" he asked.

She slithered to a stop and he was forced to stop beside her. "You've thought of that, too?" she demanded.

"Well, Jess, he is a chemistry teacher, and we know nothing about him except that he's generally a pain in the ass," Tom panted. "How convenient for everybody if it turned out that he was supplying his students with drugs. He'd go to jail and we'd have our house back to ourselves."

She narrowed her eyes. "You really hate him that much?"

"It's not a matter of hating him," Tom protested. "It's just that he's in the way all the time, never offers help, never does his share."

"He pays his rent."

"So do I. I also do the shopping, make the repairs, take out the garbage, listen to everybody's troubles—"

"We listen to yours. Over and over again," she said pointedly.

"Hah!" was all he could manage over his shoulder.

They grunted and slithered the rest of the way into town in silence.

When they reached Main Street, they removed their skis and carried them over their shoulders, as both street and pavement were relatively clear.

Once they hit the residential area, they had to redo their skis and follow what appeared to be ski runs over the lawns and side streets to the high school. Far from being unusual, skiing seemed to have become a popular mode of movement at the moment. They passed several other people, suited and goggled, sliding along under the snow-laden trees.

They had to sidestep the last few hundred yards, as the

school stood on a gradual slope that neither of them ever recalled noticing before.

"I suppose it's because we drive in all the time," Tom
gasped. For the last half mile he'd been convinced this entire
expedition was not only stupid and pointless but rapidly ap-
proaching a near-death experience. He fully expected to
leave his body any moment and look down on the two of
them floundering in the deep snow. Jess, on the other hand,
seemed quite comfortable for someone who spent so much of
her life sitting down at a quilting frame.

Now that they had stopped, he was beginning to get some
oxygen from the air he dragged in. He was also getting a
great deal of pain. I don't want to reach tomorrow, he
thought. Tomorrow I will be as stiff as a board and will lie
all day in bed weeping and thinking of ways to kill the
woman I love. This is a definite plan. I may even start
tonight.

Jess, too, was feeling the effects of their trip, but was
damned if she was going to admit it to anyone, especially
Tom, who would never let her forget that it was her idea and
her fault that they now faced their old age with rheumatism
confirmed. All she wanted to do was go to the toilet—that
was of primary and rapidly growing importance—and then
sit in her office and cry for a little while all by herself.
Everything hurt. Even her earlobes. It hadn't seemed like
such a daunting task when she'd thought of it. This kind of
thing was for the young, and she had stopped being young
just outside Helen's Bookshop on the corner of Main and
Thistle. Now she felt old, very old and very broken. It wasn't
normally this far to school, was it? After all, she drove it
every morning in just a few minutes. Of course, she suddenly
realized, the storm must have blown the school at least fourteen miles into the next county. That would explain it.

Suddenly Tom said, "What the hell? Look, up there." He
pointed with his ski pole.

There were moving figures on the left-hand corner of the

roof, and every few seconds a cascade of snow would shoot over the parapet and shower down past the windows, sparkling in the bright sunlight.

"There are people up there," Jess said. "Shoveling."

When they reached the parking lot, they found a collection of four-wheel-drive vehicles clustered in the near corner, and a broken snow trail leading up to and around the side of the school itself. They disengaged their skis and trudged around, to find the trail led them to the service entrance.

Digger Wells popped out of his office like a badger from his sett: short, fat, with a long inquisitive nose and a low widow's peak pointing down between bright little black eyes. His skin, where it showed, was seamed with fine black lines of coal dust, and his gray hair sprang up around his ears.

"You two come to help out?" he inquired hopefully.

"Help out at what?" Tom asked cautiously, already guessing the answer.

"Clearing the roof," Digger said. "I got practically the whole football team up there now, shoveling. After what happened ten years ago—" Digger was obviously deeply concerned. "Heard creakin'," he said lugubriously, his fat cheeks wobbling with importance. "Went up there this morning and saw *bulges*."

"There will be even bigger bulges with the whole football team up there as well as the snow," Tom pointed out. "You should have sent just a few at a time and spread them out, instead of concentrating them all in one place."

"You think so?" Digger asked with a worried frown that brought his widow's peak even closer to his eyebrows.

"I know so," Tom said with a sigh. He had hoped to get away with a cozy chat in Digger's lair while Jess went through Chrissie's locker. Now it looked like he had to climb not only to the top floor but onto the roof itself. "Come on—we'll see if we can work out a pattern of efficient distribution before somebody goes through."

Digger glanced at Jess and grinned. "Kind of takes charge, don't he?" They looked after Tom, already halfway down the hall to the central stairwell. "Wait up, Mr. Brady," he called after him. "I'll just get a couple more shovels."

Jess chuckled. That should keep Tom off her back for a while. She propped her skis next to his and wrestled off her ski jacket, leaving it hanging over Digger's chair.

Putting first things first, she headed toward the nearest girls' lavatory. There was a thin skin of ice on the water in the toilets, she noted when she'd reached that sanctuary. A nasty moment came when she thought she would have to call for help to remove herself from the toilet seat, but she clenched her teeth and literally tore herself away, emitting a brief shriek as she did so. She didn't dare look, but contented herself with the thought that she would go to her grave with an interesting scar.

"And I will never explain," she announced to her reflection in the mirror, which immediately hazed over with the warmth of her breath.

What had driven her to make this idiotic journey, to do the thing at all? Chrissie had been afraid of something, guilty about something, hiding something. And Chrissie was gone. *Somebody* had to get involved.

Jess made her way alone through the long halls, her clumping bootsteps echoing strangely from the metal doors of the lockers that lined each wall. It was odd to see the normally clotted halls free of adolescent aggregate.

Shafts of light fell across the hall at regular intervals, dusty, pale, and angular as they came through the glass panels of each successive door. As she passed each classroom she felt herself illuminated but not warmed. Bright reflected snow light came through the outer windows, flooding the empty rooms. It silhouetted the seats and desk, fell on blank blackboards and notice boards, slanted across posters that informed no one of past triumphs and coming events. Cloisters, Jess thought. The bars of light are like the ones you see in a cloister, and instead of the faint tinkle of a fountain we have the distant shouts of large muscular young men on the roof. She imagined she could hear Tom's voice among the others, telling everyone what to do and how to do it.

Dear bossy Tom.

The office was locked, but she'd had the foresight to borrow Digger's keys. He had been reluctant to part with them, but when she explained, and when Tom reminded him that the roof could go anytime, he had handed them over. It took her a few minutes to find the listing for the lockers, and found that Chrissie's was on the top floor, quite near her own classrooms. Number 408. To her delight, she found that alongside the assignment was the combination to the padlock that Chrissie had been issued along with the locker.

She climbed the stairs and went down the long shadowy top-floor hall until she came to the rank of lockers she wanted. Chrissie's was more or less in the middle, and the padlock was in place. Jess spun the wheel, and the lock fell open. She swung the locker door back and peered inside.

The book bag was there.

For some atavistic reason she had stayed in the center of each successive hallway (in case there were alligators loose in the building), and then clung to the banister on the endless stairs (in case a sudden tidal wave should sweep her away), reaching the top floor breathless and with a foolish feeling of being chased by shadows, stalked by ghosts. Now the feeling that she was being watched by disapproving spirits was even stronger. She snatched the book bag and slammed the door shut, closing the lock and snapping it shut.

Even her own classroom seemed strange and slightly inimical. The stoves with their eye-like dials seemed to watch her pass through, the shrouded sewing machines were like gnomes crouched to leap, all bathed in the incredible white glare of the snow light that poured through the tall windows.

She reached her office with considerable relief, falling into her elderly but serviceable chair with a long sigh. It took several minutes to restore her oxygen levels to something approximating normality, and then she was able to open Chrissie's book bag and begin to excavate.

Books, of course. A makeup bag, well stuffed with expensive lotions and cosmetics and messy throughout. A brush and comb, two headbands and a scarf, four hair clips. A half pack of cigarettes and a gold lighter. Notebooks, and a loose-leaf folder divided into subject sections, with her class schedule pasted inside the cover. Wadded-up tissues, newspaper clippings, candy wrappers, broken pencils, and pens made up the bottom layer, along with a handful of unidentifiable crumbs and bits.

No pills. No marijuana. No magic mushrooms.

Just the usual.

Disappointed and annoyed at herself for expecting anything more, Jess fingered her way through the collection again. She smoothed out the newspaper clippings, but they proved to be tips on skin care and other female preoccupations. Suddenly she stopped and stared. The notebooks—two of them, with soft leather covers—were not schoolwork, as she had presumed. A glance at a few random pages showed them to be diaries—one for activities (Chrissie was a busy girl), the other a personal journal, in Chrissie's familiar, breathless misspelled style.

Quickly Jess turned to the end of the latter. The last entry was dated the previous Thursday night and read as follows:

> *J coming over tomorrow night. God! he's so gorjous! Hope he likes the new pills. Had a few bad minutes after dinner last night, in front of the TV. Nobody saw. Scary but okay after. Had popped no pills, so maybe no connextion after all. Can't wait to see J and have him in me again, so wild and beautiful together!*

So there *was* someone, and he'd probably been with her on

Friday night. If so, was he responsible for her disappearance? He must know something, whoever he was. She flipped back through, looking for the first mention of "J," or of "pills."

She was scanning the second or third entry where pills were mentioned, when suddenly there was a tremendous noise from the opposite end of the floor. Startled, she leapt up and ran out into the hall.

Dust and debris were billowing out from the open doors of the chemistry lab. She could hear shouts and yells and an odd, thin screaming from within the room itself.

She ran down and looked in the door. A portion of the ceiling had fallen in, and from where she stood she could see at least two unconscious boys among the heaps of snow, plaster, and wood shards. A third, lying against one of the deep sinks, was the source of the screaming.

Looking up, she saw a corner of the lab ceiling open to the sky. Peering down over the ragged edge, from which continued to slide more and more snow, were Tom, Digger Wells, and several boys she recognized as members of the football team.

"Call an ambulance!" Tom shouted. "Hurry!"

TWENTY-ONE

He was Alan Ladd sculpted in ebony.

The ID said "Agent Leslie Brokaw." "But you can call me Les." The handsome black man smiled. And he sat down beside Matt's desk. "Hear you got a problem."

"I've got dozens," Matt said. "Pick a number."

"You made a recent telephone inquiry concerning the relocation of a person named Peter Murphy," Brokaw said, coming staight to the point. "May I ask why?"

Matt explained about finding and identifying Al Vernon's body, and the sheaf of newspaper clippings found in the dead man's suitcase. "It occured to me that maybe Vernon had been sent to pay Mr. Murphy off for his generous words in the witness box."

Brokaw nodded. "I can see where you might think that."

"And it further occurred to me that maybe Vernon found said Peter Murphy, who took unkindly to his attentions and turned the gun around," Matt went on.

"Again, I see your point of view," Brokaw agreed.

"So, since that might be the case, then I would appreciate your telling me who Peter Murphy is now, because I'd like to interview him in connection with Al Vernon's homicide," Matt finished.

"Well, now, that is where you have the problem," Brokaw said. "See, we work the witness relocation program on a strictly 'nobody needs to know' basis."

"But I *do* need to know," Matt protested. "This is homicide."

Brokaw leaned back in the chair beside Matt's desk. They were in Matt's office with the door closed, at the agent's request. Beyond the glass Matt could see Tilly and George trying to pretend they weren't attempting to lip-read.

Brokaw sighed. "It's a bitch, isn't it?" And he smiled that Alan Ladd smile again. The special smile that said, "Don't you wish you looked as good as I do in this three-piece suit?"

"Is Murphy living in Blackwater Bay?"

"No comment," Brokaw said.

"Oh, come *on*," Matt said.

"No comment," Brokaw repeated.

"No shit," Matt said. "Does this mean the Bureau is going to obstruct the course of my investigation?"

"Why, of course not," Brokaw said. "We will be glad to talk to this man ourselves on your behalf and report back to you."

"Then you admit he is in the area?"

"I admit nothing."

"Or that he *was* in the area six weeks ago?"

"We can talk to this man wherever he is."

"And whatever he tells you may or may not be taken down and offered to me," Matt said. "Is that it?"

"We like to cooperate with local law enforcement wherever possible," Brokaw told him blandly. "As long as it doesn't endanger our clients."

"Oh, is that what they are now? Clients?" Matt asked.

"It suits the case."

"I thought your protection covered what Murphy was up to in connection with the Ritto 'corporation.' He was to be let off whatever crimes he committed while he was employed by them in return for information leading to their conviction."

"More or less."

"I see. Well, is that protection now to be extended to crimes he commits afterward? Does that mean that anybody in the witness protection program can turn into a serial killer and be protected by the federal government simply because that was the deal they made?"

"No. But in Murphy's case it does mean that if something happens that has a Pescatori or a Ritto connection, we'll protect him," Brokaw said. "If this Vernon was sent to kill the man we are talking about, it is *because* of his testimony, and we undertook to protect him in that connection."

"To the point of committing murder?" Matt demanded.

"Sorry?"

"Well, I could take what you just said to mean that you would kill somebody like Vernon if he tried to kill your precious Peter Murphy."

"I certainly did not say that." Brokaw's perfect features arranged themselves into gentle reproach. He was disappointed in Matt. "Let us speak hypothetically."

"*Oh, let's,*" Matt agreed. "Goody, goody."

Brokaw refused to rise. "We are eternally grateful to any man who proves to be useful in one of our investigations, particularly when it leads to the successful prosecution of a known criminal or criminals."

"Criminals plural?" Matt asked.

"It can happen," Brokaw nodded. "It has happened. It will undoubtedly happen again." Brokaw examined the odd arrangement of shelving behind Matt's desk, trying to work it out.

Matt's eyes narrowed. "Do I read this right? That this Murphy may still have something to offer the government? Is that why you're taking this attitude?"

"What attitude?" Brokaw shrugged his shoulders. "I have no 'attitude.' I am sympathetic to your plight—"

"My plight," Matt echoed.

"—but you have to understand mine in return. With no disrespect to you or your staff, we cannot afford to trust local law enforcement with someone's new identity. People can be bought."

"You ought to know."

Brokaw stopped smiling. "I beg your pardon?"

"Witness protection is just another name for payoff," Matt said. "You offer freedom, a new life, temporary support—what is that but a bribe?"

"We think it is very different. And, by the way, it's a lot more expensive than a bribe. Bribes are one-shot deals."

"Whereas, as you are presently proving, federal protection goes on and on and on, no matter what."

"Look, there's no need to get shitty," Brokaw said, finally sounding almost human. "I said we'd talk to the man for you, and if there's anything you need to know you'll get it."

"And if he tells you he killed Vernon?"

"We'll talk again." Brokaw stood up.

"If Murphy admits to killing Vernon?"

"We'll talk again," Brokaw repeated, and he turned to go.

"What's the Bureau's attitude on kidnaping?" Matt asked in a casual voice.

Brokaw stopped, turned, and sank back down on his chair. "Same as it's been since 1934," he said. "You can call us in anytime you like, but we come in automatically seven days after a ranson demand on the presumption of interstate passage. Have you got a kidnaping?"

"I don't know," Matt admitted. "Maybe."

Brokaw looked at him for some time, then produced his card, writing another number on the back of it. "You can get me anytime, day or night," he said. "Does this connect with Vernon?"

"No," Matt said. "That is . . . no, I don't think so." He briefly outlined his thoughts on Chrissie Falconer.

"I haven't had much experience with kidnaping," Brokaw said. "But I think you're off base on this one."

"Yeah," Matt admitted ruefully. "And I can't say I'd be disappointed to be wrong."

"This seems like such a nice, quiet place," Brokaw said, standing up again.

"You obviously thought so when you set Murphy up here," Matt said. "See how appearances can deceive?"

Brokaw gave a brief laugh, went out of the office, collecting his elegant overcoat on the way. He went through the outer office shrugging it on, glancing neither to right nor left but heading for the door and going straight through it, closing it behind him very, very discreetly.

Matt watched him go, then gestured to George, who jumped up so fast he nearly knocked over his wastebasket.

"What?" demanded George, hanging from the door frame.

"Follow him," Matt said.

"Hot damn!" George nearly sang with delight.

"As far as you can," Matt added.

George's face fell. "Don't you think I can stick to him?"

"I think it will be difficult," Matt said resignedly.

It was.

The phone rang.

"What's this I hear about you losing one of your pretty local girls?" It was Jack Stryker, a lieutenant in the Homicide Division of the Grantham police who had helped Matt out on a local investigation the previous year. His fiancée had a house on Paradise Island and they were up there frequently for weekends—the last time being at Thanksgiving. He and Matt had struck up an unlikely but firm friendship, and when the name Blackwater had come across Stryker's desk, he had made it his business to take an interest. "Getting kind of careless, aren't you?"

"Don't tell me you've found her?"

"Sorry," Stryker said. "We're keeping a good lookout for the car, though."

"Thanks."

"What the hell is going on up there, anyway?" Stryker went on in an amused voice. "First we hear you've got a floating ice cube who turns out to be come small-time snot from the Big Apple, and now this APB on the girl and the car. I tell you, Gabriel, a little snow and you fall apart."

Matt could imagine him, feet up on his desk, receding prematurely white hair and matching mustache full of electric energy. Stryker was compactly built and usually firing on all cylinders. Matt grinned at the phone, glad of the connection, the friendship, and the news. "Didn't you get any snow down there?" he asked.

"A flake here and there, but we're used to these things. We are always prepared."

"Ha ha," said Matt, knowing the city had gone through its own troubles during the long storm.

"This girl," Stryker said. "I gather she's not just your ordinary, everyday runaway?"

"No," Matt said. He told him about the party, the drugs, and Chrissie's medical background. "She might try to get some of her medicine somewhere," he concluded. "Or she might show up as an emergency in one of the hospitals."

"I'll make sure they know about her," Stryker assured him. "I'll also notify Vice."

"Oh, God," Matt said. "I suppose you'll have to."

"Girls who come to the big city with no money in their pocket . . ." Stryker didn't continue. He didn't have to.

Matt had checked Chrissie's bank account, and there had been no withdrawals since the previous Friday, when she had taken out fifty dollars after school—her usual Friday amount. This told him that at that particular time she'd had no intention of leaving town. The bank had been alerted to report any withdrawal from anywhere else in the state, or from any affiliate out of state. He had also notified her credit card companies, asking them to let his department know if there were any purchases, but so far there had been nothing. What was Chrissie living on? If, of course, she was still living.

"How's Kate?" Matt asked. Kate Trevorne was Stryker's fiancée, a professor of English at Grantham University who had spent all her summers growing up on Paradise Island. She and Matt were old friends.

"Feisty as ever," Stryker said. "Thanks for your Christmas card, by the way. Kate's had it framed, as it's an original Daria Shanks Grey watercolor. She says it will pay for our retirement."

Matt grinned. His fiancée was an artist with a growing national reputation who had returned home to Blackwater the previous year and now ran a gallery on Main Street. "Wise move," he said. "Althought I have to tell you she painted about twenty individual cards for our favorite friends, so keep investing in those pension bonds."

"Fair enough. Is there anything more I can do for you on this missing girl?"

"Just the usual—put all your vast resources at my private disposal."

"You wish."

"Indeed, I do," Matt said. "I know girls run away every day, but this one . . . I just have a bad feeling about this one."

"You think she's dead?"

"I think she's . . . in trouble." He paused, then went on, "You had any new drugs appearing on the scene down there?"

"Every day in every way they're getting weirder and weirder and weirder," Stryker said. "According to the guys in Vice, you could turn yourself on and send yourself to the moon for less than ten bucks at the moment—should you care to take a chance on also dropping dead. Why?"

"Anything like a pink and blue capsule?" This had been the odd one out at the party, one of several pills they'd sent to the state forensics lab for analysis and/or identification. So far they had not heard back—another failure of communication due to the blizzard presumably.

"I don't know—I'll ask. Does it have a name?"

"If it does I don't know it," Matt told him.

"Okay. Anything else . . . wait a minute." Stryker covered the phone while he dealt with someone in his office.

When he came back Matt asked, "Do you know if Luca Ritto has any connections in Grantham?"

"Of course he has," Stryker said. "He must have—all the rest of them do. Being in jail doesn't slow those boys down much, you know. Your floater had connections there?"

"Yeah. Could you . . ." Matt began.

"I'll have one of the boys do you a package," Stryker said, knowing exactly what he would want. "I'll tell him to fax it up ASAP, okay?"

"Thanks," Matt said. "I'd offer a favor in return, but—"

"You could go out and take a look at our place on Paradise," Stryker suggested. "See if the roof's okay."

"I'll do that," Matt promised. "Are you and Kate coming up for the Ice Festival this weekend?"

"I don't know. We'd like to, but it depends on the weekend schedule."

"We made a bet, remember?" Matt said.

"Oh, yeah—I'd almost forgot that. Wife-sliding, wasn't it? Do fiancées count?"

"You know they do. Fifty bucks says mine goes further than yours."

Stryker laughed. "Okay, okay—I'll see what I can do. Call you later in the week. Or sooner, if we locate the girl for you."

Half an hour later George returned, muttering, "Even in the snow, even in the goddamned snow," and Matt didn't need to ask where or when he'd lost Brokaw.

George hung up his jacket, threw himself into his chair, and glared at Matt. "Well, what the hell do we do now?"

Matt sighed. "It's more like what do we do first," he said. There was a noise from overhead. In a small square opening in the ceiling by the back wall appeared Max, the office cat. He dropped gently through this special "door" and descended by way of the oddly placed shelves that had so puzzled Brokaw.

Matt and the big ginger tomcat lived in a newly constructed and decorated apartment over the office. During the alterations Matt had instructed the builders to make the small opening in the floor/ceiling, and had arranged bookshelves in the office below to make a kind of stairway for the cat to come and go as he wished. The door was left open during the day, closed at night, and there were cat flaps to the outside at the rear and front of the building both upstairs and down, as Matt was paranoid about the cat being trapped in a fire.

When they'd first moved into the new apartment, he and Max had spent several hours setting up the shelves and practicing entrances and exits, to the vast amusement of them both.

Matt was glad Max had waited until now to appear, for it had given him great pleasure to see Les Brokaw, supposedly brilliant FBI agent, trying to fathom why there were so many gaps in the bookshelves and why there was a hole in the ceiling.

"From what that agent said—and he wasn't saying much—I think Murphy is living in Blackwater Bay."

"Great," George said. "Shall I bring him in?"

"He wouldn't tell me who or where he was."

"Why the hell not?"

"I think it's because Mr. Murphy has more to tell," Matt said slowly. "I think they're planning on using him again—which may be why he suddenly became a target for Vernon. Out of sight he was safe—but if Ritto found out that he was

going to give evidence against him in *another* trial, maybe
one with, say, a much longer sentence connected with it—"

"Like what?"

"Like fraud or tax evasion, then it might be worth risking
a further killing. Murphy testified first to homicide—that
always takes precedence—but that sentence is bound to be
reduced soon, because of Ritto's 'good behavior.' No doubt
he has convinced them he intends to take up social work
when he's released."

George grinned. "In a way, that would be the truth."

"Yes, well—if the feds are lurking with this other charge,
Ritto has even more to gain by killing the only witness
against him."

"It hangs together," George agreed.

"The thing is, will they tell us—or will they simply move
him out?" Matt muttered. "They can't risk exposing him to
being charged with a murder—not yet. They might want to
shift him somewhere else until this next trial is over . . ."

"You don't think they killed Vernon, do you?"

"Don't you think I asked?"

"And did he—"

"Well, of course not. But he didn't get angry enough to
make me think it was true," Matt said. Max jumped up onto
his lap for a bit of attention, and he stroked him absently
while he thought.

"It's no good. I've been falling down on the job, George."

George was puzzled. Matt seemed all right to him. "What
do you mean?"

"Well, let's face it. Al Vernon was not exactly Mr.
Popular. His employers disavow him, he has no family demanding justice, NYPD don't give a damn about him now
they know he's dead. No public outrage attended his
demise—other than a passing morbid interest in the bizarre
method of his recovery. Therefore nobody has been pushing
me for a solution to his homicide. I've been so distracted by

the blizzard and then Chrissie Falconer, that I haven't been giving the proper attention to our iceman."

"I have," George announced.

Matt looked at him in surprise. "You have?"

"Yup. I've been making a list."

"A list of what?"

"Of all the guys in town who could be Peter Murphy," George said proudly. "Guys of his age—"

"What age?"

"One of those newspaper clippings said he was around thirty, so I took twenty-five to forty," George said. "Then I took 'moved into town in the last two or three years.' Then I took 'educated,' because he was some kind of office guy for Ritto, not a bum like Vernon. And stuff like that. I've been building up a list."

"How long is the list?" Matt asked.

George's self-satisfaction wavered slightly. "Well—" he said.

"How many?" Matt asked.

"Seventeen," George said with a sigh. "And that doesn't take into account one other thing."

"What's that?"

"Well . . . what if he had a sex change?" George asked. "This guy Peter Murphy could now be a woman, couldn't he?"

Matt gave him a look. "Don't be . . ." he began, then stopped, a look of dismay on his face.

"I'm right, aren't I?" George demanded, triumph returning to his boyish features. "He could be, couldn't he? She? They? It? I'll tell you something for nothing—as a disguise it knocks hell out of a new nose and a big hat." He flipped his pencil up into the air and caught it.

"We can't think like that," Matt muttered. "We'll go nuts if we start thinking like that."

"Yeah," George agreed, suddenly somewhat subdued by the scope of what he'd just proposed. "I read it takes years, anyway." He stopped flipping his pencil and granted a big concession. "Okay, we'll forget that. Let's just concentrate on these seventeen guys."

"That's seventeen in Blackwater Bay?"

"Yeah."

"What about Hatchville? Peskett? Oscogee? Lemonville? Kisco Beach?" Matt wanted to know. "What about the farms in between?"

"Well, gee whiz, I've been busy, too," George protested.

Matt nodded. "What did you base your list on?"

"Asking around, people . . . you know."

"Did you check the local tax offices? Voter registration? Realtors?"

"Uh—no. I should have, right?"

Matt reached across Max for the phone. "Let's start with Fran Robinson over at Century 21. She knows everybody. And let's see that list, George—it's a good beginning."

"Oh, yeah?" George was pleased.

"Yeah. The problem is, I think we're going to end up with a lot more than seventeen Peter Murphys—probably more than we can possibly handle. Single white males are probably among the most mobile group in the population. And while we're checking out all the wrong ones, Brokaw could be moving the right one on, in which case we'll *never* know any more than they're willing to tell us. Still . . . we have to try."

"Absolutely," George agreed.

Matt's hand hesitated over the phone buttons. "There's one other thing, of course."

"What's that?"

"Brokaw may be so tight-mouthed about Murphy because he's afraid Ritto has sent *another* killer after him. We have no idea how big the contract on Murphy might be." His hand descended and he continued pressing buttons. "Always assuming Vernon was planning to kill this Murphy in the first place, of course. There's still the possibility that he was after

Vic Moss. Or somebody else altogether. Or not after anyone at all. There's a thought. Maybe Al Vernon simply came to Blackwater to visit his dear gray-haired old mother, or just dropped around for the fishing and fell in, or . . . "

"Wait a minute—I'm getting confused," George interrupted.

"Welcome, George," Matt said wryly. "Welcome to the wonderful world of modern law enforcement."

From down the street, there came a thin wail, rising and falling. The volunteer fire department siren, calling the faithful to serve—NOW!

The howl of the siren reached the body trapped under the ice as a thin spiral vibration. The body did not respond, and the fish did not cease their feasting.

TWENTY-TWO

The Blackwater Bay Volunteer Fire Department was more or less a holding outfit, bringing on-the-spot attention to a fire until—if required—more sophisticated equipment could get there from Hatchville, eighteen miles away. The men were trained in first aid as well as fire fighting, but in addition brought many individual talents to the scene of any disaster.

So it was that Les Price, who in daily life was a carpenter, and Vernon Stokes, who was a building contractor, brought their particular expertise to bear on the unusual problem of extracting the three injured boys from beneath the remains of a ceiling and roof plus about a ton of rapidly melting snow. It took a while, and involved a lot of heaving and levering of timbers, but eventually the three boys were freed from the mess.

Jess, who had been trying her best to help where she could, was surprised to see both Fred Naughton and Claude Trickett among the volunteer firemen. Then she recalled that Fred had been a volunteer before he left town, so presumably had rejoined when he returned, and that she'd heard Claude giving a talk about fire safety at one of the morning assemblies. She hadn't thought him the volunteering type, his nature being chirpy rather than compassionate. He seemed to have been caught in the middle of a party, for under his hastily donned uniform Jess glimpsed what was unmistakably a silk shirt that cried out for a cashmere smoking jacket. The latter, no doubt, had been discarded in favor of the heavy oilskins. Fred, on the other hand, wore a more sensible ensemble of heavy sweater and corduroys under his Standard Issue, Fireman for the Use Of. He was very red in the face from unaccustomed exertion, but was making no complaint.

Both men were surpringly athletic, and she was impressed by the way they worked alongside their younger colleagues. She was even more surprised to see the new vet among the volunteers, and was then relieved when she saw him kneel down beside the injured boys. He obviously would be a valuable asset to the fire department. At least he probably knew something about physical trauma in man as well as beast.

The air within the building, while not warm, was considerably more temperate than that outside, and the mass of snow that had fallen in with the ceiling/roof was melting rapidly. Runnels of water snaked across the floor of the chemistry lab and out into the hall, where they joined and coiled in a small river that ran down the tiles toward the stairwell, creating in turn a delightful little waterfall that nobody was in a mood to appreciate. The melt was also seeping between the floorboards, wetting and weakening the ceiling of the classroom below. The firemen had opened the windows of the lab and were throwing armfuls of snow out as fast as they could, but it looked as if the problems were going to get worse rather than better.

"This one has spinal trauma," one of the paramedics announced as he bent over the boy who had remained strangely quiet during his rescue, although wide awake. "We'll need to brace him before we move him any more. It's only pins and needles at the moment, but we don't want it to get worse. You should have left him where he was."

"We asked him if he was in any pain," one of the firemen protested. "He said no."

"Better if he had been," the paramedic snapped. "Then you might not have moved him. He could have had a broken neck."

"And he could have suffocated where he was," Tom said with equal anger. "He was under a piece of rotten roof timber and it was cutting off his air. What would you have done?"

The paramedic shrugged. "Same thing, probably."

The third boy was sitting up, wincing as the other paramedic put his arm in a temporary splint and sling. "Boy," he said. "That was some ride."

"What exactly happened?" Matt asked Tom and Digger Wells, who, with the rest of the football team, had raced down the iron staircse that led to the roof to help in the rescue efforts. They spoke in gasps as they continued to heave snow and broken laths and plaster out of the open window.

"They had moved over to that corner to start shoveling when the whole thing just went," Digger said. "We thought it was safe enough near the parapet, but—" He raised his hands, covered in a white mud of snow and plaster dust. "It wasn't."

"It happened very fast," Tom grunted, tossing out a particularly nasty bit of wood. "It just went, like he said. No kind of warning noises or anything. Just—whoom."

"There has been mold growing in that corner for weeks," said Jason Phillips from the doorway. Jess, who had been resting for a moment beside the door, gave a little shriek. She hadn't heard him come up behind her. He went on, watching them with his hands in his pockets. "I suppose there was a damp rot there."

"Nobody never told me," Digger said, outraged. "You should have *told* me."

"Sorry," Jason said, moving past Jess to look at what was

left of the chemistry lab. "I thought Mr. Trickett told you and you were just ignoring him."

"Well, he didn't and I wasn't," Digger sulked.

"I did and you were," said Claude Trickett from where he was shoveling snow out the window with a piece of cardboard. "I told you there was staining and a suspicious crack. I put a note on your desk weeks ago."

"I never saw it," Digger said. "I wouldn't ignore something like that. How am I supposed to—"

"Coming through," said one of the paramedics, at the end of the stretcher. They all stood aside for them to carry out the boy with possible spinal injuries. He looked spaced-out and strange, but gave them a weak smile as he passed by them.

Digger and Claude Trickett were now shouting at one another, trying to assign blame. "The fact is, this whole school is falling apart," Claude said finally, in deep disgust.

"I only can do what I can do, there's no money for someone to help me, I put things in front of Dutton but he says 'no money, no money,' Digger told him. "You got to understand my point of view."

"I understand the part about no money," Trickett said morosely. "That phrase sums up my entire life."

"I hear where you're coming from," Digger said. They seemed to be coming to a state of mutual despondency, freeing one another from responsibilty for the disaster and placing it where they were sure it truly belonged—on the absent shoulders of the principal, Mr. Dutton.

Meanwhile, around them, the firemen were trying to clear up, smashing a good deal of glassware and other things in the process.

"My God, be more careful, will you?" Jason complained. "This equipment costs a lot of money. Can't you use some sense?" He turned to Jess, scowling. "I had an experiment set up on that table and now they've completely destroyed it."

"How did you get here, Jason?" Jess asked, annoyed as usual by his childish self-centered petulance.

"I drove Pat's RV," he said. "I told you to wait—the snow plows came through about an hour after you left."

"Oh," Jess said in a small voice.

"Terrific," Tom said, pausing a moment to glare at her. "I nearly kill myself getting here, and he drives along in comfort. Typical."

"No problem," Jason murmured, opening and closing nearby drawers at random. "Did you get what you came for, Jess?" he called over the crashing and banging. "Chrissie what's-her-name's things?"

"Sort of," Jess said. "No drugs, but some interesting notebooks which might have a bearing on what happened to her." She turned to look for the sheriff, then had to step aside as two of the firemen passed through with a stretcher bearing the boy who had been screaming. He was silent now, very pale and apparently asleep. "Oh, dear," she said. "He looks very bad."

"They knocked him out with something," one of the firemen said. "He'll be okay." The third boy trudged behind, supported by Dr. Kelly. The boy paused and glanced at Digger.

"Sorry," he said.

"What for?" Digger asked.

"Messing up," the boy said.

"Wasn't your fault," the caretaker protested.

The boy grinned again. "You all heard that," he said, glancing around. "He said it wasn't my fault."

"So?" Digger asked.

"So now my dad can sue," the boy said cheerfully. "See you." He went off down the hall, following the stretcher.

"Oh, God," Digger moaned.

Jess pushed through the milling men and buttonholed the sheriff. "Matt, I just heard about Chrissie Falconer's disappearance."

He nodded grimly. "Bad business. We've done all the usual things, of course."

He didn't have to explain further. Jess, feeling worse than

ever, explained her interest. "I talked to her for quite a while last Friday, and I'm afraid I scared her a bit, talking about responsibility and trials and so on . . ."

"Probably no more than I said to her," Matt said.

"Well, maybe. Anyway, I came here to see if there was anything in her locker that might be helpful," she said in a low voice. "And there was. I think they might help you in your investigation. I'd like to show you what I found. It's just down the hall."

"Sure," Matt said. "I'll—"

"Can I have a hand here?" shouted a fireman who was trying to prop up a slate-topped worktable that had collapsed under the combined burden of ceiling, snow, and impact.

Matt turned to Jess and shrugged. "I'll be with you in a minute."

"Okay," she said reluctantly. She went back to her office, collected the book bag, and trudged back down the stairs, leaving the men to it. For once, she didn't feel like asserting her feminine right to interfere.

Matt found her there a little while later. He was liberally covered in white mud, and looked for all the world like a working model of some Rodin masterpiece. *Accident in a Toothpaste Factory*, perhaps.

"Sheriff, I never thought I'd see you plastered," Jess said.

"You haven't exactly escaped yourself," Matt smiled, dropping into a spindly straight chair beside Digger's desk. He coughed deeply. "Mr. Wells tells me a lot of that old ceiling contained asbestos."

"The snow probably damped it down and kept it out of your lungs," Jess observed. "Being covered in mud is certainly better than getting lung cancer."

"Yes—but it's another reason why those ceilings should have been replaced a long time ago," Matt said. "That stuff must have been sifting down on students and teachers for years."

"Oh, dear—and my classrooms are both on that floor,"

Jess said, suddenly aware of her lungs, imagining them somehow calcifying rock-solid right in her chest.

"I wouldn't waste time worrying about it," Matt said easily. "Now, what did you want to show me?"

"Ah, yes—Chrissie's things," Jess said, leaning down to pick up the book bag. She hauled it onto her lap, then paused. "I think I should explain to you why I've done this. I mean—we have rules here about breaking into students' lockers, and maybe I should have gotten Mr. Dutton's permission, but—"

"I know Mr. Dutton," Matt said understandingly.

Jess grinned. "Yes, well—the point is, I had a talk with Chrissie on Friday, and I feel I might be responsible for her running away. I came on a bit strong about responsibility and facing up to things like this drug business. It seemed to be the first time she realized she would have to go to court about it. And then—" She paused, embarrassed. "I have this theory about the drugs that suddenly seem to be appearing on the scene. When I talked to her on Friday, she seemed very . . . under the influence."

"Of drugs?" Matt was surprised.

"No—not something, some*one*," Jess said. She went on to explain about Chrissie's defense of drug usage, the words and phrases that had seemed so out of place in a young girl's mouth. "I think someone is conning these kids into taking drugs as some kind of social experiment." As she spoke Jess was fishing around in the bag. She produced the leather-covered notebook and handed it across. Matt flipped through it, then looked up, puzzled.

"This is just assignments and appointments and—"

"Oh, damn, sorry," Jess said, delving again into the dark interior. "There were two of them . . ."

But, although she turned out the book bag onto Digger's desk, and then retraced her steps, and then turned her own office inside out, she had to accept the fact that although there had been two notebooks in Chrissie's bag when she searched it earlier, there was now only one.

The wrong one.

"It was there before the ceiling caved in," she said, and then heard her own words, sounding like a Victorian melodrama.

Matt, too, saw the funny side of it. "Since when," he smiled ruefully, "everybody and his cousin has been tramping around. I assume you didn't lock your office when you went running to see what had happened? No, of course not. Is that all that's gone?"

"I really have no idea," Jess admitted. "I don't know what she carried in here. The reason I thought there might be something in it is the way she kept clutching it to her. I figured she might have felt it was safe in her locker—and it ordinarily would be. She must have taken what she needed for the weekend out on Friday—there's no purse or wallet."

"Mmmm. Let's see, we've had the fire department, several teachers, the football team, the caretaker . . ."

"Plus anyone else who felt like walking in. That service door isn't locked—and I think Digger opened the front door for the paramedics—"

"But none of these people knew you had these things of Chrissie's, did they?" Matt pointed out.

Jason did, Jess suddenly thought.

"I did have a quick look through the diary," she volunteered, blushing slightly. "I mean, I thought I ought to see if—"

"If it had been worth the effort of skiing all the way over here?" Matt asked with a smile. "Mr. Brady told me about your perilous journey. Was it worthwhile?"

"I think it would have been, if I'd been able to read it all. I only had time to look at a few entries. I was looking for anything about pills, but mostly it was about someone she called 'J,' " she said.

"I beg your pardon?"

"She wrote about somebody named J, using only the initial.

I particularly noticed because it's my initial, too. He may well
be the source of these drugs. I think she was sleeping with
him, whoever he was. She thought he was pretty wonderful."

"Ah," said Matt, thinking immediately of Joey Ritto.

"That tells you something?" Jess asked. She'd thought immediately of Jason. There was the fact that he taught chemistry, and the way he had suddenly appeared here at school,
ostensibly to pick them up when he'd never done anything so
generous before, and the way Tom hated him . . .

Why did Tom hate him?

"J might tell me quite a lot," Matt said. "If I can get hold
of him." Ditto, thought Jess.

It was much easier riding back to Perkins Point in Pat's RV
than it would have been to ski there. Tom was sunk down in
the front passenger seat beside Jason, too tired to talk or
even complain. Jess sat behind, looking at the back of Jason's
head and wondering. Could it be that their own roommate,
their presumed friend, their trusted colleague, was not only
a maker and seller of drugs but also a seducer of young girls?
The more Jess thought about it, the more possible it
seemed—and the more impossible. He was so vociferous in
his horror of drugs—camouflage? He seemed so celibate—
more camouflage?

She tried to think back. Had Jason been out on the night
of the blizzard? Yes, he had! She remembered him stumbling
into the kitchen cursing, making a big song and dance about
how frightening it had been coming back down the freeway
from Grantham, where he said he'd gone to use the university library for some research. What kind of research?

Jason himself brought it up before she could even work
out how to begin.

"Did you find what you expected in Chrissie's book bag?"
Jason asked, as he negotiated the freshly cleared road with
some caution—a thin underlayer of very slippery snow still
clung to the surface.

"No," Jess said. "There was nothing."

"Jesus wept," muttered Tom into his chest. "All that for nothing."

"Well—I thought it would be something," Jess said defensively. "And it *might* have been something . . ."

"But it wasn't," came the gruff comment.

"I thought I saw you talking to the sheriff," Jason said.

"Oh, yes—I did," Jess agreed, thinking that he must have been watching her pretty closely despite all the excitement and chaos. "I told him about Chrissie's state of mind on Friday afternoon and so on."

"And he took her bag—the sheriff, I mean?"

"Oh—yes, he did. Why?"

"I just wondered," Jason said. "Just curious."

"That's not like you," Tom mumbled.

"I have a natural curiosity like anyone else," Jason said with some dignity. "And, of course, one is concerned about one's students."

Tom opened an eye at that. "Chrissie was one of one's students?"

"She wasn't actually in one of my classes," Jason said, narrowly missing Tom's van as he pulled in beside it. They saw that somebody—probably Chip, Tom thought gratefully—had cleared the snow from around his van and the other cars. Even so, the RV had been Jason's only sensible choice for coming into town. Jason grunted as he pulled on the hand brake. "But Chrissie Falconer was a member—an active member—of the Science Club." He turned off the engine. "There," he said. "Home safe and sound—thanks to me."

"And Pat's brakes," Tom said, glowering at the narrow space left between his van and the RV.

When they had gotten inside and sorted themselves out, Jess began preparations for dinner—something fast and comforting, she thought, and pulled a quart of her spaghetti sauce out of the freezer. She could hear the voices of the other two women upstairs, laughing and chatting. Full house, then. As she filled the gigantic pasta pan with water and staggered with it over to the stove, she heard Tom go upstairs and the women's chatter cease.

He's telling them about the ceiling collapse, she thought.

There was a footstep behind her. "You should have let me carry that across for you," Jason said without much conviction.

"No problem," Jess said, as he settled himself at the table.

She began to assemble a salad. "You could slice a cucumber if you're in the mood to help," she suggested.

"All right," he said with great reluctance. She handed him a cutting board, knife, and a long spindly cucumber. "Thin slices," she instructed him. "Across the grain."

Muttering something about getting his hands all messy, he began to do as she said. After a while he seemed to become absorbed in getting each slice precisely the same thickness as the last and absolutely straight. The tip of his tongue appeared in the corner of his mouth.

"What do you actually do in the Science Club, Jason?" Jess asked abruptly.

"Talks," he said, concentrating on the cucumber which apparently had now become a major engineering project for him. "Discussions. Demonstrations."

"What about experiments?"

"Oh, of course. Several of the boys and two of the girls are doing quite interesting things," he said vaguely. "Or perhaps I should say *were* doing. The ceiling came in right on top of all their setups."

"Was Chrissie?" She had moved from tearing green leaves to dicing stale bread for croutons.

"Was Chrissie what?"

"One of the ones doing an experiment."

"Oh, no. At least, not in my lab." He was halfway down the cucumber, going slower all the time in his quest for uniformity. "She was more into biology than chemistry or physics. Why?"

"Oh," she said. "Just curious." They worked in silence for

a while. "Could any of those Science Club experiments have been a cover for making drugs?"

The knife froze and he looked up at her in astonishment. "What?"

"I said—"

"Of course not!" he said, so vehemently that in gesturing he managed to stick the point of the knife he was holding into the cutting board, narrowly missing his thumb. "Claude and I supervise any chemical experiments that are undertaken at the school. Do you think we're idiots?"

"No, of course not, but—"

"But nothing. I am very aware of what kids can get into, Jess—in my last school I caught two of them making nitroglycerin. They eventually admitted they had planned to use it to blow up a safe in some relative's grocery store. After that—"

"You're making that up."

"I damn well am not. I've told you the kind of school I used to teach in, down in Grantham. They had metal detectors on all the entrances, and there was once even talk of arming the staff. While coming here is like coming to peaceful pastures, I haven't forgotten those two amateur burglars, and I don't intend to let any student put one over on me again, believe me."

"What's all the shouting about?" Tom asked, coming in, the others close behind them.

"Jess seems to think I'm running a dope ring in the Science Club," groused Jason, returning to his precision honing of the cucumber.

"I never said that," protested Jess.

"There can't be much left of the Science Club or anything else in the lab, from what Tom's been saying," Linda Casemore said, snaffling a slice of cucumber and crunching it up.

"I'll set the table," Pat said, slipping into the dining room before an argument started. She loathed controversy of any kind.

"Is that where the Science Club experiments were?" Tom asked.

Jason had stopped slicing. "Yes," he said morosely. "And all the rest."

"What rest?" Pat asked, lifting the lid on the pasta pot to see if it was boiling yet.

"Oh, some things I was doing, one or two setups of Claude's," Jason said. "We're both very interested in polymers."

"Oh, no—not the Man in the White Suit syndrome," Tom said with a hoot of laughter, and began imitating the idiosyncratic noises made famous by the Alec Guinness film. "No wonder you were upset at the fire department swinging their axes around."

Jason shrugged. "Experiments can only be repeated if there is equipment available. It's going to cost a fortune to replace what was lost—"

"I'm sure insurance will cover everything," Pat said. "And probably a lot better than before. It may be a stroke of good luck, the roof falling in like that." She turned to Jess. "Are we ready to put in the pasta?"

"I never thought of that," Jason said, looking happier suddenly.

"Too bad the physics room is only on the second floor," Tom mourned. "If my ceiling had fallen in, I might have gotten a new portable generator out of it."

"There!" said Jason, taking the last slice of cucumber almost carelessly. "All done."

"Good Lord," Tom said, staring. "You were *helping*."

"I—" Jason was prepared to be outraged at the implication that his help was a rarity when Pat came in looking worried.

"Jess, I think something's wrong with the cats," she said. "They're literally climbing the walls."

TWENTY-THREE

Frank Nixey was pissed off and he wanted somebody to know all about it. The honor fell to George Putnam.

"First," Frank was saying, "I find a body, and nobody believes me. Then somebody else snags the body and gets hailed as some kind of a hero, but still everybody blames me for finding the body in the first place, and so we have to get Old Fishguts to do his thing, which didn't help, because I still feel funny sitting there at the water, expecting another face to look up at me any damn minute. Why hasn't the sheriff solved my case? Once I know who killed the poor bastard—"

"Your case?" George asked.

"Damn right. Wasn't I the first responsible citizen to report the body? That makes it definitely *my* case."

"Oh," said George.

"So what I want to know is, what the hell is going on?"

"There's been a blizzard, Frank," said George Putnam.

"Has it been snowing in his brain?" Frank demanded melodramatically.

"It's not just a matter of brainwork, Frank—it's footwork, follow-up interviews, waiting for laboratory results—"

"You need a laboratory to tell you a guy's dead?" Frank wanted to know. He was pacing back and forth in front of the counter, and there was no denying he was slightly drunk and had probably had another fight with his wife, because there was the gooey stain of a thrown egg on the back of his jacket. Trixie Nixey was famous for throwing things. George thought Frank had been lucky to get off this time with just an egg. He'd been taken to the hospital before now with injuries from more deadly flying objects, notably an iron skillet and a fish-gutting knife. Of course, Trixie claimed the house had a poltergeist in it. Her mother thought so, too.

"We need the lab to—" George began.

"It's no *fun* out there anymore," Frank went on. "You know Ice Festival's coming up next weekend. How are people going to feel about having a festival over a goddamn graveyard?"

"One body doesn't make the bay a graveyard, Frank," said Tilly, in what she hoped was a soothing voice.

"It does to me," Frank said flatly. "It does to me. Old Fishguts, he wasn't happy, you know. Not by a long shot. Oh, no. He said later, he said he wasn't happy. And you know what that means, don't you?"

"No, I don't," said George, interested in spite of himself.

Frank leaned over the counter, his bloodshot eyes open wide. "It means there's more to this than we know," he said in a low and meaningful voice. "There's still evil stuff going around."

"Lucky for me," George said cheerfully. "That's how I earn my living."

"Well, you're not earning it sitting there on your fat ass treating customers like they wasn't important," Frank said nastily.

"I didn't mean to imply you weren't important, Frank," George protested, resorting to the grand manner. "I just meant there are other things more vital than finding out who killed Al Vernon, that's all."

"Well, you're wrong," Frank said, hitting the counter with his fist and wincing. He hit it again, just to make sure it hurt as much as it had the first time. It did.

"See there?" he said triumphantly to George. "See there?"

"What?" asked George.

"I'm getting self-destructive," Frank announced. "It's eating away at me. Upsetting my mind."

"Not difficult," Tilly muttered into her keyboard.

"What?" Frank glared at her.

"I said it must be difficult," Tilly said, avoiding his eye.

"Frank, you have to look at the wider picture," George advised. "That body under the ice isn't our only problem. We've had the blizzard to deal with, we have a young girl missing in suspicious circumstances—"

"Well, did you ever think that maybe they're connected?" Frank asked, his bristly chin up. "Hey? Ever think of that?"

"The girl and the blizzard?"

"No, the dead man and the missing girl. Maybe the one who killed him stole her. Or maybe he's killed her already and put her under the ice like he did the first one. Maybe there's some evil monster stalking our streets—"

"The man was shot, the girl ran away after taking some kind of pills," George said.

"Maybe he gave her the pills," Frank said.

"Who?"

"My dead guy, that Al Vernon."

"He's been dead for weeks and weeks . . ."

"So maybe she saved 'em up," Frank said triumphantly. "Maybe he got her pregnant and said, 'Here, honey, take these and everything will be—' "

"She wasn't pregnant," George said wearily. "At least as far as we know she wasn't, but—"

"*George,*" Tilly said, frowning.

"Frank, go away," George said, abruptly recalling from

Tilly's expression that he shouldn't even have mentioned Chrissie Falconer. Frank Nixey was a blabbermouth, and soon it would be all over town. (Plus whatever embellishments Frank cared to add, of course, such as the conjecture that she'd been abducted by Venusian vampires, leaving behind in her room a strong aroma of grilled antelope. Frank read a lot of very strange magazines.) "Go away, Frank. We're doing the best we can."

"Well, it ain't good enough!" Frank shouted, hitting the counter again, this time giving a little whimper upon impact. "I am being torn apart, this whole town is being torn apart—"

"Frank—the whole town is just fine. Go have a drink and calm down," George suggested, in the hope that Nixey the Gadfly would move from talkative intoxication to silent stupor as quickly as possible. "Nothing's being torn apart."

"The high school is," Frank countered, having heard a garbled version of the ceiling collapse at the high school the previous afternoon. "Probably pressure from public opinion. Finally had to burst out somewhere."

"I don't think so," George said. "Goodbye, Frank."

"You'll be hearing from my lawyer," Frank shouted.

That amused George. "Oh, really?"

"You bet," Frank shouted from the door. "My lawyer will be in touch forthwith."

"Forthwith?"

"Asssolutely." The door slammed shut behind the agitated representative of public opinion and civic responsibility.

There was a moment of respectful silence. Then George snapped and began to laugh. Tilly smiled but did not join in.

"He's pretty upset, George."

"Well, what am I supposed to do about it?" George managed to choke out. "I can see the headlines now, 'Town Psycho Sues Sheriff for Failure to Act.'"

"Yes," Tilly said. "Exactly."

"Oh, come on."

"He has a lot of nutty friends, and they could stir up trouble for Matt," Tilly insisted. "They got Old Fishguts out onto the ice, didn't they?"

"He was bored and they bribed him. And Frank is just trading off some of the grief his wife gives him, that's all."

"I hope you're right," Tilly said. "I think Matt has enough on his plate without having to explain himself to Frank Nixey or anyone else."

Tilly was more right than she knew. At the very moment she spoke, Matt was experiencing an overwhelming impulse to cause physical damage to the boy who lounged in front of him with his chair tilted back and his feet on the battered oak table of the Hatchville interrogation room. The feet were in cowboy boots that had never seen a cow, and they belonged to a boy who needed breaking as much as any bronco.

Joey Ritto was a very handsome boy, whose dark good looks were marred only by his expression, his hairstyle, and the number of earrings he wore. Of course, these same three things may have been what made him so attractive to teenage girls, but to Matt he represented all that was threatening Blackwater Bay. A few steps and I could hook the chair out from under the smug little bastard, he thought. The kid's head would hit the floor with a satisfying . . .

"I got nothing to say," said Joey Ritto for the twenty-eighth time.

"Except that."

"What?"

"That you've got nothing to say."

"Yeah." Joey grinned to himself, and examined the heel of his hand, picking at it with interest.

Matt had tried several times to locate the boy, but had been unsuccessful. He was truant from school but not at home, he was "out," he was "around"—but he was never available. This in itself had been suspicious, until he'd checked with Henderson and found it was normal for the Ritto family, who seemed to run a very loose rein on their boys. Now Joey had been brought in during the early hours of the morning on suspicion of auto theft, and Chief Henderson had notified Matt immediately, suggesting he come over quickly to talk to the kid before the family lawyer—or worse, the father—could get there. They would, he said, "lose" the arrest report for a few hours, to give Matt time. Joey, cool and unruffled despite his situation, was palpably unimpressed with the sheriff. In fact, Joey was unimpressed by pretty much everything except Joey Ritto.

"Do you know Chrissie Falconer?" Matt asked again.

"I know a lot of girls," Joey said negligently. "A lot of girls say they know me, and maybe they do, but I don't always take names, you know?" (So many girls, so little time.)

"Chrissie lives in Blackwater Bay. On Runymede Road. Very pretty girl, blonde, bright, rich . . ."

"Big tits, big white house?" Joey asked. "Yeah, maybe. She saying I got her pregnant or something?"

"She's not saying anything at all, Joey. She's missing."

The hands, busy at nothing, went still. "Oh, yeah?"

"Yes."

Joey abandoned the heel of his hand and began picking at his thumbnail. He seemed to have a lot of loose ends. "Gone to make her fortune in the big world, hey?" he said cheerfully.

"Is that what you think?"

Joey favored him with a heavy-lidded glance. "Ain't it a possibility?"

"There are a lot of possibilities, some of them worse than others."

The boy shrugged. "I got nothing to say on that."

"Where were you on the night of the blizzard?"

"How the hell should I know?"

"Most people would remember."

"Oh, yeah? Well, I ain't most people."

"Doing something you shouldn't?" Matt asked.

"No."

"Then what?"

"I was at home. You can ask my family. At home, watching TV." He seemed almost embarrassed to admit to such an uncool occupation.

"And where were you on New Year's Eve?"

"New Year's Eve?" That raised an eyebrow. "What the hell has New Year's Eve got to do with it?"

"Where were you?"

"I was around. New Year's Eve—there was lots of parties. I was at a lot of them, dropping in here and there. You know how it is when you're a popular guy." He looked Matt up and down. "Or maybe you don't."

"Would one of the here or theres have been at the Falconer house, on Runymede Road in Blackwater, say around one in the morning?"

"I got no idea, I tell you. I didn't keep track because I didn't know you was interested. Had I but known—" Joey made a sweeping gesture— "I woulda kept a file. With . . . whachamacallits . . . affidavits. Yeah. With affidavits that said, 'Joey was here.' Made your life easy. Like I should care." The sneer was built-in, ex factory, standard on this model, but to Matt, for some reason, Joey seemed worse than the usual adolescent punk he had occasion to question. There was intelligence in the eyes, that was the trouble. Intelligence and scorn, a very, very bad combination.

"You've been questioned here about drugs—"

"They keep trying." This was amusing to Joey. "They keep trying but they get nowheres, because I am a clean guy. I don't do drugs."

"At Chrissie's party we found marijuana, Ecstasy—"

"Oh, man—those aren't drugs, they're necessities of life." Joey clearly felt sorry for the old guy wearing the sheriff's costume. "When I say *drugs* I mean like heroin, cocaine,

crack—those are the babies that hook you. Not for me. Like
they say, I am a take-charge person, so I don't want nothin'
takin' charge of me, you know what I mean? Forget it."

"So you're a good, clean guy."

Joey smiled. "Absolutely. Your grandmother could eat her
dinner off me."

"I'll tell her—she's always in the market for a new thrill."

The boy frowned. "Yeah. Right."

"About Chrissie—"

Joey leaned forward. "She didn't light out on New Year's
Eve."

"Didn't she?"

"No."

"How do you know?"

"It woulda been in the papers."

"Not necessarily."

"Freedom of the press, what about that?"

"What about it?"

The boy frowned more deeply. "Are you saying Chrissie
disappeared on New Year's Eve?"

"It was quite a party. A lot of damage was done."

"Yeah, but—" He stopped.

"But what, Joey?" Matt asked.

"I got nothing to say." Full circle.

"But she was there when you left, is that it?" Matt persisted. "Is that what you wanted to say?"

"I never even said I was there."

"Then why do you doubt me when I say Chrissie Falconer
disappeared on New Year's Eve?"

Joey stared at him, then looked away.

"Is it because you've seen her since then? Been seeing her
regularly? Maybe on the night of the blizzard?"

"No. I don't know," Joey said. "Dammit, I don't know.
You got no right to ask me this stuff—they got me in here
about car stealing, which, by the way, I'm innocent of doing

also. I want to see my lawyer now. I ain't saying no more without my lawyer."

"What worries you, Joey? What are you afraid of?"

But Joey was all done, and just stared back, wordlessly.

The open plan of the Hatchville police station made quiet observation a simple matter. Matt stayed around because he wanted to see exactly who came to rescue the recalcitrant Joey. He was in luck. Not only the family lawyer—Andy "Rancid" Randall, of course, the Slippery Savior himself— but also the father, Frank Ritto.

Matt had to admit, he looked more like what he claimed to be—a harassed father and shopkeeper—than any menacing criminal overseer from back east. He was a small man, balding, neatly dressed, clean-shaven, and quiet-spoken. His eyes were sad brown pools in a kindly face, and he looked at his son not with pride but with deep reproach.

"Joey," he said. "Again."

"They got it in for me, Papa," Joey whined, his earlier bravado subsumed by a new performance as the wronged and penitent son. "I was only passing by, I had nothing to do with it."

"Passing by at two in the morning when you should have been home in bed?" Mr. Ritto asked. "Forgive me, Joey, I find it hard to believe."

"But Papa—"

"I have a good mind to leave you here," Mr. Ritto went on. "Maybe that's what you need, a good shock to your system." There was little trace of either New York or Italy in the father's words, Matt noticed.

"Papa, there was also another cop here, from Blackwater Bay," Joey went on. "Asking questions about some missing girl. Was that legal? Can they do that, ask about other stuff?"

"What kind of questions?" Rancid Randall demanded sharply.

"Did I know her, when did I see her last—stuff like that," Joey said.

"Who is this girl?" Both lawyer and father wanted to know, their questions overlapping, startling Joey.

"Girl named Chrissie Falconer," Joey said, looking from one to the other.

"Did you know her?" Randall asked. "What did you say?"

"I didn't say nothin'," Joey said. "I said I didn't know."

"And?"

Joey shrugged. "And I didn't know. So?"

Father and lawyer exchanged a glance. "We'll talk about this once we get you out of this other thing," Randall said, glancing around. His eyes passed over, then returned to Matt, who was sitting not that far away at somebody's desk, pretending to look at some arrest reports. Randall stood up and came across. He was a tall, sleek man, expensively dressed, expensively groomed. Since he represented most of the criminals in the county, it was not surprising he placed so much importance on personal hygiene.

"Well, Sheriff—a little out of your normal territory, aren't you?"

"Hello, Randall. No—my authority covers the county, as you well know."

"It doesn't usually need extra cover, does it?"

"It seems to be needing it more than it used to," Matt said easily. "I'm beginning to wonder if it isn't under attack."

"Martians?" Randall asked archly, his eyebrows up.

"I wouldn't mind Martians," Matt said. "Do wonders for the tourist trade. No, I had other enemies in mind."

"Sounds a little paranoid to me."

"You get that way in this business," Matt allowed. "Into every fan a little shit must fly. Like the one you've come to get off yet again."

Randall looked over his shoulder. "Joey? A boy too full of energy for his own good, that's all. He'll grow out of it."

"Before or after it's too late?" Matt wondered.

"Now, that's exactly the kind of attitude that alienates the young, Sheriff," Randall said. "It's no wonder they rebel."

"Ah, yes—rebellion. We used to call it crime, remember?" Matt stood up and stretched. He could see Mr. Ritto and Joey watching from across the room, Joey with a sneer, his father with worried distraction. "Well, Randall, good luck with your rebel—and all those who propose to sail in after him. We'll be waiting."

"Paranoid *and* defensive," Randall murmured. "Do I detect a trace of the common conviction around here that because a family has an Italian name they are automatically part of some bigger family?"

"You said it, not I."

"I said it because it's been said to me and to Mr. Ritto just a little too frequently," Randall said with an angry edge to his voice. "I'm surprised at a man of your intelligence showing such a prejudicial attitude, arresting a boy just—"

"I didn't arrest Joey," Matt interrupted mildly. "I have tried to talk to him before, but he was never 'available.' I asked Chief Henderson to keep an eye out for him—and he notified me when the boy was brought in for questioning on another matter. I am simply pursuing my own investigation and I'd hoped Joey might be helpful."

"He tells me it concerns a missing girl?"

"Yes," Matt said. "A young girl he knew, in whose house he had been, and whose parents had warned him off seeing her again."

"Typical," Randall said. "More prejudice, more negative expectations becoming self-fulfilling prophecies."

"I believe it's called giving a dog a bad name," Matt agreed. "But when the dog keeps barking and biting . . . well—"

"I think the biting comes from the dogs on your side of the fence," Randall said. "Joey and his brothers have been the subject of a concerted campaign of harassment here in Hatchville designed to make life for my client—Mr.

Ritto—intolerable. All because he has the effrontery to come from New York and have an Italian name."

"And because the crime figures have gone up since he and his family arrived," Matt said.

"Can you prove that?"

"I expect Chief Henderson can."

"And perhaps it's just another example of wrong connections being made."

"Maybe," Matt said. "I wouldn't complain if I were you." He nodded toward Joey and his father. "We keep one another in business, counselor. Nice if we could both retire."

"We could start with just one of us," Randall suggested.

Matt smiled and started for the door. "I'll be real sorry to see you go, Randall," he said.

Within the body under the ice, gases burgeoned, pressing outward, as the processes of decomposition, slowed by the near-freezing temperature of the water around it, nevertheless continued their inexorable, natural progression. From out of the open mouth a large bubble of noxious vapor rose slowly to press against the roof of the car, then slid sideways and rose again only to be stopped beneath the ice. Gradually it dissipated against the rough translucent undersurface, becoming smaller and smaller until it vanished completely.

TWENTY-FOUR

"You're not going to believe this."

"What?"

Emily looked up from her VDU as Dominic Pritchard came ambling into the newspaper office, edged around the counter, and plonked himself down on the chair beside her desk.

"Frank Nixey has retained me to sue Matt Gabriel," he announced with some glee.

"You're joking."

"I told you you wouldn't believe it," Dominic said, stomping a clod of snow loose from the instep of his shoe. "I can hardly believe it myself."

"But why?"

"Well, I suppose you could call it a malpractice suit, sort of. According to Frank, Matt is derelict in his duty because he hasn't found out—or, according to Frank—isn't even trying to find out who killed Al Vernon."

Emily frowned. "Al Vernon—the one they found under the ice?"

"The very man."

"But what's Frank got to do with—oh. Because he reported it first."

Dominic beamed at her. "Well, good for you. Obviously your insanity runs right off the same rails as Frank's."

"No—there's a kind of logic there," Emily said reflectively.

"Oh, right—the logic of Monty Python," Dominic agreed.

"Surely you're not taking the case?"

"Nuisance cases pay just as well as righteous ones. Mr. Nixey has as much right to representation in law as anyone else."

"Frank Nixey can't afford—"

"Oh, but he can," Dominic interrupted her. "Don't tell me I know something about someone in this town that you don't?"

"Like what?"

"Frank Nixey has a ton of money, fresh supplies coming in on a regular basis."

"But he always looks like a tramp. And Trixie looks like—" Emily paused. "I must learn to be kind. She doesn't look wealthy."

"She doesn't *know* about the money, apparently."

Emily stared at him. "You're kidding."

"You seem to have formed a mistaken impression of me. I am not a comedian, I kid not, nor do I joke." Dominic sighed with mock gravitas. "Some years ago, when he was young and full of juice and vigor, Frank Nixey invented a doohickey."

"A what?"

"A whatsit, a thingamajig, a widget—a little something he forgot all about that happens to have suddenly become a required part of every internal combustion engine now in production. Fortunately he had enough brains then to patent the little wonder. The royalties are piling up in the bank even as we speak, but as far as Mrs. Nixey is concerned,

Frank is still on a fixed but generous pension arising from an award for an industrial accident which has left him unable to work for the past ten years. Something fell off the assembly line and onto his head, apparently, leaving a dent or two."

Emily began to laugh. "She'd kill him if she knew."

"That's why she doesn't know." Dominic grinned. "I gather from what he said that she's—difficult?"

"She's impossible," Emily hooted. "My God—and she has this mother who's even worse. They'd spend it all and *destroy* him."

"I think knowing that he is rich and keeping it from her is the one bright light in his life." Dominic chuckled. "The money doesn't mean a thing to him—except that he can afford to sue Matt, and anyone else who annoys him."

"I would *love* to print this," Emily said. "Local man becomes secret millionaire—I can see it now."

"But you can't," Dominic said. "It would lead to his homicide and my disbarment because it is a privileged communication. See how much I trust you?"

"Well, you shouldn't," Emily pointed out. "Suppose we break up? Look at all the things I could write then."

"Love is not having to say 'I'll see you in court,' " Dominic observed mildly.

"If he's so rich, why doesn't he just leave her?" Emily mused.

"Think about it," Dominic suggested.

She did. "Ah," she said after a minute. "Disclosure."

"Right. Her divorce lawyer—who unfortunately could now never be me—would demand disclosure of Frank's assets, and once known, would go for as much as he or she could get for dear Trixie. And Mom. And his or herself."

"What a rotten profession is yours."

"Oh, yes? Tell me, once we are married and have children and you abandon *your* oh-so-admirable profession, do you expect me to house you, clothe you, and put food on our table?" Dominic inquired.

"Yes, of course." Emily looked at him. "O noble one."

"That's better," Dominic said.

Emily sighed. "Poor Frank. Nobody knows how clever he once was and how rich he now is."

"Well, I do now. And they know at the bank, of course. I gather he goes in to visit his money every once in a while, and to discuss investments with the president of the bank." He settled back and glanced at the clock on the wall. "Are we going to lunch or not?"

"Yes, of course." Emily stood up and went over to get her coat. "You know, Frank has a kind of point," she said, as she came back struggling to get her arm into a recalcitrant sleeve. Dominic stood up behind her. "Why isn't Matt working on who killed Al Vernon?"

"Oh, I guess he probably is," Dominic said, turning her around to button her up like a little girl. "But he doesn't have to announce every move he makes, and he has had other things on his plate—like clearing up after the blizzard. And finding that young girl who disappeared."

"Chrissie Falconer," Emily said, permitting him to treat her like a child, because it brought him nearly close enough to kiss—or bite—on the nose, but he was too quick for her.

"Yes. Apparently when Frank went in to ask about the Vernon case, George Putnam said that Chrissie—as he put it—'took some pills and ran away.' Does that sound right?"

"It sounds like something Jess has been babbling about," Emily said, following him toward the door. "She thinks some kind of experimental drugs are being handed out to the kids at the high school. She called me up last night to find out if I'd heard anything about it."

"Have you?"

"Not a damn thing. And it's been driving me bats ever since she called. There's a story there, and I can't get an edge on it. Jess is behaving very peculiarly, even for her. She was right there at the school when the roof fell in, and she gave me plenty of details on that. Then she threw in the pill thing so terribly casually I knew it was important, but when I questioned her she just shut up and changed the subject." They crunched along the pavement and crossed the street, arm in arm.

"You are mad, bad, and dangerous to know when it comes to getting a story," Dominic reminded her. "Maybe she was just being discreet."

"I'm her sister, for pete's sake! She should have known I'd pick up on it. We've grown up with the paper because Dad owns it—journalism is in our *blood*!"

"Maybe Jess is different."

"There's no maybe about it, she's different all right. And getting more different every day. I wish to heaven she'd marry Tom and settle down."

"Why Tom?"

"Because he'd be good for her, if she only realized it. Instead she bent my ear last night going on and on about the new vet and how she's lusting for him."

"New vet?" Dominic asked blankly.

"Yes. Dr. Kelly. Apparently he had to make a house call last night, because Jess's cats went crazy."

"How could they tell?" Dominic asked.

Emily grinned. "I know they're a little eccentric—all Jess's cats have been—but this time they really did go nuts. According to her, they were running up and down the curtains, careening around the rooms without hitting the floor more than once every twenty feet, and generally behaving like lunatics. She couldn't even get near them. The good doctor Kelly came out, calmed them down with something or other, and stayed for dinner. Jess was full of it. Personally I don't like red hair."

"He has red hair?"

"So she says. And eyes as green as the sea." Emily imitated her sister in raptures.

"Sounds bad," Dominic agreed, opening the door of the Golden Perch for her.

"When Jess falls for someone, it usually is," Emily said.

"You, on the other hand, have unerring good taste." Dominic took their coats over to the coatrack and hung them up. "You chose me."

She looked at him. "Actually I was thinking of choosing the Caesar salad."

"Yet another wise decision," he said, and steered her toward a vacant booth.

Things were slowly returning to normal. The roads were progressively cleared and it became possible for people to move freely on them once again. However, as the air temperature hadn't risen, there had been no thaw, so there were still great walls of snow lining every road. In the countryside it was rather like driving down dry riverbeds, with only the occasional tree or farmhouse roof visible on the far side of the high banks. In town it had been better, for there the plows and blowers had concentrated the heaps of dirty snow on the street corners, enabling pedestrians to leave their homes once again—those, that is, who needed or cared to venture forth into a blinding white world of treacherous ice and frozen noses.

Radio and television stations were still broadcasting warnings about driving cautiously and not shoveling snow. The weather forecast was for clear skies ("so wear your sunglasses, folks!") and temperatures remaining in the low teens ("Baby, it's cold out there!"). Over most of Blackwater County there remained a great stillness, except for the squish of slowly increasing traffic, the hum of helicopters taking fodder to isolated herds, and the shouts of children freed yet again from school. Sidewalks in direct sunlight melted slightly, only to refreeze at night. Icicles in direct sunlight dripped intermittently, only to grow longer once the sun had moved on. Children in direct sunlight got overheated and caught colds. The frozen surface of the bay in direct sunlight occasionally twinkled as the light caught a jagged ridge of ice, or the water in a temporarily open lea where a dedicated fisherman had drilled and chopped a hole for a quick few hours of peaceful contemplation while holding a line.

Either the highway department thought well of Vic Moss or he had a very efficient grounds crew, for the entire length of the River Hill Country Club drive had been cleared, and Matt had no trouble driving up to the graceful building, its beauty enhanced by the deep fall of snow.

The club parking lot was similarly free of snow. There were several cars in place, even at this early hour—or were they holdovers from the night before? One of them startled Matt, as the last time he had seen that particular Mercedes sedan it had been in front of the Falconer house.

Had one or both of the grieving parents sought solace in gambling or socializing? He had heard that Bill Falconer was something of a highflier in Blackwater terms, and he knew that Mrs. Falconer was socially ambitious—but to be out so soon after what had to have been a terrific shock in addition to a continuing source of pain and worry? Or was there something sinister in this visit to Moss? The specter of Chrissie having been kidnaped had never really stopped haunting Matt. He had asked the bank where Falconer had his accounts, both business and personal, to notify him if any really large withdrawal was made. The manager had looked at him in some surprise, as if the likelihood of Falconer being given a large amount of money was a remote one. That, too, had interested Matt. Now the man was here at River Hill. Seeking solace? Or finance?

As he and his "escort" went down the hall they encountered Bill Falconer and *his* escort coming toward them. Falconer looked bad—drawn and gray beneath his winter tan, and far from happy. He was trudging along with his head down, carrying a briefcase, but when he glanced up and saw Matt, his face changed and he reached out to grab Matt's arm.

"Have you found my little girl yet?" he asked. The two assistants who had been accompanying them exchanged a glance and stepped discreetly aside. Whatever else Moss did, he made sure his men were trained in exactly how to handle the rich, the edgy, and the dangerous in any given situation. All his boys were well groomed, well mannered, well dressed, and, Matt assumed, well armed.

"We've done all the usual things," Matt said. "Newspapers and radio and television, plus all the official notifications. They're not making too big a thing of it at the moment, and I think that's best. It's very possible that she doesn't *want* to be found, and a lot of screaming headlines would make it that much more difficult for her to change her mind and ask to come home."

Matt had been surprised that Falconer hadn't been complaining about the low-key media treatment of Chrissie's disappearance. His lack of concern had fed Matt's suspicions about Chrissie having been kidnaped. Falconer, in fact, had not been in touch with Matt at all since the first call. Not since his wife had opened that letter that had upset her so much. Matt had called them several times, but had been coolly received. It was very odd behavior in his eyes. He went on.

"Chrissie is eighteen, and has a right to do as she pleases as long as she doesn't break the law. Fortunately she did break the law on New Year's Eve, and the fact that she has a court appearance coming up has enabled me to do more than I might ordinarily have done for a simple adult disappearance. You understand that?"

"Yes, yes—about the drugs at the party."

"That's right. We're also waiting for the laboratory reports to come back."

"What sort of reports?" Falconer asked.

"Well . . . there was evidence that Chrissie had engaged in

sexual intercourse sometime before she disappeared. There was semen on her sheets."

"You mean she was raped?" Falconer asked in horror.

"There was no evidence of force being used."

"I can't believe—" Falconer began in a dazed voice.

"She did keep condoms in her bedside table," Matt said gently. "These days—"

"Oh, yes, yes, I know kids are different today, and it doesn't surprise me that Chrissie wasn't a virgin. I just meant—well—she wasn't seeing any special boy before we left on vacation, that I do know. I don't think Chrissie would sleep with anyone she wasn't involved with emotionally, and that takes time, even today."

"We have some indication that she felt strongly about someone she referred to as 'J.' Does that mean anything to you?"

"The name Jay or the initial?"

"The initial."

Falconer started to shake his head, then his eyes narrowed. "That dreadful Hatchville boy—Joey. He could have come back into her life."

"At the New Year's Eve party?"

Falconer was thinking, and he was apparently not happy with the trend of his thoughts. "I suppose even after we banned him from the house, she could have gone on seeing him secretly. We gave Chrissie a pretty free rein because she was always such a good girl . . ." He flushed, and there was real pain in his eyes. "At least, we thought she was."

"I'm sure she was," Matt said. "Just about every teenage girl falls for somebody unsuitable at some time or other, don't they? I was talking to one of her teachers and she said—"

"Who was that?"

"Miss Gibbons."

"The home ec teacher? Isn't she one of Granger Gibbons's daughters?"

"Yes. She said it was about the most common form of rebellion in girls, after bizarre dressing, and that it usually blew over pretty quickly, as long as the parents didn't make a big fuss—"

"Which, of course, we did," Falconer said with some bitterness.

"Don't blame yourself for that," Matt said. "I've met and spoken with the Ritto boy, and I can understand your reservations, believe me."

Their two escorts had been standing to one side while Matt and Falconer spoke, but at the sound of the name Ritto both their heads came up sharply. Matt caught the movement out of the corner of his eye.

"Was that his name, Ritto?" asked Falconer vaguely. "I don't think we ever knew." He sighed. "I caught him pocketing something once—a silver table lighter—that was when I banned him. I always got the feeling he was . . . what do they call it? Casing the joint?" He gave a wry smile. "He said . . . well, it doesn't matter what he said. The lighter was in his pocket and there was no pretending anyone else put it there. I just can't imagine Chrissie . . ." He shook his head, then looked up suddenly. "Did you say you've talked to him? What did he say? Did he admit—"

"He admitted nothing, said he might have met Chrissie somewhere but—"

"There, you see? Lies right away. Typical." Falconer was disgusted. "You keep after him. I bet you'll find out he knows more than he's saying." Anger was beginning to replace grief, and Falconer was holding on to it like a sheet anchor, giving himself something to fight against, something to hate. "If he had anything to do with her disappearance . . ." He left the specific reaction unspoken, but the threat was clear.

"Then I will find out and I will deal with it," Matt said with quiet emphasis. He glanced at Vic Moss's two assistants, who were trying to look as if they weren't listening and were not succeeding very well. "I have an appointment with Mr. Moss."

Falconer nodded and leaned a little closer. Matt could smell his aftershave, and an underlying bitterness that might have been nervous perspiration. "Vic might know something about this Joey," he said in a confident tone. "He knows a lot of very odd people."

"Oh, I expect he might," agreed Matt with a wry smile. "He knows you and me, after all." The joke didn't take— Falconer just stared at him. "Have you been a member here long?" Matt asked quickly.

"Yes, almost ten years now. The wife likes it." Falconer suddenly seemed to recall he was late somewhere. "Well, please let me know as soon as—"

"We'll be in touch," Matt assured him.

"Ritto," Vic Moss said, and the contempt in his voice could have stripped varnish.

"They insist they have no connection with the Ritto family in New York."

"I heard that," Vic said. "You'll pardon me if I suspect differently."

"You and Chief Henderson both. Do you know something?"

Moss shook his head. "Nothing specific."

"They say it's a common Italian name—"

"I believe that's true," Moss agreed. "I believe it means 'upright,' as in 'okay.' Luca Ritto made it *not* okay the minute he tried to take over the Pescatori interests. Sending people like this Vernon along to make trouble—" He stopped abruptly.

"Then you did know Vernon?" Matt asked.

Moss's assistant stood beside him, hands clasped loosely in front of him. Vic was behind his desk, elegantly dressed as always, his face devoid of expression. He was considering something, staring down at his hands. "What I'm about to say to you I didn't say to you," he finally said.

"All right, you didn't," Matt agreed.

"I run a clean house here," Vic said. "Maybe some things go on you wouldn't like, officially speaking, but as long as nobody gets hurt I make sure you don't get bothered by them, officially speaking."

Matt nodded, accepting "officially speaking" as defining what was legal and what was not. He leaned back in his chair, waiting for Vic to continue. Vic, slowly, did.

"Sometimes the things that go on here require funding. This I get from various sources, and occasionally I pass it along. Some, for instance, I passed along to Mr. Falconer, who was just here."

"You loaned money to Falconer?"

"A legitimate loan, all open and aboveboard, no problem there."

"In cash, by any chance?"

"I only deal in cash," Moss said. Of course, Matt thought. No records.

"Did he say what it was for?"

"He wanted to expand his business. I took an interest, became a silent partner. I have a lot of silent partners. I used Falconer just as an illustration, you understand. He is a good member of the club, spends a lot of time here."

"He didn't say anything about needing money to pay ransom for his daughter?"

Vic looked startled. "No, he didn't."

Matt shrugged. "It's just . . . never mind."

"Are you telling me she's been kidnaped?"

"No. I don't know whether she has been or not. It's just a possibility I can't completely dismiss, and if Falconer is looking for a large sum of money, well—"

"He said nothing about that. I would tell you if he had, because kidnaping is a filthy game. I really would tell you."

Matt believed him.

"To continue—because I think it's important that you understand where I am on this, all right?"

"All right."

Vic nodded. "This club is very popular, winter and summer. That means it's profitable, which pleases me and the Internal Revenue Service. But that means certain people who are looking to expand—like Luca Ritto and maybe others—look at an operation like mine and think what a good thing it would be to take part in it. Not open and aboveboard like I did with Bill Falconer, but in their own way. First they send people—maybe like the Ritto family—to check things out and soften things up. I've seen this before, believe me. Next they send someone like Vernon, who's very up-front about it and walks right in and says 'gimme.' With me, people like that get nowhere and go away empty." He fixed Matt with a basilisk glare. "They go away empty. The reason they go away empty is not because what they offer isn't a good business proposition—it often is—but because you never take the *first* offer of anything, right?"

"You mean you were prepared to take an offer sometime?"

"Absolutely not. I'm just stating a general business principle."

"Oh." For a minute Matt thought Vic Moss was going to smile, but the moment passed and the smile did not get any further than the corners of Vic's eyes—maybe. Matt wasn't certain he'd seen anything, anyway, so he wasn't disappointed.

"Now, it occurs to me that sometimes people like Luca Ritto kill the messenger if they don't like the message. Or maybe for other reasons, like he's on the take, maybe skimming a little from the top, maybe trying to set up his own action, whatever. Who better to enact retribution for such trangressions than a young kid who has to make his bones and prove his loyalty? That's merely a suggestion, of course."

Matt stared at him. "Are you saying that Joey Ritto killed Al Vernon on orders from Luca Ritto?"

Vic Moss shrugged elaborately. "It's a possibility, that's all I'm saying."

"I don't think so," Matt said. "I've met the boy and I don't like him—"

"Nor do I," said Vic. "A cocky little shit."

"But I don't see him as a killer."

Vic raised an eyebrow. "No?"

"No."

Vic shrugged again. "And the Ritto family?"

"I've had some information passed to me by a friend in another city. And according to this information, the Ritto family now living in Hatchville is simply the Ritto family now living in Hatchville. No connection with Luca Ritto, or at least one so thin that it's invisible."

"That's the best kind," Vic said.

"They've been accused of the connection before, and moved away because of it."

Moss looked at him for a long time without speaking. "This information is solid?"

"As solid as it can be," Matt said. "I believe it."

"Then I'm sorry I spoke," Vic sighed. "I know what it means to be pushed around for something you didn't do."

"We all know that feeling," Matt agreed.

Vic shrugged again. He was apparently fond of shrugging and had made preparation for it because his suit fitted beautifully before, during, and after each shrug. "It was only a suggestion."

"I appreciate it. Meanwhile, I still have a body and no collar. I also have a drug problem."

Vic's face darkened. "I have nothing to do with drugs."

"These are what I believe are called recreational or designer drugs."

"Ah." This appeared to be a different case. "I occasionally tolerate a little cocaine on the premises because customers bring it in, but as for myself, I prefer to avoid it in any connection. It's a personal thing—a personal distate, you could say."

"Then you'll appreciate my problem. Someone is getting to the children, Vic. The missing girl—"

"Bill Falconer's girl."

"Yes. She had access to these drugs and she has a medical problem that has been made worse by them—and now she's disappeared."

"Do you want to know the truth about the girl?"

Matt was caught off guard. "The truth?"

"The reason I mention this at all is because of what you said about kidnaping. I don't buy kidnaping, I do buy the right for people to make a new life, even if it's a bad one."

"What do you mean?" Matt was surprised to see Vic Moss was actually looking uncomfortable.

"The girl is hot, Matt. A very beautiful girl, but she can't keep her knees together. They threw her sweet-sixteen party here, and she was casing the talent the minute she was through the door. Not just her little chums, but every male in the place, young, old, fat, thin, handsome, ugly. She knew what she was looking for, and she found it. My men caught her upstairs with her choice not once but *twice* in the same evening—and not the same guy, either. She liked it. She was crazy for it and didn't care where it came from. A girl like that goes to the city—"

"You've heard something?"

"No. But it would be the logical place for her to go."

"She was a smart girl, Vic. I don't think she would have gone on the street. Too dangerous."

"Not the street," Vic agreed. "But good places are always on the lookout for new faces—"

"Are you?"

They stared at one another. "I wouldn't have her," Vic said. "Too close to home. Same goes for the Doll House and the others around here."

"She asked?"

"Oh, yeah. About three years ago. She asked Uncle Vic where did all the pretty ladies come from and what did they do to get all those beautiful clothes." He gave Matt a wry look. "Or words to that effect. I told her to go play with her dolls."

"She's eighteen now. Has she asked recently?"

"No." There was a short silence. "How time flies," Vic said mildly. He took a deep breath and looked around at his desk as if searching for something. "You want me to ask around?" he finally said.

"Please. They'd tell you." Matt knew the madams of Grantham wouldn't tell Stryker or any of the vice cops about adding a nice, new girl to their stable, an eighteen-year-old beauty queen with natural talent and an unnatural appetite. He found it difficult to believe Vic, but he could see no reason for him to lie about the girl. It put a whole new slant on the problem. "If you could find out anything, I'd be grateful."

"And Joey Ritto?"

"I'm still working on Joey," Matt said. "We'll see."

Direct sunlight did not reach the body under the ice. The darkness prevailed, the currents swirled around it, and overhead, thin cracks appeared in the ice beneath the weight of the new snow.

TWENTY-FIVE

The Golden Perch was surpringly busy, considering the difficulties patrons still faced in reaching it. "Just goes to prove how bad the TV is these days," Harlow Wilcox said to his assistant barman. "Drives 'em right out of the house."

Jess and the handsome Dr. Kelly had managed to grab a booth and were enjoying a perch fry, draft lager, and one another. When the vet had arrived at Perkins Point the previous night, he had been greeted with a scene of complete chaos— five adults chasing two cats who seemed intent on flying to the moon straight through the ceiling. He'd made everyone sit down and remain still for ten minutes, during which they'd all gotten stiff necks from following the antics of the frenzied felines.

Finally, when Cleo and then Twister had ventured into range, they had been grabbed and injected with a tranquilizer. This was followed by a general collapse of all and sundry, including said cats, who were then bundled into cages in the back of Kelly's station wagon.

"I'll take them in and give them a thorough going-over," he had said. "I think two brain tumors are a bit of a coincidence, but two viral infections aren't. Neither is the possibility that they've gotten hold of something outside, so a complete blood workup is called for, too. I'll try everything I can think of."

"At what price?" Tom asked.

The vet smiled. "Flat diagnostic fee. Call it fifty, plus lab costs. That seem fair?"

"Absolutely," Jess said with a glare at Tom. He'd been full of snide remarks ever since they'd left the school, and now seemed to have taken an instant dislike to the vet.

"They're just a little high-strung," Tom objected.

"I'm sorry, but I think it's more than that," Dr. Kelly said. "Miss Gibbons—"

"Jess," Jess interrupted with a smile.

Kelly smiled back at her. "Jess brought them in once before after something like this—the day the blizzard started, I think it was. Now, cats are generally pretty calm creatures—"

"These two are usually more interested in sitting on laps than doing laps around the room," Pat Morrison put in with a grin.

"Exactly," Kelly agreed. "That is one of a cat's more endearing characteristics. Are any of you on drugs, by the way?"

There was an amazed silence.

"What the hell do you mean by that?" Tom demanded.

"I meant are any of you taking medication for anything?" Kelly said patiently. "Tranquilizers, sleeping pills, painkillers, anything like that? Say where a pill or capsule might have fallen from a shelf or bottle . . . something the cats could have picked up and eaten?"

There had followed a brief pharmaceutical interlude where they compared medicines, illnesses, and complaints about doctors, during which Kelly made some brief notes. Jason, it turned out, had trouble sleeping and was prone to migraine, Pat was suffering from a painful wrist, all three of the women were on birth control pills (this brought forth some blushes, if only because they all complained loudly and frequently about the lonely life of the unmarried school-teacher), Tom had ulcers, and he and Jess both had allergies.

"You see what I mean," Kelly said. "Any given household is a chemical minefield, especially when you throw in the usual array of oven cleaners, paint strippers, toilet bowl cleaners, et cetera, et cetera. It's a wonder any animal survives, frankly. Shows they have more basic good sense than most humans." He turned to Jess. "Could I have a look through your kitchen cupboards?"

She had taken him off on the ten-cent tour. It was during this tour that they had moved their relationship forward to a date for dinner the next evening.

Now Tom glared sourly at them through the crowd at the Golden Perch. He was sitting at the bar next to George Putnam, nursing a beer and a grudge. They had both been there for some time, even before Jess and the vet had arrived. Jess had seen Tom, but ignored him. He knew why—because she was afraid he would horn in on her date.

Hah! Tom thought. He wouldn't do that. Would he do that? He wouldn't do that. "Moves right in, doesn't he?" he said aloud.

George turned around on his stool and looked over at the booth, where Jess and Kelly were laughing together.

"Smart-ass," George agreed. "He's on my list, all right."

"What list is that?" Tom wanted to know.

"I gotta little list," George said, echoing his role in the high school production of *The Mikado*, years back. It had been a brief moment of glory, and remnants of the experience often crept into his conversation, summoning up applause only his ears could still hear. "I'm on the lookout for guys moved in around here inna past two or three years. He's one."

"He certainly is," Tom agreed. After a pause he said, "One what?"

"One of the guys moved in inna past two or—" George repeated.

"Oh, yeah. Right."

More beer flowed down their dry throats.

"Why?" Tom finally asked.

"Why what?"

"Why do you have a list of guys that moved—"

"Could be secret-hiding-out guy onna witness protection thingy," George said. He leaned closer, nearly coming off his stool. "Could be this Peter Murphy guy who testified in that big gangster trial in New York and put Luca Ritto inna pokey."

"No!" Tom said, glancing over his shoulder in furtive astonishment. "Him?"

"Why not?" George wanted to know.

Tom considered this. "You're right," he growled. "Why not?"

"Zactly," George said. "Now, you're all right, you been here all your life."

"Not a recommendation," Tom said, glaring over at Jess. "Apparently."

"But I am looking for these two–three-year guys because maybe one of them is this Murphy and maybe this guy under the ice came to bump him off and got bumped off himself instead."

"You're kidding me," Tom said.

George shook his head hard, and regretted it. "Nope. Trial four years ago, then Murphy goes underground, undercover, whatever, he goes under. Disappears. Has to go someplace. Why not here in Blackwater Bay? Nice, innocent little community, good place to settle down, wouldn't you say?"

"Sure," Tom agreed. "Great place."

George leaned closer still and had to grab the bar to remain upright. "They say Luca Ritto hasa contract out on this Murphy, been looking for him, but the Fibbies, they got him stashed, see?" Pushing himself back to the vertical he told Tom about the FBI agent who had come to the office. "Very mysterious," he confided. "Wouldn't give anything away."

"Not supposed to," Tom pointed out. "His job."

"But to a fellow officer of the law? He could have whispered in Matt's ear, sworn him to secrecy—"

"On his Captain Midnight Code Ring," Tom chortled.

George frowned. "Be serious. Serious thing, witness protection program."

"I know that," Tom said righteously. "*I* know that."

"But he didn't."

"Didn't what?"

"Didn't whisper in Matt's ear."

"Not surprised, Matt would have given him a quick smack in the chops—" Tom began.

"I meant figuratively speaking." It was tough going, but George managed the phrase without dropping a vowel. "Would not even tell the sheriff of the goddamn *county*, for crying out loud. Why do you suppose?"

"I don't know."

"So do I," George said, banging the bar for emphasis.

There was a pause while they both tried to figure out where they were in this conversation.

"I could help you," Tom finally said. "With your investigations."

"Not a deputy," George frowned. "Not sworn."

"I swear I will help you to the best of my ability," Tom said, raising his glass in one hand and a pretzel ring in the other. He then hung the pretzel over a pencil that was sticking up from his shirt pocket. "My badge of office," he announced.

George peered at it. "Needs a shine," he said, and they both burst into laughter loud enough to draw stares.

"But seriously," Tom said when they had recovered from their own hilarity. "I could find out stuff. Especially if this

Kelly is going to be hanging around our house and something tells me he is." He scowled over his shoulder.

"Well, why not?" George said. "Harlow, my good man,
another beer for myself and my fine upstanding colleague
here."

"Listen, you two," Harlow said, advancing down the bar
with a threatening look on his face. "Keep it down, all
right?"

George made a big thing about looking down the front of
his trousers. "Can't keep a good one down long, Harlow."

"Uh-oh," Jess said, looking up as another burst of laughter
emanated from the pair at the bar. "Tom and George are feeling no pain."

"As a medical practitioner I approve of no pain," Geoff
said. "However—"

Jess frowned. "Yes, exactly. I don't know what's gotten
into Tom lately. He's so bad-tempered. Even his laughter
sounds angry to me. It's not like him at all. I've known him
for years and he's always been sweet-natured and fun—"

"Trouble at work?"

Jess shrugged. "No more than usual. Teenage kids are always difficult, we're underfunded, overcrowded . . . pretty
normal for a high school these days. Mind you, according to
Jason we're living in Paradise compared to things down in
the city. At least we don't have security guards and metal detectors on the doors. Yet. In his last school, I gather they
were dealing drugs in the halls."

"Oh? Where was that?"

"Down in Grantham—one of the inner-city high schools.
The way he talks about it, you'd think he just recently escaped from jail or something. He's a funny bird, really. Nice,
but . . . odd. Tom hates him, for some reason. But then, at
the moment, Tom . . ." She stopped herself before she said
"hates everyone."

"Jason is new in the area, then?"

"Yes. We seem to have had quite a few new faces around town lately." She smiled at him. "Some of them nicer than others."

"I will take that personally," he said, grinning at her.

"Good idea," she agreed. Then—"Oh, Lord, they're going to get thrown out if they aren't careful." This in response to yet another, louder burst of hilarity from the Bobbsey Twins at the bar. She glanced in some embarrassment at Kelly. "Harlow likes to keep the Golden Perch sort of . . . well . . . classy. You know. There are plenty of other bars in town where nobody would notice that kind of behavior, but here . . . Tom should know better."

"Laughter not permitted?" Kelly raised an eyebrow.

"Not rowdy laughter. Not—uh-oh."

"Not falling off barstools?" Kelly suggested as George Putnam did just that. "I see."

"He'll get in trouble with Matt for that," Jess said as Harlow Wilcox hustled George and Tom out the door with a suggestion that they could use some fresh air. Tom protested that fresh air was one thing, frozen air was another, but they went without much more ado. Tom gave Jess one last glare over his shoulder before the door closed.

"He seems to be angry at you," Kelly said mildly.

"Yes. He does, doesn't he?" mused Jess. "I don't know why."

"You said he'd get in trouble. You mean Tom?"

"No, I meant George. He's a deputy sheriff, and I don't think Matt would approve of him being seen like that, even off duty."

"I see," Kelly said. "Is he the only deputy?"

"Oh, no—there are quite a few, ever since we had that trouble last summer. Somebody noticed how efficiently Matt ran things and decided he was setting a bad example, I guess. Now he has more deputies than he knows what to do with, normally—although I must say they've come in useful during the blizzard, helping out and all."

"Too many cops spoil the . . . what?"

"Sloth?" Jess suggested.

"Maybe that's the trouble," Kelly said. "Maybe now that there are so many deputies, George there doesn't have enough to occupy him, so he gets drunk now and then."

"George Putnam doesn't need to be drunk to get into trouble," Jess said.

"There's his goddamn car," Tom announced as he and George ambled across the parking lot on the bias. "Let's take a look."

"Why not?" George agreed owlishly. "Let's take a *good* look. Probably all kindsa violations on that old jalopy."

They made a circuit of the vet's station wagon, and Tom put out an exploratory hand. "Trusting sort of guy," he said. "Not locked."

"Very foolish," George said. "If somebody was to break in, his insurance would be invalid, did you know that?"

"No," said Tom, sliding into the front passenger seat. "I didn't know that."

"You're invisible," George said, glancing around the parking lot.

"I am?" Tom marveled, opening the glove compartment and thrusting his hand in. "Imagine that."

"Well, *I* can't see you," George said, leaning against the car so as to shield Tom from anyone leaving by the side exit of the Golden Perch. He gazed up at the sky and addressed the moon. "Which is a good thing, because if I could see you I would have to arrest you for vehicular trespass."

"Sounds painful," Tom said, moving his hand around inside the glove compartment. " 'What have I got, Doctor?' 'You have a nasty case of vehicular trespass, I will have to remove your front wheels.' Ouch!"

"Front wheels can be—" George began.

"Wasn't my front wheels," Tom complained, pulling his hand back out and ducking down to look. "It was this." He reached in, more cautiuosly, and extracted a used hypodermic syringe. "Oh, God," he said, sobering instantly. "Do dogs get AIDS?"

"No, but cats do," George said nervously, his own beer-induced jollity quickly dissipating. "Here—" He looked around and spotted a pile of newspapers stacked beside the Dumpster that stood by the kitchen door. He went over, pulled a folded section from the middle of the stack, and returned, holding it out so that Tom could drop the syringe into it. "Did he just have that lying loose in there?"

Tom was crouching down now, holding up his lighter. Country vets didn't run to luxuries like lighted glove compartments. "No," he said, drawing out a plastic box marked with a large red X. "It was probably in here, but the box must have come open when he hit a bump or something. Oh, great, I'm going to get rabies," Tom wailed.

"Calm down," George said, looking around nervously. "I'll send this off to the lab and have it checked out. Don't worry—I'm sure if it was something really nasty, the guy would have made sure it was safe. He's a vet, he knows the dangers."

"Probably in there to foil burglars," Tom continued mournfully, staring at the back of his hand. "I'll probably turn purple or green tomorrow so he can pick me out of a lineup."

"Say—that's quite an idea," George said, brightening. "Maybe somebody could develop something like that."

"That's revolting," Tom said. "What a revolting idea."

George shrugged. "Crime doesn't pay if you don't patent it."

"What?"

George looked confused himself. "Something like that, anyway. Anything else in there?"

Tom was poking around with his pencil now. "No. Couple of maps, notepad from some pharmaceutical company, flashlight—*now* I find the flashlight—gloves—there's an oddity, gloves in a glove compartment."

"That proves it—the guy's obviously nuts," George said wryly.

Tom completed his inventory of the glove compartment, and kneeling beside the car he slid forward over the doorsill on his belly, looking under the seats. "Uh-oh," he said.

"What?" George asked.

"A gun," said Tom, his voice muffled, as he reached across the transmission arch to the driver's side of the car floor.

"*Don't touch it!*" George snapped in such an authoritarian voice that Tom froze, his fingertips only an inch from the gun.

"What? What?" asked Tom. His face was so distorted from being pressed against the seat that it came out "Whart, whart?"

"What kind of gun is it?" George asked.

Tom rolled over and looked back at George. "A revolver. Looks like a .38 but all guns look like .38s to me because I don't know anything—"

"Get out of there, let me look," George said.

Tom wriggled out and stood up. With a quick look around, George took his place. "Yeah, you're right, it's probably a .38. Damn."

"What's wrong?"

George wriggled out and stood up. "Well, I can't take it because I didn't have a warrant or just cause to search the car. We're breaking the law here, Tom."

"Oh, yeah?" Tom asked. "Didn't you see that little fire on the floor where the cigarette lighter fell out of the dashboard and set fire to the carpet? A lot of smoke in the car. Remember?"

"Tom . . ." George began.

"It was right down here," Tom said, bending down and playing a jet of flame from his lighter over the carpet. He stepped on the smoldering area, grinding out any tiny sparks and obliterating the pattern of the lighter flame.

Then he took the cigarette lighter out of the dashboard and laid it in the center of the charred area. "Could have been nasty," he said. "Good thing we were here."

"Yeah," George said slowly. "Damn good thing."

"Do you have a license for the gun?" George asked Dr. Kelly.

"Why, yes, I do," Kelly said. "It's here in my wallet." He got it out and unfolded it.

" 'For personal protection,' " George read. "Protection from what, Dr. Kelly?"

"Rabid dogs, for one thing," Kelly said patiently. "Also I have to make occasional night calls. I used to live in New Jersey and there's a lot of urban crime there."

"Where in New Jersey?"

"Paterson."

"But you've got a gun license from *this* state," George said.

"Of course. I applied for it just after I arrived. I'm a law-abiding citizen," the vet said. "Look, I don't understand all this. We're in there having a quiet meal—"

"Did Tom put you up to this?" Jess demanded, her arms wrapped around her as they stood beside the car. George had come into the Golden Perch and asked Kelly if he would step outside for a minute, and Jess had followed.

"Tom?" asked George innocently. "Tom who?"

"The Tom who you were having such big fun with about twenty minutes ago," Jess said in a nasty tone. She looked around angrily. "The same Tom who is probably standing somewhere watching us and having a great big *laugh*!" She ended on a shout, still glaring around the parking lot. Tom, who was indeed crouched behind a car but not laughing at all, crouched down further, wincing as it put a strain on his bad knee.

"I told you. I came out and saw smoke in your car. Fortunately—in this case—you hadn't locked it. I opened the door, stamped out the sparks—and then got down to see if I'd missed any. That's when I saw the gun."

"Well, thank you for your vigilance, Deputy . . ." Kelly paused.

"Putnam," Jess said in an accusing tone.

George looked at her. "Now, Jessie—"

"And don't call me that!" she snapped. "George Putnam, you are a sleazy, childish, annoying brute."

George rolled his eyes at Kelly—the beers were regaining the upper hand. "She loves me, really," he confided.

"I'm sure she does," Kelly said, amused. "Are you happy about the gun now?"

"Yes," George said, although he wasn't. What he *really* wanted to do was confiscate the gun and have a ballistics comparison run on it to see if it matched the bullet found in Al Vernon's skull, but he had no legal basis for doing so. He just had to leave it there. "Although," he added in a gruff tone, "I would prefer to see it stowed more safely than just lying under your seat, Dr. Kelly, especially if you're not in the habit of locking your car. Perhaps locked in the glove compartment or in your medical case?"

"I'll see to it," the vet agreed. "Can we go back in and finish our meal now? Miss Gibbons is slowly freezing to death, and so am I."

"Come on, George, your bluff has been called," Jess said. "Nice try, but no teddy bear."

"Better lock the car now," George suggested.

The vet did so. "Happy?"

"No," said George. "But happier."

"George," Jess said sweetly.

"What?"

"You're an idiot." She smiled, and putting her arm through Kelly's, she went with him back into the Golden Perch. The bright lights from within shone out momentarily, and the sound of happy talk floated out on a rich scent wave of beer and sizzling beef, engulfing George, who suddenly realized he was very hungry.

Tom stood up slowly, easing his sore knee. George stared across the car tops at him. "Did you hear that?" he asked sulkily. "I'm an idiot."

"She's a cruel woman," Tom said, limping toward him. "A cruel and heartless woman. You don't want anything to do with her, believe me. It will only lead to heartbreak and ball-break and every other kind of bad break you can think of."

"How come you live in the same house as her, then?" George asked as they trudged across the parking lot toward the sheriff's office.

"Because I, too, am an idiot," Tom enunciated, his arm held theatrically across his chest. "Because of that unkind female I have a hole in my hand, another in my heart—"

"And an even bigger one in your head," George said unsympathetically.

Tom sighed. "*Et tu*, sleazy, childish, annoying Brutus?"

TWENTY-SIX

Jess sat crouched over the sewing machine in her big attic room, quilting a double bedspread she was doing on commission. The school had reopened, but her classrooms—along with all the others on the third floor—were not available while the work on the roof was going on. Rather than try to teach the practicalities of cooking and needle-work in unsuitable surroundings, Mr. Dutton had allowed her to cancel her classes until the following week, when the worst of the construction would be over and warmth and quiet would return to the top floor of the school. The repairs were temporary, because it had been decided that the entire roof would be replaced during the summer recess.

The other top-floor courses, including chemistry, had plenty of straightforward classroom work that could be done anywhere, so Jason—among others—was denied the extra holiday. This suited Jess just fine, because she wanted him out of the way this morning.

Her attention drawn by a sudden noise from outside, she stopped her stitching and looked out over the gray surface of the lake. Preparations were under way for the Ice Festival, scheduled for the coming weekend. At the moment they were attempting to clear the worst of the snowfall from the surface of the ice to make room for the racetrack and the booths and—particularly—for the snow sculpture competition. The participants in that contest were perhaps the only people in Blackwater grateful for the blizzard that had dumped so much raw material on their doorstep. Two bulldozers were out on the ice compacting huge mounds of snow into solid cubes in preparation for the artistic work that lay ahead. By Sunday—wind permitting—each huge cube would be transformed into something weird and/or wonderful for the judging. It was her favorite part of the festival. The Perkins Point team had actually won last year, with a glorious depiction of Snow White and the Seven Dwarfs. This year Pat had designed an even more ambitious offering—a fairy-tale castle, with a drawbridge, a courtyard, and pointed turrets with little ice-lattice windows, standing over seven feet high at the top of the highest tower. Jess had already made the little banners that would fly from each flagpole.

A fairy-tale castle belonged in the movies, not on Blackwater Bay, Jess thought. Girls no longer waited for that special prince to come. Instead they gave themselves up to the first smooth-talking smart-ass who had the nerve to ask. And ended up like Chrissie Falconer, hooked on drugs, maybe pregnant, so afraid to face reality that they have to run away. As she gazed over the busy scene below, Jess once again thought about why she wanted Jason out of the way today.

Geoff Kelly had been rather apologetic when she'd collected the cats from his office yesterday. He'd told her that they were physically fine, although still a little woozy from their tranquilizer shots. X rays had revealed no inner physical abnormalities, and he'd spent that afternoon going over each cat inch by inch, finding nothing wrong externally, either. "Not even fleas—congratulations," he'd said.

It had been something Geoff had said again, about human medications and other deadly chemicals found around the house.

Weren't there even more deadly things found around chemistry labs? What if they had been brought home on Jason's clothes—on all their clothes the night of the roof collapse—or worse, brought home deliberately by Jason himself?

She had been trying to remember all the times that the cats had acted peculiarly before. She realized, now, that there were quite a few instances when their behavior was not normal—althought perhaps not as wild as they had been the night before last. Geoff said there were a number of drugs that might have caused the cats to behave strangely, because animals did not always react the way humans did to chemical stimuli.

"Even humans very in their reactions," he said. "One person's painkiller is another's sleeping pill and a third man's nothing at all. I've sent some of the cats' blood away for analysis—that should give us some guidance. But their metabolism is so much faster than ours that whatever sent them into their spins might have been used up by the time I drew blood. And, of course, the tranquilizer complicated things, too. I'm sorry I can't be of more help. It may be psychological, of course."

"Can you recommend a good cat psychiatrist?" she'd asked.

"I'll have a serious talk with them tonight," he'd smiled down at her. "When I pick you up for dinner. Seven o'clock, wasn't it?"

"Seven o'clock," she'd agreed, smiling back. She'd gazed up at him. Such a nice man. Such gorgeous green eyes. Such a nice, warm, firm mouth. Such sure, gentle hands.

And that had been a nice moment.

Until, from beyond his white-jacketed shoulder, she'd caught sight of Mandy Turkle glaring at her, obviously enraged because Jess was getting the full benefit of Dr. Kelly's charms and, apparently, going out to dinner with him.

Because her mother had always taught her to be a gracious winner, Jess had given Mandy a *very* nice smile when she left.

Now, as she came to the end of a run she sighed and took her foot off the sewing machine control. Daydreaming was very pleasant, but it would be better not to put off her task any longer. The sooner she started, the less risk there would be of being discovered.

It was the policy at Perkins Point that everyone's room was his or her private domain, to which each had his or her own key. But because Jess had given up her bedroom to Jason, she still had a key to it.

As she expected, the room was almost unnaturally neat, to the point of his bedroom slippers being lined up precisely in front of his easy chair, ready for the evening's relaxation.

What she was after, first of all, was the jacket Jason had been wearing when he'd come to pick them up at the high school on the day the roof had fallen in. She remembered how he'd acted while everyone else was trying to look after the injured boys or clear up the mess. Jason had complained—perfectly normal for him, of course—and had gone around the room opening drawers and taking things out, peering into smashed cupboards and poking around.

Why?

Had he been afraid something he'd hidden there would be discovered? His private "experiments" had been smashed by the falling timber and masonry. Was he making certain that no incriminating evidence was left behind of what he had actually been making under the guise of "polymer research"? He'd told them about his speech to the Science Club about drugs. Had he told them everything about it? Had he in fact been encouraging the students to try something he'd created himself, had tested on her poor cats and now wanted to have tested on human guinea pigs? Before he'd come into the chemistry lab the other day, had he made a brief stop in her office to remove Chrissie's diary because it contained incriminating evidence of his seduction of her? Was Jason Phillips Chrissie's wonderful "J"? He was physically attractive, with that wayward fall of golden hair on a well-shaped head. He might dress like a fifty-year-old, but beneath the tweeds he had a long lean body, and his soft, deep voice could easily adapt to a bedroom whisper. Had he been at the party, high on drugs with the rest of them? Was that why Chrissie had been so evasive about the so-called gate-crashers? He'd been somewhere, that was certain. In fact, Jason was *always* somewhere—especially, Tom would claim, when there was work to be done around the house.

Thinking back, Jess realized that Jason had often been out at night with no explanation, taken phone calls in a low voice, been first down to collect the mail. Nobody had known him well enough—or, frankly, cared enough—to ask questions. Had he encouraged their indifference?

In the past day or two she'd been looking at Jason with different eyes. Everything he did, everything he said, seemed now to have another, more sinister meaning. He'd been behaving as he always had—but now his self-absorption seemed secretive, his pettiness defensive, and his solitary nature furtive and sly. Had the signs always been there for her to see? His outer jacket, the goose-down one, was not in the hall downstairs—he'd obviously worn it to school today. The inner one, the blue-gray tweed with the leather patches on the elbows, she found in his closet, hanging neatly between the greenish tweed and the brown tweed. Jason was very into the British Look. Being the neat man he was, he had obviously brushed the worst of the dust of the semidestroyed chemistry lab from the surface of his clothing (and onto the cats?), but there must still, she thought, be some residue left.

Having taken the trouble to supply herself with several plastic bags, large and small, she carefully placed the jacket inside the largest plastic bag and shook and struck it repeatedly, until she could see a layer of dust at the bottom of the bag. She removed the jacket and tied up the plastic bag, sealing the dust inside. Then she carefully reversed each pocket into a small plastic bag, brushing out what dust, lint, and bits she found and securing the little bags shut with tape. In one pocket she discovered a small plastic box containing several pink and blue capsules. She gazed at them in triumph. Pink to chase away the blues, or blue to put you in the pink? So she'd been right.

Oh, Jason, she thought. You stinker, you absolute stinker! Giving drugs to innocent kids, impressing them with your position and what passed for a personality, seducing the loveliest of them. You are beneath contempt.

When she finished with that jacket and hung it back up, she went through all his other clothes, but found nothing as incriminating as the pink and blue capsules. She did find one of the cloth mice that he'd brought home for the cats, though—and bagged that as well. For all she knew it was full of marijuana rather than catnip! Satisfied she'd secured what physical evidence she could, she turned to the rest of the room.

The surface of the desk under the window was clear except for the blotter (unmarked) and a tray of pens and pencils. The first drawer she opened—the wide shallow one—was a model of efficient stowage, with every item carefully aligned. Paper clips, felt-tip pens, staples, all consigned to their proper places. Control freak, she thought. The second drawer held stationery, and the third held a number of pornographic magazines, an expensive camera, and several rolls of exposed film. Now, that presents a dilemma, she thought. Do I steal the film and get it developed? What might it be? Innocent views of the countryside? Or shots of poor, vulnerable Chrissie Falconer in varied states of undress and drug-induced ecstasy?

But oh, the allure of an older man to an impressionable girl of that age. And the thrill of "getting off" with a teacher. It was too much to bear. Her hand went forward, then back, forward, then back as she debated whether to take the film or not.

No. She would tell the sheriff about the rolls of film, but it would be up to him to get a search warrant to secure them. After, no doubt, he told her off for poking around in some-one else's possessions.

The fourth drawer was locked.

There was no key anywhere, so presumably he had it on his key chain. She wondered whether to break into the drawer, but knew she could not. At least, not without giv-ing away the fact that she—or someone—had been in his room. Well, it had been worth it, she thought, reluctantly straightening up. She probably had the goods on old Jason, child seducer and cat intoxicator, right there in her little plastic bags.

His infamy would not go undiscovered much longer. Not if she had anything to do with it. But first she had to be cer-tain of what she had. And for that, she needed help.

She was pretty sure she knew where she could get it.

"I tell you, the gun was there!" George protested.

"So?" Matt asked.

"So what's a vet doing with a gun—"

"Just what he said," Matt told him in some exasperation. "Look, George—Kelly came to me a few days after coming to town and filled out the application for a gun permit and I endorsed it. No problem. He doesn't just deal with cats and dogs, you know—what about a bull that's gone berserk in the heat, or a horse or cow that has to be put down?"

"Well . . ." George was reluctant to let it go.

"What you did was wrong and you know it. I'm not going to make matters worse."

"But you could ask for the gun for purposes of elimina-tion," George said, trying again.

"On what grounds?"

"That he's new in town, that we don't know his background, that he could be this Peter Murphy. Ask the FBI if he's the guy."

"I don't have to ask the FBI. How would there have been time for Kelly—or Murphy—to train as a vet? It's only been four years or so since the trial began, after all, and he'd have had to get into veterinary college—presuming he had a qualifying degree to begin with."

"Maybe he was a vet before then."

"Oh, sure—and made a career change into being an accountant for a gangster because he was tired of being nice to cocker spaniels? That's really likely, isn't it?"

"All right, all right." George's headache from the previous night's carousing with Tom Brady was still pounding in his temples and there was a strange taste in his mouth, like he'd been licking a galvanized-tin bathtub. The end of the evening had been pretty much of a blur, so licking a bath was as likely a source for the taste as anything else.

"What were you doing out with Tom Brady, anyway?" Matt asked curiously. He hadn't been aware that the two were particularly friendly.

"Oh, Tom's okay," George said.

"I didn't say he wasn't."

"He's just a little hung up on Jess Gibbons is all," George continued. "Which is understandable."

"Is it?"

"Sure. She's . . ." George paused. "Well, you've seen her."

"Yes." Matt conjured up an image of Jess—small, dark, and . . . what would be the best word? . . . sexy? No. Vivacious? No. Mischievous? Closer. Challenging? Yes. Made a man want to square off with her and end up laughing, maybe in bed. "See what you mean," he said, although he hadn't noticed it before.

"You have to think about it," George said, as if reading his mind. "She doesn't hit you right off, but . . ."

"But don't they live together?" Matt asked.

"Oh, yeah, sure they live together, but they don't *live* together, if you see what I mean," George said, rather ob-
scurely. "That's the trouble, if you ask me. And now she's
gone sweet on this new vet and Tom is pissed off."

"I see," said Matt, who didn't see at all.

"To be honest, I think that's really why Tom wanted me
to find out something about him. He's hoping he's an escaped felon or maybe has four wives in another state."

"Something small but damaging," Matt said wryly.

"Yeah. Also there was this hypo thingy," George continued, producing the newspaper-wrapped item. "I said I'd
have it analyzed, but maybe—"

Matt half stood and reached across for it. "Where did you
find this?"

"In the glove compartment."

"George," said Tilly with a frown. "That was very
naughty." She'd only been half listening, but when Matt
reached out for the folded newspaper, her interest had sharpened.

"The car was on fire," George said defensively.

"And what did you expect to find in the glove compartment, a fire bell?" Tilly asked.

"Kelly might have had a small extinguisher in there,"
Matt pointed out in George's defense, unfolding the newspaper. He viewed the empty hypodermic syringe with surprise. The overhead light glinted on the naked needle. "This
was just rolling around loose?"

"No, no—it had been in some kind of box, but had come
out somehow. The box was only plastic, not too tight a fastening," George explained. "You can see how it happened.
Tom is terrified he'll catch something, so I said we could
have it checked out for him. Can we?"

"Why didn't you just ask the vet?" Matt wanted to know,
eyeing George.

George reddened. "Well, I didn't want to say
we'd . . . that is . . ."

"George," Matt interrupted.

"What?" George said, looking miserable.

"You're improving," Matt told him. "You're definitely improving."

"What do you think?" Jess asked.

Claude Trickett was sitting on the edge of his chair. He reached out and poked a finger at the plastic bags that lay on the glass-topped cocktail table that sat between the chair and the sofa. "I think it's . . ." He paused. "Frankly, Jess, I don't know what to think. Jason Phillips is an unknown quantity, I agree, but he came through the right channels with all the right recommendations, and so on. I never noticed anything suspicious about his work. He keeps himself pretty aloof."

"That could be a pretense."

Claude managed a slanted smile. "It seems pretty genuine to me. He has a very high opinion of himself, as opposed to his opinion of the rest of us poor mortals."

"Exactly," Jess said. "And that's just the kind of person who thinks himself above the laws of society!"

"Oh, really?" Trickett leaned back and reached for the cigarette box on the small table beside him. He opened it, offered it to Jess, who shook her head, then took one for himself and lit it with the old-fashioned green onyx table lighter that sat beside the plastic bags. "I suppose you're right. It hadn't occurred to me. Or to you, obviously, as you took him into your own home."

"Well, at the time he seemed all right, just a bit lost and out of place. Coming in at the middle of the term isn't easy, and we thought it was just that."

"We?"

"Oh, Perkins Point is more of a cooperative than anything else," Jess explained. "We talked it over and everybody decided it would be okay to have Jason. In some ways it has been, but in others—" She thought of Tom and the eternal

battle of garbage duty. "I think one of the other girls was
sort of interested in him—I can't remember which one
now—young, reasonably attractive single men aren't exactly
thick on the ground here in Blackwater. Not in winter, anyway."

"And now?"

"I expect she's learned her lesson like the rest of us," Jess
said. She sat back and looked around the room in some surprise. Claude was head of the science department, but she
didn't think his salary was all that much higher than her
own. The furnishings in his house, and the house itself, said
otherwise. She was about to say something when she remembered that his ex-wife had been from a very wealthy
family, which would explain the expensive look of the
room—and, perhaps, the fact that it was beginning to look
rather threadbare. Apparently, when Claude's wife had left
him several years earlier, she'd taken her money with her.

That the room had been designed by a professional was
evident—the Art Deco theme was too consistent to be otherwise. Claude and the ex-wife might have been ardent Art
Deco collectors, for all she knew, but it took a real artist's eye
to combine what was a modern interpretation of a look with
genuine examples of a particular period, and it had been
done beautifully here. "This is a lovely room, Claude."

"Yes, I suppose it is," he said vaguely. "Harriet did it.
She's an interior designer, you know. Well—she was profes-
sionally qualified, but never practiced, except to do the odd
room for friends now and again. It was really only a hobby,
until she left me. Now she's a big success down in
Grantham. I obviously held her back from fulfilling her true
destiny. That's what she said, anyway—among other
things." He sighed. "I don't find this room particularly restful, though." He lowered his voice as if keeping a secret from
the absent Harriet. "I have a messy little study of my own
that I much prefer." He smiled grimly. "Harriet thought

chemistry was a smelly, nasty business that should be kept in its place—and that was not in her home."

Jess nodded, wanting to get back to the point. "The thing is, Claude—I thought maybe you could help me by analyzing this stuff. That way, if I'm wrong, it won't be official."

"On the contrary, as head of the department I'll have to take it very seriously."

"Oh, yes, of course. But I think if I took this to the sheriff he'd be legally bound to talk to Jason . . . and if I'm wrong, well . . ."

"Life wouldn't be very pleasant at Perkins Point," Claude finished, with an understanding smile.

"Exactly," Jess said. "I knew you'd understand. It's terrible to suspect a friend . . . well, a colleague . . ." She sighed. "I feel so . . . sneaky. And so . . ."

"Guilty?"

"Well, yes." She grinned. "Tom is always accusing me of going off half-cocked, and most of the time he's right, but this time . . . well, it's a lot more serious. Those pills, for example—they could be for allergy or simple antibiotics. But Mr. Deaner at the pharmacy didn't recognize them. He couldn't find anything like them in his reference books, either. He wanted to hang on to them, but I said I was taking them to the sheriff, and that seemed to satisfy him. I don't know, Claude," she said, wavering. "Maybe I am being an idiot—but if Jason has anything to do with Chrissie Falconer running off like she has, for instance—"

"Very serious stuff," Claude agreed. He sighed, running a hand through his sandy hair, now more gray than beige. "Frankly, Jess, I can't help you. I'm just a high school chemistry teacher. Whatever I learned about qualitative analysis in college I've long since forgotten—except what I teach, of course, which is very basic stuff."

"Well, mostly it's those pills—"

He pushed a finger between the bags and came up with the one that contained the small pink and blue capsules.

"They look harmless enough—but then, all pills look harmless. Even arsenic only looks like sugar, hence its popularity as a method for dispatching rich bad-tempered relatives in Victorian times."

"But not today, presumably."

"So we're led to believe. And, I must say, with the advances in forensic science, it must be pretty challenging for the modern poisoner. He or she has a pretty wide choice, but technology has a pretty long reach, too. My profession has a lot to answer for—we're very good at producing deadly poisons for other species that just happen to kill humans as well. Hence my own rather pathetic little researches into safe, organic pest control."

"Oh? I thought Jason said you were researching polymers."

"No." Claude looked puzzled. "He said that?"

"I know zip about chemistry, Claude, but I'm pretty sure he said you were both 'into' polymers. Are insecticides made from polymers—whatever polymers are?"

"No, they're not." He suddenly looked reflective. "Although there's a thought there. Sticky fibers . . ."

Jess shrugged. "Well, I've probably got it wrong. Maybe it was one of the kids in the Science Club he meant."

Trickett's face cleared as he came back to the present. "Ah, that would be it. Chrissie Falconer was interested in polymer textiles."

"He said she was interested in biology."

Claude shook his head. "Absolutely not. She was an excellent chemistry student, aside from her spelling, which in chemistry can get you into a lot of trouble, of course. The difference between an *ite* and an *ate* is a lot more complicated than a single letter. But other than that she was very sound. I suppose the fabric thing was because of her work with you."

Jess grinned. "The person who comes up with a synthetic

fabric that equals cotton will make a fortune. So far nature is in the lead and looks like it's staying there for some time."

"Don't you believe it. Students like Chrissie will be changing . . ." He paused, then frowned. "I forgot for a moment that she was missing."

"Could she have made up those pills herself?"

"No. Pharmaceutical chemistry is beyond a high school student—even a good one. Beyond me, if I'm honest. Anyway, where would she have gotten the ingredients?"

Jess was reluctant to let go of her prime suspect. "She was having an affair with someone," she said slowly. "It might have been Jason."

Now Claude was really surprised. "Phillips? I can almost believe chemical shenanigans of him, but I can't believe *that*."

"It's happened before."

"With him?"

"No . . . oh, no . . . at least, not as far as we know." She thought about that for a minute. "Maybe I should check out his last school, though," she said, half to herself.

Claude leaned back in his chair and fiddled with lighting his pipe. "Why the sudden urge to detect, Jess?" he asked with some amusement, brushing ash from his plump little stomach.

"Oh, it's not sudden," Jess confessed. "I think it's just that I read too many murder mysteries. It's a terrible vice, second only to my passion for chocolate."

He laughed. "Which can lead to equally dangerous results—such as an expanding waistline." He patted his own, rather complacently. "Harriet used to keep an eye on me—since she left I've literally gone to pot." He laughed again. "And I love it!"

Losing a wealthy wife certainly didn't seem to have upset Claude Trickett. Jess found that a refreshing change from her various friends and acquaintances who went on at length about their unhappy marriages and/or love affairs. She had long ago decided that she possessed one of those faces that seem to invite confidences. She was always interested, but sometimes even her patience wore thin. She thought, suddenly, of Tom.

Was that what was wrong with him? She couldn't recall him mentioning a new girl—or even an old girl. As a matter of fact, he'd been singularly unforthcoming lately about his feelings, not at all like his old, easy, open self. Was *everybody* in her life turning into a mystery?

"I beg your pardon?"

Claude had been speaking to her. "I said what you need is a professional qualitative analyst, not a worn-out high school chemistry teacher." He paused for a moment. "Say—I believe an old friend of mine from college went into analytical work. I wonder if I could track him down for you?"

"Oh, that would be marvelous," Jess said, brightening.

"Mind you—for all I know *he* could be working in the state forensic lab," Claude said with a twinkle.

"Oh." Jess was taken aback.

Claude relented. "No—I'm sure he went into a commercial outfit. Shall I try and track him down? If I don't have any luck—say by Monday—then you'll have to go to the sheriff. How's that?"

"Well, I'd be grateful for whatever you can do," Jess said.

"Right." He patted the plastic bags. "Leave these with me, and I'll do my best."

Jess stood up. "Thanks, Claude. And if you see Jason, don't—"

"Ask him whether he's a seducer and poisoner?" Claude grinned. "I think you're safe, Jess. It isn't exactly the kind of question one can work into the average conversation, is it?"

Under the ice the rotting seat belt gave way, and the body rose upward for a few inches, then came to rest, bent almost double against the roof of the car. The sudden movement startled the ever-attentive fish, and they darted away, circling in agitation. After a few moments, however, they began to return . . .

TWENTY-SEVEN

"You have no right to arrest my son!"

"I'm not arresting your son, Mr. Ritto, I just want to talk to him," Matt said patiently.

"All the time we're getting this harassment," Ritto went on. "I'm telling you, I'm going to sell the house, I'm going to take my family and find a *decent* place to live." Ritto was really rolling now, his face that of a man on the verge of apoplexy.

His wife, a plump woman in her late forties, stood behind the storm door, looking from one to the other through the glass, her hands gripped tightly beneath her apron. For one brief second Matt wondered whether she had a gun under the flowered fabric, then dismissed the thought as unworthy. She looked frightened, worried for her husband and her son, and Matt was sorry he had upset her.

"Look, Mr. Ritto," Matt began.

"Forget it," Joey muttered out of the side of his mouth. "He can't hear you."

Mr. Ritto was still raving, his initially faint accent becoming progressively stronger as his outrage increased. "In

New York we get this, in Pennsylvania we get this, in *Indiana* we get this—I thought maybe here, but no. No! Everywhere we get treated like scum, like vermin—"

"Your sons do have a history of troublemaking—"

"And whose fault is that? The police, everywhere, picking on my boys, saying they did this, they did that, they did everything bad and we're bad parents to let them. We do not let them do bad things. Always they are good boys—"

"Papa—" Even Joey couldn't accept this version. "Papa, sometimes we did the things they said." He glanced up at Matt. "But not this time."

"You don't even know what I want to talk to you about," Matt said, feeling more and more on the defensive. Out of the corner of his eye he could see curtains twitching as Mr. Ritto's outraged voice carried from the porch out into the neighborhood.

"About the missing girl, right?" Joey said. "About Chrissie."

Mr. Ritto suddenly stopped and stared, his hand on his chest, his face paling. "What is this?" he asked in a voice gone abruptly soft and unbelieving. "A girl . . . you ask about a girl?"

"It's nothing, Papa—a girl I knew in Blackwater ran away from home—"

"We don't know that," Matt said quickly. "We're just trying to talk to all her friends, people who knew her and may have known what was going on in her mind."

"Yeah, that's all, Papa. The girl disappeared and they want to know if she . . . was depressed."

"You think she killed herself?" Mr. Ritto was quiet now, shocked into a kind of stillness.

"It's possible," Matt said. But, of course, Joey was wrong—he didn't want to talk to him about Chrissie. Not this time. Today, he wanted to talk to him about Al Vernon. And he wondered grimly what Mr. Ritto would say about *that*.

He took Joey to the Hatchville station and borrowed an interrogation room. They sat on opposite sides of the battered table and stared at one another.

"I had an interesting suggestion made to me recently," Matt began.

"Oh, yeah?" Joey sneered. "I can think of a few suggestions to make to you, myself."

"I'm sure you can. This suggestion didn't concern me—it concerned you." Matt watched the youngster for a reaction, but Joey managed to keep his sneer intact, up to and including his eyes.

Matt continued, keeping his tone conversational. "The suggestion was that you shot the man we found floating under the ice."

That *did* get a reaction—one of utter stupefaction. After a moment Joey managed to get his jaw back under control. "Who the hell said that?" he wanted to know. So complete was his amazement that he forgot momentarily to maintain his smart-alec pose.

"Oh, a local businessman," Matt said.

Joey leaned back. "Hah," he finally said. "Somebody got it in for my old man, I suppose. Again."

"Not quite."

"Jeez," Joey said, continuing to sound almost like a human being. "We get this everywhere we go, you know? My dad keeps thinking about changing his name now, he feels so bad."

"How would you feel about changing your name?"

Joey looked at him. From behind the mask there now peered two rather intelligent eyes. "You mean, do I get off on having the same name as a big crime boss?"

"Something like that."

"Maybe I do, a little. What else have I got going for me?"

"I don't know. Brains?" Matt had taken the trouble to look into the boy's school records. Despite frequent absences, he was carrying a high B average, and according to his coun-

selor he could have been an honor student if his attendance
had been better.

"Oh, yeah. I should get big glasses and a pocket protector
full of pens and act like some wimp, hey? This would be *impressive,* I suppose."

"Afraid nobody would like you if they knew you were
smart, Joey? Afraid you might get left out of all the fun like
stealing cars and shoplifting and the other intellectual pur-
suits you and your friends have been getting into? Afraid
your little brothers wouldn't want to follow in your footsteps?"

"You don't understand," Joey said wearily. "Where I grew
up, it was—"

"You haven't grown up yet," Matt interrupted. "*You're* not
eighteen yet, and lucky you, because at eighteen these little
games of yours start to get serious penalties, right? What are
you going to do, go straight on your birthday?"

Joey suddenly grinned. "Exactly."

Matt felt like doing a little jaw-dropping himself.

Joey laughed out loud, briefly, and a little patronizingly.
"Like you said, I got brains. Look, we moved maybe four or
five times in the last eight years. My dad, he's excitable, always looking for new things to do. Before this he ran a
clothes shop. Before that a restaurant. Each time my brothers and me, we had to hit a new neighborhood, a new school.
Pretty quick I decided the way not to get pushed around was
to be the guy who pushed. Not hard—just enough. And
also, when I worked out what my dick was for, I found out I
like the brassy bitches, the high-assed numbers, you know?
And they don't go for wimps, either." He shifted in his seat,
folded his arms, and leaned forward onto the table. "But
about six months from now there will be a revolution. I'll
straighten up, I'll go to college, I'll make a million before
I'm thirty. Legit, too. That's the thing, see? We are a legit
family, and that is why I don't want to change my name, be-

cause it is *my* name just as much as it is his, the stupid bastard. Luca Ritto—fuck him."

"So there's no connection."

"No connection," Joey agreed. "Oh, maybe back in Italy there's some connection a long way back. There had to be one father and mother of all Rittos, right? Good thing they can't see how some turned out."

"And your father—"

"—is just a little Italian guy trying to get along," Joey finished for him. "Sorry to disappoint you."

"I'm not disappointed," Matt said. "Believe me, I'm not."

"Well, terrific," Joey said, his sneer returning. "Can I go now?" He started to stand up.

"What about Chrissie?" Matt asked.

Joey's face went a little blank. "What about her?"

"She wasn't a brassy bitch."

"No? Think again."

"She was a good student, Homecoming Queen, a good daughter, devoted to—"

"Chrissie was the brassiest bitch of them all, man," Joey said. "She scared the hell out of me."

"Oh?" So Vic Moss had been right.

Joey actually flushed. "Man, I couldn't keep up with her. She was insatiable. Something wrong there, man. Something not right upstairs. She had all you adults conned into thinking she was Miss Prim, but we knew. Jesus, we *all* knew. That party of hers you kept asking me about? The one where everything got busted up? Okay, you asked, I'll tell you. It went wrong because a bunch of guys got tired of waiting for their number to come up."

"What are you saying?"

"I'm saying that by midnight Miss Chrissie Falconer was as high as a kite, and announced she was going to auction herself off, that's what. Promised to do it with anyone. Said she was going to set a record, and she wrote numbers on little pieces of paper. The highest price went for number one, the next highest price got number two, and so on. She sold numbers up to twenty-five. She said it was for charity."

"How . . . generous," Matt managed to say.

"Oh, very," Joey agreed in an arch tone. "Almost civilized, right?" Matt couldn't work out for whom Joey felt the most contempt—Chrissie, Matt, or himself. "But while she was enjoying herself—I think she'd got up to about number eight—number six was a girl, by the way—a few guys from Hatchville dropped in and started to fight over the remaining numbers."

"I can't believe this," Matt said, trying to draw the boy out. He thought back to the scene of the party when he'd arrived— wanton destruction everywhere, and Chrissie whimpering like a little girl, saying how some *awful* boys had ruined her *nice* party. He'd been looking for all the wrong explanations in all the wrong directions—obviously the girl had run away to Hollywood.

"Believe it," Joey said flatly. He shook his head in deep disappointment. "You adults, you think you're so smart. She was good at that Miss Perfect act—she had you all fooled. That interested me at first—you can see why it might—but she was out of *my* league, man. She was out of everybody's league." He shook his head and stared down at the table.

Matt leaned back in his chair. Vic Moss's assessment of Chrissie Falconer had been a true one. He had thought that he was unshockable, but this threw him completely. Not the facts—but the façade.

"The secret life of kids," he murmured.

Joey's head came up. He began a slow smile. "Yeah," he said softly. "Peekaboo."

For once they were all together for dinner at Perkins Point that night, and because Jess had been home all afternoon she made a special effort with the meal. Well, she thought to herself, if Jason thinks I was cooking all day, he won't suspect me of having searched his room, will he? The others would just get the benefit and never know why.

But things had not started well. Jason startled her in the kitchen by coming up behind her and taking hold of her shoulders as she stirred the gravy. "You smell good enough to eat, yourself," he said into her ear.

"Why, thank you, kind sir," she'd said.

"Don't let us interrupt you," Tom had announced in snide tones from the door, making them both jump. "But we've set the table and we're ready when you are."

She'd turned and glared, not allowing her heart to soften at the sight of him. He was obviously suffering the aftereffects of his night before. Served him right, too. The idea! Egging George Putnam on in his drunken way to hassle Geoff, dragging him out of the restaurant like a common criminal and demanding to know why he carried a gun in his car. Tom had been in on it, she knew it. He'd left with George only minutes before. Tom didn't like Geoff, for some reason, and that had been his funny little way of showing it. The stinker! And he *knew* she'd guessed his part in it—because he'd carefully avoided her all day.

"Had a bad day at Black Rock?" she'd inquired sweetly. "I could make you an Alka-Seltzer, if you'd prefer that to roast beef *au jus* with Yorkshire pudding and apple pie after."

"Oh, God," Tom said, turning away. "Leave it alone."

"With pleasure," she snapped.

Jason raised an eyebrow. "Lover's tiff?"

"No—just general disappointment in the standards some people fail to set for social behavior!" she said, raising her voice to end in a shout to make sure Tom heard her.

As a result of this odd beginning, dinner was conducted in a rather grim silence—the others aware that something was wrong but not certain enough of what it was to venture conversation, lest they inadvertently set off the fireworks that were obviously primed to explode at the least thing.

"Would it burden you too much to pass the green beans?" Jess asked Tom icily.

"I think I can manage it," Tom responded grimly.

Pat, Chip, and Linda exchanged puzzled glances.

"How's the hangover?" Jason asked finally, trying just a little too hard to be cheerful. "Still throbbing away?"

Tom shot him a venomous look. "Nice of you to care."

Jason managed to look arch as well as smug, glancing around at the others. "Well, you will go out on these toots—"

"I did not go on a toot, a tweet, or any other form of aural expression," Tom informed him with some menace. "I had a few beers with a buddy, that's all."

"A few dozen," Jess snorted.

"It could have been a few hundred and still been none of your business," Tom growled. Wasn't it just his luck that everyone was home for dinner that night, so that they could sit and gloat, full of their natural good health with not a throbbing head or swaying stomach among them. "Leave me alone."

"With pleasure," Jess said. "I just wish you'd left Geoff alone."

"Ditto," mumbled Tom.

"And what's that supposed to mean?" Jess inquired.

"Nothing."

"What?"

"Don't shout!"

"I would like to know—"

"So would we all," Jason said brightly.

So Jess told them.

Jason looked puzzled. "The vet carries a gun?" he asked. "That seems a bit extreme."

"Not really," Jess said impatiently. "He needs it in his practice. For his own protection when he has to make an emergency night call."

"And to put down animals, I suppose," Pat said.

"But why a gun?" Jason persisted. "Don't they have some special thing they use? I seem to remember at horse races—"

"A humane killer? That's just another kind of gun you use point-blank," Chip said. "A pistol would be better, you could use it at a distance. You wouldn't want to get too close to a rabid dog, for instance."

"Surely we don't get many rabid dogs around here," Linda said, looking uneasy.

"Oh, I don't know," Tom said. "There are a few walking around on two legs."

Jess had been speaking without looking in his direction, but now she turned to face him. "You know, you are being pretty silly about all this. What, exactly, do you have against Geoff Kelly?"

Tom shrugged. "I don't like him."

"Why?"

"I don't know. He seems . . . I don't know. Wrong. Too . . ."

"Too what?"

"Too many teeth," Tom finally summoned up.

Everybody laughed, and some of the tension eased.

Tom was slightly encouraged. "George wanted to take a test firing of that gun, but—"

"What for?" Jason asked.

"Well—for comparison with the bullet that killed the guy they found under the ice, for one thing."

The tension returned.

"Are you telling me that George suspects *Geoff* of killing that gangster?" Jess asked, astonished.

"Was it the same caliber?" Jason asked.

"George thought so," Tom said. "A .38."

"Saturday night special," Jason said reflectively. "Just about the most common handgun there is out there."

"Exactly," Tom said. "All the more reason to test every one they find."

"Need a court order or something like that, wouldn't

they? Reasonable suspicion and all that," Chip said. "Now, aside from having too many teeth, what exactly makes the deputy so suspicious of our earnest young veterinarian?"

"Well—George wouldn't say much, but it has something to do with a list he has of single men between twenty-five and forty who've moved into the area in the last two years," Tom explained.

"Say, I'd like a look at that list," Pat said with a ladylike leer.

"Me, too," Chip said with a grin.

"That list would include me," Jason said slowly. "What's the list mean? What's it for?"

"I have no idea," Tom said.

"What about those who have moved *out* in the last two years?" Jason persisted.

Tom shrugged, a motion which obviously did not help his hangover. In fact, he was beginning to think it was really the flu, probably caught during that insane ski trip to the school. Another fine mess Jess had gotten him into. He scowled at her.

"Well?" Jason said.

"Well what?"

"Did the list include men between twenty-five and forty who have moved *away* in the past two years?"

"He didn't say anything about that. Or, if he did, I don't remember," Tom growled. He threw his napkin down. "Why would it matter, anyway, if they've moved away? The hell with this. I'm going to bed. I think I'm coming down with something."

"Probably got caught in a draft," Jason called after him. "Draft beer, that is."

"He doesn't look very well," Linda said with some concern.

"It's just a hangover." Chip was dismissive.

"Tom doesn't usually get ill," Pat said, looking worried.

"He doesn't usually get so drunk, either," Jess snapped. "Pass the potatoes, please."

"You're not very sympathetic," Chip said disapprovingly. "What's with you and Tom, anyway?"

"There's nothing 'with' us—I just think he's behaving abominably, that's all. I finally meet someone who's pretty special—"

"You're not the only one to think so," Linda said. "I hear Geoff Kelly has been quite the heartbreaker since he arrived. His receptionist seemed to have the inside track at first, but now every available female with a sick animal runs the risk—"

"If it be risk," Pat put in.

"—of getting asked out," Linda finished.

"He seems to be sizing up the entire town," Chip said.

"Are you saying I'm just one on his list?" Jess asked.

"It's just as well to be warned," Pat told her gently. "If he's the kiss-and-run type, well, fine—as long as you know."

"Well," Jess said smugly. "He hasn't started to run yet. He's taking me into Grantham on Friday night to see a show. So there."

"So he's spending serious money on you?" Jason put in. "That says something."

"Ah—but what?" Chip asked. "That's the question."

"He thinks I'm devastatingly attractive, intellectually stimulating, and as sexy as all get-out," Jess said.

They stared at her. "He told you all that?" Pat asked.

"Of course not," Jess said with a grin. "But he will, he will."

Tom, pausing on the stairs, grimaced. He wished George had test-fired that gun of Kelly's—preferably straight into the vet's knee. A man who coolly dispatches animals every day probably has a hard heart, he thought. Probably he could kill a man as easily as a rabid dog. But he didn't really believe it. He knew the source of his animosity toward Geoff Kelly— simple jealousy—and he wasn't proud of it. He reached his room and shut the door on the sound of the talk and laughter from below.

"I've got to get out of this place," he muttered, throwing himself on the bed. "I really do."

When Jess tapped on his door an hour later and then looked in, she saw him asleep, still fully dressed. She slipped in and removed his shoes, then pulled one of the quilts she had made for him up to his chin. You bad-tempered pain in the ass, she thought, looking down at him. Why do I care what you think? She went out, closing the door quietly behind her, then nearly jumped a foot when she turned and found Jason behind her.

"Is he all right?" he asked.

"I think so," she said edgily. She was certain Jason had guessed she'd been in his room that afternoon. Something about the way he'd kept looking at her during dinner. "He's asleep."

"I certainly would like to know more about that list," Jason said.

"Why?"

He shrugged. "I just don't like the thought of being on somebody's list, that's all."

"It could be a perfectly innocent list—"

"Oh, come on. It's something to do with that murder, isn't it?"

"Yes, well—why should you worry? You arrived *after* that man was killed, didn't you?"

"I don't know. When was he killed exactly?"

"I don't know—exactly," Jess admitted. "But they said the body had been under the ice for . . . weeks and weeks . . . and you came in the middle of November."

"Mmmm. So, you see, I could have killed him on the way in to town, right? Hey, mister, is this the way to the high school, bang bang, and I drive off singing?"

She had to smile. "I suppose so. If you're the kind of person to kill perfect strangers for no reason at all."

"Oh, I am, I definitely am. Can't you tell?"

"Why—have you got some guilty secret?" Jess asked before she could stop herself.

"Actually I am an escaped prisoner from the chain gang," Jason said, adopting a bizarre leer.

"Oh—then you'd be on the escape-from-the-chain-gang list," Jess said. "As opposed to the Colombian drug dealer list or the big bad bank robber list."

"Of course," Jason said, feigning relief. "Now, why couldn't I have realized that? Every man to his place." He went along to his door. "And this is mine. Care to come in for a nightcap?"

Jess just stared at him in astonishment—he'd never asked her into his room before.

"Or not, as the case may be," Jason said lightly, taking her silence as a refusal. With a faint smile he went inside, closing the door softly behind him.

What was going on? Was she sending out signals? Had she finally hit on the right perfume at last? She started along the corridor to the attic stairs, then stopped, appalled. Of course! Perfume!

When Jason had come down to dinner he'd made that comment to her about her smelling good. Oh, Lord—that was it! He'd smelled her perfume in his room—she always wore the same one, Anaïs, Anaïs, people often commented on how it reminded them of her. So he had known she'd been in his room.

The question was—did he know why?

TWENTY-EIGHT

The lab reports were back.

The "donor" of the semen on Chrissie Falconer's sheets had type AB negative blood, and there was a sufficient amount of the sample to get a DNA profile should it be necessary. In addition to the semen stains, there had been blond and dark pubic hairs, a couple of long blond hairs, and several short red hairs, all human. In addition to *those* there had also been animal hairs—dog, cat, and horse.

The collection of tablets found at Chrissie Falconer's party had yielded nothing spectacular—just the usual assortment of low-grade stimulants and mind-benders that were passing through the clubs right now. There was a note at the bottom, however.

> We noticed some dust in the bottom of one of the containers and analyzed that as well. There wasn't enough of it to really analyze in depth, but from what we could ascertain, it was a high-grade stimulant of considerable strength which had probably been contained in capsule form.

Matt stared at the sheets of paper. The dog hairs he could explain—Shandy, the family retriever. He hadn't seen a cat, nor had the Falconers mentioned one, but that didn't mean they didn't have one, cats often being furtive family members when dogs were around. But *horse*? A call to the Falconers elicited the information that yes, they had owned a cat but that it had died a few months ago, and yes, Chrissie did go riding, but only in the summer.

"I wish all my deductions could be as easy as this," Matt said, standing up and tossing the lab reports onto his desk.

As he and George started out the door, the phone rang and Tilly called him back. "It's Agent Brokaw," she said.

"Hey!" George said.

"I'll take it in my office," Matt said, scowling at George. "You go warm up the car."

When he joined George ten minutes later, Matt had a thoughtful look on his face. "Well?" George demanded.

Matt shrugged. "No news is good news," he said.

"What the hell does that mean?" George wanted to know.

"It means drive to the corner of Pacific and Main," Matt said, leaning back and closing his eyes. "Wake me when we get there."

"It's only going to take five minutes," George said grumpily.

"Then drive slow," Matt suggested.

Twenty minutes later, Matt settled a hip on the metal examination table and spoke wearily. "Come on, Dr. Kelly—I can stand here as long as you can, so you might as well get to it. You're the "J" that Chrissie Falconer was expecting to see on the Friday night before the blizzard, weren't you?"

"What do you mean, the jay? Is that some kind of local slang?" The vet had been annoyed at their intrusion, coming as it had when he had a waiting room full of clients, and even more annoyed when they refused to wait or come back later.

"I mean that in her diary Chrissie referred to her current

lover by the initial 'J.' But she was a terrible speller. It was you, wasn't it? Geoffrey with a 'G,' not a 'J.'"

Kelly turned away and looked out of the window at the snow-heaped parking lot beside his building. "Yes. *Yes*, all right, Chrissie and I—were good friends."

"Where is she?"

"I have no idea."

"When was the last time you saw her?"

"I don't know, exactly."

"I think you do. I think you *were* with her the night before she ran away. Was it Friday or Saturday night?"

There was a long silence. Then Kelly spoke, his tone resigned as he reached for a chair and sank down onto it. "Okay, I'll tell you what happened. But I promise you that when I left Chrissie, she was asleep in her own bed, breathing evenly, and perfectly all right—that is the honest truth."

"Go on."

"I met Chrissie last autumn. She had to bring Shandy in regularly for his shots. We were attracted to one another. She was . . . so perfect, like a soft peach at just . . . Anyway, it was such a strong physical attraction that it took us over. She knew her parents wouldn't approve, they had great plans for their darling girl that did not involve getting attached to a small-town vet twice her age. Frankly I thought the attraction was so intense that it would burn itself out pretty rapidly, but it didn't. I told her up front that I was married but separated—so she had no expectations. I'm always very honest about that."

"Nice of you."

"She was not a virgin, Sheriff," Kelly said with a steely note in his voice. "And it was not a romantic attachment. I was not the first and believe me, I wasn't going to be the last. That girl loved sex and everything to do with it. She craved physical adoration—and I did my best."

"Good for you," Matt said sarcastically. Always nice to hear about a man doing his best.

Kelly sighed and shook his head. "Anyway, yes, I went to see her on Friday night. And she was fine and everything was fine . . . and then, suddenly, after we'd made love . . . she had a seizure. An epileptic seizure. She'd told me about having what she called small attacks, and I'd assumed she meant some sort of dizzy spells or something similar. I wasn't prepared for anything like grand mal with all the trimmings. I panicked a bit, to be honest. I looked in her medicine cabinet and saw that her doctor had prescribed phenobarbital, a tiny dosage in tablet form. Well, there was no way I could have gotten pills into her. But I had phenobarb with me in the car—it's standard stuff—so I gave her a small, a very small, injection. And she came out of it just fine. She was absolutely fine. Awake, but sleepy—fully *compos mentis*, though. I wanted to call her doctor, of course, but she said it wasn't necessary, that all she needed was to rest, so I sat with her until she fell asleep. Her breathing and pulse were perfectly normal."

"Not exactly regulation, all this," Matt observed.

"No, I suppose not, although vets are allowed some latitude in human emergencies. The risk isn't with the authorities, it's in getting sued by the patient. But I *was* concerned about her. I was going to call her doctor once she was asleep—" He looked up, and Matt met his eyes. Green eyes, transparently honest if you believed in the tooth fairy, and worried now. Very worried.

"But you didn't."

"Well, frankly, I never got the chance. My beeper went and when I called in, it was Mandy saying that one of Riley Newcombe's herd was calving and it was a breech, so I had to go."

"Leaving Chrissie alone in the house."

"She was fine when I left, dammit. I wouldn't have left, otherwise."

"And what time did you leave?"

"It was just after ten-thirty. I got to the Newcombe farm just before eleven, and I was there for most of the night. You can check that. And you can check my beeper call with Mandy, my receptionist."

"Oh, I intend to, Dr. Kelly. I intend to check it *all*."

"The injection I gave Chrissie was no stronger than a Valium at best and certainly couldn't have harmed her. I'm not saying I wasn't concerned about her. I was. I called the house three or four times the next day, to urge her to see her doctor, but only got the answering machine."

"Did you leave a message?"

"No. I assumed her parents were back by then. She had expected them back on Saturday, although I should have realized the blizzard . . . Anyway, I think I assumed they'd taken her to the doctor and that was why the machine was on. I never really thought it through—I should have, but Saturday was a damned busy day. And I should have gone over there rather than telephoning, but—what would I have said to her parents if they had been there? What possible excuse could I have used for suddenly appearing at their door?"

"But they didn't get back."

"So I understand." He sighed again. "What I don't understand is how or why she's disappeared."

"Neither do I," Matt said. "You injected her with phenobarbital. Weren't you worried about it being affected by the other drugs?"

Kelly flushed suddenly, and it was all the more noticeable because of his previous pallor. It occurred to Matt that redheads must have a particularly difficult time when it came to lying. "Ah," Dr. Kelly said. "You know about those."

"I know that Chrissie was into something new, something dangerous—"

"Oh, no—it wasn't dangerous. At least, not to a normal person. Quite a few of her friends had taken it, apparently, with no problems."

"What was it—Ecstasy, Nexus, Bromo?"

"No—that is, similar in effect, but much more . . . how can I put it . . . much more concentrated. More *controlled*, somehow. Time-specific, too. The perfect drug for lunchtime sex. Great for the bored businessman who wanted to swing and still attend a board meeting in the afternoon. It was . . . very good, I must admit. Added to Chrissie's natural talent, well . . . "

Matt looked at Kelly in disgust. "You're quite a piece of work, aren't you?"

Kelly looked affronted. "She offered them to me, Sheriff, not the other way around. Kids are very savvy about this kind of thing these days. They're looking for new sensations all the time—and they find them. She said it was something someone at school was selling—"

"Did she say who?" Matt asked quickly.

"If she did I've forgotten it. The name meant nothing to me. She said she'd taken them several times and they really gave you a buzz."

"Taken what?"

"I have no idea what they were. She called them Little Wonders. Well, they might be wonderful for some people, including me, but I told Chrissie that she mustn't take them again. That attack scared the hell out of me. I told her that they could well be the cause of her epilepsy and that they might cause her real damage if she took any more. She argued with me, so I took away all she had, just in case."

"I'd like them, please."

"They're perfectly legal."

"Are you sure of that?" Matt stared at him until the vet shrugged and took out his wallet. He extracted a small plastic envelope and handed it over. Matt inspected it—there were three blue and pink capsules—then put it into his pocket. "Go on about that night, please."

"Well—we took one each, and she was right. It's amazing stuff. It worked very fast—a solid one-hour mind-high with every nerve ending singing the praises of nature, and then—bingo—straight again. It left you really clear, that was its

big advantage. I wasn't at all worried about driving or de-
livering that calf."

"I see. You say she argued with you about the pills being
dangerous. Is it possible that she held some back from you?
That she took another one after you left and felt equally confident to drive somewhere?"

"I doubt it. I think I eventually scared her enough to stop
her taking any more." Kelly frowned. "Maybe she didn't go
then. Maybe she went the next morning."

"No. We found a neighbor who noticed the garage door
open when he arrived home at three o'clock on Saturday
morning, so she must have left sometime between when you
left and then." He regarded the vet with some contempt.
"Why weren't you worried about leaving an eighteen-year-old
girl who'd just had an epileptic attack alone in a house with
no one to attend to her? What if she had another attack?"

Kelly stood up, shaking his head. "Because I was sure the
injection I gave her would have prevented that. She was fine
when I left her. Just fine."

Matt straightened up and headed for the door. He took a
step out into the hall, then turned back. "Tell me, Dr.
Kelly—would you have left a *dog* alone under the same circumstances?"

When Matt got into the car he glared at George. "Remind
me to reregister Max with another veterinarian," he said in
disgust. He didn't care whether Kelly was competent as an
animal doctor or not—as a man, Kelly had not impressed
him. Obviously he was a natural philanderer with a fine line
in self-justification, and it seemed to Matt that if he would
excuse one lapse he would just as easily excuse another. Max
might just be a beat-up old tomcat to some people, but to
Matt he was a friend and companion. You didn't entrust a
friend to someone used to making excuses.

"Oh," George said, obviously disappointed.

"What?"

George looked embarrassed. "Well—his receptionist—"

"Yes, who is she?" Matt asked. "I thought she looked familiar."

"Mandy Turkle," George said. He'd stayed out in the reception area talking to the girl and staving off the glares of the waiting-room inhabitants, both two- and four-legged. "Not all that bright, but what a pair of—"

"Turkle," Matt said, as if that explained everything. Her resentful manner when he'd asked for verification of Kelly's Friday night story had been definitely negative. "No wonder she looked at me like that."

"Now, come on, Turkles aren't *all* bad," George protested. "Some of them are really good people."

"The trouble is, you can't always tell just by looking," Matt reminded him. "Kelly looks okay, but he's really one of life's pleasure-seekers—only out for what he can get, I think. He may be an okay vet—although he'll never be a match for Dr. Marlow—but I wouldn't leave him alone with a wife or daughter of mine."

"But Mandy likes him," George said in surprise. "She thinks he's wonderful. In fact, I think she's in love with him. Every time I tried to get her interested in me, she started talking about him."

"Too bad," Matt said, suppressing a smile. Poor George, outflanked again. They were all waiting for the day when George would realize that bragging about himself was not the best way to interest nubile young women—at least, not the nubile young women of today. George started the car and backed out onto the road.

"Well, maybe Mandy is one of his conquests," Matt said. "He seems to like them young. He was definitely the one who slept with Chrissie before she ran away. They'd been having quite an affair, according to him." Briefly he relayed his conversation with the vet.

"I don't know about that younger-woman stuff," said

George when Matt had finished. "Jess Gibbons must be coming up to thirty."

"What's Jess Gibbons got to do with it?" Matt asked.

"Why, he was having dinner with her the other night," George said, getting more outraged the more he thought about it. "When we found that gun of his, she was with him. How about that? No sooner does one run out on him than he starts up with another."

"Do you think that's what happened?"

"What?"

"That Chrissie ran out on him? Maybe when he met Jess Gibbons, he decided to dump Chrissie, and told her so that Friday night, and that's why she ran away. Maybe she was more in love with him than he thought." Matt scowled. "I wish I'd known about Jess before I talked to him."

"You want to go back?" George asked, slowing the car.

Matt shook his head. "No, go on. I'll let him stew for a while, then we'll call him in for further questioning. Meanwhile, I want to go back to the office and call the state lab. I've got some nice pink and blue pills, and it seems to me that there might be a way of tracing who made them. If we're lucky."

Jess went into school that afternoon to see if the work on the roof had progressed sufficiently for her to resume teaching after the weekend. She found Digger Wells walking the upper floor, keeping an eye on things. Full of importance, he assured her that "the seal" would be sufficient for him to have her rooms to full heat by then.

"As full as it gets, you mean," she said with a smile. "Now, if someone would care to replace all the windows with new frames . . ."

"Fat chance," Digger said. "I still don't believe they're actually going to put on a whole new roof next summer."

"Probably the law of diminishing returns," Jess suggested. "Cheaper to replace it than to keep repairing it.

Although to the bureaucratic mind, that's the wrong way around."

"I don't know," Digger said, gazing upward. "Sure it caved in, but the circumstances was unusual. Modern stuff sometimes ain't as good, ain't as solid as what they built in the old days. They could fix it and in a few more years—blooey!"

"We'll just have to cross our fingers and carry big umbrellas, I suppose," Jess said. "Anyway, you promise I can get back to what passes for normal in this place next Monday?"

"Barring further incidents of the type we had, yes," Digger said, hedging his bets. "I mean, another blizzard could put us right back, you know?"

With this cheery thought, Jess fled the chilly upper regions for the familiar shabby warmth of the faculty lounge.

It was past eleven and most teachers were in their classrooms, trying to dun a little learning into the brains they optimistically hoped were lurking under this year's hairstyles. Jess still smiled every time she thought of Betty Hardwicke's description of one of her students as "a clump of hair with a boy hanging from it."

She herself tended to get the more conventional female students in her classes, as "the wild ones" were more into technology and political science than cooking and sewing. Sometimes she felt like a blacksmith or a thatcher, teaching old dying crafts to a devoted few. But there had been a recent resurgence of interest in the domestic arts, a backlash from the materialistic eighties and a sign of the ecologically aware nineties, she supposed. Or perhaps it was a sign that the feminist movement had grown up sufficiently to support the notion that the woman who stayed at home and the woman who went to work had equal dignity and status. Whatever the source, she appreciated the fact that quilts and quilting were achieving artistic appreciation. Indeed, she and Margaret Toby both had quilts hanging in Daria Grey's art gallery, and several had been sold for quite amazing prices the previous summer. The fiber arts in general were beginning to be reviewed in some of the more prestigious magazines. Maybe the mainstream was wending their way at last. Maybe she could eventually teach part-time and devote more of her energy to her own work, to create—

"Now, what could produce a smile like that, I wonder? Thinking of me?" It was Jason, of course, standing in front of her and holding out a cup of coffee from the machine.

"No—I was planning a new quilt," Jess admitted, taking the coffee gratefully. She was still chilled from standing in the freezing upper hall. "Thanks."

He sank down on the old sofa beside her. "Tom didn't show up this morning."

"I know. I left him at home in bed with a hot water bottle and a stack of old *Scientific Americans*," Jess said. "Feeling very sorry for himself, I might add."

"Not just a hangover, then," Jason observed. "Flu?"

"Maybe. I don't know. He's a stranger to me at the moment," Jess said. "He's been behaving so oddly."

Jason shrugged. "He's a complex man."

She stared at him over the edge of her cup. "Tom? Complex?"

"Sure. Underneath that loony exterior lurks an even loonier interior," Jason said. "He's too bright to be teaching high school, but possibly not quite bright enough to achieve funding for research—presuming he has a subject for research. He needs direction, encouragement—and he's not likely to get it teaching in a small-town high school. I can't work out what keeps him here—he could be earning a lot more money in industry."

"Could he? I don't know anything about physics," Jess admitted.

"Neither do I, but I do know about chemistry, and this coffee is definitely a precipitate of gluck—speaking technically, of course." He put his own cup down with a shudder.

Jess laughed. "You seem to know a different Tom."

"Maybe I see him differently simply because he's unfamiliar to me. You've known him all your life, haven't you?"

"More or less."

"That's the problem. You don't see—"

"Thank God—it's cooler in here!" Pat Morrison burst in, looking very flushed and cross. She threw herself down in an armchair opposite them. "I don't know what Digger is up to, but it's about a hundred and forty-three degrees in the art room—I dismissed my class early for lunch before we all melted into the floorboards." She puffed out her cheeks and blew her hair up off her forehead.

"Digger's on the top floor, supervising the builders, although they don't know it," Jess said. "It's freezing up there."

Jason stood up. "He's probably blasting three floors of heat into two floors of classrooms. I'll track him down."

Pat watched him go. "That's not like him. Usually he'd just sit there and give us a lecture on the dynamics of heating. Or the state of the Union."

"I know." Jess looked after Jason. "I'm beginning to think I'm a very, very bad judge of character."

The noon bell rang through the corridors and after a minute or two, more teachers arrived in the lounge, looking flushed and warm. Somebody even suggested opening a window.

"I think we're all in danger of catching pneumonia tomorrow," Chip said reflectively. "Getting overheated all day here, and then standing around on the ice all day—"

"Good heavens—it's the Ice Festival tomorrow!" Jess said.

Pat raised an eyebrow. "Had you forgotten?"

"Yes, to be honest."

"Do you think Tom will be well enough to help us with the sculpture?" Chip asked worriedly. "We need everybody."

"Oh, I think so. He wasn't running a fever or anything. I think he's what my mom used to call 'peepsick'—like a little bird going peep, peep, peep, wanting to be fed and comforted."

"And did you?"

"Did I what?"

"Did you feed and comfort him?"

"I told him there was food in the cupboard and fridge," Jess said.

"Still angry with him?"

"Well—not happy. We're speaking—and that's all." Jess sighed. "I just don't understand him."

Pat's eyes twinkled. "You always used to."

"I know. That's why . . ." Jess caught sight of Pat's expression. "What? What's so funny?"

"Oh, nothing. There are none so blind . . ."

"Are you entering the Ski-doo race tomorrow, Jess?" Milly Hackabush asked.

"You bet," Jess said. "I told you last year I'd beat you."

"And you didn't," Milly laughed.

"Well, I will this year," Jess said stoutly. For Jess the Ski-doo races were one of the highlights of the Ice Festival. She had been entering them ever since she was a teenager, and had yet to achieve first place. Neither, for that matter, had Milly—but they had a running competition of their own each year. They mostly ended up vying for last place in the early elimination runs.

"Now, now, ladies," Claude Trickett said in passing. "Talons in, please. You know I'm going to win, so why argue?"

"No," Decker Mosely said in his deep, grave voice. "I will win. It is manifest destiny. Resign now, Trickett."

Claude grinned. "The hell I will."

"I am taking bets on those teachers foolish enough to risk their necks on the Ski-doo track tomorrow," Betty Hardwicke announced. "I will list odds on the bulletin board before three o'clock this afternoon." They all looked at her in amazement. She smiled demurely. "I worked it all out on the computer. *I* intend to be the real winner out of all this."

"Roll on tomorrow," Claude said. And he winked at Jess.

TWENTY-NINE

It was a bright blue day. The sun shone down and managed to melt a few stray edges of snow, but the air was still so frigid that it made very little headway against the huge rim of snow that surrounded the area cleared for the festival. The inner edge of the bay was now festive with many colors made even more vivid by the clarity of the morning. The Ice Festival always began early because of the shortness of the day, so things were in full swing by nine o'clock, many people bringing a portable breakfast with them so as to enjoy everything from start to finish.

The few remaining huts of the ice fishers had been joined by booths dragged out on sledges. These were draped with bunting and their occupants were busy selling many items: hot, cold, consumable, or collectible.

Down toward Paradise Island stood the huge blocks of compressed snow which the sculpting teams were already hewing into shape while covertly eyeing each other's efforts and trying to ascertain ultimate designs from the first hacks and slices.

The surface of the racetrack gleamed where the bulldozer's

blade had scraped it smooth. It was a long, wide oval at the back of the grounds, allowing plenty of room for the Ski-doos to maneuver, which was just as well, because while the first heats were generally conducted in an orderly manner, the final race inevitably bore the stamp of a day's alcoholic consumption.

There was quite a crowd gathering for the first wife-sliding competition. In this, wives were seated on the ice on top of burlap sacks which their husbands swung around several times and then let go at the ultimate moment. There were plenty of fallers as wives shot in all directions and cannoned into the crowds, but most of them managed to stay on the marked-out track. The first heat was won—as usual—by Frank Nixey, who managed to slide Trixie some forty-three feet by virtue of whipping the burlap sack on which she sat with a snap that nearly dislocated both his wrists. He straightened with a groan, and had the satisfaction of seeing her whiz into the lead and then into the legs of Councillor Berringer, with whom Frank had been having a running battle about an extra tariff imposed on his garage. Berringer went down with Trixie in a flailing knot of arms and legs, much to the consternation of Mrs. Berringer, who'd thought she had him under control for once.

"Just like you to get tangled up with a fast woman," she shouted, clipping him on the side of his knitted cap. "Can't take my eyes off you for a minute, can I?"

"Nice one, Frank!" shouted Harlow Wilcox, who had taken the morning off from the Golden Perch and looked like a leftover Santa, stuffed as he was into his red ski outfit. Only lacked the beard and the bells, someone said. The bag of goodies by his side was yet another of the many pretty young girlfriends he seemed to have standing by for festive occasions.

"How does he do it?" Frog Bartlett wondered aloud.

"Do what?" Shad Billmore wanted to know. This was his first Ice Festival and he was already regretting the effort he'd

made to rise early. He had to admit it looked attractive—
rather like a medieval fair, including the roasting pig which
someone was turning on a spit over a specially built barbecue—but as far as he was concerned, snowmen were for children and wife-sliding was definitely antifeminist, even
though the poor dears seemed to enjoy it.

"Get all those pretty girls to hang around him," Frog said
glumly. "He's big and fat—"

"And rich," Shad pointed out.

"Just runs a damn bar."

"And rich," repeated Shad.

"I guess," conceded Frog, who wandered away toward the
barbecue stand for a bucket of drumsticks. An unusual
breakfast, but one designed to keep a man warm until lunch,
when the ribs would be ready. Of course, later on, the ice
around the barbecues would become slippery, what with
meltwater from the reflected heat and spilled barbecue
sauce. Procuring refreshments then would become another
spectator sport, but for the moment it was relatively safe to
approach.

The big danger, aside from the specific events, was from
children, and it seemed to Matt that most of his and his
deputies' time was spent in catching and admonishing
them. Some on skates, most on foot, and all moving fast, the
kids darted in and out of the crowds, shrieking and yelling
and snowballing. Some years there was only clear ice on the
bay and snowballs were few, but though the bulldozers had
done their best, there were those high dunes of blizzard snow
left around the edges of the festival that could be drawn on
for ammunition—and the packing was good, too. Icy spher-
oids shot everywhere, making life more adventurous than it
need have been for the fairgoers.

Jess and the others were hard at work on their snow sculpture, using a two-handled saw to take out the larger sections.
They set these carefully aside to saw into blocks for later
construction. Everyone had turned out, even Tom, although

he looked a little pale, still, and hadn't much to say for him-self.

"Maybe we should have gone for something simpler," Chip said, straighening up to wipe his forehead.

"Oh, come on, drippy," Pat said encouragingly. "I thought you were super-fit and ready for anything."

"Anything athletic," he agreed. "But this artistic stuff is too much like hard work."

"Oh, shut up and keep scraping," Jess said, digging him in the ribs. "We don't want to lose the trophy, do we?" The trophy she spoke of had been residing on the mantelpiece at Perkins Point for the past year—a huge white plastic snow-man with a nauseating grin.

"Oh, could we?" Tom asked. "Please?"

"Absolutely not!" Pat cried. "He may not be beautiful—"

"There's no maybe about it," Linda muttered.

"—but he represents a triumph of the artistic spirit," Pat concluded, and was immediately inundated with snowballs from the others.

Old Fishguts was enjoying himself. Having assembled a goodly part of his regalia for the earlier exorcising of Frank Nixey's fishing hole, he had decided to get it all out and do the thing right for the festival. As a result he was a thor-oughly splendid multicolored figure, moving among the crowd with a tail of fascinated children strung out behind him. He tried to maintain a cheerful attitude, but some-thing bothered him. There was a bad feel to the ice beneath his feet, and tension in the air—as if a storm were due. The weather report, however, had been for clear and dry. He kept smiling, but could not keep his feet still on the ice. It itched but could not be scratched.

Claude Trickett and Fred Naughton were standing by the Ski-doos, which were drawn up in ranks near the starting line. "I see you've got a new model," Fred said, eyeing the red machine over which Claude bent, adjusting something.

Claude straightened. "I had to do something to get an advantage, didn't I?" he said. "I'm tired of getting everybody else's ice spray in the face."

"Set you back much?" Fred asked, walking around the little machine admiringly.

"Too much," Claude said. "As usual."

"Yeah, I know what you mean," Fred agreed. "Still, you get other use out of it, don't you?"

"Sure. It came in real useful after the blizzard." Claude straightened up and stuck the polishing rag into his mackinaw pocket. "Only way I could get around—my house is back on Woodhaven Lane, and that's always the first road closed and the last one opened."

"Wasn't much better in town, you know," Fred said, and proceeded to tell Claude far more than Claude wanted to know about how difficult life had been on Firwood Avenue, Blackwater, during and after the blizzard.

About midday, Matt turned at the sound of a friendly voice and encountered the cheerful faces of Jack Stryker and his fiancée, Kate Trevorne. "You made it!" he said, banging Stryker on the shoulder enthusiastically.

"Why is it every time I see you, you beat the living hell out of me?" Stryker inquired with a grin as he rubbed his arm.

"You just have that effect on me, I guess," Matt said.

"He has that effect on everyone," Kate commented. She was a bright girl with a bright eye. Her curly brown hair was almost confined under a knitted cap, and she wore a red toggle coat. "One glance from those beady eyes and they're punching him out."

"My eyes aren't beady," Stryker protested.

"No, they're kind of pink and watery at the moment," she agreed, banging her arms together against the cold. "My Lord, I always forget what it's like up here. Ten minutes on the ice and I'm freezing to death already!"

"I liked it better in the summer," Stryker said. His parka

was more suited to city than country temperatures. "Let's go home."

"Oh, don't be such a wimp," Matt said, knowing Stryker was nothing of the kind.

"Yeah, okay. Listen, I brought you that information about those small-volume chemical suppliers you asked for, including the home numbers," Stryker said, handing Matt an envelope. "And when I dropped by your office on the way over here, there was a fax for you from the state forensic lab, so I told your deputy—whatsisname—Duff?—that I'd play mailman."

"Thanks. What does it say?" Matt asked.

"There are a lot of words I couldn't read, and one I could—overtime. They seem to be cross with you," Styker said, turning away to survey the scene. "I can't believe all this," he said. "It's eerie, seeing it frozen over and people and things on top of it when a few months ago I was swimming *through* it." He glanced down at the ice under his feet. "Are you sure it's safe?" He bounced a little. "It gives," he said, looking rather alarmed.

"Not much," Matt said, folding up the papers and stuffing them inside his jacket. "It's over two feet thick, Jack—you're not going to fall through. Come and have something to eat."

They approached the food area, Stryker taking each step with immense caution. He eyed the structure supporting the rotating spit, which by then had warmed itself about four inches into the ice. "I suppose we'd better get some before it goes through."

"Stop kvetching," Kate said. "That smells wonderful—whose recipe is it this year?"

"Mr. Naseem's. Bit of a cultural problem there—he would have preferred lamb rather than a pig—"

"Oh, of course," Kate said.

"But he bowed to convention in the end, which was

damned nice of him," Matt said, steering him closer. "Daria! Look who's here!"

Daria Grey, her face pink from the heat, was taking her turn at the barbecue, basting the rapidly diminishing pig from a large bucket of sauce while Harlow Wilcox hacked pieces off and placed them on the plates held out by the people who stood around with eager and hungry faces. "Hi!" she shouted, waving her ladle and managing to splash herself with barbecue sauce.

"She's just about finished her stint," Matt said. "I think Mrs. Toby takes over from her in a few minutes. We'd better get ours while we have a friend on the ladle."

"I'll get the plates," Stryker said, reaching for his wallet. The food arrangement at the barbecue was that you bought a plate, and then could have it filled as often as you liked from the spit or from the constantly replenished buffet table. Alternatively you could buy a waxed bucket of ribs or drumsticks, or anything from pizza slices to doughnuts to hot dogs to hush puppies at the other food stands.

When the four of them had secured their portions they wandered over to the racetrack, where one of the Ski-doo semifinal heats was about to take off. The snarling buzz of the Ski-doos was deafening, as eight abreast stood revving and ready to go.

"Go, Jess!" shouted Daria, waving to Jess Gibbons, who waved back and nearly missed the start. The starting pistol went off with a crack, and the little machines shot forward with ferocious roars, throwing a glittering shower of ice crystals into the air behind them.

Jess had been astonished to find herself in a semifinal heat, having seen Milly Hackabush off when the latter's old green machine had finally given up the ghost on the third circuit of their first heat. She herself had managed to maneuver between Art Turkle and Fred Naughton and secure a place in the first four, right behind Tyrone Molt. She had shuttled between the snow sculpture and the racetrack, keeping up with other heats as best she could.

Now she was up against seven more who wanted to grind her into the ice—including her prospective brother-in-law, Dominic Pritchard, and Debbie Robinson, the most daredevil girl on the bay. With Debbie in the running she didn't have a chance of making it to the finals, but having gotten this far she was going to give it all she had.

She couldn't see who the others were. Riding a Ski-doo on ice was far more risky than skimming over nice soft snow, and as a result everyone had to wear protective headgear. The rule didn't specify which type of headgear, so several of the riders were topped by full motorcycle helmets, while others opted for jockey helmets and goggles. Jess herself wore her cycle helmet—she often cycled to school in the summer—and an old cashmere scarf wound several times around her face, so that only her eyes showed, protected by ski goggles. It was fortunate, she thought, as they rounded their first turn, that nobody was in it for looks.

As they completed the first lap in a blur, she caught sight of Tom, hands jammed in pockets, watching her intently, his face pale above the dark blue and green of his ski suit. He looked stricken, and she wondered why on earth he bothered to watch if it worried him so much.

Then she was rounding the end turn again, roaring into the backstretch, the wind of her forward progress icing its way in tiny lances between every gap in scarf and helmet. Her eyes watered with the cold and the need to hold on tight to the vibrating, shaking, skidding little monster that at any moment threatened to throw her to the winds.

As they came up on the far turn, a machine came up from nowhere and hung close on her inside. Suddenly it swerved and began to force her to the side, driving her closer and closer to the high icy banks of snow that surrounded the track. Wide and wider she swung, shouting through her scarf at whoever it was to give her room. But the machine—

ridden by someone in a visored motorcycle helmet—kept relentlessly forcing her out, further and further, away from the smooth bulldozed track and onto the rough surface of the unprepared ice.

"Stop it!" she screamed. "Stop it!"

She tried to swerve, slow down, speed up—but it was no good. He—if it was a he—was pushing her further and further away from the safety of the track. She tried to pull her ignition safety cord out, but it wouldn't come. Suddenly a white wall of snow was in front of her. She tried to skid sideways but the steering wouldn't respond, it was frozen, stuck . . . she couldn't turn away. Just then there was a low spot in the banked snow and rather than going into it, she went up and over it in a flying leap. Her ignition safety pulled free and she parted company with her Ski-doo, hitting the ice hard and at speed. She slithered forward, spinning and tumbling, then felt rather than saw or heard the ice begin to go mushy beneath her. She began to slow as slush built up around her. This would save her, she thought with relief.

But it was too late. As she continued forward, the ice beneath the slush began breaking up. It was cracking beneath her weight, glittering liquid seams opening like fast-moving zippers, spreading out around her, starlike.

The freezing water hit her like a fist, and she was going down, down into burning cold, into the deep black heart of the river channel that flowed out into the bay beneath the heavy gray carapace of the ice.

THIRTY

One, perhaps two minutes and she would be dead, from the cold of the water, from the water in her lungs, from the hard grip of something in the depths that held her down, held her under, kept her from the air and the light . . .

Jess turned and thrashed in the water, shocked by its icy grasp around her chest. She was encumbered by her thick sodden clothing and her heavy boots, and tried to rid herself of them, but her fingers were stiff from holding onto the Ski-doo, her muscles rigid with cramp from the cold. Desperate to reach the air before the ice closed over her, she felt herself being pulled at by the current that could take her away from the broken area to a place where the implacable armorplate of the frozen bay would trap her.

As she struggled to free herself, she could not, would not believe what she saw in the faint light, a shape so impossible, so horrible, that she closed her eyes to it and kicked away at it, wanting to scream. A face, a ravaged face, and long, flowing blond hair drifting and tumbling—

And then strong arms were around her and she was free, she was rising.

With a roaring gasp she broke into the air, supported and held by someone who was pushing aside the broken floes of ice, holding her against his chest, his own choking breath loud in her ear.

"Kick off your goddamn boots," said a wheezing voice. She tried to, but could only shed one. Her limbs were heavy and she could not seem to maneuver herself. Nothing seemed to be working properly, including her lungs.

"Chrissie . . . " she managed to whisper. "I saw Chrissie—"

"Take this!" someone shouted. "Grab this!" someone else cried. A long line of knotted scarves snaked its way over the ice, long poles snatched from fishing huts or food booths were extended toward them, what seemed like a hundred helping hands reached out for them.

Jess stretched forward, and as she wrapped clumsy hands around a scarf, so the person holding her grabbed the end of a wooden pole. Slowly, slowly, they were dragged from the sucking, greedy grasp of the ice-filled water, across the slushy thin ice, which groaned and cracked beneath them, to thicker, stronger, safer ice, where they could be helped up, supported, and wrapped in blankets that appeared from nowhere. Staggering, sliding, half falling but always held upright, they were guided across the ice to the warmth of the barbecue fire. Then and only then did Jess look up to see who had saved her.

It was Tom.

And though it seemed impossible, she was not surprised.

"This wind is bad," Stryker said. "Let's get them indoors."

"They should go to the hospital," Matt told him. He knew what shock from a sudden, icy immersion could do. "And as fast as possible."

"I'm all right," Jess tried to say, but could not get it out. She looked at Tom, who did not look at her, and apparently could not speak either.

"Oh, sweetie, are you all right?" It was Emily, pale, clutching at her, hugging her. Behind her, Dominic.

"I don't know . . ." Jess tried to say, trembling so badly she could not coordinate her lips. "Chrissie . . . I saw Chrissie . . ." But it came out in a garbled wail, and nobody seemed to understand.

"What happened?" people were shouting. "Are they all right?" "What happened?" "What happened?"

All around them a melee, chaos, as people crowded close, asking one another for details, talking, shouting, giggling with the humorless laughter of relief, of excitement, of shock. Jess felt herself shaking, could not stop, could not breathe—

She felt herself picked up bodily and looked up into Chip Chandler's face. He strode ahead, pushing through the crowd.

"Tom—" she managed to say as she snuggled into Chip's broad chest, grateful for his strength and his anger. It did seem to her that someone should be angry, and she was far too tired.

"They're bringing him," Chip said brusquely. "He's okay."

"Chip—I saw Chrissie," Jess managed to say through her chattering teeth. "And I think you'd better tell the sheriff."

"Sure, honey, sure."

"Ask Tom," Jess said, struggling. "Ask Tom!"

It was not until Jess and Tom were safe and in a police car on their way to the hospital that Matt looked around for the other Ski-doo rider. And found only confusion facing him.

Dominic Pritchard, who had been just ahead of Jess before the incident began, was pretty certain it was a red Ski-doo that had been directly behind him and next to Jess. But someone else thought it had been a black one. All were certain the rider wore a motorcycle helmet.

But Dominic was definite about what had happened. "It was deliberate," he said. "The guy forced her off the track, tried to tip her over." Several spectators agreed with him.

Frog Bartlett spoke up. "I was in the middle of the track," he growled. "It was deliberate, all right. The guy was driving to win and he didn't give a damn who got hurt. Jeez, it was just a semifinal heat."

"And who was it?" Matt asked. He turned to one of the judges.

"I got his number," Frog said. "Twenty-three."

"There! Over there!" Dominic started to run after a figure that was hurrying from the scene. Several others joined in the chase, which was brisk but brief. Dominic marched the figure back toward the sheriff, rage in every line of his body. They could see him and then hear him cursing steadily as he forced the helmeted number twenty-three to face the sheriff.

"Don't blame him for trying to get the hell out of here," Frog said. Everybody murmured agreement. The Ice Festival was for fun, not for glory.

"Well?" Matt took hold of the helmet visor and pushed it up. A girl's face looked out at him, half-defiant, half-terrified.

"Mandy!" said Geoff Kelly, who had been one of the men who'd joined Dominic in the chase. "My God, Mandy! You nearly killed her!"

The girl pulled her helmet off. "I didn't mean to, I didn't mean to!" she said, tears of anger and frustration running down her cheeks. "I just wanted to beat her."

"And maybe break her neck in the bargain?" demanded Emily Gibbons. "My God, let me at her—" She started forward.

"Okay, okay—settle down," Matt said, grabbing Emily's shoulder before she could scratch the eyes out of her sister's near killer.

"She could have turned back," Mandy insisted. "There was room, plenty of room. She *could* have turned but she didn't. She just went straight on."

"I can't believe you'd do something like that," Geoff Kelly kept saying. Matt turned to him.

"Not *all* cats are alike in the dark, are they?" he said. "Some of them have sharper claws than others. I'd have thought you'd have realized that at some time in your . . . career."

Kelly flushed. "Are you charging her with anything?"

"It depends," Matt said, letting go of Mandy. Obviously the negative side of this Turkle had momentarily taken over. Whether charging her with something—he wasn't sure what—would make her better or worse was hard to say. Women in love, he thought. No sense at all. "Why don't you take her home while I decide?"

"But I—"

"Geoff, please . . ." Mandy said tearfully.

"Oh, all right," Kelly said gracelessly. "Come on." He took hold of the girl's arm and led her away.

"But it was attempted murder!" Emily Gibbons said. "Arrest her!"

"No—she was right," Dominic said reluctantly. "Jess *did* have time to turn back, and she didn't. It looked like there was something wrong with her Ski-doo steering. I could see her struggling with it."

"Oh," said Emily.

"There are several more heats to run," May Berringer said diffidently. "Or should we just forget the whole thing?"

"No—you go on with the races," Matt said. "The break in the ice is far enough away for safety, I think."

"What do you mean, you *think*?" Stryker asked nervously. He was strictly a city-streets kind of man—all this nature stuff made him antsy. You had no control over it, it just sort of swept down and blew you away to Oz or drowned you or squashed you or made you fall on your ass. Goddamn treachery, everywhere you looked, and changing, always changing, not a leaf stood still.

"Let's move back onto the land," he said, edging sideways.

"Don't worry," Matt said. "You're safe if you stay on this

side of the snowbanks. It's odd that the ice should be thin over there, though . . ."

"There's something down there," said a voice. Matt turned to find Chip Chandler standing behind him. "They both saw it, they both told me."

"What?"

"A car," Chip said. "And Jess said—" He stopped and took a breath, looking around at all of them beseechingly, as if to excuse the insanity of the message he was bearing. "She said Chrissie Falconer was in it."

Everybody agreed it was the highlight of that year's Ice Festival. First George Putnam went through the break in the ice in his frogman's outfit and came back looking sick. This was followed by long discussions between George and Matt and some black guy wearing a three-piece suit underneath a quilted fur-lined raincoat.

Then it got *really* good. Police cars parked around the break in the ice, and a helicopter from Greenleaf Air Force base swooped low from across the bay, hovering while two more frogmen went into the water.

Then, as darkness fell, the police cars turned on their headlights, and cables were dropped and there was a long wait while the frogmen attached things.

And at last came the slow raising of a white sedan through the hole in the ice, water cascading from windows and doors as it turned and swayed beneath the helicopter, the passenger door hanging open.

The other door was closed, however.

The driver's door.

The one still holding a body inside the car.

Then, and only then, did Old Fishguts go home.

THIRTY-ONE

"I think it's him."

They stood in the mortuary, looking at what was left of the body in the car. "How can you tell?" Matt asked.

"Hair, ring on his finger, height, clothes, car," Agent Brokaw counted off. "We'll know better when we get a dental match, of course, but I think it's Murphy, all right."

"It would explain a lot," Matt said.

"It would explain everything," Jason Phillips said.

"Not quite," Agent Brokaw observed. "But at least we now know why we couldn't find him."

The three men walked out of the mortuary into the parking lot, huddling into their coats as the wind clacked the branches of the trees overhead. It was very late, very windy, and very, very cold.

"Do you think that was the gun that killed Vernon?" Jason asked. "The one we found in Murphy's coat pocket?"

"Right caliber," Matt said. "Ballistics shouldn't take long, but if all you tell me is true, I think it's pretty likely."

When Brokaw had first admitted to him that they couldn't let him talk to "Peter Murphy" because they themselves had lost track of him, Matt had thought it was just another stalling tactic. Then, when Brokaw had explained that Murphy had been sent to Blackwater as a chemistry teacher named Ed Martin, he began to believe it, because he knew that Ed Martin had left town shortly after the Howl. He had been, apparently, a complete dud as a teacher.

"But what happened?" Jason wanted to know. "How did they end up down there?"

Matt unlocked his car and they all got in—Brokaw in the front, and Jason—as befitted his junior status—in the back. They were all relieved to get in out of the wind, and for a while nobody spoke as they blew out their cheeks, rubbed and banged their hands together, and generally settled themselves.

"Well," Matt said as he started the engine, "I imagine that Murphy killed Vernon."

"We figured that a long time ago," Brokaw said.

"Yeah, well, it was nice of you to let me in on that eventually," Matt said with only slight reproach in his voice.

"I didn't want to compromise Phillips's investigations," Brokaw said.

Jason Phillips, who had proved to be, as he claimed, a good teacher, had also turned out to be an FBI undercover agent. He had been sent to see if he could find out why "Ed Martin" had disappeared so suddenly and so completely. He had soon stumbled on the drug thing, and thinking it was connected with Murphy/Martin, had been gathering evidence ever since.

"However," Brokaw went on, "when he found that the Gibbons woman had searched his room and removed the capsules he had finally managed to get, there was no point in keeping anything back."

"I wish we could have stopped her," Matt said. "She could have drowned out there."

"Thanks to Tom, she didn't," Jason said wonderingly. He, like Chip and several others, had started for the hole in the ice, but only Tom had persisted and done what had to be done without hesitation or thought for himself.

Matt swung out of the parking lot and started back toward Blackwater. There was very little traffic on the road at that late hour, and the night was clear, so he put his foot down. A warm bed and a few blank hours made a tempting goal.

"When did he kill him?" Matt wondered. "And why?"

"Oh, I think that's pretty straightforward," Brokaw said. "From what we understand, Vernon was a braggart—he liked his victims to know he was going to kill them. What he didn't count on, obviously, was Murphy being ready for that. Peter knew he was still in danger—he took self-defense lessons, that kind of thing, to protect himself. I understand your local mayor is some kind of expert?"

"Oh, yes." Matt smiled. "Mayor Atwater took an Olympic gold medal in judo some years ago. A lot of my men work out in his gym."

"Do you?" Jason asked.

Matt smiled again. "Occasionally." He turned onto the main highway. "So you think Murphy simply overpowered Vernon."

"Yes."

"And then shot him in *cold blood?*"

There was a long silence. Finally Jason said, "Yes."

Brokaw stirred in his seat. "Peter Murphy wasn't exactly an easy person."

"He was a pain in the ass," Jason said flatly.

"You were his local contact?" Matt asked over his shoulder.

"For my sins," Jason said. The pedantic manner had disappeared, and his usually immaculate appearance was ruffled now, and relaxed. Jess would not have recognized him, except for that same beautiful lick of fair hair that persisted in falling over his forehead. "He'd be on the phone four or five times a week with complaints—he didn't like teaching, someone was following him, he hated Blackwater, it wasn't safe enough, he wanted to move somewhere else—the whole bit. God, he was an asshole."

Brokaw chuckled. "We get them like that sometimes. Most people we put into witness protection are damned grateful, but some are never satisfied."

"He thought he was a big hero, bringing Luca Ritto down," Jason said in disgust. "As if he'd done it all on his own."

"Not so?" Matt asked.

"Damn right not so," Jason said. "It was a big operation. Still is. That is to say, still would be, if Murphy was alive. We'll never get Ritto on those other charges now."

"Some you win, some you give up on," Brokaw said philosophically. Jason just grunted.

"I can try to guess the rest," Matt said, slowing a little as they approached Blackwater. "The bay had frozen over and a few ice fishermen had braved drowning by getting their huts out early. Murphy, not being local, thought this meant the ice was safe enough to drive on. I suppose he figured to drop Vernon's body down somebody's fishing hole—we'll never know for sure. But he drove out too far and went through the ice. What was the actual date he finally left the school?"

"I can get it for you. I know he packed up and left town— or we thought he left town—on Thanksgiving weekend," Jason said.

Matt nodded. "I thought that might be it. The bay had frozen by then, and we had a big storm over that weekend. If he drove out in a snowstorm—and that would be a good time to do it if you didn't want to be seen—then after he went through the ice the pieces would have floated together again over the hole, confined by the surrounding ice. Snow filled in the cracks little by little, so that by the time the storm had blown out, it would have been hard to see where the car had gone through. It was damn lucky that nobody drove over that spot again all winter—but the locals know enough to avoid the river channel area because the current means the ice is always a bit thinner there."

"Murphy didn't know that, obviously," Brokaw said.

"Neither did I," Jason commented, and shivered.

"Well, Murphy did one good thing," Matt said.

"In addition to killing Vernon, you mean?" asked Brokaw. Matt glanced over at him. "That was good?"

Brokaw nodded. "Pest control," he said bluntly.

"He also blew a second whistle," Matt pointed out. "Taking his place meant you caught on to the drug thing."

"And I was on my way to proving it, if my dear friend Jess hadn't interfered," Jason said. "What do we do for proof now?"

"I think I can help you there, but it might mean getting a lot of people out of bed," Matt said, smiling as he pulled up beside Brokaw's car, which had been left at the entrance to the bay taken by the ice fishermen and the festival crowds. "We dumb local cops occasionally manage to have ideas, you know."

The slamming of the cars' doors broke the Sunday morning peace of Woodhaven Lane, and a clump of snow fell from one of the large trees that surrounded the house. Somewhere in the distance a dog barked, and there was a faint rhythmic chunking in the air as far away someone chopped wood.

"You know, this drug business is really a local problem," Brokaw said as they trudged up the walk. "Now that we've found out what happened to Murphy, we really no longer have an interest."

"How about pure nosiness?" Jason suggested. Brokaw grinned.

"Well," he said, "I do hate leaving before the movie's over."

"I wonder if he'll put up any resistance?" Jason said.

Matt shrugged. "He might be willing to try."

"He was willing to nearly kill Jessie," George pointed

out. "The son of a bitch." They'd retrieved Jess Gibbons's Ski-doo when they'd pulled up the car, and found the steering *had* been tampered with.

The house was an oddity out there in the countryside, the show home of a projected twenties development that had never developed. Two stories of Art Deco design in dirty white, with glass-brick inserts breaking the rounded lines. What had been a decorative steel-ribbed porch was now just rusty spikes, and the garden—which might have softened the austere lines of the place—was still covered with deep snow, offering no relief. Alongside the house was a double garage, with a car parked in front of one door, a mere mound under the snow. Beside it, in a cleared area in front of the second door, was a large four-wheel-drive RV.

Matt glanced over at it and frowned. "Now, why would he leave one car out like that?"

"Probably got a boat in the other half," said George. "On a trailer or something."

"Mmmm—I suppose," Matt conceded. It was a common practice in this lakeside community for small boats to be wintered over in that way. Large boats either required boathouses or dry-docking. "Just a minute." He waded through the snow and peered through the side window of the garage. The others saw his back stiffen and he stood there for a minute, quite still. Then he turned and came back to them. "I think you'll be glad you came," he said to Brokaw grimly. "There a back door to this place?" The walk led up to the front, but there were no branching paths that he could see.

"Must be," Duff Bradley, one of Matt's deputies, said. "I'll go see." He started to plow through the deep snow.

"Keep an eye on it if there is," Matt said. "Come on, Brokaw, let's have a talk with Mr. Trickett."

They approached the house, mounted the stairs, and rang the bell. There was no immediate response. Matt rang again and banged on the door. "Police," he shouted. "Open up."

A long silence.

"We have a warrant, Mr. Trickett," shouted Matt.

Silence.

"We'll break in if we have to."

There was a sudden sound behind the door and it opened to reveal Claude Trickett, smiling and shaking his head. "My goodness, no need to do that, Sheriff. Come in, come in."

They went in and stood in the circular hall, looking up at the chrome staircase that rose around the perimeter. "Come through to the living room," Trickett said. "I'm sorry it took me so long to answer the door. What is this all about?"

"Maybe it's about sabotaging Jess Gibbons's Ski-doo," George said abruptly.

Trickett looked confused. "I beg your pardon?"

"We know you were hanging around the Ski-doos yesterday morning," George went on. "Several people saw you there."

"But of course—I was in the race. I was checking over my own vehicle." He smiled and raised his hands slightly. "I didn't realize one could be arrested for that."

"You—"

"Never mind, George," Matt said, touching his sleeve. "Where is she, Trickett?"

"I beg your pardon?"

"Where is Chrissie Falconer?"

"Who?"

"Chrissie Falconer. She's been missing for a week. Her car is in your garage. Where is she?"

There was a moment of silence, then Trickett shrugged. "I have no idea where she is now," he said, abandoning his chirpy pose. "She left her car there because she was afraid to drive it. She'd started out to drive to Grantham but the snow was getting heavier and heavier. She begged me to take her into the city, and I did so."

"When was this?" Matt asked.

"The day the blizzard began. She had decided to leave home, and had some sort of appointment in town."

"Why should she come here?"

"When the snow interfered with her control of that little car, she wasn't far from here and turned to me for help."

"She knew where you lived?"

"Of course. We had meetings of the Science Club here in the first month of the term, when it was still warm. I have a pool, and the boys and girls liked to have a swim."

"I bet that wasn't all they had," muttered Jason.

"Why didn't you come forward with this information when you knew we were looking for her? You must have seen the notices on television or in the *Chronicle*."

"I've been too busy this week for reading or watching television," Trickett said huffily.

"There was plenty of talk about it at school, Trickett," Jason said. "You knew her parents were worried."

"She asked me to be discreet," Trickett said. "I was respecting her wishes." He glared at Jason. "And I don't see what it has to do with you, Phillips."

Jason smiled. "Agent Phillips, FBI," he said with what was obviously tremendous satisfaction.

Trickett's mouth opened, but no sound came out.

Matt turned to George. "Search the house."

Trickett managed a sound at last. "You have no right—" he croaked.

"I have a search warrant," Matt said, producing it. "Gentlemen?"

They proceeded to search the house from top to bottom, with Trickett pattering after them, protesting and babbling like a housewife caught with her dust showing. And dust was surely present in all but one bedroom and bathroom. The kitchen was tidy but it was clear it was sparingly used. There was no sign of Chrissie Falconer or of a laboratory where

Trickett could have produced the drugs they now knew he had been making. A check of invoices—produced by Principal Dutton under great protest—revealed that some very unusual chemicals had been included on the autumn orders for supplies to the science department. Chemicals that were no longer on school property.

They all returned to the living room and stared at one another. Trickett looked at them triumphantly.

"There," he said. "All for nothing. I'd like you to leave now."

"This is ridiculous," Brokaw said, ignoring him. "He must have rented space somewhere."

"No way," Jason said. "I checked all that out with local real estate agents. It has to be here. I found almost nothing at the school, except those few capsules in the back of his locked cupboard. And I wouldn't have found *those* if the roof hadn't collapsed."

"Acts of the merciful gods," Matt murmured.

Trickett was looking from one to the other and had gone very pale. "I'm going to call my lawyer," he said.

"You have every right to do so," Matt agreed. "Tell him you are going to be held for questioning on suspicion of illicit drug manufacture and possibly kidnaping."

Trickett exploded. "That's outrageous! I merely drove the girl into the city, that's all. She was over eighteen and had a perfect right to leave home if she wished."

Brokaw glanced at Matt. "You believe that?"

"No," Matt said. "But we didn't find her or any trace of her."

"Maybe she's out there in the car," Glen Hardwicke suggested.

"My God, that never occurred to me," Matt said. "Go take a look."

"Your search warrant doesn't cover the garage," Trickett protested.

"I'm afraid it does," Matt said. " 'And premises,' it says."

They stood there, waiting, until Hardwicke returned, shaking his head. "Just the car," he said.

Trickett smirked. "Kidnaping, indeed," he said, and went to a telephone on a table on the far side of the piano.

While they waited they stood looking around at the Art Deco decor. "This cost plenty of money," Brokaw said.

"Not worth it," George grumbled, looking around the austere geometry of the room. "Place is like a damn hospital. Even smells like one."

Brokaw and Jason exchanged a glance. "*Ether*," they said together. And beamed.

"I don't know why I didn't notice it before," Jason said.

"What's ether got to do with it?" George asked.

"Ether is used in refining cocaine," Brokaw said. "Whatever his pills contain, it's likely they contain that or something very like it."

"A derivative, probably," Jason added. "Let's see if we can tell where it's coming from."

They sniffed their way around the room, all finally coming together near the inner wall, on which there was a large, if faded, mural of jazz musicians.

"Look for straight lines," Jason said.

"You seem to know a lot about it," George said suspiciously.

Jason grinned. "I read a lot about Prohibition." He ran his fingers over the mural. "Hey," he said. "Here—look—" He caught his fingers in the edge of something and pulled.

"Here—what are you doing?" protested Trickett from across the room. "That mural cost a fortune—"

"So did this door, I imagine," said Matt dryly, as a section of the wall swung open, revealing a flight of stairs going down into darkness. He turned to look at Trickett. "Care to give us a guided tour?"

"There's nothing down there," Trickett said.

"It sure smells like something," Jason said, sniffing. "Ether, acids, bases . . ."

"Just storage," Trickett said quickly. "And wine . . . I keep my wine down there."

"Uh-huh," Matt said. He reached into his pocket, extracted the warrant, and waved it in Trickett's direction. "Premises," he said.

Jason had been feeling along the inside wall and located a switch. Lights came on below, and they descended. Matt paused. "Coming, Trickett?"

"I—"

Glen Hardwicke took hold of the man's arm. "He's coming," he said.

"Holy shit," said Jason when he reached the foot of the staircase. "A subsidiary of Du Pont."

The basement was a large one, and filled from end to end with laboratory equipment. Two broad slate-topped benches ran the length of the room, with a wooden-slatted walkway between them. Glasswear gleamed everywhere under the brilliant overhead lights. Some of the tubing and retorts were active, bubbling gently. There was a steady drip of distillates while snowfalls of precipitates settled silently.

"I think we might just have a little look around," Matt suggested. "Look for signs of the girl."

But there were no separate rooms where Chrissie Falconer might have been held, no bins or boxes into which she might have been forced, no sign of her ever having been there at all. At the far end of the right-hand bench, however, Brokaw found plastic boxes full of pink and blue capsule halves, waiting to be filled and joined.

"I can't make head or tail of this setup," Jason admitted, looking back up the length of the lab. "I was barely keeping ahead of the kids in class, as it was."

"We'd better call in some experts from the DEA," Brokaw said.

"Fine," Matt agreed. "But is there enough for me to arrest?"

"Oh, I think so," Jason said. "I found about ten ounces of cocaine back there in—"

"Hey!" Hardwicke shouted.

They all looked back toward the stairs and saw Trickett had managed to get away from the deputy and had reached for a large gallon jar of something on the shelves that ran around the room. He picked it up and threw it straight into the center of the right-hand bench, where a burner was running blue under a bubbling retort. The gallon container smashed and there was a sudden overpowering smell of ether, followed by a whoosh of flame that ran along the bench and poured over the sides. Glassware began bursting and popping and spattering chemicals.

"Look out! Some of that is acid!" Jason shouted.

Matt, George, Brokaw, and Jason ducked down, holding their arms up to protect their faces. At the opposite end of the room they could see Hardwicke trying to wrestle Trickett to the ground, but the latter's desperation was more than the older man could handle, and Trickett broke free. He grabbed two more gallon containers from the shelf and retreated up the stairs.

"We've got to get out of here," Jason said, glancing up at the now-blazing bench from which vapors and smoke were pouring. "That stuff must definitely be bad for one's personal health."

In the end they made a run for it and reached the fallen Hardwicke with their clothes smoking. "Come on, Glen," Matt said, helping him up. "There's only Bradley outside and he won't understand what's happening.

Jason and George grabbed fire extinguishers from the wall and were attempting to put out the bench fire, but the rivulets of burning ether had soaked into the wooden slats on the floor and they were alight, too. It was too much for the extinguisher to handle.

"Leave it, leave it!" Matt said.

They ran up the stairs, only to be met by flames coming

at them. Trickett had poured some chemical over everything in the living room and set fire to it, hoping to create a wall of flame to hold them back while he escaped. They had no option but to run through it before it got any worse.

It was not a pleasant ninety seconds.

They hit the outside running and rolled in the snow. Behind them they could hear the roar of the flames taking hold of the house. Windows were breaking, and smoke poured out over them.

When Matt lifted his face from the welcome iciness of the snow, he could see that Bradley was in one of the cars radioing for help. He turned his head and saw that the RV that had been parked in front of Trickett's garage was gone. He struggled to his feet and ran toward the cars, shouting the time-honored question.

"Which way did he go?"

THIRTY-TWO

They had two cars, and they called out others as well, but it was hopeless. Claude Trickett had made good use of his brief head start. "Time to call out the troopers," Matt said.

Two hours later the state police called. After a few minutes' conversation, Matt stood up. "They're pretty sure they've spotted the RV in the Little Hills State Park. What the hell he's doing there, God only knows. Come on—bring the skis."

They slowed to a stop behind two state police cars that were in a parking area set aside for visitors. The lot was nearly full, for the park was a popular area for winter sports, and the hills around them were alive with casual sledders and skiers for whom the big official runs and slopes of the northern part of the state were too daunting or too expensive. The blizzard had made some people happy, at least.

"How the hell are we going to pick him out of all that?" asked George.

"Beats me. Maybe that's why he came over this way," Matt said. A couple of state policemen came across the slushy parking lot toward them.

"You Sheriff Gabriel?" one of them called.

"Yeah."

"I'm Mallory, this is Palmer." He gestured toward the RV. "We got some witnesses who say that your man went off on skis and was wearing a hefty backpack. We reckon he might be making north and then east into Canada over the frozen channel in the dark. You really want to go in with us?"

"I damn well do," Matt said. "He killed a young girl."

"Is that the girl that was missing?" Palmer asked.

"Yes," Matt said grimly. They'd found Chrissie in the end. The heat of the burning house on Woodhaven Road had melted the snow around it for several feet—revealing, at last, the frozen body of Chrissie Falconer, curled up like a baby, the bruises of strangulation still vivid around her slender throat.

She had been put out with the garbage.

"Which way do we go?" Matt asked, impatient to get on with it. George looked at him—he had never seen him so grim.

"There was no way we could make out his trail among all these others—we think that's what he hoped. So we sent up a chopper. There are quite a few cross-country skiers in the hills, but the witnesses told us he was wearing turquoise, so we should be able to spot him eventually—especially if he turns toward Canada."

They bought some coffee from a machine, and about twenty minutes later they were hailed from a state police car. "They think they've spotted him," shouted a trooper. They ran across and got the location. "You bring your skis?" asked Mallory.

"We brought them," Matt said. "Give us a minute."

Five minutes after that they were moving away from the more populated slopes and into the inner reaches of the park. Soon they'd left the shrieking, laughing Sunday snowbunnies behind them, and were into the silent back hills, where the snow lay unmarked and deep, and many of the trees were bent low with their burden.

After an hour's chase, Mallory and Palmer stopped and waited for Matt and George to come up to them. Mallory had been periodically talking on a mobile phone, and now he snapped it shut and stuck it in a leather pouch on his belt. "They spotted him from that helicopter up there," he said, pointing overhead to where a machine hovered high in the bright sky. "He's gone into that wooded area over there. They've been watching but he hasn't come out yet. They can see all the perimeter. We've got people moving in from the other side, too. It's just a matter of flushing him out." Mallory didn't seem too worried about it, as if he hunted men in the deep snow every day. Maybe he did, Matt thought, as he tried to catch his breath.

"Let's go, then. He must have heard the chopper looking for him. I bet he's holed up in there waiting for it to get dark."

"Okay," Mallory agreed. "Now, if we spread out, maybe ten feet between us, we can cover quite an area. And listen, there's bound to be a lot of undergrowth in there, and most of it is covered by snow. You could get snagged if you aren't careful."

They spread out and moved forward.

"The woods are dark and deep," Matt muttered to himself as he slid forward between the trees. "And we've miles to go before we catch that bastard."

In fact, it was exactly one and three-tenths miles, and they found him in a hollow, sitting on the snow with one leg twisted under him. His backpack had slid from him and come open. From inside protruded a broken cardboard box from which had spewed a fountain of capsules, some blue and pink, others of different hues. They lay scattered on the snow, melting.

"Well, hello there!" Claude Trickett said cheerfully. "Nice of you to come looking for me!"

They stood and stared at him. His face was pale except for two bright spots of red high on his chubby cheeks. Sweat streaked his face, but he seemed oblivious to it. In fact, to all intents and purposes, Claude Trickett seemed to be having a ball.

"I've broken my leg, you know," he confided as they moved toward him. "Silly thing, really—I was skiing to my winter place. Hoped to make it before dark, but I suppose that wasn't realistic."

"Where is it?" George asked—he couldn't help himself.

"Bear Claw Lake," Claude said. "Know it?"

They all looked at one another. Bear Claw Lake was a good two hundred miles north and east of where they stood, well into Ontario.

"Heard of it," Mallory managed.

"Yes, yes—lovely place," Claude said happily.

"Claude Trickett, I have here a warrant for your arrest for the murder of Christine Mary Falconer . . ."

"Oh, no," Claude said. "Oh, no . . . I didn't murder her. It was self-defense. She came at me like a wild thing and I had to protect myself." He leaned forward. "She wasn't a very nice girl, you know. Blamed me for ruining her life, said I turned her into some kind of cripple. Went on and on about never being able to have sex without having a fit or some such thing. I mean, what kind of thing is that for a young girl to be worrying about? She might have been Homecoming Queen and all that, but the language was strictly gutter. I don't mind telling you I was shocked. And, of course, it wasn't true. Not at all. I didn't do anything to her, she did it to herself. I didn't *make* her take the pills, did I?" He babbled on, while over his thin, hysterical voice, Matt droned out the words informing him of his rights.

"They all *chose* to take the pills. It was in the interest of re-search. All I asked was for them to tell Chrissie about their reactions so she could report back to me, but do you think the lazy little monsters could do that? Oh, no, not one of them bothered. And so I told her that if they didn't come through for me, then I wouldn't come through for them, I mean, a bargain is a bargain and they were getting a bargain all right, why, my pills were the finest thing available." He leaned back a little—the broken leg didn't seem to be bothering him much, and if it were not for the sweat that ran down his face, Matt and the others might well have thought he wasn't in any pain at all.

The jagged bone sticking through his ski pants said otherwise.

Matt stepped forward and glared down at Trickett. "Did you send a ransom note to the Falconers?" he demanded.

Trickett looked up at him. "So what if I did? She'd be found sometime—I had to get what I could while they were still ready to pay up." He was entirely unrepentant, his voice reasonable, as if explaining to a child that the world was round. "I picked it up last night, as a matter of fact. Right where I told him to leave it, good as gold." He patted his backpack with obvious satisfaction.

"You bastard," Matt snarled.

Trickett shrugged. "Obviously you don't understand how expensive research is. Money has to be found somewhere." He straightened his shoulders and looked around at his attentive audience. "It's very important research I'm doing, after all. It could change the world. Oh, yes. When I perfect these drugs they'll be after me for the formula, but I won't come cheap, oh, no. I'll show her I didn't need her money. She'll come back begging, you watch and see. When *I'm* the rich one and she is only a little interior decorator, *then* we'll see, all right."

It was clear he had taken more than a few of his own drugs. He was high on his own creation. High beyond high, into the stratosphere of high, sick, manic, made foolish and deadly by his own hand, his own brain, his own greed. Matt slapped him, hard. "You put Chrissie out in the snow like some dead animal," he shouted, his voice flattened by the snow and the trees.

Trickett looked up at him, almost pityingly. "Well, you have to, you know. They go *off* if you don't freeze them."

Matt began to shake. George came forward and took his arm. "Come on, Matt. These guys will take care of him."

"He's mine," Matt said.

"Yeah, of course he is. But look at him. He'll have to go to the hospital and stuff like that . . . let them do it. They're good at cleaning up messes." He glanced around at Mallory, who nodded. "Come on, Matt," George said gently. "Let it go for now. We'll deal with the charges in the morning."

More state police had arrived from the other side of the forest. A ring of scowling uniformed skiers stood around in a circle while the center of their attention, Claude Trickett, late head of the science department of the Cecil G. Heckman Memorial High School, Blackwater, told them how he was going to be the savior of suffering mankind and a very, very, very, *very* rich man, richer than his wife had *ever* been, wasn't that *wonderful*?

Slowly, Matt turned away and, following George, skied back through the woods.

It was a long trip home.

Tom was released late Sunday afternoon and wanted to go home, but Chip insisted they go up and see Jess.

"She needs to rest," Tom protested.

"Five minutes won't hurt," Chip said, propelling him along the hall. "And I'm certain she'll want to thank you."

"Oh, for crying out—" Tom said weakly.

He knew it was a mistake the minute he saw her lying back against the pillows, her dark hair curling loosely around her face. She looked the way she always looked after a bath—flushed and dewy and vulnerable—when it had been the most difficult to keep his hands to himself. His heart crashed upward against his throat and then thudded back into his chest, making it hard to breathe. Or perhaps that was just the result of all the ice water he'd swallowed.

"Tom," she said. "Thank you."

"Okay," Tom said gruffly.

"My God," Chip said in exasperation. "You'd think you were a couple of strangers. Jess Gibbons, this is Tom Brady, a friend of mine who likes to swim in cold water. Brady, this is Jess, an idiot who thinks she can ride a Ski-doo. Now *talk* to one another. I'm going to get myself some coffee." He went out, grinning.

"Did they find the . . . did they . . . ?" She didn't want to think of it but had to ask.

"Yeah, they pulled it up," Tom said. "Not nice."

"No," Jess agreed. She struggled with the words, but finally got them out. "Was it . . . was it . . . Chrissie?"

Tom shook his head. "No—it was a man." He came a little closer to the bed. "Chip said he heard it was Ed Martin, the chem teacher we all hated." He shook his head. "Damnedest thing."

"All that blond hair . . . I thought . . . "

"Yeah, well . . . he used to wear that ponytail, remember? He thought he looked like Fabio, you once said," Tom said in disgust. "Speaking of hair, guess what? Our Jason turns out not to be a teacher after all, but some kind of government agent, looking for Martin. Who turns out to have been someone called Murphy. And maybe something else before that. He was in the government witness protection program apparently. Because of testifying against some New York crime boss. According to George, he was the one who killed the first guy they found. It's kind of complicated—Chip wasn't too clear on all the details."

"Chrissie—" Jess said.

He sighed. "You've slept through a lot, Jess. Chrissie is dead, I'm afraid. Claude Trickett killed her."

She struggled up onto her elbows. "*Claude?*"

"Yes. You were right about the drugs, but wrong about

where they were coming from. Not our Jason, but Claude Trickett. He apparently had hatched a scheme for becoming some kind of drug baron, and he was using Chrissie to distribute his various experimental drugs. Research, he called it. Jason came looking for the missing guy in the witness protection program and stumbled onto the drug thing, too." He grinned. "Apparently you messed up his investigations by going through his pockets looking for something you thought he'd poisoned the cats with? I didn't know you went through our pockets, Jess. I'm ashamed of you."

Jess managed a smile, but was too shocked and tired to defend herself. All these horrible revelations were more than she could bear. He looked shocked, too, telling her about them. They'd been too cozy, just as she had thought, thinking themselves safe in their small world, never suspecting its real size. Nowhere is safe, she thought.

She looked at him, familiar and unfamiliar Tom. The one Jason said she'd always looked at but never really seen before. What was *he* looking at—the old Jess? Or the new Jess—the one who had wanted to take hold of her life—and instead had stumbled into briars, hot coals, and stinging serpents.

Tom came even closer to the bed, concerned by her bleak expression. He cursed himself for telling her about Chrissie and Claude. He should have left it for tomorrow or the next day. When things were back to normal. "You all right? Want anything from home? Chip and I can go get whatever you—"

"No, I'm fine. Emily brought me in some things." She looked up at him. "I'm a little cold, still."

"Yeah." He managed a smile. "I know what you mean. Went right through to the bone, didn't it?"

"Tom . . ."

"Say, listen—we were damned lucky," Tom said, sitting awkwardly on the edge of the bed. "Okay? No big deal . . .

A lot of people started for you, I just . . . happened to get there first."

"You're a lousy swimmer," Jess reminded him. "I'm a good swimmer."

"You weren't doing too well when I grabbed you," he said reprovingly.

"I know." She reached out to him. "Give me a hug—I need a hug."

He hesitated, then leaned over and hugged her, letting go rather quickly. She eyed him. He sighed, and hugged her again. "Okay?" He straightened up.

"Why are you such a grouch?" Jess suddenly snapped. "You've been sniping at me for weeks. If I'm such a pain, why the hell did you save my life?"

"I didn't save your life, I just helped keep you afloat while the others—"

"My foot was caught in the car, Tom," Jess said. "If you hadn't freed me I would have drowned."

"Well, all right—maybe I—" He stood up. "It doesn't matter, anyway. The point is, you're okay and I'm okay and that's the end of it."

Jess had had a long talk with Emily, who was better-sighted than she was. Emily saw a lot of things other people missed. She decided it was time to find out whether Emily was right or not. Time to find out a lot of things, in fact. "Come here," she said. "I want to see something. There's a mark on your ear."

He reached up and rubbed at his ear.

"No—come here," Jess insisted. He bent down, obedient as a child, but instead of looking at his ear, she put her hands on either side of his face and kissed him.

"Hey," he said, trying to pull away.

"Hey," she said softly. "That's what I thought." And she kissed him once more, holding fast to him, not letting go. Not ever letting go again. After a moment he stopped struggling. After another moment he sat back down on the bed and put his arms around her. After quite a few more moments the kiss ended.

And the new life she'd been looking for began.

Frank Nixey sat at the bar of the Golden Perch, shaking his head. "Crazy," he said. "Just crazy. First one floats up, then another one comes up . . . the goddamn bay must be littered with dead guys. I mean, there was room for *five* in that car."

"I don't think you have to worry," Harlow said reassuringly, as he served Frog Bartlett.

Frog agreed. "I think it was just the two of them, Frank. The other guy, the driver, he was held in by a seat belt. That's what kept him down so long. The one come up in your fishing hole, he come out the open passenger door eventually. He forgot to fasten up."

"He was already dead," Harlow pointed out.

"Oh, yeah," Frog said. "So he was."

"I don't know," Frank Nixey said morosely, reluctant to give up his image of a bay crammed with corpses. "It's crazy."

"I'm sure they'll be able to figure it out," Dominic Pritchard said, sitting down on the other side of his client. He'd just dropped Emily at the hospital, but had been too restless to stay long himself and had come to the bar in search of a nightcap. "We'll be able to read all about it in the *Chronicle*. Don't you think so, Billmore?"

But the insurance man was not forthcoming. He sat at the end of the bar, nursing his third double Scotch. Standing on the ice in the windy darkness the previous night, watching the retrieval operations, he had had a nasty shock. He had recognized the car as it came up out of the water.

He had written the policy on it himself.

Old Fishguts sat on his storm porch overlooking the fast-moving silver-singing river. Behind him the living room was brightly alive with the sound and sights of the starship

Enterprise countering yet another alien invasion. Before him lay the dark supple velvet of the Black River valley, winding down to the frozen flats of the Mush and the scarred heavy gray ice of Blackwater Bay, glimmering in the moonlight. He sat still, his glass of Scotch in one hand, a beaded strip of leather in the other.

He was listening.

Faintly, he thought he could hear voices, more a rushing through his blood than a sound, more a slow throb in the brain than words. What the sound told him was, "All right for now." What it warned was, "Be watchful until next time." He wished he could hear more clearly, *listen* more clearly, but he was growing old, and it was hard to focus on such a faint message.

He sighed, remembering the itchiness of the ice beneath his feet that had suddenly ceased, leaving him comfortable at last. And the long ride home, when he wondered if he had done the right things with his life.

His grandson came out onto the porch. "Hey," Billy said. "You missed a really good episode."

"If you want a great story, *I* can tell you one," Old Fishguts said.

"Oh, Grandpa," Billy said impatiently. He was thirteen, he had things to do. But he came over and sat down beside the old man, who handed him the beaded leather strip, still warm.

"You should listen to this," Old Fishguts said.

And Billy listened.